# Red

## HOUSE OF MISFITS

# CAMBRIA HEBERT

Published by Cambria Hebert
http://www.cambriahebert.com

Interior design and typesetting by Classic Interior Design
Cover design by Cover Me Darling
Edited by Cassie McCown
Copyright 2022 by Cambria Hebert

HOUSE OF MISFITS
CAMBRIA HEBERT

I'm a cop. He's a criminal.

We're the human equivalent of oil and water.

Staying away from him would be the obvious answer. Too bad we share a one-bedroom apartment. It's an unfortunate situation I didn't choose but can't do anything about. When my best friend, Earth, moved out, he offered his room to his big brother who had rolled into town from Korea to kill him… but then ended up saving him.

And now we're all supposed to be one big happy family.

Except Daeshim is not my brother and never will be. And no one has any idea who I really am. For years, I've been Beau the hacker. Beau the agreeable, quiet one in the corner.

I am those things. But I'm also a cyber crimes specialist with the FBI.

Surprise!

My real identity is a secret no one can know. Because the second they find out who I really am, my cover will be blown, everything I've been doing will come to light, and the found family I desperately want will toss me on the street.

Or worse.

But Daeshim won't stop staring, dissecting me with his perceptive dark eyes. I can't stand him, yet the heavier his attention gets, the more I crave. The more I begin to wonder if I'm just nervous he will find out my secrets or somehow get into my heart.

I'm starting to crumble, the weight on my shoulders too much to hold alone. His stubborn, unruly presence challenges me, scares me, yet also somehow calms me.

When danger gets uncomfortably close, I realize the only one strong enough to save me is the very criminal I'm not supposed to trust.

HOUSE OF MISFITS

# CAMBRIA HEBERT

## ONCE UPON A TIME

Black roses dripped blood, but that was okay. Red was his color.

# PROLOGUE

---

## MANY YEARS AGO...

*LITTLE RED*

"THERE'S A JOB."

"I already have a job."

"Yeah, it's to do what I tell you to do."

Silence reigned. A heavy sigh filled the air. Wooden chair legs scraped over the floor, creating a nails-on-chalkboard sort of effect.

He swung his leg over the seat, sitting down with the back pressed against his chest. Leaning closer, teetering on two legs instead of four, he said, "You're uniquely qualified for this job."

I gave him a sidelong glance. "How so?"

"You look innocent."

I scoffed. "I'm not."

"Exactly why you'll fit in where I need you to go."

I glanced up, intrigued. "You need me to go somewhere?"

He smiled, and I realized I gave away my interest too soon. Still, I couldn't help but ask. "Where?"

The smile grew wider. "Into the forest, Little Red. Into the forest to catch the big bad wolf."

# 1

---

*DAESHIM*

THE LATE-NIGHT HOUR QUIETED THE STREET. SHADOW shrouded the city, making me feel like I was walking through an old black-and-white film. It was an in-between hour, the previous day over but the new one not yet begun.

It was these moments of ambiguity I liked most because the black and white bled into gray, and it was in this cloudy wash I felt most at home.

Abruptly, the quiet rippled with disturbance as though somewhere up ahead a large stone hit the center of a calm sea, causing ripples to bloom out across the surface. Everything in those moments still looked the same, but when the first ripple hit my boot, the hair on the back of my neck spiked.

Shattering glass broke the sensation of limbo, and I started to run. Adrenaline spiked my heart rate so fast, and my breathing grew labored in my ears. I didn't even know what was happening, but every single cell in my body knew it was bad.

*Ping-ping-ping.* Broken shards of glass hit the sidewalk up ahead, the light sound exceptionally loud.

I didn't look at where it fell, instead focusing on where it came from and the man half dangling out of the newly busted window. He was there all but two seconds, his body disappearing back inside almost as quickly as he'd appeared. I shouted, but the sound went unheard because it was violently wiped out by another.

The unmistakable blast of a gun.

A howl ripped through the dark, the sound so raw it silenced the bullet. It also made my presence known.

"Shit! He's here!" Someone panicked.

Tearing into the building, I bounded up the stairs toward the apartment. Partway there, two men burst into the stairwell in a panic, black masks covering their faces. The second they saw me charging, they started back the way they'd come.

Leaping forward, I grabbed them both by their backs, slamming their bodies together so hard I felt my wrist bones vibrate. Both of them swayed on their feet even as they tried to run anew.

Planting a boot in one's gut, I slammed him into the wall where he slid toward the floor.

Spinning toward the other, I grabbed the lapels of his black jacket, yanking him forward. "Who sent you?"

"It doesn't matter now."

My blood turned frigid, the blast of cold making me numb. I tossed him over the stair railing like a rag doll, ignoring the way his body cracked and smacked on its way down.

Heaving, I turned toward the man trying to crawl away.

"P-please," he whimpered.

I growled and picked him by the back of his neck. "At least die with some dignity," I spat, burying the blade I always carried deep in his gut.

It made a wet sort of sucking sound, and blood spurted from between the man's lips, saturating the black mask covering his face. I twisted the handle. He gurgled, and his eyes rolled back in his head. He was dead before I yanked the metal from his lifeless form.

Leaving him lying where he dropped, I stormed the rest of the way to the top floor. The front door was partially open, gritty light spilling from the crack.

I kicked it open, barreling through. I felt rather than saw the movement off to the side and lunged at it. The cold, hard metal of a gun pressed into my belly as I pinned the man against the wall. His eyes bulged when I sent the metal flying out of his hand, skittering somewhere into the dark. Oh, I reveled in the way his windpipe gave beneath my hand as I squeezed.

"You bring a gun to my house?" I snarled.

His bulging eyes flared.

"*Pussy*," I spat and then tossed him out the busted window.

The pavement below silenced the last scream he would ever make.

*Cough. Wheeze. Cough.* "Daeshim."

I spun, eyes going directly to the huddled body in the center of the ransacked room. The only light came from an upended lamp with a partially busted bulb.

A strangled sound ripped from my lips, and I dropped to my knees beside his body. "Hoon—ah," I whispered, pulling the man into my lap.

"I'm glad you're here," he rasped, his voice sounding oddly wet.

"Hospital," I said, preparing to lift him off the floor.

His blood-slicked hand grabbed mine. "No."

My eyes crashed with his. Even in this shitty light, I saw.

*He isn't going to make it to the hospital.*

Rocking us a little, I glanced at the gunshot wound ripped crudely in his middle. Blood pumped out at a steady rate, and for the first time in my life, the sight of blood made me sick. Slapping my hand against the wound, I applied as much pressure as I possibly could.

"Ow." Hoon winced.

"We have to slow the bleeding," I told him.

He smiled, teeth outlined in blood. "I gave them hell."

A hard knot formed in the center of my chest. It was hard to breathe around it. "I'm sure you did." I pressed harder against the wound as if I could heal it with sheer will. "Who sent them?"

He coughed. Blood splattered my chin.

"Kiss me before I die."

"Who sent them?" I yelled, pulling his body farther into mine.

"I think we both know." His voice was weak. In just moments, there would be more blood outside his body than in.

A broken sound ripped from me, and I curled around him. Weak, bloodstained fingers tangled in the front of my shirt.

"I'm sorry," I rasped against his ear.

"Daeshim."

My lips grabbed his, kissing ferociously. His jaw went slack, and a broken sob left me, but then he made a sound, and I was kissing him with renewed force. I tasted nothing but blood as I tried to give him something he wanted but never had to give. The lack of it never bothered me before, but now that he was dying, my heart clenched with anger and despair.

When I lifted my head, there was blood smeared all over us both, and I dully wondered if I would ever taste anything else.

Hoon smiled weakly, his hazy eyes clinging to mine. "I... don't regret it."

The fingers in my shirt loosened. Life faded out of his eyes, turning him into an empty shell.

"*No,*" I rasped brokenly, curling around him again. I didn't bother begging him not to die. I never got what I asked for, and his death was just more proof.

"I'm sorry," I confessed, the words too late because he couldn't hear.

Tears mixed with blood, and his body turned cold.

*I don't regret it.*

I was glad he died with no regret.

I would live with enough for both of us.

# 2

---

*BEAU*

NOT EVEN THE NOISE-CANCELING HEADPHONES COULD DROWN out his shout. My fingers paused in flying over the keyboard but resumed when nothing else followed.

A moment later, he yelled again. I glanced up out of the blue-toned bubble the monitors always surrounded me with. He was not a peaceful sleeper. I normally ignored him, but tonight I couldn't. Tonight he was annoying me more than usual.

Shoving back one side of the headphones, I listened anew.

"No," he wailed, and something twisted in my gut.

I tossed the headphones onto my desk, moving out from behind my setup, adjusting the beanie I wore as I strode toward the bedroom. Pushing open the door without knocking, I folded my arms over my chest in the doorway.

"Hey," I called.

He seemed too big for the bed as he thrashed around,

breathing heavily and muttering too low for me to understand.

Sighing, I stepped into the dark room out of the light spilling in from the living room. His forehead was damp with a sheen of sweat, his messy dark hair matted in it.

"Wake up," I intoned, still staring down.

His body stilled for a brief moment, making me think I'd managed to wake him. "I'm trying to work," I bitched, turning away.

A keening sound filled the room, followed by a broken sob. Footsteps faltering, I turned back, realizing he was still trapped wherever he was. The pain etched in his features made my chest tight, and a sudden need to comfort had me leaning over him.

"Daeshim," I called.

His face softened just a bit, and it made something inside me ease.

"Daeshim." I called out to him again, this time reaching out to tap his cheek.

He moved so fast I didn't even realize what was happening until I was on my back, pinned beneath him. The mattress was soft, but maybe it only felt that way because the body pinning me in place was rock hard.

"What the hell are you doing?" I grunted, trying to shove him off.

His eyes snapped open, but there was no one home. An uneasy feeling wormed around inside me, my fight-or-flight response coming in hot.

I shoved at his shoulders again, watching his face contort in menace. Daeshim was basically a gangster. A criminal and an asshole. He was also my roommate. I'd never been scared of him.

But as his hands shot out, locking around my neck to squeeze, fear bloomed.

I opened my mouth to yell at him, but all that came out was a strangled sound. Panic assaulted me, bursting over everything else and making me feel like I was fighting even though all my physical movements stopped.

*Get it together!* A voice demanded inside me, effectively stopping the absolute control of the panic.

Grunting, I twisted under him, but his weight pushed me harder into the bed.

Wheezing and eyes bulging, I grappled at his arms, digging my nails into them, trying to pry away his hands.

The set of his mouth was grim, and his eyes glittered with that creepy, empty, nobody's-home look.

"Dae—" I wheezed, twisting and slapping his arm. "Daeshim."

He blinked, and I was able to drag in some air before he started strangling me anew. He was in there.

*I just have to—*

The thought cut off as spots started to swim before my eyes. It was do or die. Literally.

Letting my body go lax under his, I put every last bit of effort into the fist I clenched at my side.

Then, just before this asshole overpowered me, I launched a right hook into the side of his head.

## 3

*Daeshim*

One moment, I was cradling him in the protection of my body, and the next, pain exploded over the side of my face.

I fell sideways, sagging a little as my cheekbone burned like it was on fire. Gasping, my hand came up to feel the spot, confusion muddling my brain.

Something shifted under me.

*Hoon.*

I reached out but was met with resistance, my hand slapped away.

"Jesus Christ," he wheezed, twisting to try and get on his side.

Chest squeezing, I reached for him again. *"Hoon."*

"This is what I get for trying to be a good roommate." *Hack. Cough. Hack.*

The voice brought me up short.

I sat back a little, blinking. Awareness washed over me,

and the dream faded away, revealing the familiar walls of Earth's bedroom—no, *my* bedroom.

I glanced down at the body I was straddling. Even in the dark, I could see his red locks.

"Beau?"

He wheezed.

Even though I was straddling his hips, he was twisting away from me at the waist. My hand covered his shoulder, pushing him flat into the bed.

His chest rose and fell rapidly, and his cheeks flushed pink against his pale skin.

"What the fuck are you doing in my bed?"

If looks could kill, my funeral would be tomorrow. "You were having a nightmare."

"I don't have—" My cheek throbbed. "Did you punch me?" I roared.

*Wheeze.* "That's what you get for trying to kill me!"

"Kill you?" I scoffed.

"Get off me." Beau pushed at me, his voice raspy, arms weak.

A veil of grimness draped over me. Instead of moving to let him up, I held him down and leaned in. His eyes flashed with wariness, but it was gone almost as quick as it appeared. It didn't matter that it only lasted a second. I saw it, and… I didn't like it.

"What did I do?" I asked, harsh.

"Nothing. It's my fault for coming in here."

His unusually hoarse tone drew my eyes to his throat. It was too dark in here, so I shifted to snag my cell off the nightstand.

"What the fuck? Get off me," Beau bitched, trying to get up.

I shoved him back, pinning him with one palm flattened on his shoulder, and activated the flashlight on my phone. He squinted against the intrusive light, turning his face away, the action revealing some of his neck. A rough sound rumbled out of me, making him struggle all over again.

My stare snapped up, colliding with his. "Let me see."

I was prepared for more bitching, but charged silence swelled in the tiny bedroom. Even though our eyes stayed locked on each other, I became *very* aware of his body under mine.

Tension coiled at the base of my spine, tightening all my muscles and hardening my jaw. Green eyes glittered with anger as they stared, but then suddenly, he relented. I felt the loss of the emerald gaze so significantly my breath whooshed out of me, making me feel like a deflated balloon. His chin tipped up, the action pushing his head farther into my pillow as he bared his throat.

My nostrils flared as something possessive yet wholly satisfying slammed into me. The hand pinning him to the bed left his shoulder, sliding down to fist in the T-shirt against his chest.

I swear I heard the seams on the fabric groan under the force with which I bunched the material, but neither of us moved or reacted. I remained on top of him, and he stayed still beneath me, displaying his neck. Surrendering.

Heart pounding, I directed the light down toward the skin. There were already bruises. A swollen red ring around his otherwise pale flesh.

Something inside me whined, and the sound slipped out between my lips. Regret rushed to the surface, pushing out all reason until all that was left was instinct.

Leaning down, I nuzzled the mottled skin, breathing out so my breath fanned over the injury.

Beneath me, Beau went rigid, his body so tense I could feel it vibrate. "What the fuck—"

I nuzzled him again, and the words broke off. Against my

nose, his Adam's apple bobbed as though he couldn't swallow.

A sympathetic noise filled the bedroom, and my lips brushed over the struggling knot. He sucked in a sharp breath. I could feel his pulse hammering, practically hear the blood rushing through his veins.

Abandoning the phone, I slid my hand between his neck and the bed, cupping it gently. Stroking my thumb over some of the marks, I nuzzled him again. "I'm sorry."

All rigidity melted away, and his body went boneless. I swear to God, I heard the beginning of a purr build deep in his throat, and blood rushed south in anticipation of that sound.

Catching us both off guard, Beau jackknifed up, scrambling out from under me. In his haste, he pitched off the side of the bed, nearly face-planting, but I caught him around the waist and towed him back.

He scrambled out of that hold too, knocking me away and rising to his feet. Chest heaving, eyes wild, his hands balled into fists at his sides. "Are you insane?"

Whatever spell I was under burst and dropped me so hard into reality I had to pause to take a breath. "What happened?" My voice was strained.

"You wouldn't stop shouting. I came in to wake you."

My eyes slid to his neck, then snapped back up. "I didn't ask you to do that."

"Yeah? Well, next time, you're on your own."

Hot anger practically wept from my pores, turning my movements stiff and jerky. Picking up the first T-shirt I saw, I banged out of the room, stopping long enough near the front door to pull on my leather jacket before throwing the locks and wrenching it open.

I felt rather than heard or saw Beau come out of the

bedroom. The urge to turn and look at him was so strong it pissed me off all over again. Without even the slightest glimpse backward, I stormed out, the entire doorframe rattling beneath the force with which I slammed the door.

## 4

---

*BEAU*

IT HAD BEEN MONTHS SINCE EVERYONE MOVED OUT AND LEFT me here with him.

We argued. We bitched and yelled. Sometimes we fought. Mostly, we ignored each other. Very few times, you might have caught a smile.

But... this?

*What the fuck just happened?*

# 5

---

*DAESHIM*

I HAD NO IDEA WHAT TIME IT WAS. I DIDN'T CARE. THE SKY WAS black, the city hushed. It wasn't yet morning, but the previous day was already gone.

I brushed off the thought because it made a shiver run down my spine, reminding me of things I couldn't get away from even in sleep.

I didn't think about where I was going, just that I had to get out. But when I finally looked up after a subway ride and a walk in the freezing temps, I wasn't surprised.

Without pause, I went up the stone steps leading to the brownstone. The light over the arched front door was off, darkness enveloping me like a familiar friend.

*Bang! Bang! Bang!* I pounded on the door. After several moments, I banged some more.

A light flicked on, spilling down the stairs I knew were just inside. The door shuddered when it was wrenched open. Obviously, he wasn't at all concerned about who might be on the other side. I wasn't sure if he was just brave or stupid, but honestly, I didn't give a damn either way.

The air whooshed when he yanked back the door, his face angled so his scars were the first thing to be seen. "What the —Daeshim?"

I merely stared from beneath the rim of the black baseball hat I wore and said nothing at all.

"What's wrong?" Ander asked instantly, body language changing from defensive to alert. Leaning out, he surveyed behind me, expecting to see more of the family.

"It's just me."

Frigid air whipped around, whistling through the small covered alcove above the door.

"Ander? Should I get my bat?" Emogen's voice floated down the stairs.

My lips twitched.

"That fucking bat," Ander muttered before turning to call up to her. "It's just Daeshim. Put the bat down and go to bed."

She appeared at the top of the stairs, her shapely legs on full display underneath a T-shirt. "Daeshim? What's wrong? Is there any emergency?"

"Woman, where the hell are your pants?" Ander bellowed, seeing her teetering above us.

"Probably wherever I left them," she sassed, then looked at me. "Daeshim?"

I held up my hand. "Everything's fine. I just… ah, couldn't sleep. Had something to say to Ander."

Emogen relaxed instantly and waved me in. "Well, get in here. We aren't paying to heat all of Brooklyn."

I came inside just enough for Ander to be able to close the door behind me. He was wearing nothing but a pair of loose sweatpants and a hoodie he hadn't even zipped up on his way to the door. It hung open to reveal his bare chest, and some of the scarring on his upper body peaked out from the open edges.

"I'm going back to bed. If you want to talk to me, come back when the sun's up," Emogen announced, already on her way back upstairs.

"Come on," Ander said, gesturing toward the living room.

I shook my head. "I'm not staying. Just came to say something."

Sensing my mood, Ander crossed his arms over his chest and regarded me steadily. "So say it."

"You killed my mother."

A beat of thick silence followed my words. Lowering his arms to his sides, Ander frowned. "Daeshim, that was—"

"Thank you."

Flabbergasted, he shifted, trying to read me, but I knew he couldn't. "What?"

Pulling my hands out of the pockets of my coat, I extended one between us. "She was an evil bitch who deserved what she got. So thank you." *Thank you for doing something I wasn't able to do.*

Ander wrenched his gaze from my face to stare dumbly at my hand. Slowly, he pushed his hand into mine. His skin was warm where mine felt like ice.

I pulled back and turned to the door.

"You can stay."

"I know," I replied, pulling the door open anyway and stepping out into the winter.

"I didn't mean to kill her."

I stopped, slowly pivoting. The light coming down the stairs cast a warm glow behind him, making his wild blond hair a halo. But that was all that was angelic about Ander Todd. The scars mottling his face saw to that. He was a beast trapped in the body of a man, but even still, he was no killer. That title belonged to me.

How ironic that it was him who'd been able to kill my greatest enemy.

"I'm thankful just the same." I jogged down the steps and toward the night's inky tentacles reaching out to claim me.

Ander's bare feet slapped over the stone steps as he followed me into the dark. "Hey."

I didn't turn around, but I listened.

"I'm not sorry I bit you."

Cold air smacked against my teeth when I smiled. Tension I didn't realize I carried loosened just a bit. "Fuck you."

"Come back anytime." There was amusement in his voice, but underneath was sincerity.

I didn't listen for his door to close as I made my way down the Brooklyn street. The air was so cold it stung my esophagus with every breath. I walked with no destination and with no hope of clearing my head. It wasn't the dream, though, that disturbed me. No, that dream was a familiar friend. Tonight, I had a new companion, and a friend it was not.

The bruises bothered me.

They bothered me more than the echo of the gunshot that had ripped through my dream.

*Because you caused the bruises.*

*Yeah? Well, that gunshot was your fault too.*

Flashes of his bobbing Adam's apple taunted the backs of my eyelids. And it wasn't so much the vision of it but the way it made me feel. How could a two-second flicker of a memory pull me into a feeling? A feeling that hummed beneath my skin and flipped my stomach.

*Remnants of the dream.* I reasoned. Leftover emotion spilling into that moment and muddying up my brain.

*It's not him.*

Taking an exceptionally deep breath, I welcomed the

stinging cold as it stretched all the way down toward my stomach. It was so frigid it made me cough. Just before dipping my head against the wind, something caught my attention down the block. *Someone.*

A flash of red stood out against the night, seemingly appearing out of nowhere. Through narrowed, interested eyes, I stared at that beacon of color as it retreated farther away.

There was something infinitely familiar about the body moving beneath that hoodie. Something I sensed rather than saw. The same sensation that flipped over my stomach earlier crashed over me again, making my eyes narrow.

Ducking into the nearest alley, I pressed into the rough brick. After waiting a few seconds that felt like longer, I leaned around the corner, eyes immediately finding him again.

The hoodie-cloaked man stopped walking, hesitating the briefest of seconds, then glanced over his shoulder imperceptibly before disappearing through a nearby door.

Moving at once, I strolled down the street, keeping my head down but attention trained on the spot where he'd last stood.

There was nothing special about the building he went into. It looked like an ordinary row house like all the rest. Inside my pockets, my fists clenched with the desire to stop and glance in the windows. Hell, to even pull open the door and gaze inside.

I knew better, so I kept walking, pretending I was just an ordinary guy walking down an ordinary street. That I was a guy who hadn't just seen the roommate he'd nearly strangled an hour ago duck into a building that was *not* where we lived.

Sure. Sure, it could be innocent.

But oh, I knew it wasn't.

*Oh, Red. What are you up to?*

## 6

---

*Beau*

I STARED AT THE COMPUTER MONITOR WITHOUT SEEING. I didn't blink. Or think. I just stared off into nothing, trapped in a place I probably should have hated but didn't.

A familiar sound snapped me back, eyes focusing on the screen. I watched as everything I had pulled up blinked out and then a million tiny pixels converged into the center, one by one piecing together an image at rapid speed.

A low curse dropped into the quiet room as I stared at the wicker basket, the tiny pixels making up the stupid calling card already pulling apart to disappear as if they'd never been there at all.

It all happened in less than thirty seconds, and then I was sitting there staring at the screen looking exactly as I'd left it.

My eyes strayed toward the bedroom.

*Exactly as it was when I went to wake him.*

Where'd he even storm off to in the middle of the night? I was glad he'd left. Not only was his presence worse than a fried hard drive, but now I wouldn't have to worry about him noticing me leave. What the hell was I even being summoned for?

Irritation made my neck muscles tight and an unwelcome jitteriness zing beneath my skin. Flying over the keyboard, I backed up everything I had going on and then powered it all down.

After tugging on a red hoodie, I reached up to adjust the beanie, but my fingers met hair instead. Patting around on my head, I realized it wasn't even there. *It had been...* My eyes strayed back toward the bedroom.

My stomach somersaulted, which in turn made my back teeth slam together. Ignoring it all, I stalked back into the bedroom and over to the side of the bed. The blankets were rumpled and partially twisted in a heap. The single pillow was wrinkled and indented in the middle.

It smelled different in here than the rest of the apartment. A deeper, muskier scent. The air was also tinged just slightly with sweat, and it made me think of the way his hair had clung to his damp forehead.

A gruff noise vibrated my throat, but a twinge of soreness cut off the sound. Suddenly, I was very aware of my neck. The bruises I'd yet to look at throbbed lightly as though I had a second heartbeat.

Throat tight, I turned my attention, easily finding my hat. It was bunched up on the pillow, halfway lying in the indent left from his head.

*Or maybe it was mine.*

Flashes of how he'd pinned me down, of how he'd looked over me, made me jolt. Swiping the beanie up, I stalked out of the room, pulling it over my head to conceal my hair.

Red hair was memorable, and I was the kind of guy who shouldn't be remembered.

I locked up the place and left a lot less dramatically than

Daeshim had just a short while ago. It took a little longer than necessary to get where I needed to go because even in the forest, you need to cover your tracks.

I ended up not far from Ander's place, and it only served to further spoil my mood. Just before I went inside, an inkling of awareness brushed over the back of my neck, and the bruises throbbed anew.

The glance over my shoulder might have appeared cursory, but it satisfied my instincts that I was safe. I walked in without knocking, following the light to the back of the townhouse where three men sat waiting around a table.

"Took you long enough," Rogers intoned the second I walked in.

"Do you want me to get here fast, or do you want me to get here without an audience?" I replied, keeping my voice mild. He grunted, and I shoved the hood back, revealing the black beanie. "What do you want?"

"Now, is that any way to talk to your family?" McClaren tsked.

My back teeth ground together. "Summoning me like that in the middle of the night is reckless."

"It's untraceable, and you know it," Woods said, pushing away from the table to stand. Pursing his lips, he gave me a hard stare. "Unless you're losing your touch. Is that what you're saying, Rogen?"

I stared at him levelly. "I think we both know better."

The coffee machine on the counter across the room hissed, breaking up some of the tension. "Help yourself to some coffee," Rogers invited.

I shifted more comfortably into my stance and stayed there. "I'd rather you just tell me why I'm here."

"You don't seem so glad to see us," McClaren said, a hint of suspicion underlying his tone. "You starting to forget where you come from?"

I matched his tone. "I know exactly where I come from."

"So, Little Red." Woods began. "What kind of bread did you bring in that basket of yours?"

Maybe I didn't like the unspoken challenge in McClaren's tone. Maybe I was tired, or maybe I was pissed off that I had to drag my ass all the way to Brooklyn in the middle of the night. Whatever the reason, it seemed infinitely more difficult than usual to act as if that stupid nickname didn't get under my skin.

"I wasn't aware I was supposed to bring refreshments," I remarked.

Woods's eyes narrowed into slits. If he wanted to intimidate me, he'd have to work a whole hell of a lot harder than that. "Cut the shit, Rogen. What have you got?"

"Nothing."

Silence went around the room, stopping at each man who sat and stared. I remained relaxed and unbothered, waiting out their quiet.

"What the hell do you mean you got nothing?" McClaren spoke first.

I shrugged one shoulder. "I need a few more days, maybe a week, to crack the Stein case. Whoever they had install their safeguards knew what they were doing."

"You saying you can't get in?"

"I'm saying I need a couple more days."

Rogers sat back in his seat. "Someone is losing his touch."

The tight control I had on my irritation since walking in frayed almost to snapping. "You want me to just crack into their databases full throttle and alert a bunch of child traffickers that someone is on to them? You want to be on the team that cleans up those bodies when those men decide their product has to disappear?"

"Enough." Woods grunted, giving Rogers a hard look. "No

one is questioning your ability. Just send the info when you get it. Make sure it's ironclad."

As if I'd send anything less than that—especially when kids were involved. A rogue vision of Ivory distracted me for a few seconds, her smiling as she lovingly palmed her belly. She was only a few months pregnant, but her usually flat middle was beginning to round. The thought of anyone hurting my niece or nephew the way this scum was hurting kids made me want to hurl.

"When I'm done, there will be no get-out-of-jail-free cards for any of them," I intoned.

"I have no doubt." Woods assured me, then cleared his throat. "But that's not the info we want, and you damn well know it."

Bitterness tossed itself up the back of my throat, and I pressed my lips into a line. "I just handed over the Black Rose a couple months ago, plus a couple petty arsonists as a bonus."

"The Black Rose wouldn't even have been setting up shop if not for one reason."

A hard knot formed in my stomach, and I kept my voice as neutral as possible. "I told you he's clean."

McClaren made a rude sound. Rogers sighed loudly and helped himself to the coffee. And Woods? His stare tried to drill a hole through me.

I stared back, unblinking.

His lip curved up at the side. "Your poker face is a hell of a lot better than it used to be."

*I learned from the best.*

"I wasn't aware we were playing cards."

Anger flashed in his eyes, making his back straighten. "We both know he's not innocent."

I inclined my head. "No one in the Grimms is. But if I

brought everyone in for their petty crimes, there'd be no one left in the ghetto."

"He's a killer!" Woods yelled, the words punctuated by his palm slapping down on the table.

Behind him, Rogers and McClaren froze. I could almost feel them trying to make themselves smaller to avoid his wrath.

"I've yet to find any solid proof of that. Unless you count the man he admitted to killing in self-defense."

Woods moved fast, shoving his face into mine. "You covering for him?"

"Why would I do that?" I asked very quietly.

"Maybe McClaren is right. Maybe you've been deep too long. Maybe you're forgetting where you come from."

Panic welled in my already tight throat, making me panic more. I struggled internally for long seconds, grappling for any semblance of control.

"I'm insulted," I returned, my voice very quiet, and if it was a bit raspy from anger and swollen vocal cords, well, let that tone hammer my point home. "I've brought in more scum than everyone in this room combined. And I did it from a one-room dump in the middle of the ghetto. Maybe the problem isn't with my work but with yours."

McClaren whistled low, but I didn't look in his direction. I kept my green eyes calmly on my superior.

"Excuse me?" Woods intoned.

"You got some kinda hard-on for him that no amount of release seems to wilt. I've done everything asked of me. I've been watching. Listening. Hell, I've solved four murders you were convinced he committed."

Woods's tongue ran over his teeth, clearly unhappy with my little recount.

"And what about White?" I said, adding salt to the wound.

"If he'd been the one hired to off her, wouldn't she have known? She sure as hell wouldn't be spending the holidays with him and calling him brother."

"How convenient Audra White expired in a cell," Woods spat, pacing away.

"You trying to blame that on him too?" I mused.

"He went to see her weeks before she died!"

"And I told you Audra hired the Black Rose to kill Ivory, and he got caught in the crossfire. My s—" *Fuck.* I let out a cough to cover the slip. "Virginia almost died because of it."

McClaren made a harsh sound. "That's the worst part. He's using a sad gimp to make himself look more human."

There wasn't even a chance to think, to even hold myself back. My shoulder clipped Woods as I shoved forward, hand closing around the front of McClaren's half-washed dress shirt to throw him onto the counter. The mug he'd been using tipped over and fell to the floor with a thump. Coffee splashed over my feet and jeans, but I didn't even notice.

Pinning him to the counter, I leaned over his out-of-shape torso. "The fuck you just say?"

McClaren smiled, proud he'd managed to get beneath my skin. My fist plowed into his nose. The sound of bone cracking wiped the triumph right off his jackass face. Blood spurted almost instantly, rushing over his top lip.

"Rogen." Rogers materialized behind me.

Breathing hard, I shook his hand off my shoulder, not tearing my eyes off of McClaren.

My upper lip curled, and I leaned in so close, enjoying the fear flickering deep in his pupils. "I ever hear you say something like that about my sister again, I'll knock every one of those coffee-stained teeth out of your face."

"Beau!" Woods barked.

I shoved off, pacing across the room. Agitation clung to

me like a second skin. There wasn't even room for regret to set in yet. No, not regret about busting his nose—he deserved it. If Earth had heard him, he'd have gotten a hell of a lot worse. The regret was because I'd shown emotion. That was something I never did.

*But what he said about V...*

"You've been under too long."

My head snapped up, reality rushing in. "What?"

"You're getting too close."

"I am not."

"It was bound to happen. Frankly, I'm shocked it took this long." Rogers agreed like the kiss-ass he was.

I glared at him over my shoulder, and he shrugged.

"You sure about that?" Woods asked, stepping up to fill my line of sight. "It wouldn't be the first time an agent was corrupted."

"I've been bringing in criminals for years, and you think I'm corrupt?" I laughed.

"All of them but the one I sent you in for."

*Into the forest you go, Little Red. Go and catch the big bad wolf.*

I made a sound, shaking out the hand I used to break McClaren's nose. "Is it really that hard to admit the wolf you were after isn't actually the wolf at all?"

Woods was silent a moment. Then he held out his arms as if taking in the room. "Then where is he, Rogen? Where's the killer we've been searching for?"

"Maybe he doesn't exist."

Silence descended upon the room. My superior's eyes dropped to my throat, taking in the bruises I didn't bother to cover. He stared at them a while before lifting his stare to meet mine.

I said nothing.

He said nothing.

The sound of McClaren's whistly nostril breathing filled the room.

"Finish up the Stein case, and once it's wrapped, you're out."

My entire chest constricted, making my voice sound weak. "What?"

"It's been years, Rogen. If there's no wolf to catch, then I guess it's time for Little Red to come out of the forest."

They wanted to pull me out. They wanted me to leave the Grimms?

*No. No, I can't do that.*

"But what about all the other cases I've closed?"

"You can do that from headquarters."

Headquarters was not home. "It's easier to find info when people think you're one of them."

"Well, you're not one of them. You're one of us. It's about time you remembered."

"I am. I do," I echoed, the responses so conditioned into me that I uttered them without blinking.

"Then what the hell's the problem?" Woods snapped.

Schooling my features, I shrugged. "No problem."

He grunted. "Good. Let me know when you're finished, and get the hell out of my sight!"

I pulled the hood up as I went to the front of the house, dully registering Woods snapping at someone to clean up all the blood.

Slipping out onto the street, I started walking without pause. Frigid air seeped through the material of my sweatshirt and cut through the shirt beneath it. I'd walked right out of the apartment without a coat. My thoughts had been too muddled to think to grab one.

Now they were even worse.

I noticed my pace stuttering and glanced down at my

sneakers faltering against the pavement. A small smile caught me off guard when I looked at the shoes. The shoes Fletcher used to borrow when his wore out.

The thought was like a shard of glass puncturing my chest, so I abandoned it swiftly and looked up. The choked sound disappeared in the wind as I realized exactly where I was, exactly where my feet had hesitated.

Ander and Emogen's brownstone towered beside me, the little alcove over the door dark, but through the window, I could see the dim glow from a light in the stairwell that they must have left on.

The puncture in my chest stung anew, and suddenly, the street around me turned heavy and slow. Everything grew muffled except for that sharp feeling stabbing my heart. I was dragged under as if a riptide caught hold of me and tugged down, down, down.

I didn't know it was possible to drown on dry land, but here I was, fighting against emotion so heavy it was impossible to breathe.

Bending just slightly at the waist, I tried to suck in air. Instead, my throat seized up, and my lungs overflowed with more panicked anxiety. Despite the frigid temperature, my skin grew hot, my forehead clammy.

An unsteady hand slapped against my neck, ready to rip open a new way to breathe. My fingers found the bruises instead, and I grasped almost desperately at the swollen flesh.

I wheezed greedily, finally finding air. After sucking in a few breaths, my heart rate began to slow. Straightening, I let my fingers slip down, but the sharp grip of panic slammed into me all over again.

The pads of my fingers brushed over the bruises once more, my entire hand lightly curling around my own throat. An odd sense of relief wrapped around me as though I'd been yanked free from the sea in which I'd been drowning and wrapped up in a towel.

If I hadn't already been completely pummeled, it would have freaked me out. I desperately needed reprieve. That meant accepting that the reprieve I intensely needed came from the bruises another man had put on my skin.

## 7

*Daeshim*

The locks disengaged one at a time. The second he slipped inside, I sensed it. Something was off.

I tracked his movements as he shut the door and leaned against it. He didn't bother with the locks, just stood there almost like he was numb, staring off into the darkness. Eventually, he pushed off the wood, pivoting toward the little corner of the room he'd commandeered.

*Click.* The sound of me switching on the lamp stopped him in his tracks. A flicker of surprise widened his emerald eyes before it succumbed to whatever else was cloaking him.

"Where have you been?" I inquired, dropping my hand back into my lap.

"You left first," he retorted. Then I almost, *almost* saw him grimace at the childish reply.

*Oh, how I love getting under your skin.*

"I went for a walk."

"Too bad you didn't get lost," he grumped.

"Stopped by to see Ander."

His footsteps faltered on his way to his desk, but he used the movement to kick off his sneakers as if it were his plan all along.

He was wondering... *Did he see me?*

Scoffing, he asked, "Did Emogen meet you at the door with her bat?"

I laughed under my breath. But then our fake attempt at conversation died a swift death, and I asked again, "So where were you?"

"Newsflash. I don't report to you."

"Who do you report to?"

His head snapped up at the quiet question. "What?"

Lazily, I pushed up from the chair to stroll casually toward the kitchen. "If you don't report to family, then who?"

"You aren't my family."

"What would Fletcher say if he heard you?" I mocked.

"Leave Fletch out of this!" The sudden sharpness in his tone was surprising.

Was this somehow about our little brother? Pondering that, I headed toward the fridge, standing in the open door, looking between the beer and water, not really thinking about the drinks but purely focused on the man whose eyes I felt.

"Can't you put on a shirt?" he barked, and a slow smile curved my lips.

Reaching in, I snagged a water off the shelf, pushing the door shut with my foot. Keeping my back to him, I uncapped it, making sure to ripple my back muscles as I did and then again as I took a long drink. Suddenly, I was *very* dehydrated.

I could feel his eyes on the ink covering my back. He stared a lot when he thought I wasn't looking. I didn't know if he liked it or it unnerved him, but it *always* drew his eyes.

"Better to see you with," I said quietly, knowing he would hear.

He made a rude sound and stalked into the kitchen, reaching around me to pull out a beer. After ripping off the cap, he pushed it against his lips, pouring nearly half down the back of his throat.

I stared unabashedly, raising an eyebrow when he lowered the half-empty bottle.

"I'm gonna need a hell of a lot more than half this beer if you want me to believe you got that wolf tattoo thinking it would watch your back for you."

I shifted around so we stood facing each other. "He sees a lot more than you realize."

His eyes narrowed until the green pretty much disappeared. "You think?"

I stepped forward. "I know."

"Whatever," he spat and started away.

I grabbed his arm, restraining him. Quietly, he looked down at my hand, then back up at my face. "I already punched you once tonight. Want to make it twice?"

"That why your knuckle is busted?"

"What?" His face went blank. Then something flared in his eyes. The beer lifted as he gazed down at his puffy, split knuckle.

As he stared, I spoke quietly. "I didn't think you hit me that hard."

He wrenched away, but I grabbed him again, this time tossing him against the wall. Seconds ticked by. Then the fridge kicked on, and the hum of the appliance cut through the thick tension as we stood rigidly measuring each other.

Beau jolted forward, but he didn't get far before I slapped both palms onto the wall on either side of his head, effectively caging him. The muscle in his jaw ticked, and his full lip curled up in a half snarl. The room turned almost humid with frustration and something else, our bodies coiled and ready to fight, yet neither of us moved to strike.

"No one ever wonders what it is you do on that screen all day every day," I observed, angling my chin just slightly toward his workstation in the other room.

He scoffed.

"No one ever notices you coming and going in the middle of the night."

He stilled.

"But I notice." My voice was low. "I notice a lot of things you think I don't."

Rearing back, he shoved me hard, but my body remained firmly planted in his space.

Reaching up, I ripped the beanie off his head, tossing it over my shoulder. "I notice you keep these fiery strands covered up almost every time you leave the house." His scowl turned startled when I pushed my fingers into the uncombed ginger locks, noting how they immediately curled against my skin.

He pulled away, but I dug my fingers in, and he bit off a groan. *So tense*. Not at all the laidback one he purported to be. As I massaged his scalp, he seemed to forget he'd been trying to flee, and some of the tension in his body ebbed. When his chin dipped toward his chest, I smiled.

Moving slow, I leaned in until my lips were right beside his ear and whispered, "I know you're hiding something, Red."

The beer bottle thumped against the kitchen floor when he jolted up. I stumbled back, body knocking into the table and chairs in the center of the room.

He was almost to the front door when I caught him at the back of the couch. With rough hands, I shoved him into the wall that was covered in a mural painted by Neo. He fought like the fiery redhead I knew him to be, making me grunt and twist. I don't know why I didn't just let him go, this challenge between us going much further tonight than it ever had before.

But I couldn't. Not tonight.

Suddenly, the fight drained out of him, and he went limp against the wall. I kept my hands pressed against his shoulders, not giving in just because he did. He wasn't going to fool me.

"Now is your chance to tell me what it is."

Mutiny lit his stare on fire, and I prepared myself for more fight. From the first day I'd stepped into this apartment, from the first time I'd met the man everyone announced was my new brother, I knew.

Beau wasn't as easygoing as everyone believed. Beau didn't have an addiction to the internet; he had unparalleled focus.

And also…

Beau was most definitely *not* my brother.

I felt his eyes drop from my face to my shoulder, that jade gaze trailing down toward my chest where it lingered on the black rose inked into my chest.

He seemed to wilt, staring at the flower. The smattering of freckles across his cheeks and nose suddenly seemed darker as color leached from his already pale skin.

The mood clinging to him earlier when he snuck into the house, not knowing I waited, bloomed tenfold, and it turned him weary.

His anguished whisper filled the space between us. "Isn't it enough today?"

Every ounce of challenge I pulsed with was replaced with the intense need to comfort. So much so that my entire body reacted. The second I lifted my hands off him, he sort of slumped, somehow turning smaller right before my eyes.

I communicated with only a gruff sound, using gentle hands to grasp his arms.

He glanced up but then away almost as fast.

"It's okay." I assured him, one hand skimming across the top of his shoulder to slide against his neck. Those bruises on his throat had been an accident, and even if they hadn't been, I normally wouldn't care. But I did. Even still, my attention kept returning to them, not because I worried they hurt him but because I liked seeing the marks I'd left on his skin.

*Mine.*

Just like earlier tonight, he shifted so a little more of his throat was bared to me, an action that seemed to have the ability to bring me to my knees.

My entire palm wrapped around the side of his neck, the pad of my thumb brushing gently over the worst of the bruises. "Do you hurt?"

The purr I'd been certain I almost got before cut quietly through the room, the vibration of it rubbing against my thumb and effectively denying any pain.

The bottom fell out of my stomach, and a few other parts of me went with it. Sight turned into a secondary sense as others I didn't even know I had took over. Instinct demanded the hand not caressing his neck curl around his hip and pull him in. Instinct demanded I revel in the way his forehead dropped onto my shoulder and preen under the weight he shifted for me to hold.

I felt his Adam's apple bob in his throat, the pads of my fingers brushing reassuringly over the nape of his neck. A low snuffle met with a sigh, and some of whatever he was feeling was expelled, tickling my bare chest.

I didn't think to ask him anything with words. Instead, my body shifted closer, telling him I was there. Another deep breath brushed over my skin, and then tentative fingers curled around my hip, sliding up until his skin met mine and he lightly gripped my waist.

A singsongy croon rumbled out from deep within me, ferocious enough to offer a shield but gentle enough to also give reprieve. Satisfaction imprinted on my pounding heart when he nuzzled just a little closer, turning his head so it was tucked into my neck.

I didn't think about why he was acting this way or what caused such vulnerability to bubble up. As suspicious as I was of him, I didn't care.

Suddenly, it didn't matter.

In that moment, I didn't think at all. I only listened to what he was telling me without words and answered in the most basic way I knew.

For in those unexpected moments in the middle of the night, I was not Daeshim, and he was not Beau. We were not roommates, enemies, or brothers.

As the dark enveloped us, I enveloped him, and there was only one thing we could be:

Red and his wolf.

# 8

*BEAU*

A SKINNY KID, I WALKED THE STREETS, MY PAPER-WHITE SKIN *only colored by a smattering of freckles, green eyes, and a mop of red locks. My pale, slight appearance made me more like a ghost. Even when people looked at me, they didn't see but rather gazed through me to find something else worth their attention.*

*The only time I was really noticeable was when someone wanted something, whenever they wanted to take.*

*The tiny internet café was more of a small smoke hole for the man who owned the place. The air was thick and polluted, the plaster on the wall crumbling in some places. The hard metal chairs were torture on the ass, and the heat only sometimes warmed. Even if the PCs were outdated, the internet was fast, and that's all that really mattered.*

*I spent more time here than the place I slept, and my ghost-like coloring only turned paler from the lack of sun.*

*"I'm gonna start charging rent." His craggy voice floated over*

my shoulder, bringing me back from a world where there were no people, just numbers and codes.

I barely glanced over my shoulder. "I'm paid up."

He made a sound. "I'm starting to wonder where you get the money to pay for internet when all you do is sit here all day."

"What do you care as long as I pay?" I muttered, turning back.

A heavy hand slapped on my shoulder. "What you doing on that computer all hours?"

I shrugged him off. "Did you run out of cigarettes? Why are you bothering me?"

"'Cause I'm starting to wonder what's so interesting."

"Nothing. I just like computers."

"Bullshit."

"Whatever," I muttered, grabbing up my backpack and preparing to leave.

He shoved me back into the chair, the force making it bang into the shitty little table. "You doing something illegal?"

"No." It was only illegal if I got caught.

He studied me a long minute. "I'm raising my prices."

I scoffed.

"Twenty bucks an hour."

My eyes bulged as my cheeks heated. Inwardly, I prayed my stupid skin wasn't showing my anger. "That's more than double!"

He crossed his arms over his chest. "So? Don't like it? Don't come back."

"No one will pay that."

He smiled, his teeth brown from tobacco. "New prices only affect you."

The chair skittered back when I jolted up. "You can't do that!"

"Yeah?" He leaned in, his stale breath brushing over my face. "Who's gonna stop me?"

Feeling my face flame, I grabbed my bag and shouldered past him. "Give me a cut of whatever you're doing, and I'll keep my prices the same."

*"Fuck you!"*

*His meaty fingers slapped between my shoulder blades, taking a fistful of my jacket to pull me back. "What did you just say to me?"*

*Anger swelled, making my breath come in heavy gasps. I'd been coming here for months, and he never cared before. But the second he decided I might be worth something, he changed his tune.*

*"Fuck. You." I enunciated both words, not once looking away.*

*Sure, it was stupid, but I was beyond caring.*

*My head snapped back, and the warm rush of blood trickled from my nose to pool over my top lip. Pain radiated in my head, but adrenaline kept it dull.*

*He reared back to hit me again, but I didn't wait around, instead ducking under his arm to flee out onto the street. He followed me as far as the door, his smoke-ruined voice carrying behind me as I ran.*

*"Don't come back here, you little freak!"*

*I ran a few blocks until my leg muscles burned and I needed more than just gasping breaths. Stopping in an alley, I dropped my bag at my feet, bending at the waist to catch my breath. You'd think after all these years on the streets, I'd be better at being a street rat by now.*

*But the truth was my brain only worked in numbers and codes. The real world was too chaotic and hard to understand. There was no equation or formula to make it easier, and street smarts couldn't be found on a computer screen.*

*I walked a few more blocks. The fading adrenaline left me tired, and my stomach growled, reminding me I hadn't eaten all day. I needed to head back home—if the place where I slept could even be called that.*

*I'd have to find a new internet café, and just the idea of it made me more exhausted than I already was. Bitterness tossed itself up the back of my throat, burning my esophagus.*

Snatched off the streets only to be thrown back to the wolves. Except there are no wolves here, just assholes.

*Without thought, I tugged the beanie off my head, stuffing it partially into my coat pocket. Cold air nipped at my exposed ears and the tip of my nose turned icy. I should put the cap back on, but I hadn't been wearing it for warmth anyway.*

*It didn't take long. It never did.*

*No one heard my resolved sigh as it became part of the city noise. A hand fell on my shoulder, and I wondered how bad it would be this time.*

*Spun around with aggression, I took in the faces even as I stumbled.*

Three of them. Worse than usual.

*"Hey, jackoff, what are you doing?"*

*"Passing through."*

*"There's a fee to use my street."*

*The resolve I'd felt suddenly disappeared with a snap. What was it about me that seemed so easy? My size? My red hair and pale skin? The fact I didn't roll with a crew?*

*I was sick of it. This wasn't what I signed up for.*

*Knocking away the hand still gripping my shoulder, I straightened. "Yeah? Well, I'm not giving you shit."*

*Surprise filtered his features before he laughed. "You don't have to give it to me. I'm gonna take it."*

*I swung first, hitting him in the jaw. His head rocked back, and as he moved, I kicked him in the dick. A high moan slipped from his lips as he bent toward his junk.*

*A set of hands grabbed me from behind. Jumping, I kicked out both feet, slamming them into his chest. He stumbled back, then snarled. "Hold him!"*

*The hands tightened around me, and I struggled to get free. A fist snapped my head to the side, and then another snapped it back.*

*The tang of blood coated my tongue, and I spit it on the hands binding me.*

*The man whose nuts I crushed stumbled to his feet, eyes dark with fury.*

*He lunged. I winced.*

*The hit never came.*

*A deep groan. A sharp slap. A thud.*

*Peeling my eyes open, I stared down at the body at my feet. More grunts and the sounds of flesh on flesh drew my attention, and I saw a dark figure raining down hell on the other man.*

*The hands holding me slackened, and I took my chance to rip free, spinning instantly and throwing out a fist.*

*It caught him but only because he was staring wide-eyed at the beating his friend was receiving. The second the body dropped next to his friend, the man who'd been pinning me started to back away.*

*"Hold him," the newcomer said, his back still turned, a hood over his head.*

*It took me a second to realize he'd been talking to me, but the guy attacking me seemed to know right away.*

*I might have been small, but I was fast, and I caught up to him, leaping up onto his back, closing my arms around his neck. He bucked like a bull, gagging as I held tighter, refusing to let go.*

*Movement ahead made him still. He swung around, taking me with him, to watch the approaching figure. He was dressed all in black: jeans, boots, hoodie, and leather jacket. The hood concealed his identity, but something inside me whispered that I knew exactly who he was.*

*As if to prove my intuition, he reached beneath the leather, coming out with a wicked-looking blade. I thought the man I was restraining would freak out, but it was as if he were too afraid to even run.*

*"What did I tell you about running on my street?" the voice inside the hood intoned. He had a slight accent, one I didn't know.*

*"I-I'm sorry! It was Jenkins!" he burst out, pointing a shaking finger to the man on the ground.*

*"But you're the one I'm talking to."*

*A squeal burst out of him, and then suddenly I was flipped, the* cold, hard cement slamming into my back and momentarily robbing me of sight and breath.

A low grunt brought me out of it, and I rolled onto my stomach. The two men were so close they were touching, and as I stared, the one in leather pulled back his arm, bringing with him a blood-drenched blade.

Stepping back, he held it at his side, staring at the man he'd just stabbed.

"Y-you stabbed me!" he wheezed, slapping both hands onto his side.

"I see you back here again, that ain't all I'll do."

The wounded man turned to stumble away.

"Hey."

The retreating man stiffened, turning back to the figure who stood there so calmly even as he held a dripping knife.

"Take your trash."

He stumbled over to his friends, blood starting to seep between his fingers. After nudging them with his toe, he fell onto them, which ironically woke them up.

It took less than one minute for them to realize what was going on. I stiffened, thinking they would charge him to avenge their friend.

They didn't. They picked up his body and ran off.

Silence settled on the street, and I realized I was still lying on the sidewalk, staring.

Sensing my attention, the man with the bloody blade rotated, pulling back his hood as he moved. The thick, dark fabric fell against his back as he lifted nearly black eyes to me.

"If you're gonna run these streets, you need to learn how to take care of yourself," he said.

I nodded and continued to stare.

"What are you looking at?"

"You're Asian," I observed, basically proving I was completely socially inept.

"Yeah, and you got red hair," he deadpanned.

Wiping the blade on his jeans, he returned it under his coat and started to leave.

"Wait," I said, pushing to my feet.

He stopped but didn't turn around. His hair was as black as his eyes.

"Thanks," I said because I'd stopped him and had nothing else to say.

He grunted and walked a few more steps.

The jingling of a bell made me look up. In the doorway of some rundown-looking place, he glanced over his shoulder, around a lock of inky hair. "You want a beer?"

He didn't wait to see if I would answer as though he didn't give a damn either way. I rushed off after him, watching as he stepped behind a half-finished bar.

"The beer tastes like shit," he told me, plunking down a bottle for me to drink.

Poisoning Guaranteed the label read. I glanced back up, noting the way he stared as he lifted an identical bottle of poison to his lips.

Following his lead, I grabbed the longneck, taking a mighty swig. He was right. It tasted like shit. So bad that I coughed, making it spray out over the bar.

Slapping a hand over my mouth, I looked up wide-eyed.

Already pissing off the wolf.

His lips twitched just enough for me to notice before he turned away. "Clean that up," he barked.

When I was done, he stared at me again. His glare was intense and unnerving, yet I wasn't afraid.

"What's your name?" he asked.

"Beau," I told him.

When he said nothing, I did. "What's your name?" I asked.

He was silent so long I thought he wasn't going to answer. But then finally, he did.

*"Earth."*

---

IT WAS AS IF THE DREAM CONJURED HIM UP. MY EYES SPRANG open, blurred from sleep but still making out every sharp angle of his features as he stared down from over the back of the couch.

He looked older than in that dream, and it took a moment for the past version of him to blend with the one I knew now. It was probably that realization accompanied by my sleep-addled brain that loosened my tongue. "You don't have an accent anymore."

Earth's frown deepened, his near-black eyes turning into half-moon shapes. "What?"

All clinging remnants of the dream fled, the violence of being thrust into reality stiffening my muscles. I pushed up, attempting to swallow down the entire lumpy orange lodged in my throat. "Nothing. I was dreaming," I muttered.

*"Oomph."* All my breath expelled when a large weight sprang on top of me, halting my attempt to get off the couch. Snort's impressively loud mouth breathing drowned out every other sound as his warm, wet, and textured tongue licked up the side of my face.

His entire back end was wiggling, and I winced away from his tongue even as I scratched behind his ear. "Hey, Snort."

The mouth breathing grew louder with the acknowledgment, and his smooshed nose nudged my hand for more attention.

"What the hell are you doing on the couch?" Earth asked, still towering over me from behind the sofa.

I gave him an *ain't it obvious* look and said, "Ah, sleeping?"

"You sick?"

Snort licked me again, making me grunt. "Dog breath."

"Come get some bacon, Snort!" a sunshiny voice beckoned.

Snort leaped off the couch instantly, his nails clicking over the floor as he raced off. Sitting up, I looked over the cushions toward the kitchen where Virginia was near the small table, a white paper sack in her lap.

"He's going to get the shits," Earth told her.

"He's hungry," V retorted, giving the dog an entire piece of bacon. Then completely ignoring Earth's glowering, she smiled at me. "Sorry to wake you, but we brought breakfast!"

"Is it for us or the dog?" Earth bitched.

"I'm giving Snort your portion!"

He muttered under his breath, but I saw the way his lips twitched.

Virginia laughed when Snort put his front paws up on her lap, sniffing enthusiastically at the bag. The wheelchair she was sitting in slipped backward under the force of his weight.

"Snort," Earth warned in a quiet yet ominous voice. The dog jumped down immediately, then gave a small lick to V's fingers like he was apologizing.

Her hair was in some sort of braid that wrapped around her head, and there were flowers stuck in the woven pieces. Her sweater was a light shade of purple, and her cheeks were flushed pink. "Good boy," she crooned, giving him more bacon.

Last night stole over my head as I looked at her. The insult McClaren had so easily spat about her made me pissed off all over again. I should have done more than bust his nose.

Abandoning the couch, I went into the kitchen, dropping beside the wheelchair where my sister sat. Without thinking too much, I reached out and wrapped her in a hug. Her small frame jolted in surprise but then relaxed almost immediately and hugged me back. She smelled like flowers. Which kind, I didn't know, but it was nice, much better than the cigarette smoke that clung to the inside of my nostrils.

If I'd been thinking clearly, or maybe even more awake, I wouldn't be doing this. It was very rare for me to be affectionate, but I was off balance. Last night. The dream... *Daeshim.*

It was almost as if just the whisper of him inside my head made me all too aware of his presence. Following that awareness, I gazed over Virginia's shoulder where he was leaning against the counter, a cup of coffee in his hand.

The same hand that offered comfort just hours before.

Our stares met and held for the briefest of seconds before I wrenched mine away. Swallowing down the awkwardness I was saddled with, I tugged back from Virginia and smiled. "Coffee?"

Her face fell a little. "I didn't bring that. I figured you would already have made some by now."

It was true. I was usually up by now, logged in and working away as the sun rose. Today I was in no hurry to get behind that screen.

"No worries. Daeshim already made some."

"I brought donuts!" she said, twisting around to flip the lid off a white box. "And sandwiches."

Straightening, I reached for a glazed pastry.

Earth's hand fell onto my shoulder, spinning me around. "What's wrong with you?" he demanded.

I blinked. "Nothing."

He made a rude sound, his eyes practically calling me a liar. "You sick?"

I made a face. "Why would I be sick?"

His face twisted like he was constipated. "Because you aren't behind that desk," he said, punctuating his words by jabbing toward my workstation and then at the couch. "And because you were sleeping on the couch when I got here."

I usually slept over near my desk on a rollout bed I kept there. When he still lived here, Fletcher slept on the couch.

Out of the corner of my eyes, I glanced at Daeshim, who just stood watching us all like we were some kind of movie. He felt my attention, though, openly staring at me while lifting the mug to his lips.

Forcing my attention back to Earth, I shrugged. "So? I fell asleep watching TV."

The lie rolled right off my tongue. I was so used to telling lies that sometimes even I believed them.

But not that one.

The truth played in my head, and the feelings just the memory conjured fisted around my chest.

*We didn't speak. He didn't ask despite the vulnerability leaking from me and filling up the room. His hands were warm and confident. His even breathing secure. All the energy he'd put into challenging me suddenly shifted into something else. I felt it ripple under his skin. He wasn't wearing a shirt. I fit into the crook of his neck, asking for a reprieve, so relieved to find it that I didn't question why it was him who offered it. No one else could give it anyway.*

*My limbs grew heavy as he soaked up the worst of my exhaustion like he was a sponge with endless capacity. When I swayed a little on my feet, the soft noise he made had my eyes slipping farther closed. I let him guide me the short distance to the couch. I let his body press mine into the cushions, sighing with relief when he stayed close for a few minutes more. Sleep held out its hand when a blanket draped over me, trapping in the warmth his body left behind. I let it pull me down, taking the reprieve I'd never allowed myself before.*

"Liar." The one-word accusation cruelly pulled me out of that place I'd slipped back into, though a part of me yearned to stay. I shot a look at Daeshim, panic clawing in my throat. He wouldn't dare tell Earth about last night... *Would he?*

Earth divided his dark stare between me and his brother.

Pushing away from the counter, Daeshim helped himself to more coffee, the last of what was in the pot. Smirking, he turned back. "Beau's exhausted because he left in the middle of the night and was gone for hours."

*Asshole.*

Earth turned the weight of his stare fully on me, but I wasn't intimidated. I'd lived with him for too long to ever be truly afraid. "Why were you out in the middle of the night?"

Turning away from him and Virginia, I moved casually to the fridge. Reaching in, I grabbed a bottle of creamer we mostly kept here because Fletch liked it—but maybe I did too.

Everything inside the icebox rattled when I shoved the door closed. Popping the lid off the top, I told the room, "Guess I needed some air after Daeshim here tried to strangle me."

I heard his intake of breath and fought the urge to smirk. Instead, I watched Earth's eyes drop to the bruises on my neck and then widen.

Off to his side, Virginia gasped, which made Earth's jaw turn to granite. Looking at his brother, he asked, "You did that?"

Daeshim kept his posture relaxed against the counter, but everything else about him was alert.

Lifting the creamer, I added a few dollops into the mug Daeshim was holding. His relaxed posture stiffened, his stare dismissing Earth so he could look at me like I was insane.

I smiled like a hungry cat who'd caught a mouse. *Two can play at this game.*

Abandoning the bottle to the counter, I took the mug from his grasp. *If* our fingers bumped together and *if* a shot of awareness zinged up my arm toward my chest, well, I didn't notice.

"That's mine," he growled, and oh, a delicious sort of heat unfurled low in my belly.

Over the rim of the mug, I stared as I took a long sip. "Not anymore."

His eyes flashed as though he would lunge, but my soft words stopped him in his tracks. "Better to taste you with."

The pupils in his eyes dilated when I drank from the mug once more.

*What the fuck are you doing, Beau?*

Trying to unsettle him the way he unsettled me last night. It was reckless and stupid, two things I defied every single day… but two things I ultimately would always be.

A hard hand slapped onto my shoulder, and my swallow turned into a choke. The cough turned strangled when Earth's hand wrapped around my throat, quickly sliding up to grasp my jaw and push, baring my throat to his stare.

Even though he wasn't rough, I started to choke anew. *Wrong, wrong, wrong.* It wasn't a thought but an instinct, something I could not ignore. It eclipsed everything around me as if my brain just dropped offline.

Muffled curses, the splash of something hot, and a thud dully registered, but none of it was strong enough to bring me back. My brain only blinked back on when instinct allowed, when that horrible wrongness I'd known was gone.

"Stop it!" Virginia wailed, making me lift my eyes.

Following her stricken expression, I took in everything I'd somehow been present for but wholly missed. All my attention zeroed in on the wolf tattooed across Daeshim's back. I felt its eyes as if they were far more than ink on skin.

A ripple of chaotic calmness washed over me, and my muscles began to relax.

Until, that is, I noticed how the wolf and his owner were snarling at Earth who he had pinned roughly against the wall.

# 9

---

*Daeshim*

Behind every action is a thought. And behind every thought is some kind of desire.

It was becoming frighteningly clear to me I was able to skip over all thought and go right to desire. Right to instinct.

I understood it was borderline irrational, but it made it no less potent. If anything, it made it more. The second Earth grabbed Beau's neck, the very second another man bared his throat, thought ceased. Thought was steamrolled by desire so pungent it unleashed the type of instinct I truly thought only animals could know.

*Protect. Claim. Own.*

Mine.

It didn't matter Earth was my little brother. It didn't matter he was the only family I had left. The sight of those fingers on Beau's freckled, pale neck incited me. Blind rage took over, and before I knew what was happening, I had him pinned to the wall, my entire body coiled for battle.

"Don't touch him like that," I snarled, barely recognizing my own voice.

There was not an ounce of fear emanating from my brother, and it sort of pissed me off. He should be afraid. Afraid of what I would do to protect what's mine. "You mean look at the bruises *you* put on him." He challenged.

Off to the side, Virginia made a sound, and she must have started forward because Earth's entire body went rigid.

"Stay back," he demanded, using a tone he probably never did with her.

Immune to guilt, wildness still had a hold on me. I felt it rushing in my veins, mixing with my blood, making me feel invincible.

"Beau," Virginia whispered, her tone pleading. But it wasn't her tone that cut through. It was who she called for.

I faltered, thought finally trickling back into my brain. What the fuck was I doing?

With a grunt, I shoved off Earth, looking over my shoulder to where Beau stood. His green eyes were owlishly wide, coffee plastered his shirt to his chest, and a broken mug lay at his feet. His normally pale skin was flushed red, nearly matching his uncombed hair.

I stiffened when a memory flashed behind my eyes from just moments ago, and I knew just from the way my heartbeat tripled that it was likely what set me off.

He panicked.

The second Earth grabbed his neck, distress took over. It paralyzed him like an electric shock. All he could do was stand there and know how terribly wrong it was to be vulnerable like that to someone else.

Someone who wasn't me.

*Instinct took over him the way it took over for you.*

I caught the noise trying to claw its way out of my throat but couldn't stop myself from rotating toward him.

Earth stopped me midway, shoving me back. "You try and kill him?"

"Earth, *please*." Virginia's small voice broke all the emotion controlling the room.

With a grunt, Earth shoved away from me to go to his woman's side. The second he lowered beside her, she practically threw herself into his chest with a low sob. "It's okay, sprite," he murmured against her flower-filled hair as he stood with her in his arms.

Glittering, black eyes as hard as diamonds gazed over the woman he cradled. "Fletcher was worried about you two. I told him you were fine. You make a liar out of me?"

I cursed.

Virginia's small hand curled up around Earth's neck.

Tucking her a little closer, he glared at us still. "I want a goddamn explanation, and I want it right now."

"Brothers shouldn't fight like this," Virginia said, lifting her face out of Earth's chest.

Up until this point, Beau had said very little, and it wasn't because he wasn't bold enough to get between us. He was likely as shocked as I was.

So when he cleared his throat and spoke, I couldn't help but turn in his direction. "It was an accident."

"An accident." Earth's echo told us we were full of shit.

Stepping over the mess, Beau went to the table to snatch a donut and take a huge bite. "He was having a nightmare. I tried to wake him," he said, smacking his lips. "I knew better."

Virginia pulled herself out of Earth's chest to look at me with wide eyes. "You were having a nightmare?"

I didn't want to talk about it, but if we upset her any more, I'd probably end up with Earth's knife through my shoulder. Again. "Yeah."

"It must have been horrible. Do you get them very often?" she asked, empathy dripping from her voice.

*More than I wish I did.* I shrugged. "It's no big deal."

"The bruises around our brother's neck say different," Earth rebuked.

"He's not my brother," we both said at exactly the same time.

Earth's eyes narrowed, the reaction a lot more unsettling than the much louder one that came from the tiny woman in his arms.

"What? How can you even say that?" Virginia practically yelled. "I know you two argue a lot, but this is too much. How can you say you aren't brothers?"

"What do you dream about?" Earth followed her question with one of his own.

Both were landmines, so I turned my back and busied myself making another pot of coffee.

Since, you know, someone took mine and then dumped it all over the floor.

*Better to taste you with.*

The base of my spine tingled when those words echoed through my head.

*"Hyung."* It always got me when Earth called me that. Older brother. Someone who was respected and looked up to. Revered even.

I slammed the carafe down on the burner and turned. "I'd rather not talk about it," I said, sliding a quick glance at Virginia.

It was a dirty trick because if Earth thought for a second whatever I dreamed about would upset his girl more, he would drop the topic right there.

"It obviously must be horrible if you would strangle Beau," she said.

"I shouldn't have tried to wake him. The bruises are just as much my fault as they are his," Beau said, gazing at the coffeepot as though he could will it to brew faster.

"And that's why you went out in the middle of the night," Earth surmised.

He nodded once. "I just needed a breather."

I grabbed a clean mug and the coffee pot, which was still brewing, to pour out what was already done. I knew it was a bald-faced lie... yet I believed him.

I thought about how he felt curled into my chest, how everything in me was compelled to protect. Probably why I was so keyed up this morning.

Perhaps it wasn't a lie after all. He did need a breather. Just not the one he led Earth to believe.

The creamer was still open on the counter, and I added some into the mug before carrying it over to Beau, holding it out. His eyebrows shot up as he stared at what I offered.

"Just take it," I snapped.

He did, and even though I was annoyed as hell, I felt some innate sense of satisfaction when he drank what I gave him.

"Maybe you should come stay with us for a while," Earth suggested to Beau.

I paused mid-pour, the carafe hovering over my new mug precariously as the machine hissed and groaned for me to hurry up.

"Me?" Beau echoed.

Earth grunted.

"My computer is here," he said simply.

I started pouring again.

"Daeshim, then," Virginia suggested, making me turn.

Earth tilted his head, studying me. I could practically hear him trying to decide if it would be safe to have me in such close quarters with Virginia.

Part of me was offended by it, but the other part knew he was right.

Life had left me with a short fuse and a violent nature. Virginia was soft and fragile, and my brother loved her. And because of that, I would never hurt her... at least intentionally.

A few seconds ticked by, and then Earth nodded once. "Yeah, how about it, Hyung?"

I cocked my eyebrow. *You really trust me with her?*

He cocked one back. *Fuck this up, and I'll kill you.*

"No," I said out loud.

His eyes flared, and I shook my head once, telling him I wasn't refusing because I thought I was a danger to Virginia.

"Might be good for you to, ah, let whatever it is between you two cool down." He pressed.

I glanced at Beau, noting that the bruises seemed darker today. They probably ached more as well. The redness in his cheeks was gone, and the thousands of freckles dotting his skin were on full display. We'd been at each other's throats for months. I hated being his roommate, and he hated being mine.

But he was hiding things. Secrets. After last night, I was surer than ever.

If I left now, I might not figure him out.

"Want to have the place to yourself for a while, Beau?" Earth asked.

My fingers tightened around the mug so tense they ached as I lifted my gaze to look at my roommate. He squirmed a bit under the gaze of three people, and I could practically taste the stress being put in the middle caused.

I could have offered to leave for a while and just ended it right then. I didn't. Instead, I watched him struggle for long moments until something became very clear.

He didn't want me to go. But he couldn't ask me to stay.

If he did, he would have to go against Earth and then explain why he wanted to keep rooming with a man who nearly strangled him in his sleep.

*He doesn't want me to go.*

The realization made me slightly euphoric even if I did think this was insane.

Clearing his throat, he looked between me and Earth, and I knew.

*It's okay, Red. I'll be the big bad so you can be the good.*

"No," I announced, slamming my hand onto the back of an empty chair. "I'm not moving out. If you want me out, you can make me."

Earth stood, shoulders tight. "I can."

"No," Beau said, his mug clinking down on the table. "I'm a grown-ass man, Earth. I don't need you to take care of me."

Earth scowled.

Beau's next words were quiet. "You already taught me how to take care of myself."

That seemed to take some of the fight right out of him. Earth backed down, his ass hitting the chair. "If I see any more bruises on either of you, I'm kicking out both your asses."

"Whatever," I spat and poured the rest of my coffee down my throat. "I'm going to the bar. I need to stock."

"What about breakfast?" Virginia called after me as I fled the kitchen.

"I'm not hungry!"

"You sure about this?" I heard my brother ask after they assumed I'd gone.

My hands clenched and unclenched at my sides, waiting for Beau's reply.

"Yeah," he said after a minute. "I'm sure."

It was hardly a ringing endorsement. It sounded more like a resolved sigh. But damn, if it didn't make being the asshole feel good.

## 10

*Beau*

My eyelids felt like sandpaper. Every single time I blinked, another layer of my already-dry eyeballs was scraped away. The ever-present glow of the monitor was beginning to make my skin feel tight, and the dull throb in my temples annoyed me.

I didn't even know how long I'd been sitting there. Twenty-four hours? Forty-eight? After Earth and Virginia left the other morning, I'd all but chained myself to this desk. Daeshim came and went a few times. I registered his presence like a light in the dark, but I pretended to be blind to him.

The fault lines between us shifted, becoming so precarious that even the slightest change would set off a cataclysmic earthquake the likes of which would transform everything forever.

Desperately, I tried to ignore him, the soreness in my throat reminding me I could not. You'd think I would have jumped at the chance to get out of this place, away from the man who nearly choked the life out of me.

It seemed, however, that as valiantly as I tried to stay away from him, something much stronger kept me in place.

It was confusing. It was irritating. It made me hate him more.

I was relieved when he refused Earth's offer so adamantly.

As loathe as I was to work—a first time for me—I imprisoned myself at this desk to break the case that would likely end my life as I knew it.

I felt guilty for not wanting to work. The kids being abused needed me to work fast. I understood the damage to them was done. They would be scarred and damaged forever, and me breaking this case wouldn't fix that. But I could prevent further scars from happening. I could prevent kids not yet stolen from suffering the same fate.

That was the bigger picture here. More important than what ending this job would cost me. And so I used it as a distraction and continued pecking away while ignoring the gritty feeling in my eyeballs and everything around me I didn't want to acknowledge.

Whoever this scum hired to do their cyber work was really good at their job. Three attempts at getting into their networks, files, and systems had failed. Three attempts at getting irrefutable info to bring down an entire ring of child endangerment, pornography, and abuse thwarted.

They might be good, but I was better, and I refused to give up. If anything, I channeled all the wild, churning emotions pummeling me into absolute resolve to bring these fuckers down.

My chair creaked when I sat back, letting out a heavy sigh. Snatching up the Red Bull, I drained the rest into my mouth, tossing the empty can onto the floor where it joined all the others.

*I know you're hiding something, Red.*

His words echoed in my head as they often had since that night. The nickname hit so close to home, nearly terrifying me with what he could know. But that bone-chilling fear was also underscored with something else.

Something even more frightening.

The true reason I was so eager to hide behind this monitor, bathed in artificial light with sharp toothpicks keeping my eyes from closing.

Clarity.

As if after all this time someone truly looked at me, past the lies I disguised with truth. Deeper than who I was to a part even I barely knew. And upon that discovery, the hate he always snarled at me with morphed into something else, something not even hate could withstand. Not love. No, this was far much more. I didn't know what it was, but it was heavier than anything I'd ever known, nearly suffocating but not quite. It was also addictive. So heavily addictive it consumed me from the very first second.

My scoff filled the empty apartment. *If he really knew, he wouldn't accept. If he really knew, you'd be dead.*

Yet I stayed in this apartment, flirting with the idea of being found out because, as I said, I was suddenly addicted and because the one-in-one-million chance he actually might accept eclipsed the idea of even death.

I was fucked.

A brief buzzer-like sound filled my ears and cut off all my thoughts. Instantly, I looked back at the screen at the small red X that flashed up inside a small white box.

"Son of a bitch!" I fumed, ripping the headphones off my head and throwing them across the room.

Chest heaving, I rocketed up out of the chair so fast it hit the wall behind me with a loud bang. The urge to swipe everything off my desk was so strong I vibrated with it. My arms shot out, and my palms slapped the table.

Just before I did it, I wrenched back, stomping away into the living room where I punched the top of the couch.

Breath heaving, I straightened, pinning my hands behind my head to pace.

I was not this guy. I was not explosive and volatile. I was laidback. I was chill. I kept my emotions on lock. I never let it get the best of me.

*Until Daeshim nuzzled your throat.*

*Until your coworker called you family and insulted Virginia.*

*Until Daeshim shouldered the crippling anxiety you couldn't contain without even caring where it came from.*

*Until they told you to pack it up.*

How was I supposed to leave?

*Little Red sent into the forest to find a wolf, but instead, he found home.*

A broken sound ripped out of me, and I stopped pacing to stare at the wall. How the fuck did my life get like this?

And how the fuck did those douchebags kick me out of their system again?

*Screw them.* The thought made me grunt, and I pounded back over to my desk. I couldn't control a lot of shit in my life, but this? This I could fucking own.

"You want to play a game, little boys?" I intoned, my fingers flying over the keyboard at a speed even I found impressive. "Play with this."

My finger jabbed into the key with finality as I straightened, crossing my arms over my chest to stare at the screen with a smirk. "Here I come," I sang.

Calmed a bit by the epic move I just pulled, knowing that no matter what they did, I was breaking in this time made me feel more in control.

It would take a while—likely hours—for what I just did to crack into their database, but it would happen. And in the meantime, I could grab a shower and something other than energy drinks.

Maybe I'd call Fletch and see if he wanted to hang. I could take him to that fancy hot chocolate place he loved so much. My stomach tightened a little at the thought of my baby brother. At the thought that my time with him was probably limited.

On my way to the shower, I called up his number on my cell. Just before I dialed, I noticed the time. Almost two a.m.

Spinning, I glanced at the window, but the curtains were drawn. Swearing beneath my breath, I tossed the phone on the couch. I didn't even know what time it was. Hell, what day it was.

Calling Fletch would have to wait.

Another thought had me turning toward the bedroom. Was Daeshim here? When was the last time I felt his presence? Frowning, I tried to remember. It seemed like a while. Like he was avoiding me too.

If he was here, I'd know.

Was he down at the bar? The Rotten Apple was still Earth's place, but Daeshim put a lot of time in there. He often took the late-night shifts so Earth could be home with Virginia.

I was halfway through undoing all the locks on our door when a muffled bang had my head lifting. Cocking it to the side, I stood silently, listening.

*Thud. Shatter.*

Did a fight break out in the bar? It wouldn't be the first time.

A loud shout.

*Daeshim.* My hands flew over the rest of the locks, and I

flung the door wide, not even pausing to pull it shut behind me.

The sounds of a struggle grew louder and louder as I ran down the stairs.

Another grunt—wholly Daeshim's—filled my ears, and without hesitation, I threw myself into the fight.

---

## 11

*Daeshim*

THE ROTTEN APPLE WAS A HOLE-IN-THE-WALL BAR MY brother owned in a shitty building that sat below our rundown apartment in an equally shitty part of the ghetto. It had brick walls and ugly multicolored string lights draped around the place.

He served beer he brewed and bottled himself, the label claiming it would poison you.

It made me proud.

Proud that I shot him all those years ago and dumped his body so our fucked-up family thought he was dead. I'd do it all over again if it meant he would end up here, running this place on his own terms.

I made a lot of mistakes in my life. In fact, most everything I did was reprehensible. But getting my little brother out of the Black Rose was something good. Even if I was heavily punished for it.

Even if he had turned into a contract killer, it was still

worth it. Because as I said, he lived on his own terms. For my entire life, living like that had been just a dream... until I'd come here prepared to die. Now I lived on my own terms too. It wasn't as easy as it looked, but it was still better than the alternative.

Since he moved up the block into a renovated building with Virginia, I'd taken over his bedroom and closed the bar a lot. He still did it sometimes, but it made him scarier than usual because leaving Virginia at home alone late at night made him murderous.

Murderous didn't sell a lot of beer.

Not that I was charming, but they were used to Earth's asshole disposition, and since I was also an asshole, the regulars got used to me well enough too.

For a while, my presence actually drew in more business. People were curious to meet the brother no one knew Earth had. They wanted to see if I was as intimidating as him.

They learned real fast that I was.

In my opinion, I was far worse than Earth, having done more despicable things than he, but he was top dog on these streets, and I had no desire to one-up him. Besides, it was good not to show all the cards in your hand because someday you might need the surprise they held.

I let the regulars linger tonight, in no hurry to close up shop. Going upstairs and seeing Beau hunched behind those fucking monitors made me feel about as murderous as Earth.

After I flat out refused to move out, we settled into an odd sort of avoidance, if you could call it that. We pretended not to notice each other. We pretended not to see the sidelong glances, and we evaded the hard fact that we stayed in close proximity to each other even while we acted like we didn't.

Keep your friends close but your enemies closer.

Beau wasn't my friend or my enemy. He was something else. Something far more.

Around one thirty, I finally kicked out the last drunk and went behind the bar to clean up. When that was done, I went to the back for more longnecks to stock the cooler.

My intuition was piqued the second my arms reached into the icebox, cold air caressing my bare arms like a frigid kiss. But it wasn't the low temp that made the hair on the back of my neck stand or the bolt of awareness glide down my spine.

Cocking my head, I listened, silence the only sound I heard.

Silence, though... Oh, silence could be a capable liar. Silence was very good at disguising the truth.

But vibes, they never lied. *Ever.*

And my normally impeccable instincts had been even more honed as of late.

*Because of Beau.*

I shook my head, banishing the thought. Now wasn't the time.

*Focus.*

Taking the silence for what it was, I continued. The bottles in the box clinked together as the cooler door banged shut behind me. Arms full of cardboard and poison, I scuffed my boots along the floor on my way back out front. The muscles in my neck were so tight my ears started to feel hot, but I maintained an unhurried pace. The bar was empty just like the silence purported, and I practically dumped the box of beer onto the counter.

The ugly Christmas lights were still on around the room, the poisoning guaranteed neon sign over the bar still lit in red. Music from the sound system fought with the silence, but it was a pathetic fight.

And seriously, the music playing was pathetic too. Earth needed some better shit.

Boots sticking to the linoleum floor, I reached beneath the bar to push open the cooler tops, the rush of icy air saying hello.

Sniffing, I reached into the box, closing my hand around a longneck, then spun, firing the bottle over the bar toward the inky shadow breaking free from the small darkened alcove where the bathroom sat.

The beer hit the target, eliciting a grunt before bouncing to the floor and shattering.

The man dressed all in black burst forward, knocking over a barstool, and leaped over the bar as though he were a parkour expert.

A fissure of familiarity made my gut heave, but I shoved that back because now was no time for distraction.

Launching up, his feet hit the edge of the counter, and he propelled himself forward, leaping at me like some kind of toxic frog.

I sidestepped his attempt, and he hit the ground like a cat, straightening up and spinning without any loss of balance. More familiarity befell me, and again, I denied the distraction to plant my foot in his midsection and shove, sending him backward into a cooler. His back bowed over the edge, and as he straightened, he pulled out a bottle from the open case and pitched it at me.

Sinking low, I avoided the glass, and it splintered loudly against the back wall just over my head. Droplets of beer splattered on my back as I hurled forward, taking us both to the ground.

He landed a sucker punch to my gut, making me grunt, but then I landed a hit of my own. He was wearing a black ski mask, which I thought was a pussy move. If you wanted to come at me, then come on. Don't hide.

Sinking my weight into the thinner man, I yanked my fist back to deliver another blow, planning to rip off the fabric the second he was in la-la land.

Midway through the swing, my arm faltered as pain lanced through me, sharp and familiar but pungent just the same. Hand still fisted, I glanced down at my chest and the rip in my T-shirt. Blood made the dark fabric look wet.

Tearing my eyes up, I saw the small red-stained blade clutched in his gloved hand.

Time was suspended for a few seconds as we stared at each other, sort of like neither of us could believe the audacity of this asshole. But then it was over, and the blade came slashing at me again. I knocked it out of his hand, sending it sliding under a cooler.

I slammed my fist in his face, feeling satisfied when the back of his head thumped off the hard floor.

Taking a fistful of his jacket, I dragged his half-conscious body from behind the bar and farther into the room, dropping him between a few tables. There was nothing gentle about the way I ripped the black mask off his face and tossed it aside.

The very second my eyes lay upon his features, shock rendered me motionless. Betrayal rocked me on my heels. I'd known he was familiar... but this wasn't familiarity. It had been friendship.

I stood there for long moments, spiraling, knowing I had shit to demand. *Who sent you? What the fuck are you thinking?* I didn't get the chance.

His whole body whipped around, legs slamming into mine and swiping me onto the floor. I landed with a heavy groan, the gash in my chest choosing that moment to burn. He was on me in seconds, pinning me to the ground and pulling out yet another blade.

This one was bigger.

"Dangsin-eun dangsin-ui seontaeg-eul haessda. Geuligo ije nae geos-eulo mandeul-eossseubnida." The man spoke in Korean. Since it was my first language, my brain didn't have to struggle to keep up. *You made your choice. And now I've made mine.*

But the rest of me?

I seemed to be in shock.

The blade came down, and I stiffened, snapping out of it a little too late.

A body I hadn't heard coming, a person I didn't expect, soared over me, crashing into my attacker at full speed. The knife landed off to the side with a clatter, and a series of grunts and groans rose toward the ceiling.

Scrambling up, I watched Beau—who was fucking barefoot and straddling the ninja, red hair all wild—deliver a swift punch to the man under him.

The ninja fought, bucking up as if Beau weighed nothing at all, his body bending and bowing. Somehow he got out from under him, and the two locked together like two bulls about to fight to the death.

One hit. That's all it took.

One fist into the side of Beau's ribcage, and I saw black. With a howl, I threw myself into the fight, Beau's shirt tearing under the force with which I grabbed him, tossing him back.

Heart thundered. Chest dripped with blood. Black eyes pierced the man I used to call friend.

He knew.

He knew he'd done something to flip the switch inside me, and now he would never, ever stand a chance. Whatever choice he'd made by coming here tonight—it was a choice made in vain.

His eyes widened a fraction, then slipped over my

shoulder toward Beau, maybe trying to figure out if he was the reason I'd suddenly transformed.

The sound of his neck cracking was so loud it reverberated off the walls. I moved so fast his eyes never even made it to the red-haired man standing behind me. The crack seemed to echo even after the dead man crumpled to my feet. His dark eyes stared off at nothing, the last thing he would ever see.

It took a single heartbeat for the rest of me to catch up to what I'd done, but even as I stared down at the lifeless body, I felt no remorse.

It hadn't been my plan to kill him, but he went after Beau.

*Beau.*

Sucking in a breath, I turned, ready and willing to boldly face his reaction, the expression in his eyes from just watching me kill.

*This is who I am.*

His green stare was unreadable as it flicked to the body, then back up to mine.

And then?

He ended me.

"The better to see you with," he whispered.

Surging forward, my lips locked on his, my deep growl twining around us before I even knew I moved. My fists were so tight in the front of his shirt the bones in my fingers screamed in pain, but it only made me grip tighter.

I kissed him ferociously, forcing his lips wide and crawling inside. My God, he was warm and sweet, and the texture of his tongue made me growl again.

The full mouth I always tried to ignore was the perfect place for my lips, having just enough padding to cushion the violence with which I devoured.

A noise vibrated his throat and his nostrils flared, hot breath expelling over my top lip. Those details only spurred me on. I licked deeper, fucking into his mouth with wild abandon, getting lost in his taste until a very vague thought penetrated the haze.

*He's kissing back.*

My tongue jolted. His chased. My eyes popped wide even as we tangled anew. He heard the silent call, and then I was drowning in those goddamn green orbs, falling into their depths, the greatest fall I'd ever known.

Sucking in a breath without disengaging our lips, I unknotted one hand from the front of his shirt to splay it over the side of his jaw. One finger landed on his pulse point, and its hammering matched the beat of my heart.

He watched me still, so I tilted my head just slightly, pushing the pads of my fingers farther into his skin. His lashes swept down, breaking the spell of his jade gaze but shackling me with something else.

The kiss shifted and changed. The air around us grew thick and hot. What first was violent and demanding became insistent and effortless. I didn't have to take... He was offering it up.

Groaning, I stroked my tongue over his, our lips slipping together like two halves of a whole. The silky skin on the inside of his lips was my kryptonite, the softest sensation I'd ever experienced.

Lazily, I tugged his lower lip between mine, fingers tightening against his head. Dear God, his lips were plump and ripe, forbidden fruit I'd longed to take a bite of.

The kiss went on, and he swayed a little on his feet. *No.* He rocked gently back and forth as if his senses were overloaded—overloaded by me.

When I released his lip, his tongue chased, and I made a broken sound. His bare feet hit my booted ones when I tugged him close. His long fingers whispered over my shirt, gliding up toward my chest. Oh, his hands on me felt like sin as if he blazed with the same fire in his hair and the flames scorched my skin.

The smacking sound of our lips breaking apart didn't register. In fact, nothing did until my tongue stroked his again, but I came up with air.

"You're bleeding," he announced, voice husky.

"What?" I echoed dumbly, reaching for him again.

A choked sound left his throat, and he denied the attempt. I might have turned hostile if the rip of my shirt and the brush of cool air didn't distract me.

Glancing down, I watched newly opened fabric fall to the sides of my waist, and Beau's hand came palm up between us. His fingers were smeared with red.

Gasping, I grabbed his wrist, a murderous rage overtaking it all.

"It's yours," he said, his voice probably the only thing capable of penetrating that particular haze.

"What?" I rasped, still gripping his wrist so hard it likely hurt. But he didn't complain. He didn't even wince.

"The blood is yours. What happened?"

Still slightly muddied in the head, I grunted. "Knife." Releasing his wrist, I noted the gash on my pec, the smears of crimson over my olive-toned skin. In the center of it was the black rose tattoo… and I stared fascinated as fresh blood welled, seemingly right out of its venomously-colored petals to drip over its leaves.

"The Black Rose bleeds red," I muttered, the words not really a thought but somehow bringing it into existence.

"That's okay. Red is kinda my color."

Possession so strong hit me, and I took a step back. Curling my hand around the back of his neck, I anchored us together and went in for his lips.

He made a sound and turned his face, my kiss landing against his freckles.

*I like that too.*

But it was his mouth I wanted. Wanted to feel it under mine, wanted to grind us together until we were nothing more than a single flavor.

"You're bleeding." He reminded me, voice quiet, eyes refusing to meet mine.

*Oh*, I liked when his eyes were slightly downcast when he spoke to me.

"I don't care," I snapped, reaching for him again.

His eyes came up like a pair of flashing emeralds. Clearly, he was willing to surrender, but he would also never hesitate to fight back. "I do."

I sat in the nearest wooden chair, my breath expelling the second my ass hit the seat.

Beau went into Earth's office and came back with a white kit. He completely ignored the body of the man I'd killed to drag an identical chair up to mine. The kit flopped open on the tabletop. Beau rifled through without any kind of organization. Bandages and white packets fell everywhere. A small tube of something rolled free.

His hands were shaking.

"Hey," I murmured, voice as soft as that skin on the inside of his lip.

He stilled when my hand covered his jittering one, but his eyes refused to meet mine.

"Did he hurt you?" I asked, and the second the idea took root, the need to defile a dead man's body became fierce.

"No."

I let that soothe some of my harshest thoughts, a frown pulling my lips. "I killed him right in front of you." I didn't think that was the problem, but my mind went there regardless.

He made a rude sound. "It was him or you."

"Are you glad it wasn't me?"

His hand pulled free of mine to begin rummaging in the kit again. After laying out a few supplies, he used his teeth to rip open an alcohol pad. "I don't like this blood."

*My blood. He didn't like my blood.*

The need to pull him down on the floor and push him under me was so strong I slid forward on the seat. His hand flattened on my shoulder and shoved me back, the alcohol-drenched pad slapped onto the gash.

"Oww!" I roared, bucking up.

"Don't be a baby."

"A baby!" I fumed. "I'd like to see you take that torture liquid to an open knife wound without screaming."

His eyes finally met mine, and I swear a little of me relaxed. One ginger brow arched roguishly up his forehead. *He has millions of freckles there too.*

"You want to see? I'll show you."

Leaning down, he grabbed the blade my old friend tried to filet me with. Dropping the pad into my lap, he flipped his arm palm up and brought the blade down.

The chair I was in skittered wildly back, knocked into another, and took them both down.

"No!" I shouted, ripping the knife from him and throwing it across the room. Chest heaving, I glared at him. "Are you out of your fucking mind?" I roared. "I broke his neck for punching you, and you want to slice yourself open in front of me?"

He laughed.

He fucking laughed.

I hated that sound.

*I love it.*

"Sit down, drama queen. You're bleeding again."

The emotion he pummeled me with was so wild and so omnipotent I lashed out. My hand closed around his throat, squeezing just enough to make my presence known.

His cinnamon lashes widened, showing the whites around his insanely green orbs.

I growled. "What the fuck did you just say to me?"

Even though I had him by the throat, he smirked. The lips I'd just kissed smirked.

My fingers tightened.

I'd already nearly strangled him. The yellowing bruises still ringed his throat. But he wasn't afraid. Not at all. In fact...

He tilted his chin back.

Offering more space to control him.

I straddled his lap, dropping onto his thighs without thought. The hand around his throat gentled, the hold turning into a caress. His chin was still tipped back, his face —his lips—on full display.

I descended upon them like nighttime in an evening sky. The first brush was just a taste, and then I used the full width of my tongue to lick over the seam where his lips met. He made a low sound and parted instantly, and then we were kissing again. I was sinking deep, reveling in how he fit between my legs. Because his head was thrown back, my hand cradled it, supporting all his weight.

In that moment, he became my pulse. His existence my air. His lips became my salvation and his heartbeat the clock by which I lived.

*This is it. What Hoon always wanted but I never had to give.*

The thought jarred me so hard our lips popped apart, and I sucked in air as though my lungs weren't already full. The hand curled around my side kept me in place. It didn't matter how horrendous, how life-shattering my thoughts were. Beau's touch would always, always be stronger.

*This is way more than I realized.*

"Shim." His voice was soft. The use of the new nickname

beckoned like the most beautiful of sirens in the midst of a dark and stormy sea.

I made a sound. It was all I was capable of.

"Red is my color. Not yours."

It took a minute for his words to penetrate. But then they did, and I saw how he stared at the bleeding rose on my chest. How it clearly bothered him.

I forced myself out of his lap, found another chair, and pulled it close.

We both ignored the body lying just feet away as he went about cleaning the knife wound and then dressing it.

If he used more alcohol to disinfect it, well, I didn't notice.

# 12

*Beau*

I WAS REALLY GOOD AT COMPARTMENTALIZING. REALLY GOOD at covering up my chaos with silence.

And those kisses?

Napalm-level chaos.

The kind of chaos that would bring me to my knees. I could already feel the panic creeping, already unable to draw in a deep breath.

So I retreated. I threw up my walls and did what I did best. Turned the tables.

"Who is that?" I asked, giving a cursory glance to the man Daeshim literally murdered in front of me.

Maybe I was starting to corrupt because watching him do it, hearing the sharp snap of that man's neck, didn't make me horrified. In an odd twist, it made me calm. Violence like that was absolute. Nothing could pass a man willing to kill to protect.

Perhaps that was why I could compartmentalize so well

in this moment, even as that kiss lay in wait to destroy me.

He grunted. "No one."

"Don't lie to me."

"Why? You're lying to me."

Forgetting about the man and the pile of bandages, I looked up. "What?"

"We both know it."

"Don't you think I have a right to ask about that?" I pointed to the body.

"No."

"Why the hell not?"

"Because I didn't ask you to get in the middle of my fight."

"He was going to kill you." I fumed. Was he fucking serious? Try and help a guy out, and this is what I get. Scolded.

"He wasn't."

I said nothing.

Daeshim sighed. "I didn't even get to question him."

"Like that's my fault," I retorted.

"You got yourself punched."

I rolled my eyes.

Shooting forward, he caught my chin between his fingers, forcing me to look at him. His bottomless, black irises were simmering and scorching hot. "And what would you have me do, Red? Should I just allow someone to touch what's mine?"

The chained-up chaos broke its restraints, flooding me so fast it was like a punch of adrenaline punctured straight into my heart. I sucked in a breath, feeling literally everything but unable to form those feelings into thoughts.

I was overwhelmed. Inherently so.

I was so knotted up I would never be able to untangle.

"All right now." His voice was like a purr, and it cut through the thickest part of my panic. The hand left my chin, curled around the base of my neck, and tickled the strands at my hairline. My eyes slipped closed as he pulled me in, my forehead hitting his bare shoulder.

The urge to lick him was more of an instinct, and I couldn't stop my tongue. His skin was slightly salty, smooth, and warm. He gave no reaction at all when the whole of my tongue slid over him, so I did it again.

His fingers tightened a little in my hair, a silent message it was okay.

But it wasn't. I was licking him without thought. Kissing him without inhibition. I'd never been so out of control.

The tip of my tongue jutted out, sampling what was left of him on my lips. We stayed like that for uncounted minutes, until the worst of the chaos shrank toward its chains.

Only when I felt I had enough control did I speak.

"I'm not yours."

He was silent for long moments. Then his voice brushed against my ear. "If you say so."

## 13

---

*DAESHIM*

WE GOT RID OF THE BODY TOGETHER. IT WAS THE KIND OF thing that could bind anyone—but not us.

We were already bound. He was already mine even if I let him think otherwise.

Deep down, he knew. This was a most basic instinct that was basically DNA.

That's why Hoon always wanted what he couldn't have. I couldn't give away something someone else already owned.

And yes, Beau owned me before we even met. He was mine likely from the moment he came into this world. I didn't know how. I didn't know why.

But even me—a born gangster, a killer, and a crime lord—couldn't fight against this.

It was why we fought so long. Why we fought still.

Succumbing to that kind of pull... it could never be undone.

When the body was gone and the bar was locked up, we

trudged up the stairs maybe an hour before dawn. The second the locks were thrown, he started toward his corner.

A hand between his shoulder blades stopped him. I didn't even have to fist into his shirt.

"No," I said, quiet, not a demand but also not a request.

He hesitated for perhaps half a second before changing direction. We didn't speak as we shucked off boots or the clothes we'd put on after we'd showered somewhere that wasn't home.

He slipped under the blankets in my bed, wearing nothing but his boxers, turning onto his side and showing me his back.

Wearing exactly the same, I slipped in behind him, shifting forward so my chest met his back. I thought he might move away when my arm curled around his waist. He didn't. He eased closer.

We shared the single pillow.

We didn't speak a word.

We slept pressed together, two bodies… but one.

# 14

*BEAU*

THE ENTIRE APARTMENT HAD THREE WINDOWS. NONE OF which were in the bedroom where I'd spent the night. I'd lived in this tiny place perched above a bar for roughly five years, and this was the first time I'd ever slept in the bedroom.

It was also the first time I'd slept with another man.

And no, Fletcher didn't count. He's my brother. Don't be a perv.

In these last five years, I lived in close proximity to other men. First Earth and Snort, then Neo when one day Earth brought him home. Then Neo brought home Fletcher, and soon there were five of us (counting the dog, of course) filling a minuscule one-bedroom apartment. We were all basically on top of each other all the time, but never once did I feel like this.

Like there wasn't enough air for everyone to breathe. Like the presence of someone else made my skin hum so relentlessly I sometimes wanted to rip it off my bones. I never got frustrated and annoyed. I never got sick of Fletcher's chip-chomping, Snort's loud mouth breathing, or the fact this apartment always smelled so pungently of paint because Neo was forever slapping it on every surface.

Then Daeshim showed up.

He was quieter than the others. He never made a mess. He walked around without a shirt, and the art on his body was somehow way more distracting than the giant paintings Neo splashed on the walls.

Just his presence ruffled my feathers. I automatically went on defense whenever his eyes slid in my direction as if I just knew he was planning an attack.

He was suspicious of me. I sure as fuck was suspicious of him.

We eyed each other with derision, circling the other like tigers tossed in the same cage. Occasionally, we would lunge at each other, but it was never a full-on attack.

Earth said he was good people. Earth called him family. I trusted his judgment, so much that I put it above my own. And so I settled into this uncomfortable existence with a roommate that made this house feel so much smaller than the four previous tenants combined.

And now?

Now I opened my eyes to a dark, windowless room, in a bed that was not mine.

In his bed. With his frame spooned against mine, the heat radiating from his skin was so delicious it attempted to lull me back to sleep.

I was out of my mind, I knew. But sleep still had enough of a hold on me that I couldn't find a reason to care.

How long had it been since I felt so calm?

Outwardly, I always appeared carefree. It made a really

good shield. Truth was I was never calm or relaxed. Behind the walls I showed to the world, I lived in a state of chaos.

But not right now. Right now I felt boneless against the sagging mattress, reassured with the heat of the body against mine. The even rise and fall of his smooth chest against my back was a cadence I could admit in this sleepy state that I rather liked.

He was unpredictable. Bossy. Mean. He unleashed sharp barbs off his tongue, and they never missed their mark. His obscure black gaze never missed a thing, and his instincts were arguably more honed than even Earth's.

He made me nervous. Angry. Confused.

I'd been on the receiving end of his asshole demeanor more times than I could count.

*But oh*. Oh, when all that he was suddenly shifted and became a shield. When all that intensity normally firing at me fired at someone trying to do me harm.

He literally killed a man just for punching me.

*Safe. Calm. Surrender.*

Not words. Feelings. They echoed through my body, rousing that sleeping calm I so loved to set off shrill alarms in my head.

Eyes popping open, I wanted to swear at the interruption, but my brain kicked on and the survival mode I existed in forced everything else away. Fighting the urge to tear myself out of bed, I slid out carefully, trying not to wake the sleeping wolf at my back.

Dealing with him was not something I was prepared for. After last night, I might never be.

Memories of the kiss assaulted me, making me tumble back onto the edge of the bed. Dropping my head in my hands, I exhaled a shaky breath.

More images assaulted me. Him straddling my lap. His

hands in my hair, on my neck, and his tongue twirling around mine.

*Jesus.*

And then what did I do? I crawled into bed with him. After I helped him dump the body of the man he killed.

*The man he killed because he touched you.*

I wasn't corrupt like McClaren suggested. I was losing it. Cracking under pressure.

There was no other explanation.

*You let a man kiss you!* No. *You let a man practically eat you! You aren't even gay!*

Not that I had a problem with anyone's sexuality. I meant it when I told Fletcher I didn't care if he loved Ethan, and I even meant it when I offered to Google any questions he might have.

*You're the one with the questions now.*

I was spiraling into myself, folding like a house of cards. And even though waking up next to Daeshim was the absolute cause of it... I wanted nothing more than to crawl back under the covers next to him because deep down I knew he was also the solution.

A familiar ping brought my head up. The relief of that barely audible noise was incredible, offering me a reprieve, handing me focus.

Grabbing that offering with both my hands, I stood from the bed. I had no idea what time it was. The darkness gave no indication. Cold air tightened my nipples as I moved across the small space. My toe caught in something soft, and without a second thought, I snatched up the sweats to tug them on as I walked.

I didn't notice they were loose on me. I didn't even bother to tie the string at the waist. They were well-worn and comfortable, offering protection from the icy air.

The rest of the apartment was nearly as dark as the

bedroom. The two windows near my desk were covered so there was no glare on my monitors. There was dim light filtering in the kitchen, so I knew it was already morning.

The only other light came from the glow of my screens, the little ping I'd heard having come directly from one.

Shuffling forward, my pulse quickened with anticipation. Was I in? Had I finally, after weeks, managed to bypass the system keeping me out.

Despite how badly I wanted this, how big of a win it would be for me to crack those perverts' codes, my feet stuttered when I got to my desk.

*Time's up.*

If I walked around this desk and saw what I'd been chasing, then I would have to leave. Automatically, I glanced over my shoulder toward the bedroom I'd just left. A sick, panicky feeling tightened my innards.

*Maybe it's for the best,* something whispered inside me.

Even though every cell in my body revolted and my fingers curled into my palms, I thought, *Yeah, maybe.*

These musings were stupid and could be a waste of time because if I'd somehow been bounced out of their servers again, if my epic move was somehow not epic at all, then I was still on this job.

Barreling around the desk, I nudged my chair back enough to step forward and plant my palms on the desk. Leaning on both arms, I stared up at the screens that appeared in sleep mode. They weren't.

Stretching one long finger, I hit a button on my keyboard, and the monitors flickered to life.

I was prepared for two outcomes: success or failure.

What I got was something else entirely. Something no one could prepare for even if they were warned.

My stomach turned into this hollow, aching pit, and all my weight sort of sank into my arms still braced on the desk.

A low, strangled sound ripped out of my throat. The strain of it on my vocal cords was something I wouldn't have believed if I couldn't feel the pain.

I stared unblinking at the horror unfolding on these monitors, popping up on the screens like some kind of sick slideshow.

I don't know how long I was held hostage, how long my arms had to support the rest of my haggard weight.

Eventually, my limbs gave out, and I dropped. The chair I previously nudged back slid out from under my dead weight and flew into the wall, my ass hitting the floor.

I didn't notice the sting radiating up my tailbone or how cold the floor was against my ass. My eyes were still locked on those images. Ripping my eyes from my skull would not be enough for me to ever unsee.

Without preamble, my whole body heaved, and I lurched forward with enough presence of mind to grab the small trashcan nearby and empty all the sickness bubbling up inside me. I retched and puked, my ribs aching so painfully with every hurl. Finally, I sagged back into the floor, wiping my mouth with the back of my hand.

The wall was too far away to lean on, so I sat there hunched in. The only thing giving my body shape was the bones under my skin.

*Sick.*

*Sick.*

*Sick.*

I managed to crack their system. I had evidence that would put away all of them.

It was a good thing, right? The bureau would be happy.

But me?

I might never be the same.

# 15

*Daeshim*

Sleep let go of me slowly, and if I thought back later in the day, I would know it was trying to offer a few last moments of peace.

Eventually, my lashes fluttered, and I realized my body was no longer curled around the one I'd brought to bed last night. Instead, all I spooned was air.

*Where is he?*

The blankets fell to my waist when I sat up, rubbing a hand over my face. My lungs expanded with my inhale, but before I could even exhale, my head snapped up.

Something was wrong. It permeated the air, the stench so thick I was forced to take shallow breaths.

Shoving back the blankets, I leaped up, not bothering with clothes, and went directly into the living room. The dim lighting couldn't conceal the thickness and salty tinge sorrow gave to the air. It raised the hair on the back of my neck and caused goose bumps to climb along my bare arms.

The space appeared empty, and for a fraction of a second, my pulse spiked in sheer panic. But upon another inhale, I knew he was here. Somewhere along the way, I'd become attuned to his scent, his invisible presence, and, unbeknownst to him, his anxiety.

But knowing he was here didn't make me feel better. In fact, it spurred me to move faster. Even in his worst state, I'd never smelled this. I'd never had to practically work against the energy in the room just to move forward.

"Beau," I called, noting his desk chair was empty and so was the couch.

He didn't answer, and I shoved my fingers through my hair as I rushed into the kitchen. The room was lighter here, the window over the sink uncovered, revealing he wasn't here either. He hadn't even made coffee.

A low curse dropped from my lips, and a sense of urgency tightened my throat.

"Beau!" I yelled much louder.

It wasn't really a sound. Perhaps it was a movement. A slight ripple in the energy filling the space. I spun, and from the archway in the kitchen, I saw him—or rather, his bowed red head.

Bare feet slapping over the floor, I rushed toward him, fear slamming into me so fucking hard due to the way he sagged onto the hardwood, deflated like some kind of slashed tire, like a man who'd been hung and his body just cut down.

With a rough sound, I dropped to my knees beside him, filling my palm with the back of his head.

"Hey," I crooned. "What are you doing on the floor, Red? Did you fall?"

He gave no indication he heard me or even knew I was there. An unpleasant odor wafted closer, and I saw the trashcan nearby.

"Are you sick?" I asked, running my fingers through his hair. With my free hand, I cupped his chin, bringing up his face so I could see him.

He was so white not even his freckles held color. The glazed look in his red-rimmed eyes pulled a broken sound from me, but hot rage of volcanic proportions bubbled up inside.

"Who did this to you?" I nearly growled. "I'll fucking kill them dead."

A shudder moved through his chest, and a little bit of something flickered in his eyes.

I slid closer, my knees digging into the unforgiving floor, the wintry air nipping at all my skin. But I was warm compared to him, his skin like ice.

"Beau!" I demanded, wanting to be gentle but needing a response.

I realized then we might not be alone, that whoever had done this might still be here.

Keeping gentle hands on his head, the rest of me turned to stone. Whipping around, I looked for the intruder, not worrying about a weapon. My bare hands would do just fine.

The apartment seemed empty. It *felt* empty.

*If no one is here, then maybe whatever he did all day on these damn computers...*

Stiffening anew, I turned toward the desk to look at the glowing screen. He moved suddenly, like a crack of neon lightning tearing through a storm.

*"No!"* His yell was strangled and desperate, his hands rough when he grabbed my face, pulling me back down.

I nearly fell over, and a string of dark curses filled the room. "What the fuck—" I started, but his hands tightened on my face.

Wide, glassy green irises implored mine. I swear to Christ, I felt that stare all the way to my bones.

"Don't look."

"What made you this way is on those screens?"

He nodded once, and I felt the fine tremble in his hands. "Don't look."

The urge to look was fucking painful. If this was any other person, any other situation, I already would have shoved his face into the floorboards and been feasting my eyes on whatever it was that was so damn earth-shattering.

But it wasn't any other person.

It was Beau. My Red.

"Please, Daeshim," he begged. "Promise me you won't look."

A slight turn of my head was all it would take to see all.

I'd chew off my own arm before betraying his trust like that. Cupping his face, I glided closer, the pads of my thumbs brushing away the wetness on his ghostly cheeks. "Okay, I won't look. I won't look, okay?"

"Promise."

"I promise."

His whole body folded toward me, and I basically tugged him into my lap as I adjusted so it wasn't my knees on the floor but my ass and he was in my arms. Stroking his hair, I rocked him back and forth, whispering, "I got you," over and over again.

His fingers bit into my bicep, pinching the skin so tight I'd likely have bruises. Even as I wondered desperately why he was like this, I didn't turn to look.

Yes, I was suspicious of Beau. Yes, I knew he harbored secrets.

But...

I wanted him to tell me. I didn't want the information by default.

I don't know how long we sat there huddled on the floor, practically beneath his desk with his puke bucket nearby. I didn't count the minutes or the hours because I'd sit there as long as he needed.

When I finally spoke, my voice was rusty as though I hadn't used it in years. "You're wearing my sweatpants."

"They're soft," he whispered, still clinging to my arm.

I felt hollowed out in a way I had never been before. Lips moving in the silky strands of his carroty hair, I whispered, "You can keep them."

A little while later, his fingers went slack, and he pulled out of my chest, unwilling to meet my eyes.

"Hey," I summoned, but he ducked his head even farther.

Grasping his face, I pulled it around, drilling my stare into his.

"I don't care about it," I told him.

His eyes tried to slip away.

Giving him a gentle shake, I told him again, "Whatever it is, I don't care."

The tip of his pink tongue swiped over his chapped bottom lip. "Close your eyes."

I closed them.

He left my side, and I heard his fingers flying over the keyboard, and then a few moments later, those fingers brushed my shoulder. "Come on."

I got up, avoiding the screens, but he said, "I hid them."

*Hid what?*

"There's a matching hoodie for those pants in the bedroom," I told him when we were away from the desk.

He didn't say anything, just looked down at my pants. He was thinner than me, so they hung low, accentuating the way his hip bones jutted out just slightly.

The urge to run my tongue along those ridges was so strong I started to salivate.

"Go on," I told him with enough gruffness to make him look up. "Your skin feels like ice."

"I have my own clothes."

"It's lying on the dresser," I said, ignoring his protest.

He said nothing but went toward the bedroom, and I headed the opposite direction into the kitchen to make coffee. I heard the bathroom water running and what I was sure was the sound of him brushing his teeth. When he finally appeared in the archway, I had a cup of coffee already ready for him, and he was wearing the hoodie I'd told him to put on.

Sticking out from under the hem was a blue T-shirt. It was one of mine too.

"Sit down," I said, pulling out a chair.

I put the coffee in front of him. He wrapped his hands around it without saying anything, and if holding him on the floor beside a puke bucket hadn't already told me, that's how I knew this was bad.

Beau argued over everything. We could stand under a clear blue sky, and he would argue if I told him it was blue.

It was our twisted method of communication.

The fact that he'd willingly dressed in my clothes, sat when directed, and then accepted the coffee I made with barely a word scared me.

It's not that I didn't like Beau if he wasn't arguing. Quite the contrary. But his demeanor unsettled me. This was not who he was.

I got myself some coffee and carried it over to the tiny window over the sink to stare out at a brick building close by.

"You gonna tell me?" I asked eventually.

"No."

I basically threw my mug into the sink. The handle broke off, and what was left of the brew trickled down the drain. "Why the hell not?"

"It ain't your business."

I shot forward, but he was already up and out of the chair, turning to face me with a shuttered gaze.

"Everything about you is my business," I said dangerously low.

"No," he denied, strolling out of the kitchen as though his word was law.

Out in the living room, my scent bloomed out around him when I shoved him against the wall. For a moment, my senses went haywire, need and desire rising inside me, trying to take out everything else.

His hand slapped onto my chest as if he would push me away.

I leaned into the touch, caging his body with mine, tilting in so my lips brushed his ear when I spoke quietly. "I'm giving you the chance to tell me, Red. I did things your way back there."

"I can't," he said, anxiety making his voice slightly high.

"You can, and you will," I intoned darkly. "Because soon you won't have to tell me your secrets. Soon I'll be in you so deep there will be nowhere left for them to hide."

He made a sound, a cross between grunt and growl. My groin tightened, and I pushed a little closer.

He didn't have to fight to slip away. I let him go. My eyes, though, they stayed trained on him as he put on some shoes and grabbed his beanie.

"Take a coat," I intoned, watching him stalk to the door.

His shoulders hiked so far up they nearly touched his ears. "Fuck off," he muttered and stepped into the hall.

I caught him at the bottom of the stairs in the small hallway leading past the bar to the exit onto the street. My hands slammed the thick material over his shoulders, squeezing once before pulling back.

He didn't turn around. "This isn't mine."

I grunted. "If you wanted to wear your coat, you should have gotten it when I told you to."

He started to rip it off his body, but I made a menacing sound that impressed even me. I felt his stare angle over his shoulder in my direction.

"I'm not playing games today, Red. You take that godforsaken coat, or I'll put you over my knee."

He scoffed.

This little shit scoffed.

Shooting forward, I grabbed him up, and all the breath in his chest was expelled when I tossed him over my shoulder. The coat I'd forced on him fluttered to my feet as I brought my palm down on his ass.

The smack was solid, the material of the sweatpants hardly enough to cushion the sting. His whole body tightened, back bowing to lift him from my shoulder.

I landed another smack on his cheek, holding nothing back.

A little sound slipped out of him, and then he was knotting his fingers into my hair to pull. "You asshole!"

My scalp was burning when I set him back on his feet, taking in his wide eyes and flushed cheeks.

"Yeah," I intoned, not once looking away. "I am an asshole. But I'm *your* asshole."

He started to flee, hesitating just long enough to snatch up the coat and rush out into the city.

# 16

---

*Beau*

CHAOS GAVE WAY TO CONFUSION. OR PERHAPS CONFUSION created the chaos.

All I really knew was that things were messed up. More than ever before. Usually, I had some semblance of control. Usually, I kept it all under wraps. It was harder now as though there was too much to contain.

And my ass cheek stung. *I think I kinda like it.*

Not only was I corrupt and cracking... but I might be *depraved.*

Puking up my guts left my stomach in a tight coil, aching from the inside out. Rubbing my palm over my middle, I thought of what I'd just seen.

No. No, I wasn't depraved. What I just saw? That was the definition of depraved. In all my years as a cop, in all my years of cracking cases, putting away murderers, and spending most of my time combing the black web for the nastiest of the nasty... I'd never had to see *anything* like that.

And now I'd never unsee it. Those images were branded into me, blackening patches of my heart where they'd touched.

I knew this case was big and I knew it was debauched, but this? Not even my bitter, anxiety-addled mind went this far.

I should have been at those monitors right then, sifting through the stuff I hadn't even looked at yet. Putting all the evidence in a neat package so we could take those fuckers down. I had no idea where they'd end up because I was certain not even Satan himself would let them into hell.

I didn't really care where they ended up as long as their crimes stopped.

*You should tell them.* My brain hammered the words like it was trying to give me a second pulse. And no, my subconscious (or whoever the fuck it was whispering in my head) did not mean my "buddies" at the FBI.

*Earth. Daeshim. Family.*

If I told them, there would be no case building, no red tape. No arrests or anything. There would just be swift justice in the form of death.

*I can't let them do this.*

*Not even for a bunch of innocent kids?*

Lurching to the edge of a building, I fell to my knees, the cold of the concrete seeping through my pants as I retched up the couple sips of coffee I'd had.

Eyes watering, I gave an angry yell, punching my fist right into the pavement. Stinging pain shot over my knuckles, but I was so mad I didn't even glance at it.

Then I started to laugh. Chuckling like a madman as I shoved up off the pavement, swiping the back of my hand across my lips.

*After everything, you get pissed because you couldn't hold on to the coffee that asshole made you.*

Noticing a few curious glances from people walking past,

I tugged the coat closer around me, holding the front closed with my hands. I should just zip it up, but if I did, I'd have no reason to hold on to it.

My head shook as I started walking again, angling toward my destination. I guess that answered my previous thought.

I didn't want to risk them even for a bunch of innocent kids.

I didn't have to, though. I could take out those pedophiles myself. I could slough through all that evil to put together an airtight case.

Still, instead of going home, I pressed a button beside a spotless gold elevator and stepped into the posh car without preamble.

I came all the way here without even thinking twice. Everything inside me was so muddled and mixed up, but even so... I wasn't surprised this was where it led me.

Barely glancing at the gigantic flower arrangement on a table in the center of the foyer, I walked past to knock on the large wooden doors.

I was hardly done knocking when the door swung open and Jane—Ethan and Fletcher's house manager—appeared.

What the hell did they need a house manager for anyway?

"Master Beau," she said, eyes widening just a fraction, but besides that, she didn't seem surprised to see me. We never called when we wanted to see Fletcher. We just showed up. She was probably used to it by now.

"Is Fletcher here?"

"Yes, come in," she said, instantly opening the door wider to let me into the giant penthouse. The black-and-white marble floors were glossy, the console table nearby as polished, and the ceilings were so high sometimes we yelled just so we could hear the echo.

My eyes slid to the big Spider-Man statue they had on

display near the curving staircase. My brother's pride and joy.

"Who was at the door, J—" Fletcher called, coming around the corner. "Beau!" he hollered, a smile widening his face the second he saw me.

I knew it was coming, so I steadied myself, and then he plowed into me, wrapping his arms around my waist in a hug. "I didn't expect to see you!"

"You too busy for your brother?"

"No way!" he said, pulling back. "I just got done practicing for the event I have next week. Come in. Play a video game with me."

Jane laughed under her breath. "Well, I'll be off. I have some errands."

When I glanced around, the woman already had on a coat and scarf.

"I left sandwiches on the counter for you, Fletcher."

"Thanks, Jane!" he said, giving her a wave.

I followed him through the massive foyer and into the open-concept living area. There were floor-to-ceiling windows that looked out over a portion of Central Park. Everything was high-style, high-class, and obviously high-priced. But the place didn't feel untouchable. The couch had a couple blankets tossed over it and a few pillows that obviously were well used. Fletcher's ratty violin case was open on the large coffee table, his violin and bow lying nearby. There was no sheet music because he rarely needed it. My baby brother was quite the prodigy.

The scent of waffles lingered in the air, and even as my stomach tightened, I smiled. Fletcher loved a considerate pancake.

*Squueaaakkk!* The high-pitched sound made me nearly piss my pants, and I jerked backward to stare down at what the hell I'd just traumatized with my foot.

Fletcher smiled. "That's Gwennie's favorite," he said, reaching down to pick up the mouse-shaped cat toy I'd trampled.

I grunted and started forward, this time the toe of my shoe knocking into a ball with a bell in the center. It skittered over the floor wildly, and from out of nowhere, a white cat darted out to chase.

"She likes that one too," he said.

"Aren't you usually working at this time of day?" Fletcher asked, flopping down on the giant sofa.

They all thought I was some sort of hacker who took odd jobs that were mostly illegal. Sometimes I did take jobs like that because the longer I lived with them, the harder the lies were to tell. At least this way I was being partially honest.

I just also did more.

"Tired of sitting there, so I figured I'd stop by."

*Mee-oww!* The very dramatic sound seemed to boom overhead, making me spin toward the last place I'd seen Gwen.

But she was nowhere in sight.

"Parker!" Fletcher yelled, jumping off the couch to rush across the room toward a window. "What are you doing up there?" he moaned.

Following his movements, I looked up to see the tabby kitten clinging to the top of a curtain. All four of its legs were splayed out, and it was obvious all his claws were jabbed into what was probably a silk curtain.

"Is that a cat or a monkey?" I asked as the cat gave another pitiful wail.

"You better get down before Daddy comes home and sees you!" Fletcher intoned, jumping up to try and catch the small animal, but he was too high.

I felt my eyebrows shoot up to my beanie. "Daddy?"

Fletcher made a rude sound. "Well, that's what he is to Parker!"

Parker was the new addition to the family. Earth told Virginia she could get a cat, and well, that led to Virginia calling Fletcher to go to the animal shelter with her... And now you know why there was a wild, clawed beast dangling from the very expensive curtains.

Ethan must have been beside himself.

I started to laugh. The action caused my already tight stomach to spasm, but Fletcher jumped toward the cat again, waving his arms, and I laughed more. And with it, some of the sickness shriveling up my insides lessened.

Out in the foyer, the front door opened and shut. "Puppy!"

Fletcher stopped jumping and glared at the cat. "He's home! Get down here!"

The cat meowed pitifully again.

Ethan appeared around the corner. "Fletcher?"

"I told him to get down!" he bemoaned.

I laughed more.

Ethan sighed woefully, loosening his purple tie as he went. "Utterly disgraceful," he muttered beneath his breath. "It's like we live on a farm. A completely uncivilized farm."

To punctuate the statement, Gwen and her squeaky mouse shot into the room, zooming by Ethan's feet.

To his credit, he didn't even wince, just kept going to where Fletch and the daredevil cat dangled.

"I really told him not to," Fletcher said, looking dejected.

Ethan rubbed a hand over the back of Fletcher's head. "I know, love."

Planting his hands on his hips, Ethan's blond head tilted up to Parker. "Well, what do you have to say for yourself?"

*Like he would answer.*

*Oww!* the cat wailed.

"Well, you got what you deserved," Ethan scolded. "Now, come on. Down."

The cat meowed again.

Ethan made a rude sound and reached up. "I don't have all day."

Remarkably, the cat retracted his claws and dropped away from the curtain into Ethan's waiting hands. He gently set down the kitten, and it hopped off to attack yet another toy littering the living room.

Straightening, Ethan turned to Fletcher. I was used to their size difference, but sometimes it still surprised me.

"We don't have to get rid of him, do we?" Fletcher worried.

I stiffened, ready to jump in and defend my brother and his hellion cat.

Ethan made a sound. "As if I would get rid of something you love."

Fletcher frowned. "You love him too."

"Of course. Parker is family, and you don't just get rid of family when they do things you don't like."

A lump formed in my throat. No matter how many times I swallowed, it wouldn't dissolve.

Fletcher flung himself at Ethan, who caught him easily and lifted him right into his arms. I couldn't help but openly stare at the way they looked standing there with Fletcher's legs wrapped around Ethan's middle and Ethan smiling at him all dumbstruck.

Without thinking, I reached into the open coat to brush my fingers over the sweats I was wearing.

"I've been home a whole five minutes, and you haven't even kissed me," Ethan complained.

"Who's the kiss monster now?" Fletcher taunted.

"You, love. Always you." Ethan's voice was soft, and it

reminded me of how Daeshim spoke earlier, trying to soothe my meltdown.

*I got you.*

*But he will let you go.* I told myself. *That is if he doesn't kill you first.*

Sure, this family stuck by family—even when it was practically impossible—but this was different. If they knew who I really was, would they even consider me family?

*No. To them, you will be nothing but a traitor.*

Exactly why I should be at home, finishing this case. Finishing this case so I could go back to the real life I didn't have.

*Maybe it would be better to just let them kill you.*

No. Because then they'd go down for that.

The best thing I could do for everyone was finish this job and leave quietly. That way the only one that would be hurt was me.

"Beau?"

The close voice snapped me out of my spiraling mind, and I jolted, seeing how close Ethan was standing there, frowning.

"Are you okay?"

I cleared my throat. "Yeah. Yeah, I'm okay."

He seemed unconvinced. "What are you doing here in the middle of the day?"

"E!" Fletcher admonished right beside him. "Beau can come here whenever he wants."

"Well, of course you can," Ethan said immediately. "I just meant it's unusual."

"Well, I didn't expect you to be here in the middle of the day either."

"It's my house," he muttered but then also said, "I came home for lunch because I had a break in my schedule, and I knew Fletch was home."

I nodded, suddenly feeling homesick. "Right. Well, I won't stay. You two can—"

"No!" Fletcher cut me off. "Don't go! Just 'cause Ethan came home doesn't mean you can't stay. Eat with us."

I glanced at Ethan. He smiled. "You know you are welcome here anytime."

I swallowed.

"I'm going to go get out of this suit," Ethan announced before leaning in to kiss the top of Fletcher's head and then slap me on the shoulder on his way past.

The second he was out of sight, Fletcher pinned me with wide light-brown eyes. "What's wrong?"

I panicked for a minute before shoving it down to smile. "Nothing."

"You've never lied to me before."

That panic I'd shoved down? It came rushing back like a freaking tsunami. "What?"

"I can tell something's wrong."

"I'm just tired," I said, going to flop down on the sofa.

Fletcher was quiet a moment, then started off toward the kitchen. "Are you hungry? Jane made sandwiches."

"No, I had a late breakfast." I lied.

Fletcher appeared with a large white platter piled with enough food for twenty people.

"Good thing Ethan came home to help you eat all that," I mused.

Fletcher wrinkled his nose. "Ethan won't eat this. He'll eat a sad bowl of lettuce."

"Poor guy," I muttered, but shock made me sit up. "Those are all for you?"

He shrugged, lips smacking around the bread. He pushed the platter under my nose, but I recoiled, gut clenching.

The heavy ceramic made a thud on the coffee table when Fletch set it down, grabbing another sandwich off the tray so he had one in each hand before plopping back onto the cushions near me.

"Are you fighting with Daeshim again?" he asked, eyes never leaving me even as he shoved his mouth full.

I'd like to note that if I wasn't in a serious state of turmoil, I would totally be housing those sammies like my bro. They looked like some kind of roast beef concoction with veggies and some sort of white spread. And it wasn't like bread you got at the corner mart. It was thick and crusty.

But not even richie food could make me forget about everything else.

"Why would you think that?" I asked mildly, avoiding looking at the food.

"Because he's the only thing that ever really upsets you."

*If you only knew.* The thought sent a rush of sadness through me, and for a moment, it eclipsed everything else. It was a reprieve really, which made me sink even further into despair.

How bad had I let things get that intense sadness felt like a relief from everything else?

I couldn't even be properly miserable because I was too upset that the sadness made everything else feel better.

Fletcher watched me quietly, even his chewing somehow muted. I loved him. He was my brother, the baby of the family, but beyond that, a genuinely good person. I could count on my hand the amount of genuinely good people I knew. And he was like that even after everything he'd been through.

It was sad we'd been family for years now and he didn't really know me. I wanted him to, but it was impossible.

*I've let him down.* In so many ways.

"Beau?" Fletcher's voice was quiet.

"How did you know you liked Ethan?" I asked.

Fletcher blinked but then took another bite and shrugged. "Doesn't everyone like Ethan?"

Sometimes talking to Fletch was like talking in a circle. But he was really the only one I could ask, and if I was honest with myself, I knew this was the reason I was here. I wasn't going to chicken out because like, bro, no one wants to have this conversation... But maybe I did.

Maybe this was one way Fletcher could know me, one thing I didn't have to hide.

"Like, *like* Ethan." I clarified. "Like to date him," I said, squirming into the cushion.

Listen. Just because I maybe did want to have this conversation didn't mean I wasn't completely ape-shit embarrassed.

He stopped chewing. The food fisted in both hands lowered slowly toward his lap. "Oh." He swallowed, thinking over his answer. "He made my stomach feel weird."

"What?"

"Every time I was around him, my stomach felt like it was on a tilt-a-whirl ride. At first, it made me really nervous, but then I kinda started liking it."

I nodded, trying to understand. "Is that all?"

"I missed him when he wasn't around. I thought about him all the time. He made me feel safe."

I scowled. "You didn't feel safe with your brothers?"

His eyes went wide. "Of course!" His cheeks turned slightly pink. "But this was a different kind of safe."

*Yeah.* Yeah, I knew about that.

"And..." he said but then quickly stuffed more food in his face like that would mean he didn't have to finish.

"And what?"

He shook his head.

"Fletcher," I said, trying to sound firm, but really, it was just desperate.

"I like his kisses."

*Yeah. Me too.*

Fletcher jumped up. "What?"

I jolted in surprise, sitting back at the sudden outburst.

"What do you mean *yeah, me too?*" Fletcher demanded. "When were you kissing Ethan?"

Oh shit, I said that out loud?

"That's not what I meant," I said, pushing up.

"Ethan!" Fletcher roared.

One of the half-eaten sandwiches clutched in his grip launched at me, slapping me right in the center of my chest. I glanced down as it bounced off, the bread falling open and everything dropping onto the floor at my feet.

Dumbly, I stared down at the sandwich then slowly up at my brother. He also was staring at the food.

"You threw roast beef at me," I deadpanned.

He started to giggle, but then he pressed his lips together. "You'll always be my brother, Beau, and I love you. But you can't have Ethan."

*You'll always be my brother.* My heart cracked a little at the sincerity in his voice, and—*wait.* This conversation was completely ridiculous.

"I don't want Ethan." *He is so not my type.*

"Fletcher!" Ethan yelled, rushing into the room, bare chest on full display, a shirt clutched in his hand. "What happened? What's wrong?" he asked, eyes roaming the room for whatever made Fletcher yell. Grabbing Fletch by the arm, he spun him around so he could look him over.

"*Agh!*" Fletcher gasped. "Why are you naked?"

Then as if he were larger than Ethan and as if he could block him from view, he spread his legs and threw his arms up like he could create a giant X and hide his shirtless man.

"I'm hardly naked," Ethan said, calm despite Fletcher's absolute absurdity. "But you yelled for me like the house was caving in. Should I finish dressing next time there is an emergency?"

"I've seen Ethan without a shirt before," I pointed out dryly.

"Well, that was before you brought up kissing!"

Ethan looked at me and raised an eyebrow.

"I was just trying to have a conversation with him," I told him, pained. Turning away, I sighed. "I can't even do that right."

"Wait," Fletcher called, flinging his arms around my waist from behind when I started away. "Don't go! I'm sorry! I know you'd never kiss Ethan."

Behind us, Ethan made a choked sound. "Could someone explain?"

Patting Fletcher's hand, I turned. "Fletcher said he knew he liked you because he liked your kisses."

Ethan's face went a little soft at that, and I wanted to puke.

"And I said yeah, me too." Before anyone could get all riled up again, I hurried to say, "But I was thinking of someone else when I said that."

"Fletcher, come here," Ethan intoned.

Fletcher went to him without even a thought. I started to bristle, but then I remembered how I'd basically done the same thing over a coat.

*After he spanked me.*

*Did Ethan ever have to spank Fletcher to get him to listen?* The thought made me irrationally angry. "You better not ever hit him!" I intoned.

Ethan looked up, shock widening his eyes. "What?" The shock quickly gave way to anger. "I would never!"

I nodded, relaxing. Well, on the outside. On the inside, I was beginning to wonder why I ever thought this talk would be a good idea.

"E?" Fletcher asked, drawing our eyes.

All the hard edges and anger on Ethan's face drained away. Cupping Fletch's face, he leaned down. "You know the only person I would ever kiss is you."

Fletcher's head bobbed. Ethan kissed the end of his nose.

That stupid, stupid homesick feeling sloshed up the back of my throat. So many unpleasant feelings. And all of them seemed to live inside me.

"Did you throw roast beef on the floor?" Ethan asked a moment later.

"If we had a dog, it would already be cleaned up." Fletcher goaded him.

Ethan sighed. "I come home to find the cat dangling from the curtains like this is some kind of Cirque du Soleil show, and now you are asking me to get a dog?"

"What's Cirque du Soleil?" Fletcher asked.

Ethan smiled. "I'll get us tickets." His eyes met mine. "I'll get tickets for you too, Beau, and you can bring a date."

Suddenly, Fletcher remembered we'd been attempting to have a conversation—can you all see why I prefer to just be quiet now?—and spun, "Who do you like kissing?"

"Forget it." I half groaned. I was exhausted. Puking had been less painful than this.

"Are you wearing Daeshim's clothes?" Ethan dropped the question into the room like it was some innocent inquiry when, in fact, it was like a detonated grenade.

"How the hell did you even notice that?" I wondered.

Ethan shrugged. "I like fashion."

This was hardly fashion. But it was my new favorite outfit.

Tell no one.

Fletcher gasped, nearly tripping over his feet to come closer. Clucking, Ethan scooped him up and put him on the couch before he could fall or trample the meat into the area rug that probably cost more than I made all last year.

"That is Daeshim's outfit." Fletcher realized. "He wears it all the time."

Ethan motioned for me to sit, and I sighed.

"I just borrowed it," I muttered, sitting.

Ethan snagged a fresh sandwich off the table and handed it to Fletcher, who took it and started eating.

"I have to say I'm surprised," Ethan mused. "Although, with all the fighting, I guess I shouldn't be."

"Did you guys fight like that?"

Ethan grimaced. "Great gods, no. I would never fight with Fletcher like that."

Fletcher nodded. "I don't like yelling."

"Right." I agreed.

A frown pulled at Fletcher's lips. "So you like Daeshim? Like, *like* him the way I like Ethan?"

"I don't know," I said, confusion swirling in the center of my chest. "If I really did like him, we would be more like you and Ethan and less like the *Real Housewives of Beverly Hills*."

"You watch reality TV?" Fletcher wondered.

"Sometimes it's all that's on when I'm up working late."

Ethan grinned.

"Well, you definitely don't act like you like each other," Fletcher said.

"I wouldn't be so sure," Ethan mused, gazing at me.

I felt my cheeks heat, and I had to fight the urge to look away. But I did fight it, keeping my gaze steady on Ethan's. Just because this conversation made me feel vulnerable didn't mean I would show it.

*I'd only show that to one man.*

"There is a thin line between love and hate." The blond man went on, his blue eyes sparkling. "Sometimes the feelings are so intense it's hard to differentiate."

"I've never thought I hated you," Fletcher said, squirming backward toward Ethan.

With a gruff sound, he lifted him, settling Fletch into his lap. "That's because you're too pure for that." Looking at me, he tilted his head. "But Daeshim is a whole other animal."

A picture of the tattoo on his back immediately flashed to mind. A wolf. He's a wolf.

"Someone like him who's had such a violent life... hate is probably easier to process than love."

"Daeshim doesn't love me." I rebuked the notion instantly, even if it did make it feel like my ribcage suddenly shrunk and there was no room left for my heart.

"Do you love him?" Fletcher asked.

"Of course not." I denied it instantly, my eyes flicking off to the side.

"But you like to kiss him."

I pressed my lips together.

"You have kissed him?" Ethan asked.

I gave a single nod.

Fletcher practically shot up off Ethan's lap, but the larger man somehow pulled him in and subdued him with just a touch. I really appreciated Ethan in that moment. It was Fletcher I wanted to talk to, but Ethan's understanding was something I didn't realize I needed.

"How long has this been going on?" he asked.

"Not long."

"You must be confused," Ethan observed.

"Why would he be confused?" Fletcher wondered.

"I'm not gay, Fletch."

Fletcher blinked. "Well, neither am I."

I thought back to that convoluted conversation when Fletcher and Ethan were first getting together. I'd told Fletcher to just tell people he was bi if they asked.

He was kind of put off about it then, and I guess I kind of

understood why. It really didn't matter either way. But also, it seemed, at least to me, that putting some kind of identifier on it made it easier. Like it was less confusing if I thought to myself, *Oh, I'm bisexual,* instead of wondering why Daeshim.

But it was Daeshim. And I wouldn't even be thinking I could be bi if not for Daeshim, so did that label even apply to me?

God, I was fucking confused.

"It doesn't matter if you are gay or not," Ethan said, ever the voice of calm reason. "Attraction is attraction."

I nodded. "But why him?"

"Why not?"

"Because he's probably done worse things than Earth."

"Does that matter to you?" Ethan asked gently.

*It's my job for it to matter to me. A cop and a criminal make no kind of sense. I'm leaving, never coming back.*

The strength and confidence in Daeshim's voice earlier this morning eclipsed all my thoughts. *I don't care about it. Whatever it is, I don't care.*

"You love Earth anyway," Fletcher pointed out.

*And look where that's gotten me.*

Silence stretched on. I searched and searched inside myself. I listened to all the reasons it should definitely matter to me. The only voice I heard was his. *I don't care about it.*

My stomach was so fluttery by the time I was done, my voice came out in nothing but a whisper. "It doesn't matter to me."

Fletcher's arms came around my shoulders, enveloping me in a warm hug. "It's okay, Beau. It just means you have a big heart."

The butterflies in my stomach died. "No. I don't."

"I think you do."

I glanced over his shoulder at Ethan, our eyes meeting the moment I looked up.

"I'm sure it feels really complicated, but love doesn't have to be."

"It's not love," I repeated, pulling back from Fletcher.

"Well, then it's even less complicated," Ethan said, flippant. "Just sleep with him and get it out of your system."

My whole body went taut, but I wasn't sure if it was because the idea of sleeping with Daeshim filled me with so much anticipation or if it was because the idea he was something I could "get out of my system" was just so ridiculous.

"Ethan!" Fletcher scolded. "How can you say that?"

"What? We're all grown men."

"What's it like?" I blurted out.

Both men turned to me. My entire face felt like it was on fire, like one more tiny brush of oxygen and my entire body would just combust.

But I was so curious. So fucking... needy.

I hated it.

"Sex?" Fletcher squeaked.

"With a man," I added.

"Well, would men do it if it didn't feel good?" Ethan asked.

"Maybe it isn't about feeling good. Maybe it's about feeling like you belong somewhere." The second the words left my lips, I intensely regretted them. It was one of the most personal thoughts I'd ever said out loud.

"And you think you aren't in love," Ethan murmured.

I jumped to my feet.

"Sit!" Ethan demanded.

I sat.

*I fucking sat.*

What the fuck was happening to me?

"I get this conversation is a bit... intimate, but you clearly need to talk, and we're family. And as I pointed out, we are all grown men."

I slid a glance at Fletcher.

"I am not a baby!" He fumed, almost reading my thoughts.

"No. You aren't." Ethan agreed.

That shut me up. Sure, I knew Ethan and Fletcher got it on, but this was a whole new level of awareness.

Awkward.

Ethan cleared his throat, continuing as though he was used to leading a room. Actually, he was used to it. "You are absolutely right. Sex isn't just about physically feeling good. And to be honest, if you don't treat sex with a man with a little bit of care, then yes, it will hurt. But..." He went on. "Sex—when real feelings are involved—is more intimate. There's a bigger connection, and it does feel like finding where you belong." He glanced at Fletcher. "Am I right, Puppy?"

Fletcher's head bobbed.

Ethan seemed pleased with that and finished up by saying, "It's that emotional and physical connection that makes it the best, and usually, when you have both those things, the heart follows."

"I've had sex with women. It's never been like that," I admitted.

Ethan made a sound, acknowledging my words.

"They weren't the right person, then," Fletcher said.

"Who's to say he is?" I countered.

"That's only for you two to decide," Ethan surmised.

"Ethan," Fletcher whispered.

"What?"

"What if Daeshim is too rough?" Fletcher worry-whispered. "He's kinda... intense."

Ethan made a choked sound.

"I can hear you," I said, face literally seconds from being a torch. But then I scowled. "And who says he would be the rough one?"

Fletcher openly gaped. "You're the top?"

*I cannot believe I'm having this conversation.* "Why wouldn't I be?" I demanded.

Fletcher said nothing.

"And who says it has to be one or the other? You two don't switch?"

A squeak left Fletcher's lips, and he buried his face in Ethan's neck. Ethan laughed, but the high points of his cheekbones were slightly pink.

Thank God I wasn't the only one completely losing it.

"I think that's something that's up to the, ah, couple. There is no right or wrong answer. I guess it's about preference."

"And you prefer delivering," I deadpanned, eyes narrowing. Is that why Fletcher was worrying about me getting hurt? Because Ethan hurt him?

Ethan's eyes narrowed to match mine, the blue turning almost navy. "I don't think I like what you are implying."

"I don't like implying it."

"Yes, I'm the bottom!" Fletcher burst out, unearthing himself from his hiding place. "But that's because that's how we like it. And Ethan has never, not once, ever hurt me." He paused and glanced at Ethan. "I like it."

Ethan murmured something in Fletcher's ear and stroked his hair. Fletcher relaxed instantly.

"Good," I said. "That's, ah... good."

"I can't believe you offered to give me sex advice," Fletcher murmured. "You know less than me."

Ethan jolted. "He offered you sex advice?"

I flashed my teeth. "I offered to Google it if he had questions."

Ethan muttered something under his breath about the internet being an unreliable source.

"You're a good brother, Beau."

My stomach dipped at Fletcher's sincere words. I started to spiral again, the chaos rising, but he beat it back when he said, "Even if you are bad at sex."

I burst off the couch. "I am not bad at sex!"

Fletcher laughed. He laughed so hard he rolled off Ethan's lap into the couch cushions.

"Don't tell anyone about this conversation." I warned them both. "Ever."

"It's not something I care to repeat," Ethan vowed.

Fletcher was still laughing. I didn't bother making him promise. No one would understand what he was talking about if he tried anyway.

"I'm leaving," I announced. "Fletch..."

Fletcher peeled himself off the couch, a smile still playing on his lips. When he hugged me, I hugged him back, smiling a little at his easy affection. I'd never had so much affection in my life until I met him.

"Thank you for coming over. Thank you for trusting me enough to talk," he whispered in my ear. "Ethan too."

I hugged him a little harder and said nothing.

He started toward the door with me, but Ethan pointed at the floor. "What about that?"

Fletcher made a face and went to clean it up. "Bye, Beau! I'll come play video games soon!"

"Okay," I said, throat suddenly tight.

*I won't be there when he comes.*

Ethan made it to the door first, but instead of pulling it open, he turned around, blocking me from its path. "I want you to know that you can talk to me anytime about this stuff. I know Fletcher is a little... inexperienced, but I'm not."

I just couldn't stop the words from coming out of my mouth. "But you like it... him anyway?"

Ethan didn't seem offended or angry. In fact, he seemed a little... endeared. *Gross.*

"Yes. Very much." He cleared his throat. "In fact, most men would probably appreciate the inexperience."

I nodded, not exactly sure inexperience could be so great but unwilling to ask anything else that exposed my soul. "I actually really appreciate everything, Ethan."

He inclined his head. "I know what it's like to be someone people don't expect. To want things other people might not agree with."

The tightness in my chest returned, this time so intense my ribs felt like they might crack under the pressure. "Yeah," I said, voice hoarse.

"I'm not just speaking for myself right now but the entire family because I know they would agree. We will always be here for you no matter what. Make the choices your heart tells you to make, and work everything else out around that."

"It's not that easy."

"No, it's not. But anything less is beneath you."

I looked up. He meant it. In this moment, he was not only representing himself but our entire family, and they were behind me.

His hand landed on my shoulder, giving it a squeeze.

And then I was in the elevator, gazing at my reflection in the shiny metal door.

I wondered if he would still mean that if he knew about my lies.

# 17

---

*Daeshim*

THERE WAS A LOT I NEEDED TO DEAL WITH. URGENT MATTERS that frankly required my full attention.

I mean, someone just tried to kill me. Not just someone—a man I'd literally once thought of as my best friend.

*Betrayal is everywhere, and usually, it comes from those who are not your enemies.*

A knife wound literally festered in my chest. Okay, it wasn't festering. Beau cleaned it with care.

And *that* was exactly why even my impending murder took a back seat. How could I think of anything—*anyone*—else when he ran out of here with that look in his eyes?

Traces of intense anxiety lingered in the entire apartment, a scent that was only underscored by hints of self-loathing. He'd been gone for hours already, and the scent still clung to everything, leaving me agitated and powerless to think of anything else.

*Where is he?*

He thought he could avoid me, but we were beyond that. Here I paced, waiting half out of my mind and showing far more patience than I'd ever shown anything since the moment I drew my first breath.

However, it seemed this was the wrong approach. How ironic. The only time I tried to be less like myself was the one time it seemed all of me was required. I'd given Beau plenty of time to confess his secrets. I didn't push.

Oh, you think I pushed? *Pfft.* That was me holding back.

The longer I waited, the clearer it became. Beau wasn't going to admit anything unless I made him. And honestly? He needed my force.

Beau wasn't going to come to me. So that left one option.

I would go to him.

# 18

*Beau*

We met in the same row house as before. I had no idea who owned it, and we usually never met in the same place twice. Normally, there was a lot more time between visits, but this couldn't wait.

The place must be secure if they thought it was okay to use it again because when I signaled, this was the location I was given. I was too tired to argue, too shellshocked to even think about it, but I still had the presence of mind to watch my back. It took three times as long to get here because I'd doubled back twice and changed direction three times. The paranoia I suffered was astounding. Frankly, the worst it had ever been.

I guess seeing blatant, graphic evidence of child abuse, trafficking, and pedophilia snapped whatever hold I had on my confidence. I knew this world was filled with scum. Hell, I'd spent more time in the presence of sin than I ever spent in virtue. But what I saw this morning was next level, and I knew cracking that system put a target on my back.

I was good at my job. I might even argue I was the best. I had to be. If I'd been less, they would have pulled me out of the "forest" long ago. And so to remain in the place that felt most like home, I existed in a state of constant anxiety, constant gnawing pressure that I had to be the best, that I had to be so good no one ever questioned me.

I was successful at it, but success came with a hefty price.

A price I willingly and silently paid, but I was rapidly becoming depleted. How long could a man walk across a tightrope, balanced on the finest of threads? How long until that fragile rope suspended between two worlds was snapped—or worse, cut?

I'd grown used to the quivering of all my muscles from the exertion of staying balanced, but how much longer until I gave out? Where would I land?

I should have been more careful, but I'd been so fucking angry. Those hackers thought they could keep me out of their systems? Fuck them. I'd done everything to keep myself untraceable. I covered my tracks and hid very, very well.

But the stakes were epically high, and I'd likely pissed off all kinds of the wrong people. As good as I was, I was still just a lone man working out of the ghetto. They could be tracking me. They could be coming to end me.

*At least this way Earth won't have to put me down.*

The sensation of my palm rubbing persistently over my chest created a fissure in my dark thoughts, allowing just a sliver of light to shine through. It was enough to bring back reality, the slap of it making my feet stumble on the concrete stairs.

My chest ached. No. My *heart* ached, ached so painfully that, without even thinking, I rubbed over it, trying to find respite. There was none.

Paying close attention to my surroundings without turning to gaze around, I let myself into the brownstone, my shoes moving quietly down the hall.

The team was in the back kitchen/dining room combo just as before. The scent of shitty, scalded coffee singed my nose hairs, and I saw McClaren had a butterfly bandage in the center of his black-and-blue nose. It was still swollen, and his eyes were just as black as the middle of his face.

*Good.*

When he saw me looking at the damage I'd proudly inflicted, his lip curled slightly, but then he glanced away.

"Rogen," Woods said from his position at the counter. "What's this meeting about?"

Before the other two could inject some kind of snarky shit I was not in the mood for, I got right to it. "I cracked their system."

All three of the men straightened, varying levels of mild surprise on their features.

Annoyance made my shoulder blades come together. "You really thought I couldn't do it."

"It's been a few weeks," Rogers murmured.

I flipped him off.

Woods cleared his throat. "I knew you could, but I have to admit I thought it would take longer."

"I got impatient."

McClaren made a whining sound that seemed to come right out of his crooked nose. "Goddammit, Rogen, you pissed everyone off, and then you called us for a meeting!" The chair he'd been using clattered over when he jumped up. "Now we're all sitting ducks!"

"This is our job," I bit out.

Woods held up a hand as though he could pacify the room.

He couldn't.

No one could pacify me.

*Daeshim can.*

I shook my head against that rogue thought. No, not even a thought. An instinct. I didn't so much think about Daeshim anymore; I just *felt* him.

It was odd and uncomfortable, but it was also addictive.

"How bad is it?" Woods asked, voice low.

"I'm pretty sure I have PTSD."

"Jesus," Rogers whispered.

McClaren's hands hit the table, and he bowed over them, hiding his busted-up face.

Woods was just staring, expression inscrutable.

"To be honest, I haven't even had time to dive deep and put it all together. The first few things I saw…" My gag reflex started to jump in my throat, and I dropped my chin. An unexpected yet familiar scent rose to tease my nostrils. I sucked in that scent like I was suddenly having an asthma attack, so desperate for its comfort.

I wondered dully if the reason I'd reached for Daeshim's clothes instead of mine was because this scent contained unspoken power to calm me down.

"Then what the fuck are you doing here?" McClaren yelled.

"I felt it was impertinent to let you know I found everything and it's way bigger than even we knew."

"I want to know who the power players are," Woods barked.

I nodded.

"I want names, dates, locations. I want everything."

I nodded again.

"You put it in a safe location?" he demanded.

"Yes." And I'd sent encrypted copies to places only I knew about. Not even the FBI.

He nodded once. "Good."

"You know they're coming for him," McClaren said. "They're going to want to wipe him out before he hands over any information. Your cover is probably blown."

"We don't know that," I said.

But really, it was only a matter of time.

"I'm good at what I do, asshole. They might find me, but it's going to take longer than a couple hours," I told the room.

"That gives us plenty of time to extract you."

My head snapped up. "W-what?"

"Pull your head out of your ass, Rogen!" Woods barked. "I told you the minute you finish this case, you're out."

"But I'm not finished. I still have to go through it all—"

"All of which you can do in a safe house at an undisclosed location. A location where the bureau can keep you protected."

*They can't protect you.* The voice in my head drowned out everything else for a single astounding moment. I felt the truth of those words all the way to the balls of my feet.

The only people who could protect me from the wicked coming were those who were equally as malevolent.

I started to shake my head, panic building so rapidly my head buzzed. *I'm not ready. I'm not ready to say goodbye.*

"I told you. He's grown attached," McClaren exclaimed.

Even though it was a waste of breath, I would have argued if I could have. In that moment, everything inside me was beating down the panic attack barreling at me with startling force.

My already tender stomach spasmed painfully, threatening to turn itself inside out. A fine tremor I'd worked hard to hide stole over my limbs. I hated this. I hated how out of control I felt in my own body, how it could just betray me this way.

Everyone thought I was so laidback. So calm.

How good I was at lying.

"Beau—" Woods began.

"Someone tried to kill him." The words came out harsh as if they had to battle against the raging anxiety just to escape.

"What?" Rogers asked.

Shoving my hands deep into my pockets, I lifted my chin, ignoring the nausea, dizziness, and beads of sweat gathering on my hairline.

"Last night. Someone broke into the Rotten Apple and tried to kill—"

"I knew it was him," Woods hollered, cutting me off. "I told you, Little Red, all this time, you've been living with the baddest wolf of them all."

*It's always about Earth*, I thought bitterly.

"It's not Earth!" I practically roared.

That shut everyone the fuck up. Goddamn, I was so fucking close to losing it.

"I've been telling you for years. Earth is not the man you think he is. He is no killer." I sucked in a breath, which my lungs basically rejected. "This isn't about him. The killer was after Daeshim."

The news made everyone forget that I'd just been yelling.

"Earth's brother?" Rogers asked.

What the fuck was he even on this team for if he needed confirmation for that?

*God fucking hell.*

Inside the coat pockets, my hands fisted. The coat Daeshim forced on me so I wouldn't be cold, and now here I was selling him out to the FBI.

That little gem of a thought slashed through my throat like the sharpest set of talons. The acrid taste of metal coated the back of my mouth, and for a second, I dully wondered if I might drown in blood.

Daeshim was an asshole. He wasn't my family or my brother, and he was the worst roommate in the history of roommates. I would know. I once shared a park bench with a military veteran with mange and PTSD.

He was also a bona fide criminal deserving of the FBI's ire.

*I need him.*

Even though it was just three words, a thought not even spoken, something without any physical weight, I stumbled as if I'd been punched.

I only realized I'd sagged onto one knee when Rogers shoved a shoulder under my arm to help me back to my feet.

"What the hell is wrong with you?" McClaren demanded. Then he looked at our superior. "He's fucking cracking up."

I laughed.

Three sets of bulging eyes turned to me.

I waved them off and straightened, though it took real effort to stay straight. "I haven't slept, and I haven't eaten shit since I saw what I did. I have low blood sugar, and I'm exhausted." Then before he could use that as another reason I had to pack up, I went on. "The guy who came to off him wasn't able to finish the job. Daeshim took him out. I helped dump the body."

I had no qualms about admitting it because I had immunity from shit like that. Undercover cops lived and worked in a gray area.

"Who sent him? Why?" Woods asked.

"I don't know yet. The assassin was Korean. Like Daeshim. I'm wondering if maybe there is some kind of resurgence within the Black Rose."

Woods frowned. "Rogers, get on that. Reach out to our contact and find out what the hell is going on over in Korea."

Rogers nodded instantly.

"I need to stay longer. If I'm there, I can find out the details. Maybe it will lead us somewhere."

*Like to the man you're obsessed with catching.* The unspoken words lay thickly in the room, something I knew Woods wouldn't be able to resist.

"You think Daeshim is the one we've been after all this time?" he asked, considering the idea.

I had to work to stay upright. I had to work not to punch my own boss in his stupid face. Even still, I had to do this. If I didn't, I'd have to go.

"No," I said. Not even my own desperation would allow me to implicate Daeshim that much. "He hasn't been here all these years. But I think he could lead us to him. The fact people want him dead is proof."

"It could have been an isolated incident," McClaren muttered. "Hell, the killer could have mistaken Daeshim for Earth."

I tried to swallow, unsuccessful. "Let me stay and find out."

"And what about the people you just pissed off?"

"It would look even worse if I just disappeared. If I stay and act like everything is normal, it might throw them off. By then, I'll have sifted through everything. I'll have all the info we need to take these motherfuckers off the streets."

"I don't like it," Woods announced.

I nearly rocked back in relief. He was going to let me stay.

I blinked back the rush of sudden tears behind my eyes.

*Get it together, Beau!*

"I'll give you a week, tops. Find out what's going on, and between that, I want everything you got on this scum."

I didn't even say anything. I merely turned to leave. I felt like I was going to fucking collapse. I needed some air.

"Rogen." Wood's firm voice halted my steps, but I refused to turn around.

"Watch your back."

I grunted in reply and left.

# 19

*Daeshim*

I thought I might climb out of my skin when I finally laid eyes on him. Only to suffer through several more years while he was inside that brownstone. In actuality, he was in there less than twenty minutes, but a pregnant turtle moved faster. Regardless of the time, it was almost impossible to stay planted in the dark just watching and waiting.

I wasn't confident I was close enough to hear if he yelled. What if there was some kind of struggle and I wasn't there? The anxiety of the unknown made me chew my nails down, something I never did.

The only thing that kept me from bursting in there was the fact that I knew deep down that I did not have to hear Beau yell if something was wrong.

I would just know.

He was an instinct for me now, someone I sensed. If he was in danger, I'd know.

The moment he slipped out of the house, my back teeth

came together. He clearly wasn't in physical danger, but he wasn't okay. He needed me.

The world condensed to him alone, and I chewed down another nail as his unhurried steps carried him down the sidewalk. The wait for him to get here was so torturous I was not gentle when my hand finally shot out of the alley to yank him off his feet.

Or maybe it wasn't that I was too rough but that he gave no resistance at all. Alarms went off in my head as he fell sideways, body not even reacting. It took too long for him to snap partway out of wherever he was and start to fight. But by then, I already had him pinned into the unforgiving brick wall. With a gruff, breathless grunt, Beau went taut, ready to launch.

"It's me."

His head snapped up so fast his beanie-covered forehead nearly slammed into my nose. The glassy, faraway sheen coating the usually vivid green cleared some, allowing recognition to slam into their depths.

"Shim?" His relief was fucking palpable, and then his whole body sagged like that last bit of fight literally sucked the remaining life right out of him.

"Whoa," I said, hurrying to press my body closer.

Our chests collided as he wilted, my own puffing out to offer more support. His head drooped, face landing in the juncture between my neck and shoulder. He shook so much his body vibrated, and the uneven breaths puttering against my throat made my heart stutter.

Supporting all his weight with an arm wrapped tight around his waist, I lifted the other to palm the back of his head and tug. His neck was limp, and his cranium dropped back into my palm. Cinnamon lashes swept downward, concealing most of his jade stare, but oh, I felt his attention.

Ducking close, I nosed at the pulse point just beneath his

ear. It was fluttering too fast for my liking as it too struggled like his lungs. His pale neck was cold against my lips when I brushed them across the hammering vein.

His breath wheezed, and I abandoned the spot to hover my lips just above his. His mouth parted instantly, and pride welled in my chest. *He trusts me.*

Instantly, I closed the tiny space between us, settling my mouth firmly against his trembling one. This wasn't a kiss, though. This was more. I gobbled down his ragged breaths, matching them with much steadier ones. At first, he didn't understand, his confusion tinging the shared air between us.

"Match my breathing, baby," I whispered, keeping my lips right against his. It was hard to keep my own breaths steady and even when my heart was anything but. I felt my lungs shudder with the urge to gasp, but I denied their attempts.

If he couldn't breathe, then I would be his breath.

If his lungs had forgotten how to work, then I would teach them again.

I knew he felt the confident rise and fall of my chest. Every breath I drew in, I expelled right past his parted lips. When his breathing began to even out, his hands curled into my chest to cling.

Aware there was an entire city around us, I slid us deeper into the shadows of the alley, making absolutely certain we were tucked out of sight.

The anxiety I'd been soothing spiked again, and I ripped that fucking hat off his head so I could bury my fingers in his hair.

"I got you," I murmured, angling him tighter against me.

We stayed like that until his panting eased into long, drawn-out sighs that swirled around the small world we'd carved out. As soon as his need for air was met, a new one stirred. He was somehow small tucked against me, vulnerable and relying on me as his shield. In that moment, I would destroy anyone who even looked at him. I'd unapologetically slash apart even the slightest of threats.

Beneath mine, his lips turned restless, and I saw the unspoken plea in his heavy-lidded stare. He could take whatever he wanted from me. I'd let him have anything at all.

But Red didn't want to take anything. He wanted me to give.

His sigh was the sweetest flavor I'd ever met when my tongue slipped between his parted lips. Stroking deep, I kissed fully but gently, taking my time to explore all of his silky heat. We melted together until I really had no idea where he ended and I began. His mouth no longer tasted like him alone but us.

One of his hands glided up to rest against my neck, the feel of his palm a grounding sensation in an otherwise weightless moment. His lips, though slick, clung to me like I was made of Velcro, making my heart feel as though it was suddenly inverted. He was greedy even though I controlled the kiss, taking everything I offered, chasing after my tongue for more.

The pads of my fingers tingled as I massaged against his scalp, his auburn strands curling around my fingers like vines growing toward the sun. I could stay tangled up in him forever, taken over by red vines and held prisoner by a needy tongue.

A loud bang at the opening of the alley made him jolt. Our lips were forced apart abruptly even as I hunched around him and spun. Using my body as a shield, I glanced over my shoulder to see a large flatbed truck stopped out on the street.

When I turned back, Beau was staring at me with an unreadable look locked on his features. The color in his cheeks was better, and despite the fact that I'd gone from filling his lungs to kissing him breathless, his breathing was steady.

"Did you follow me?" he demanded, voice like sandpaper. "There's no way you followed me."

Paranoia was not a good look on him. In fact, I never wanted to see it again.

"I don't need to follow you."

His brow furrowed for a fraction of a second before realization dawned to burn bright in his expression. An unmistakable air of wariness entered our space, his eyes probing.

I nodded slowly, answering that, yes, I had seen him the other day.

Suddenly, it was like watching a two-hour movie play over his face in just mere moments. Anger, panic, resolve, and even relief flickered rapidly. They fought and clashed as if he couldn't decide which emotion was the most important, so he spiraled into overload, which looked a hell of a lot like the panic I'd just pulled him out of.

"I don't care." I reminded him. "Whatever the fuck it is, I don't give a damn." Reaching between us, I grabbed his hand. "Come on. We're going home." *Where I can get answers.*

His hand yanked away, body tumbling back into the wall.

"Red," I intoned, spinning back, about to lose my cool.

Whatever I would have said died before it even formed on my tongue because the way he bowed under the weight of whatever he carried scared the shit out of me.

I'd never seen Beau like this. So... *defeated.*

"They still in there?" I fumed, stabbing a finger in the direction of that fucking brownstone. "They're dead."

I swung around, ready to attack.

Long fingers snatched my wrist as I spun, the grip weak but his hold on me strong. "I gave you up." The broken, hollow tone made my stomach bottom out.

I rotated toward him, making no move to dislodge his grasp on my arm. "What?"

"It was the only way I could stay." His sheer misery pounded me like a level-five hurricane.

I stood there taking the beating, barely feeling it at all. All I heard was that he used me to somehow protect himself.

The broken sound I made fell heavily at our feet, and I trampled it on my way to him. "It's okay." I assured him, cupping his head. "You did what you had to do."

A jagged sob ripped free as his forehead fell onto my shoulder. "I think I might need you," he whispered.

I grabbed him fast and ferocious, lifting him off his feet. His long legs clamped around my waist, arms looping around my shoulders, and his face hid in my neck.

*He's starved for touch.* The realization cracked a piece of my already battered heart. Thank God I'd been here. It was painfully clear Beau couldn't ask for what he needed. Hell, I wondered if he even knew.

With him still stuck around me like an octopus, I rotated to watch the street over his shoulder. I couldn't carry him home like this. It would draw too many stares.

Not that I gave a shit about people looking, but I still wasn't sure what he was caught up in, and discretion was clearly essential.

I'd have to hail a cab, which wasn't ideal, but it seemed the best of our severely limited options right now.

"Shim?" The nickname was more of a breath whispering across my bare neck.

Prickles of awareness tingled over my scalp, making my eyes lower to half-mast. Of all the things in life I managed to survive, that little nickname just might be the thing to take me out.

"I'm here, Red," I promised, sitting down right there in the alley, leaning against the wall with him in my lap.

Over his shoulder I kept watch on our surroundings, making sure we stayed alone.

"You'll leave when you find out," he said ominously as if he could chase me away. I wondered if he realized that even as he tried to scare me, his body settled farther into mine.

I laughed beneath my breath, finding him cute as hell. He thought sinister would frighten me, but sinister was just a midnight snack.

"Rest for a while," I murmured, lazily stroking up and down his back.

"Who's afraid of the big bad wolf?" he intoned, words slurring like he was suddenly drunk.

My hand paused mid-caress causing him to make a sound of distress. I started stroking again, and instantly, he settled.

"Are you?" I asked, curious for his response.

"No."

I was mildly surprised. "No?"

He pushed farther into my neck with a hum.

"Why not?" I pressed.

He stayed quiet so long I thought he'd gone to sleep, but then his quiet confession left fingerprints on my heart.

"I like him. He scares the chaos away."

## 20

---

*BEAU*

I MUST HAVE FALLEN ASLEEP FOR A WHILE BECAUSE WHEN I woke, color was draining from the city sky and the already cold temperature had turned frosty.

Daeshim's arms wrapped around me underneath the coat I wore, and the heat his body generated was delicious. With a small sound, I settled farther into him, loving the way his warmth seemed to seep into my body.

Fingertips lazily drew small circles against my side, and my eyes slid shut once more.

"We have to go now, Red." The baritone of his voice was so close it tingled my scalp, massaging my overworked brain.

One hand pulled free from beneath the coat to reach up and glide through my hair. A slightly startled sound shook his throat. "Your ear is ice cold."

"Someone ripped the hat off my head," I said, voice sleep-drunk and filled with relaxation.

Frankly, it was a fucking marvel I was so relaxed here and

now. We were literally in some sketchy alleyway, tucked into the corner like criminals staking out their next mark. The temperature was frigid, the air scented of snow, and we weren't far from the blatant evidence of my double life.

None of it mattered because he was holding me.

He'd given me the breath right out of his lungs, and now I was curled up in his lap, his hand dragging along my spine in the most reassuring way.

His hands pulled away from me, and my nose scrunched up in displeasure. After a moment of doing whatever, he nudged me. "Sit up."

The whine I let loose would have embarrassed me at any other time, but frankly, I was just beyond that right now. This comfort felt too good, my body too grateful for the fucking relief.

He laughed beneath his breath, and the sound made my stomach flip over. "I know, baby, but my ass is numb."

I pushed off his chest, blinking owlishly as if someone turned on a bright light.

The well-loved beanie was pulled over my head, Daeshim tugging it a little extra to make sure it covered my ears.

"I fell asleep," I said as if he didn't already know.

"Mm." He agreed, eyes roaming my features as though he'd never looked at them before.

"You didn't wake me."

"You needed the rest."

And so he'd sat down in a filthy alley, taking our weight and keeping all the cold of the concrete from my sleeping form.

"We shouldn't be out here like this," I said, once again marveling at the fact I'd literally fallen asleep with my back turned to everyone in this city that could potentially be hunting me down. That I'd fallen asleep in the arms of what was likely the biggest danger of all.

"I'll protect you," he whispered, tucking his coat around me and zipping it up. Tapping my thigh, he grimaced. "But up, yeah?"

My body was stiff when I unfolded from his, so he likely felt even more rickety than me, but his movements were fluid when he stood.

Hand settling at the small of my back, he hitched a chin toward the street. "C'mon, there's a ramen place around the corner. You need to eat. Then we're going home."

"We should split up," I said, the respite I'd had in his arms too soon fading away.

His fingers were firm when he pulled my face around. Black eyes drilled into mine without blinking and with a ferocity that left no room for any other emotion. "You are not leaving my sight. Food. Home. And if anyone even looks at you a second too long, I'm taking them out."

My stomach growled, ruining the argument I was preparing.

Daeshim's teeth flashed in a there-and-gone smile. "Good boy."

I knocked his hand away, face flaming. "Don't fucking praise me like a dog," I demanded, stomping ahead. "I'm not Fletcher," I tacked on, then inwardly winced.

My God, I'd just climbed up his body and into his lap like Fletcher did with Ethan. *Oh my God, was I going to be his bottom?*

I rocked on my feet when they planted into the pavement, halting my forward progress. Swinging around, I pinned Daeshim with an almost angry look. "Would you let me top?"

Shock made him go still. Then he blinked. Once. Twice. A slow smile pulled his wide mouth. "Why, Red, I didn't know you wanted to have sex."

This asshole.

And me? I was fucking worse. The word-vomit. *Dear God,* the vomit.

"I don't!" I roared, then started to stomp away.

My whole body was snatched from behind, hauled backward into a chest that wasn't that much wider than mine but made me feel like I was being swallowed by the Grand Canyon.

*The Grand Canyon is a nice place.*

I started swearing. Great colorful verbs that I hoped I remembered to use again later.

The thrust of his obviously hard dick against my ass guaranteed none of those words would be recalled. I stilled, fighting the urge to arch back into him, mortified at how goddamn natural the instinct was to offer myself up.

His arm held me against him, coiled around me like some kind of deadly snake. His thick fingers lifted the side of my beanie just enough so his teeth could graze my ear.

The shiver was involuntary, the sensation of his mouth on me so fucking good.

Nipping again, I felt a little sting when his canine nicked the flesh. The prick was followed immediately with the broadness of his tongue, lapping up the wound he'd just inflicted.

"Would I let you top me?" he murmured, voice sounding like a bear rumbling in my ear. "If that's what you want, Red, then yes, I'd welcome your dick."

My tongue ran across my teeth, a small hiss leaking from between my lips. That slight sound turned strangled when he thrust against my ass again, rougher than before.

Reaching around, my hand slapped against his hip, holding him there, silently reveling in the power of his throbbing rod.

A husky laugh brushed against my exposed ear, and he nipped at it again. "But something whispers you'd rather be under me, my hands all over your skin, my cum filling up all your empty places, and with every single ounce of my attention trained solely on you."

He took my weight easily as if he'd been expecting my knees to go weak. My own dick was painfully hard, the vivid picture he painted making it leak.

I didn't say anything. What the fuck was there to say? I was the one who started this, but Shim? He fucking ended it.

After a moment of us just standing there, me a quivering mess, his voice filled my ear again. "It's nice to know you're thinking about it too."

A high-pitched sound ripped loose, and I leaped forward —off his dick and away from his hold. I powerwalked the entire way to the ramen shop, staying in front of him, not once looking back.

Occasionally, I heard his predatory laughter being carried off by the wind, and I decided I would never look at him again.

My resolve lasted the amount of time it took for him to slide a huge, steaming bowl of ramen under my nose. It was my favorite kind.

Surprise made me look up, and he smiled as he unwrapped a pair of chopsticks, expertly snapping them apart. Those, too, appeared under my nose, and I reached out, planning to make sure our fingers didn't brush. He didn't let me get away with it. This man never let me get away with jackshit.

Instead, his warmer-toned digits wrapped around mine, pulling me and the sticks partway across the table. Steam from both huge bowls curled up around my exposed wrist, feeling like some sort of seductive kiss.

"You have freckles everywhere," he murmured, gazing at my hand.

I tried to tug away, a fierce blush already pooling in my

cheeks. His grip tightened to just this side of painful, and then he lowered, brushing his lips over my knuckles.

I bit into my lower lip, and though completely embarrassed, I could not look away.

"I like them," he confessed, steam wafting up to try and obscure his face. "They're pretty."

I snatched my hand back, making a face. "I am not pretty."

"You are to me."

Again, I say, this asshole. *How dare he make me feel things I've never felt before?*

"Eat your noodles, Red. We aren't leaving until the entire bowl is gone."

I snorted. As if that were a challenge. I couldn't even remember the last time I ate. And then I remembered why. The sudden lump in my throat made me stare at the food and wonder if I'd even be able to swallow it down.

He kicked me under the table, making me howl and earning us a few stares from the tables nearby.

"I said eat." His stare burned with black flames, the intensity so great the lump in my throat melted.

I slurped up a giant bite so big my cheeks puffed out.

I saw the stupid praise form on his lips, and I slotted my eyes in threat.

He grinned fast, holding up his palms in surrender.

We ate the rest of the meal in silence.

## 21

*Daeshim*

My plan to force him to talk turned into a nap and noodles.

What the fuck was this? Daycare?

But you tell me how the hell I was supposed to act when he could barely stay upright. Instinct took over, and it wasn't about the answers anymore but taking care of what was mine.

Besides, sitting in the alley while he drooled on me provided ample opportunity to watch the comings and goings of everyone around us. So far, it seemed no one was searching. For me or for him.

What a fucking duo we made. Filled with secrets, marred with scars. We spent the first several months together in forced proximity, roommates by default, brothers *not* by choice. We fought against each other tooth and nail, but in the end, we were powerless to the underlying connection somehow binding us together.

Maybe that was why the talking kept slipping through the cracks. First because I wanted him to tell me and now because it didn't matter. However, we'd come to a crossroads. This was now need-to-know. I meant it when I said I would protect him, and to do that I needed a crystal-clear picture of whatever the threat was.

The cabbie pulled up in front of the Rotten Apple, the inside of the bar brightly lit. Earth was probably wondering where I was, but bro would have to wonder.

"Go straight upstairs," I told Beau, and he pinned me with a withering look, which I fondly ignored to turn toward the driver.

Beau was already past the door leading up to the apartment when I tossed a wad of cash into the front seat and followed behind. On the other side of the wall, the bar was loud. Clearly, Earth was entertaining a packed house. The music was up, and people talked over it, drowning out any sounds we made moving along the hall.

The second my foot hit the bottom stair, everything in the air shifted. Nostrils flaring, I snapped my eyes to the top of the steps where Beau stood rigidly, staring at the unlatched door.

Endorphins blasted through my body, spiking my heart rate but narrowing my focus. I bound up to put myself between Beau and whatever could be inside, but he moved just as quick as me.

One moment, he was gawking at the partially open door, and the next, he was rushing headfirst into the unknown.

Time slowed to a crawl, and it was as if someone shoved my head underwater, turning everything slightly muted. But it didn't matter how buffered my senses were. I still heard Beau's shout followed closely by a thud.

And just like that, I was dropkicked back into Korea, back into my old life... back into that night.

The humanity I wore to mask my animalistic nature was stripped away, leaving behind the true face of the predator with the bloodthirsty appetite.

The door sagged off its hinges when I ripped it wide. The hazy tunnel vision I stared through tracked the room as if there were a visible trail.

Despite the completely black room, I found the fighting bodies instantly, locked together so close they made one shadow instead of two. The sound I made filled the room as I surged forward to rip them apart. I didn't have to look to know who was who. I didn't pause at all. I tossed Beau back, his body disappearing over the back of the couch, and settled all my ire on the man who'd tried to take him from me.

His jaw cracked when my fist slammed into it, his groan of pain only fueling my thirst for more. Even though his jaw drooped unhinged and crooked, he jumped into a spinning kick, booted foot aimed at my middle.

I caught the foot midair, using his own force against him to snap his ankle and drop him to the floor. He landed with a sharp smack, writhing facedown as he gasped for air. In his struggle, he reached up and tugged off his mask.

"*Sallyeojuseyo.*" *Please, spare me.* His Korean was garbled because of his broken face. But still, I knew what he said. I knew his voice.

The body rolled over, and the face of yet another man I'd worked alongside since I was old enough to walk looked up, pleading with his eyes.

"They made me come," he rasped, blood trailing from his lip.

The snarl I let loose was nothing short of menacing, and I watched him pathetically pretend to be intimidated, hoping to distract me from the Glock in his hand.

Movement off to the side made the man on the ground

smile, his expression more like a gruesome, gleeful gape because of his slackened lower face.

The ground dropped out from under my feet, and fear so powerful suspended me in a place that was worse than hell.

I shouted but didn't hear the sound. I moved infinitely too slow. The only thing that registered was the deafening pop of the gun accompanied by the brief spark in the dark created by the discharging bullet.

## 22

*Beau*

*They found me.*

The second I noticed the slightly open door, I knew.

*How the hell did they find me so fast?*

The run-on thoughts were followed just as quickly by the fierce flush of anger. I was so sick of this shit.

Not even trying to hide my presence, I rushed into the apartment, looking straight toward my workstation. The creeper was there, dressed all in black (shocker), and the second he heard me, his entire body spun.

Without hesitation, I threw myself at him, adrenaline giving me the energy I'd previously lacked. There was some noise behind me, but I paid it no mind, arms locking with the intruder and swiping his legs out from under him.

We went down in a tangle of limbs, him flipping me so I was pinned against the floor. Driving my thumbs into the sockets of his eyes, I rolled, flipping us again.

Before I could do anything more, I was wrenched up off

the ground at startling speed. My body was tossed away, knocking into the back of the couch and flipping over it, landing on the cushions with an *oomph!*

Stunned, I lay there breathing heavily for long moments, the sound of the fight not really penetrating until the man in black spoke. In Korean.

*Is he not here for me?*

"They made me come." This time he spoke in thickly accented English, but the pleading in his tone was universal.

*Shit! He's here for Daeshim!*

As if on cue, a sinister sound rumbled toward the ceiling, making goose bumps prickle over my arms. Rolling off the couch, I stood, automatically moving toward the sound.

A series of events unfolded at exactly the same time, seeming to be one big incident and not small simultaneous actions.

"No!" Daeshim shouted, throwing himself at the man as a gun went off. On instinct, I dove sideways onto the floor, hands automatically going over my head as I rolled.

The side of the couch exploded with a muffled boom, and white stuffing shot into the air like some kind of confetti bomb. The Glock skidded under my desk as pounding footsteps and shouting erupted from close by but somehow also so far away.

Someone made a sharp sound like he was being mauled, and I leaped up, rushing toward the men.

"Shim!" I yelled, fear nearly splitting my heart in half. "Shim!"

The overhead light flipped on, and the sudden brightness blinded me for seconds, but even in blindness, I looked for Daeshim.

"What the fuck is going on?" Earth roared, rushing into the room.

I ignored him to hurry toward Daeshim, still freaking out that he'd possibly been shot. But he was fine.

Well. He wasn't.

But he didn't have a bullet hole.

What I saw was not a man but a predator, hunched over our attacker like he would rip out his throat with his teeth. His longish hair was wild. Throbbing thick veins striped his arms, which vibrated with power. With a vicious swipe, he clawed the man's neck, then coldcocked him at close range.

"Ungh." The assailant grunted as his head knocked off the floor.

"You come into my house and try to kill what's mine?" His voice wasn't even recognizable, odious and deep.

"Daeshim." The shock in Earth's voice was tangible, but even it wasn't enough to draw my eyes.

Shim's head whipped around, his eyes cracking onto his brother like a whip. Not flinching under the aggression, Earth remained planted even as Daeshim unfolded from the half-conscious man to stalk over.

Earth held his hands out palms up, but Daeshim ignored the gesture to roughly jam his hand beneath his leather jacket to unsheathe the wicked blade he always wore. Fisting the thick handle, Daeshim towered over the man whose head lolled against the floor.

"I'd crack your neck, but you deserve to bleed," he spat.

The man's legs moved restlessly on the ground as if he could run, but even uninjured, he'd never get away. The blade whistled with the force with which Daeshim brought it down, plunging it directly into the man's chest.

The small gurgle of blood bubbling between the man's lips tripled in size when Daeshim roughly twisted the blade. The dead man's head fell to the side, fear forever frozen on his face.

A heavy beat of stunned silence settled over the room,

coating everything with a metallic taste. Daeshim's thick grunt of satisfaction filled the space and had those goose bumps flying across my skin again.

*I like his savagery. Dear God, I fucking like it.*

"Jesus, Hyung, what—" Earth muttered, but the words were cut off when Daeshim shoved off the dead body and spun toward me.

Wild eyes assessed with the kind of clarity no irrational man should have as he harnessed the same vicious energy he'd just used to kill to make sure I was unharmed.

I couldn't look away from him even as he prowled closer, even as his bloodied hands grabbed me by the shoulders to roughly shake. "Don't you *ever* do that again."

My lips fell open, but I wasn't sure I'd even be able to speak. It didn't matter, though, because he spoke before I could.

"Goddammit, Red."

His fierce grip began to tremble, and some of the killer instinct in his eyes ebbed, leaving behind a man experiencing a different kind of wildness.

Fear.

"Beau." Earth came forward, clearly worried I was hurt.

Daeshim snarled, releasing my shoulders so he could shove me behind him, stepping so close his back plastered against my front. The grip he used on my hip was punishing. There was absolutely no doubt I would have bruises in the shape of his fingerprints.

"Get out," Daeshim demanded.

Earth crossed his arms over his chest, mild boredom written on his face. "I didn't even think you were home. Then suddenly, a gun is going off, and you're up here running my blade through some asshole. I'm not leaving. Explain."

The second Earth mentioned the gun, Daeshim's body

turned into a live wire. I didn't think about what to do. My brain never would have known. Instead, I did what came most naturally to me when it came to Shim.

Slipping my arms around him, I flattened my palms against his waist. Next to his ear, I whispered, "Shim." My hands rose and fell with his exhale, but his eyes never left Earth.

"Come on," I said, tugging him toward the bedroom. He resisted, still trying to intimidate his brother, feet planted on the floor.

"Shim." I beckoned again, this time letting my lips brush the back of his ear. I walked backward toward the bedroom, keeping him in front of me, letting him have full view of the room.

Earth's eyes skipped to mine, and a low rumble built in Daeshim's throat.

"Just give us a minute," I quietly implored Earth.

"You shouldn't be alone with him," he deadpanned, not even caring his words would just rile Daeshim more.

My arms tightened when he lunged, pulling him back into me. "I need you," I whispered.

The second he relented, I dragged him the rest of the way into the bedroom. Once there, Daeshim pulled away, slamming the door with a slap. Then, as if it wasn't enough of a barricade, he crossed to the dresser and pushed it in front of the door.

I wasn't sure if the gesture was meant to keep people out or me in, but perversely, I found both those things a turn-on.

Task complete, he began pacing in front of the dresser like an animal with too much energy and not enough room to run.

"Did you do that for me?" I asked. Maybe it was about the dresser. Or maybe the way he literally filleted the man who'd shot at me. Maybe it was both.

He stopped pacing midstride, entire being rotating toward me. The breath was knocked out of my lungs with the intensity of his stare. It was frightening and exhilarating all at once as though he was on fire and would burn everything around us… everything but me.

"*Mine,*" he declared, closing the distance between us in two wide steps.

I fell back onto the bed when he pounced, his full weight settling over me. We melded into the mattress, his rough hands ripping at my coat and shirts. A sound of frustration filled the room when none of the clothes came off, creating a dangerous flash in his edgy eyes.

"*Mine,*" he demanded again, catching handfuls of the sweatshirt, prepared to rip it right off.

"Wait," I said, covering his hands with mine. His eyes narrowed into dark slits, stopping because I asked but daring me to keep him away. I pushed gently, nudging him back enough so I could sit up halfway and lift my arms overhead.

What? I told you this was my new favorite outfit.

Nostrils flaring, breath uneven, he pulled the coat, hoodie, and T-shirt over my head in one fluid motion. Cold air brushed over my newly bared skin, nipples pinching tight.

A low rumble vibrated his chest, and his eyes lit with appreciation. He pounced again, as though he'd forgotten how to human. I laughed beneath my breath, making him growl anew.

"*Mine, mine, mine,*" he demanded.

Without reservation, I caught his face, forcing it up so I could look into him. "Yes, Shim. Yours. Okay? Yours."

A whine slipped between us, and then we were kissing. The deepness with which he invaded me stole my breath and killed all thought. The width of his tongue filled my mouth, and the length seemed to reach into the deepest places no one else had been. He stroked and sucked, licked and devoured.

The sharpness of his teeth was all that kept me from succumbing to a place where there was nothing but pleasure. The way he nipped my lips shot currents of electricity into my dick, making it throb with need.

Daeshim didn't just kiss. He claimed. He claimed with his body, his instinct, and his mind. He kissed as if he knew where every single private piece of me was hidden and he wanted them too.

I gave myself up to it, kissing back with what I hoped was the same ferocity but at times forgetting to try and match his pace because, honestly, I couldn't. In those moments, I let him take, relishing in the fact he wanted so much of me when no one else ever had.

He'd charged in here tonight and killed for me. Yes, the man had been after him, but Daeshim had only gone rabid when his enemy turned to me.

Usually, I was the one doing the protecting. Usually, I was the one in a room filled with people but always somehow alone.

I'd never known what it was to be protected. Not until recently, not until he started doing it. I'd begun to waver then, but tonight? Seeing just how fucking far he'd go? I collapsed.

I was drunk when he wrenched back, pressing my stinging, swollen lips together as I stared up at him dumbly.

"I'm not stopping," he rasped, eyes flashing with defiance.

I said nothing yet everything in a language only he knew, matching his defiance by lifting my chin and baring the long column of my throat.

His pupils blew wide, making me realize that perhaps his eyes weren't always black as night. They contained a hint of chocolate. I yelped when he dove in, lips locking onto my throat and sucking with a ferocity that shouldn't have surprised me. Stinging pain bloomed, heightened by the sharpness of his teeth.

A loud knock on the door broke into our haze. "Your minute is up," Earth demanded.

Daeshim's palm settled on the side of my head, keeping me pinned and my neck exposed. "Fuck off!" he called, then was sucking deeply again, drawing from me an exaggerated moan.

With a satisfied sound, he pulled back, licking across what I was sure would be one hell of a bruise before grasping my chin to kiss my lips gently. The complete one-eighty he made from neck to lips threw me off balance, and butterflies began to flutter wildly just under my ribcage.

Straddling my waist, he stripped off his shirts, and for the first time, I didn't have to pretend not to look. His shoulders were broad and his waist was lean. He worked out almost every day but wasn't overly muscular. Still, his honed form hummed with unmistakable strength. Scars littered his upper body, the most recent on his upper arm and shoulder from when Earth stabbed him and when he was shot.

The tattoo of the black rose on his chest was obscured by the bandage I'd placed over the knife wound. The white padding was stained with red, making me momentarily forget I was checking him out.

"You're bleeding again," I murmured, fingertips brushing the loose corners of the bandage.

"Leave it," he commanded, catching my wrist.

"No." I rebelled, green eyes flashing, dislodging his light hold to rip away the covering.

The wound definitely reopened, probably when he was going wild. It wasn't bleeding profusely, but as I stared, fresh blood welled.

Grabbing my hands, he forced them over my head, pinning my wrists in one of his. "You didn't listen."

"So?" I taunted. I might be willing to surrender to him, but that didn't mean I would always give in.

"So now you'll have my cum *and* my blood all over you."

When I shivered beneath him, he smiled.

"You like that?" he crooned, leaning down to tug my upper lip into his mouth. "Tell me."

I panted, squirming under his weight. "I like it."

He rumbled in satisfaction, making my cock strain against the sweats. I thrust up, looking for friction, coming into full contact with his raging bulge. His head dropped into my neck, and we both panted while rutting against each other, sweat breaking out along my hairline.

Jesus, it had never been like this before. So fucking intense. I was going to explode, and I still had on half my clothes.

As if knowing my thoughts, he glided his hand over my sides, trailing across my abdomen to flirt with the trail of light-red hair starting below my navel.

Tracking open-mouthed kisses down my chest, he worked himself until he was off the bed, his knees on the floor. Fingers dipping into the waistband of the sweats, he tugged them off, tossing them over his shoulder.

For long, charged moments, he only stared, long enough for me to dully wonder what my dick looked like to him from where he crouched.

Overheated and hard, it jutted up off my stomach, twitching under his stare. The tip was flushed, probably pinker than most because of the natural undertone of my skin. Freckles marred even the insides of my thighs, going as far as to speckle over my balls.

My throat tightened in anticipation the second he made a gruff sound and pushed to his feet. My stare dropped to the way his hands fumbled with his jeans, popping the button and ripping them down before they were even all the way unzipped. His dick bounced out, pointing right at me, the tip glossy from his excitement. Without even thinking, my tongue darted out, swiping over my lip as I imagined what it would be like to have that gloss coating my tongue.

"I'm not a gentle man," he warned.

Why he bothered, I didn't know. I'd already consented, and he'd never let me change my mind.

Just knowing that made me want him more. *Finally, someone caught me, someone with enough strength to force me to stay.*

"At least use lube," I croaked, those butterflies still attacking my insides.

His brow arched, and he didn't have to speak for me to know what he was saying. *I thought you wanted to top.*

Face flaming, I ducked my eyes, unable to meet his gaze. Truth was I wanted this. I wanted him. In me. On me. Over me. Everywhere.

Before the thought even finished, he shoved my legs wide and dropped between them. I nearly shot up off the bed when his wide, wet tongue licked right up my crack. My strangled cry filled the room as my back arched.

Without lifting his head, one hand slapped onto my chest, bringing with it a slight sting as he pushed me back and pinned me on the bed. My eyes rolled as his tongue swirled around the tight ring of muscle, and my legs went boneless against the bed. He didn't chuckle or act smug. He just held me down and ate me like he was indeed a wolf and I was his meal.

*Better to taste you with.*

A low whine floated overhead when he left my hole to nudge the underside of my sack. He latched on to one of the soft balls, sucking the entire thing into his mouth.

I twisted, nearly choking at the pleasure-pain combination, but he didn't stop. It was like he had a one-track mind and pleasure was on repeat. Once my balls were damp from his mouth, my hips tilted, anticipating his hot mouth on my shaft.

Disappointment speared me when he went south but was quickly forgotten when the end of his tongue jabbed my entrance. Hands fisting in the blankets, he speared me again and again, his saliva making me slick. When his mouth slid over to the inside of my thigh, my weep turned into a shout as he jammed one finger deep.

Shock brought my upper body off the bed, and I blinked widely at the dark head between my legs. He bit into my thigh before lazily lifting his face, his eyes colliding with mine when he twisted his finger.

I couldn't decide if the pressure of him invading my body was pleasure or pain. All I could think about was how his thick finger was literally claiming a place no one had ever dared to explore.

Biting down on my lip, I stared, asking him how I should feel.

Holding his finger inside me, he abandoned my stare to lower his head.

The force of my groan pushed me back when his mouth enclosed my shaft. When the tip of my swollen head hit the back of his throat, I sighed. He pulled off only to plunge over me again, the muscles in my lower belly contracting so hard I felt my inner walls clamp around the finger still inside me.

Then he was gone, mouth abandoning my dick, finger leaving me empty. As uncertain as I was before, I was now positive being empty was worse.

He went to the dresser, reached into the top drawer, and pulled out a bottle of liquid. My stomach dipped watching him coat two fingers as he crossed back to me. The second his knee hit the end of the bed, more lube drizzled over my crack, sliding along me in an unusual way.

I started to squirm, but his eyes landed on mine, stilling me. Just like the first time, there was no warning. One minute, I was empty, and the next, two fingers were pushing inside me, scissoring to loosen me faster.

"Shim…" I panted, anxiety starting to creep in.

"Shh." He soothed, blanketing my body with his and kissing me slowly.

My body opened for him like my lips, and soon I was wiggling against the fingers, exploring the way they made me pant. When a third finger joined the others, I grunted, and his tongue slipped into my mouth. It didn't seem like very long, and then he was ripping free of my body, a glint of impatience in his eyes.

"Red," he intoned, moving between my knees and coating his thick cock with lube.

I widened my legs, still not quite sure what I was asking for but wanting it just the same.

He positioned me so my knees were up, feet flat against the bed. With an arm snaked around each thigh, his glittering eyes pinned me in place.

He took me in one hard thrust. My mouth fell open, but nothing, not even air, came out. My whole existence became about the stretch and burn of my body and the way it adjusted around his.

His nails bit into my thighs with the effort of holding still, but it was an afterthought because this man was invading me, a predator taking down its prey.

After a moment of stunned silence, he pulled back and plunged in again. A garbled sound ripped from my throat, my tongue suddenly thick. His hips rocked farther until I felt his balls against my ass. The pressure was indescribable, the invasion full-on.

I blew out a shaky breath, and then his hands slammed down on either side of me, his body looming to block out everything else. Forcing my eyes open, I looked up into his ravenous ones. Pride, possession, and bone-deep satisfaction shone back.

In a sudden burst of emotion, I desperately wanted to please him, something I'd hate myself for later. But here, now, in this moment with his dick stretching my walls and his body claiming mine, I wanted nothing more than to be everything he wanted.

I was so overwhelmed all I could manage was a little wiggle. Wiggling my hips and sinking down on him just a little more. I felt split open—not just my body... my heart.

I became afraid he wouldn't understand and bereft it might not be enough. So I did it again and then took a chance and looked up.

All the rough intensity in his stare gave way to tenderness, raw need, and something that looked a hell of a lot like devotion.

Satisfaction made me purr. I did that. *Me.* I milked benevolence from a savage.

His eyes bounced between mine for the span of two heartbeats. His lips brushed softly over mine for one. And then the softness he let me know existed disappeared with the single snap of his hips.

My hands slapped onto his biceps, clinging as he fucked me into the bed. The headboard banged against the wall with every powerful thrust, and I nearly choked on pleasure. Tears blurred my vision as my nails punctured his skin. His pace only slowed when I felt his hand in my hair, tugging it back to expose my throat.

He kissed and sucked down the column, making my eyes squeeze tight. The welling tears were forced out and rolled down the sides of my face. Almost as if he could scent them, he lifted his head to lick them off my skin.

I was so doused in euphoria I didn't even know where it was coming from. His tongue? His dick? The feel of his body rubbing against mine?

I was completely covered in him. His bruises. His saliva... his dripping blood.

I never knew what it was to be owned until he took me in every way.

"Shim," I whimpered, not even sure why.

He pulled back, grabbing my chin and staring into my face. "You good?"

My head bobbed. "More."

He moved fast, bending my body near in half, plunging even deeper. A strangled sound ripped out of me, and my nails dragged down his back. He did it again, and light exploded behind my eyes, my whole body electrified.

"There it is," he grunted, angling his hips and hitting the same spot again.

The sounds I let loose were inhuman, and I had not one ounce of control over any part of me. He assaulted that spot until I was writhing and begging and the only word I knew was his name.

Reaching between us, his fist closed around my aching, sensitive dick. One pump was all it took, and my entire body went rigid as pleasure unlike anything I'd ever experienced poured over me, poured *out* of me. Dear God, the fucking relief, the fucking instantaneous bone-numbing satisfaction.

"That's it," Daeshim crooned as I spilled out across my abs and chest. Just when I thought I couldn't possibly feel anything else, he'd hit that spot again, and more white ribbons would dribble over his hand.

Eventually, it was too damn much, and I swatted him away, begging for a break.

He let me go, chuckling as he dipped his head and dragged his tongue through my release. Shocked, I stared greedily as he swallowed me down.

"You taste good, baby," he murmured, pleased.

I smiled, melting back into the bed.

"Uh-uh," he scolded, practically doing a push-up over my body. "Hold on."

Automatically, my arms wound around his neck, anchoring my body to his. Inside me, his dick spasmed, and my eyes flew wide. His hips started moving, deep grunts filling the space beside my ear, and I hugged him hard as he chased his own release. It didn't take long before he shouted in pleasure, his throbbing dick filling my hole.

My arms went limp, body sliding away from his. He remained above me, shuddering with aftershocks, humming with delight.

After a while, he slipped out of me, and the second he was gone, his warm jizz started to follow. I wrinkled my nose at the weird sensation. With a gruff sound, he pushed one completely boneless thigh open, and then two fingers were scooping up the leaking liquid and stuffing it back inside me.

"You keep that in there," he said, gruff.

A fissure of heat shot into my cock, and frankly, it stunned the shit out of me. I was so spent I probably wouldn't be able to walk tomorrow, but this asshole shoves his cum back into me and suddenly I'm willing to go again?

I wanted to sputter at the ridiculousness, but I was too tired for that too.

Pulling his fingers from my body, he dropped onto the bed and hauled me up so I was draped over his chest. His palm covered the entire side of my head when he pushed it into his chest and held it there as if he thought I would escape.

"I can't walk, asshole," I told him. Not only that, but he'd blocked the damn door.

He grunted but continued to hold my head against his chest. It made me smile.

A little while later, he finally stopped pinning me, instead dragging his fingers through my hair. "Did I hurt you?"

I made a sound. "Would you care if you did?"

His hands stopped stroking. "Yes."

How many times was he going to break me apart?

It didn't matter because he knew how to put me back together again.

"No, Shim. You didn't hurt me."

He grunted, playing in my hair again. "I like when you call me that."

"I know."

"You're the only one who does."

I smiled but then remembered Earth... who we'd pretty much abandoned with a corpse. "Fuck, I forgot about Earth. We should—" I started to get up, my body protesting in ways I didn't even know it could.

Daeshim made a rude sound, pushing me back down. "It's just us right now, Red. We'll deal with everyone else later."

I snuggled back into his chest, looping my arm around his waist with a sigh. Yeah, maybe everyone else could wait.

# 23

*Daeshim*

I NEVER DOUBTED HELL EXISTED, BUT NOW I WAS SURE HEAVEN did too.

I'd put my dick in a lot of places—

*Oh,* was that too crude for your delicate sensibilities?

My apologies.

What I meant to say was I've had a lot of sex. With men. With women. Sometimes with both at the same time. I've paid for it. I've gotten it for free...

You know what sex has never done for me?

Blown my mind.

I couldn't even argue it was adrenaline, the near carnal, animalistic urge I'd taken him with. I'd been primed on adrenaline plenty of times in the past.

This was different.

This was *more.*

It wasn't even like this with Hoon.

It was almost as though I'd been possessed, taken over by insurmountable desire and the insatiable need to claim what was mine.

*When I saw that gun...* The unfinished thought made me shiver.

"Shim?" the red head resting on my chest lifted. "Are you okay?"

His green eyes were hazy from sex, pupils still larger than normal. His lips were puffy and swollen, the upper one slightly chewed. A smear of blood marred his cheek, and I knew his body was littered with bruises.

He looked like a work of art. A priceless fucking work of art.

Gliding my finger over the smattering of freckles on his cheek, I smiled. "I can't believe you let me do that."

A blush bloomed over his face instantaneously, and he ducked, shy. It was so cute I chuckled.

"Don't laugh at me," he muttered, twisting my nipple.

I laughed louder because that wasn't a punishment. His little intake of breath told me he realized, making him boldly pluck at it again.

"Don't start something you can't finish, baby."

Huffing, he pressed his cheek back onto my chest. I pushed my fingers back into the mussed strands of his hair, loving the way they felt around my fingers. Absentmindedly, he traced abstract patterns over my stomach, making everything under my skin hum with pleasure.

*Having his hands on me is everything. Being inside him is heaven. Knowing he is mine... invaluable.*

"It was the alleyway," he whispered.

"What?"

"You just sat down with me in the middle of the street. Right there. It was freezing and dirty, and I'd just admitted

I'd given you up to the cops. But you just sat down. You just gave me what I needed most."

I tried not to react. It was by sheer force of will that I kept my body from stiffening under the slip of his tongue.

*Cops.*

Behind my ribs, my heart started to hammer. *Oh, Red. This is worse than I thought.*

Slowly, I dragged in a breath and let it out. "Red, are you a nark?"

It took me pointing out what he said to make him hear it too. First, he went stiff, and I prepared to hold him down. But then, remarkably, he relaxed again. "No," he whispered.

My lips curled in on themselves, and my pounding heart began to hurt. "A cop, then?"

He said nothing.

Lifting my hand off his body, I laid it beside us on the bed, curling it into a fist. "Beau, are you a cop?"

When he sat up, I was momentarily distracted by all his bare pale skin, the freckles decorating his body, and the fresh bruises I'd used to mark him as mine.

"Yes." The quiet confession made my eyes close.

"Undercover?" I whispered, eyes still closed.

"Yeah."

I breathed in deep. Exhaled.

The silence was near crushing, the weight of his words not unexpected but still heavy. I'd known almost from day one he had secrets. I knew he was up to something, and I might have even suspected this a time or two. But not knowing for sure? It offered the luxury of not having to believe it. Of not having to look the truth in the face. Perhaps that was also why I hadn't forced it out of him until now.

The blankets started to rustle, his warm body slipping from the bed.

Eyes popping wide, I bolted forward to snatch him back. Dragging his naked ass over the small mattress, I anchored him against my chest, clamping both my arms around his waist.

"Please don't kill me." His voice was forlorn, almost resigned.

Of all the things he could have said, that never once crossed my mind.

"What?" My voice was strangled.

He tried to turn, so I gentled my hold so I could stare into his expression. It was pleading, as I guess it should have been, as anyone's should be if they were trying to save their own life.

"You'll go down for it, and I've worked too hard to keep you all out."

Shock knocked me sideways. "What?"

"I'm just going to leave, okay? I know you can't trust me, but I swear. I swear that once I'm gone, they won't bother you anymore. I'll make sure. Just let me go and keep the family together."

*He's going to leave? He thinks we can't trust him? He's been protecting us?*

I was not surprised by much, if anything. I'd seen too much in my life. Some of it I participated in. But this? This stunned me. It rendered me speechless and made my mind almost numb.

I sat there silent and rigid so long that Beau tapped me on the shoulder. "Shim?"

My eyes shot up.

He flushed, pulling back. "I mean, Daeshim."

I rasped again, "What?" I was not a dumb man, but a habit was emerging: him speaking and me uttering the word *what* incredulously.

*Get it together!*

He frowned, hurt filling up the depths of his eyes with rapid speed. "I'll just go."

That knocked me back into action. Grabbing him by the back of the neck, I threw him onto the bed to straddle his waist, holding him down.

"What are you doing?" he asked, not even fighting me at all as though he were just going to accept his fate.

It pissed me the hell off. "Don't you dare call me Daeshim again," I intoned, "or I'll spank your ass."

His eyes went wide, disbelief written all over that pale, creamy skin. Before he could utter more shit that pissed me the hell off, I spoke again. "Did you just tell me you didn't want me to kill you because then *I* would get in trouble?"

Misery clouded his face, and he looked away, robbing me of that emerald gaze. "Earth too."

"And you don't want that?"

"Why the hell would I?" he burst out.

I raised a brow, liking that some of his fire was back. "Because you're a cop."

He turned, dejected. "I don't want to be."

I frowned. "They're forcing you?"

"No."

I sucked in some oxygen, trying to find the will to remain calm. I wasn't gentle or patient. Half the time, I wasn't even reasonable. But with him, I wanted to be. As much as I could at least. With him, I wanted to be able to shield him softly even in my hardness.

It was fucking hard. Painful even. Because right now, I wanted to grab him, shake him, and scream. I wanted explanations, and I wanted them now.

I didn't want to believe he was double-crossing us. I wanted to trust him.

No. I *did* trust him, and that was why this was so hard. Because his words weren't matching up with my instincts.

My instincts had yet to steer me wrong, especially where Beau was concerned. So this was what I did…

Moving to the side, I pulled him with me so we were facing each other in the center of the bed, my legs spread out so he was wedged between them. Cupping his face, I leaned in so he could see the sincerity in my eyes.

"Just tell me this," I implored.

After a thick swallow, he nodded.

"Good boy," I said, rubbing his ear between my fingers.

He didn't scold me for the praise, and it made my heart ache.

"Where is your loyalty, to them or to us?" *To me?*

His response was immediate, not even a hint of doubt in his eyes. "You. Always with you. You're my family."

The relief that coursed through me was almost as painful as the question. A choked sound vibrated my throat, and my forehead met his. I kept ahold of his face, pressing ours together as I let his promise wash away some of the worst of my worry.

After a moment, my lips reached for his. He sat frozen. I could taste the fear and shame on his lips.

"It's okay, baby. Kiss me back," I whispered.

He melted into me with a sob, his tongue pushing past all my defenses, desperately searching for mine. I gave it instantly, trying to soothe the worst of the anxiety twisting around inside him.

When the distinct tang of salt dripped into the kiss, I groaned and kissed deeper, using my thumb to brush away the stray tear that leaked from his eye.

Our ragged breathing filled the space when I pulled back, my hands dropping into his lap. "One more question,"

"Ask," he replied.

"When you say you gave me up to the cops…" I grimaced.

"Are they like on their way here to arrest me?" *How much time do I have?*

He jolted back as though I'd slapped him. I mean, really, *he* was the one who told the cops about me!

"No! I would never," he said, angry and vehement.

The absolute abhorrence he clearly felt at the idea of having me arrested was adorable, but it also told me nothing.

"Help me understand, Red," I practically begged.

His shoulders moved under the weight of everything he carried.

*Has he been doing this for five years? No wonder he literally walks around on the verge of a crippling panic attack. Why had no one noticed?*

"I told them someone tried to kill you. I used it as an excuse to stay."

My heart seized. "They want you to leave?"

He nodded once. "They said my assignment was over and I had to pack it up." Finally, his eyes lifted to mine. "I don't want to go."

Curling my hand around the back of his neck, I pulled him in.

His forehead tucked into my neck, and he blew out a warm sigh across my skin. "I just used your attack as a reason to stay and investigate. I didn't want to use you, but it was that or…"

"Or be taken away." I finished, staring over his shoulder.

His arms slid past my waist, forearms lying vertically along my back while his palms clutched my shoulders. "I'm sorry. I'm so fucking sorry."

"It's okay," I promised. "It's okay. You did the right thing. I'd rather have you here with me than not."

He pulled back. "Really?"

Beau's vulnerability made him look about five years younger and an entire size smaller. He was usually so confident, which I now realized was not confidence but him being closed off.

The part of me I said struggled to be soft? It didn't struggle right now. In fact, the wolf in me pushed that part forward so it could envelop him.

"Yes, Red. This is where you belong. Here. With me. With all of us."

He sniffled as I peeled him off my chest. "Promise me you won't just disappear. No leaving."

Doubt crossed his face, so I used the only threat I knew. "If you leave, I will rip apart this entire city and cause so much turmoil they will have to lock me up."

He sucked in a breath, then with its release said, "You wouldn't."

"I think you know I would."

He frowned, brows creasing so hard I fought the urge to smooth them with my thumb. Thankfully, he relented. "Okay."

I didn't really know what to do with the realization that the only threat willing to keep Beau in check was my demise.

Honestly? I fucking loved it. It made me feel powerful.

A wave of tenderness had me brushing my lips across his forehead. "Let's take a shower and deal with the mess in the living room. Then we'll figure this out."

"Seriously?"

I grunted. "The body is going to start to stink."

Cleanup was the worst part of killing.

I started up, but his hand closed around my wrist, tugging me back.

"I thought you would hate me." It was a pained, almost disbelieving whisper.

Coming back onto the mattress, I leaned in, pushing some of the hair off his forehead. "Baby, if I hated you for your mistakes, then how the hell would I ever expect you to live with mine?"

Those tendrils of anxiety that had been leisurely curling around the room, looking for the chance to drag him under...

They vanished.

## 24

*BEAU*

THE WOLF WAS STARING.

The beast covering Daeshim's back was inked with surprisingly delicate lines, but together, those lines created something so fierce no one would dare call it weak.

It was a very fitting representation of the man wearing the art. No one would dare call him weak, though he did have delicate parts. No one would likely believe it, but I had glimpsed those parts even in his ire—*especially* during his ire.

And that was why the watchful, penetrating stare of his tattoo didn't unsettle me like it used to. Sometime in the last few days, I stopped fighting against this, against the intense emotion he brought out in me.

No one had ever. No one would ever. It was him and only him. Daeshim and his wolf.

His whole body stilled when the pad of my wet finger dragged over the side of the wolf's face. The water from the shitty showerhead spurted and flowed with a pathetic lack of pressure. The spray itself was loud as if it had to exert great amounts of force just to produce the little it did.

The only water droplets that made it past him were the especially unruly ones, and the tepid water felt more like icy jabs when it landed. I ignored the sound and the flick of each droplet as the scent of whatever body wash Ivory always seemed to have stocked in this bathroom swirled with the scent that was wholly Daeshim.

His head turned just slightly, not enough to see me from the corner of his eye but enough to make sure I knew all his attention was on me.

I liked it that way.

I liked being the center of his focus, the center of the wolf's focus. There was nothing quite like the attention of a predator. It was not wholesome or pure but unscrupulous and cunning. It was so much heavier than anything else. The weight of it some might find suffocating, but me?

I reveled in it.

Once caught in a predator's sight, there was no escape. They hunted you and studied you with single-minded precision... and I bet they loved the same.

Oddly, I never realized how famished I'd become. How starved for attention. For so long my entire focus was on survival, which meant ignoring some of the most basic parts of me.

Sure, I had sex. I picked up girls down at the bar or wherever and used them as outlets for pent-up energy and to take the edge off. It had been enough to help keep the chaos I lived with contained... until it wasn't.

Until Daeshim showed up and started staring. Started pressing every button I didn't even know I had. The heavier his attention became, the more I wanted, and it pissed me off. It threw me off until eventually I had to succumb.

Suddenly, it seemed stupid, all the fighting we'd been

doing for months, because in the end, none of it mattered. In the end, I was standing here on quivering legs in the back of our shitty shower, reverently tracing over the lines of a tattoo on a man I just wanted to touch.

"How long have you had this?" I asked, finger trailing over one of its bared fangs.

"A few years."

"And you got it to watch your back," I stated, repeating something I heard him say months ago.

He made a gruff noise and turned his head to stare toward the front of the shower. Underneath the design were thick, long scars, only visible up close and if you touched his skin as I was now. I couldn't help but wonder.

"Did you also get it to hide these?" I asked, rubbing a finger over one of the raised marks.

"No."

I pulled back, suddenly feeling like I was intruding on him, my stomach turning sour. Even though I was already toward the back of the ancient clawfoot tub, I took another small step away.

That small distance actually felt painful, and it scared me so much the sour churning tossed itself up the back of my throat.

*What is worse: suffering from loneliness or the misery of someone you desperately want pushing you away?*

A blast of water splashed my lower half when he spun. White suds clung to his upper body, dripping down his torso as if the soap refused to give up contact with his skin.

A surge of jealousy smacked me in the center of my chest, and irrational anger turned me hot. It was official. I was crazy. No sane man would get jealous of soap.

Off balance already, I pitched forward when he wrapped an arm around my waist to yank, bringing my entire body flush against his.

Even as I stiffened, something inside me purred.

"Don't," he intoned, a drop of water beading on the corner of his brow and slipping down the side of his face.

"Don't what?"

"Pull away from me. Don't do it."

"I wasn't," I argued.

"You were, and I don't like it. If you want to touch me, you can touch me."

Flushing, I looked away. *How'd he know?*

"Eyes on me."

When our stares collided again, I focused hard on the water droplets clinging to his short, dark lashes and tried to ignore the intensity glimmering in his eyes.

"I wasn't just saying that to get you off my back. It was the truth. I did not get that tattoo to hide those scars. And if you want to know about them, all you have to do is ask."

Surprised, I met his gaze. "You'd tell me?"

He leaned in to suck away the water dripping off the tip of my nose. "I will tell you anything you want to know."

I couldn't help it. I whispered, "Why?"

His body settled closer, fingers curling tighter against my side. "Because ever since we met, that wolf doesn't watch my back. He only watches you."

The bottom fell out of my stomach, and my knees turned to putty. The arm around my waist shifted so his palm pressed flat against my back, guiding me down until my cheek met his shoulder. Saying nothing, Daeshim grabbed the soap and started lathering me up, his hands going everywhere. My eyes slipped closed under the sensation.

Rotating us so the water flowed down my back, he cupped his hands to rinse away the soap. His palms were slightly rough and wide. The stroking motions he used likely removed the suds with just a few swipes, but he kept going as though it wouldn't wash away.

"It only clings to you like that," I muttered darkly.

"What?"

"Nothing." The urge to pout when he forced me off his chest was so strong my lip jutted out. It was so embarrassing I transformed it into a scowl. "I was talking to myself."

The side of his lip quirked up, and laughter shone in his eyes.

I snarled at him, and the laughter in his eyes burst out of his throat. A warm, fizzy sensation bubbled in my chest, and the snarl transformed into a smile.

Grabbing more of the body wash, he squirted a frigid blob onto my chest.

I jerked back. "That's cold!"

His warm chuckle sounded a lot like a growl, and my dick twitched. I shot a look down, practically threatening it to give me away.

"You're too pale," Daeshim announced, not even noticing the staredown I was having with my dick because he was too focused on the rest of me.

I scoffed. "No, that's just my skin."

He made a rough sound. "No, baby. That's because of your life."

A flush bloomed over my cheeks, the warmth of it spreading to my ears. He kept saying it. Kept calling me that. I tried to ignore it, but how the hell was I supposed to?

His sense of me was entirely too keen, indeed like the wolf plastered on his back.

His washing hands stalled long enough to tease. "Oh, that's one way to get color on those cheeks. You like when I call you that?" He leaned closer and, with a saccharine voice, added, "*Baby.*"

Sputtering, I stepped back, face still burning.

I was halfway around when his slippery finger slipped somewhere I did not invite it. "Hey!" I gave a hoarse shout, reaching around to grab for him as my knees buckled. His laugh battled against the loud shower, the sound of it making tingles race over my freshly washed scalp.

"What the hell are you doing?" I demanded, trying to pull away from the finger he'd literally just jammed in my ass.

But the more I moved, the more he followed, and the dick I'd threatened earlier? It started to side with him. Fucking traitor.

"Shim! What the hell?" I whined, body leaning back into his.

"I didn't use a condom." His husky voice rasped against my ear. And to prove his point, his finger curled in a little and pulled out like he was, ah, scooping out what was left of him in there.

"Well, why would you?" I muttered, not even realizing I spoke.

The hand not jammed in my ass grabbed my chin, forcing my face around. "Exactly. I wouldn't. Because you're mine."

The power balance between us was slipping, and I grappled to regain some of what I felt I'd lost. "I thought you told me to keep that in there."

A hazy veil dropped over his eyes, and a little bit of the animal I had in bed flickered in the deepest part of his gaze. The animal I'd managed to calm. "You like knowing I'm in there?"

I forgot I was supposed to be taking control. *Yes, oh yes, I love having you in there.*

His finger slipped back in, making me hiss. I was swollen and obviously sore. But God, if the pressure of his finger didn't take all of that away.

"Answer me, baby." He bit lightly on my earlobe.

"Yes."

"Yes what?"

"Yes, I like having you in me."

He made a satisfied sound and swirled his finger around me one more time before stroking over whatever the fuck magic spot was inside me. *Does everyone have that?*

My knees bowed for like the twentieth time, and his finger pulled free so his palm could pat my bare ass. "I'll fill you back up later," he promised.

"You're really not pissed off?" The words spilled out of me quickly, making him draw back. I mean, really, this was surreal to me.

Sighing, he pushed me around to rinse off my chest, and when his chin hit my shoulder, my heart skipped a beat.

"Obviously, I'm not happy you're a cop. You've been lying to my brother for what... five years?"

My throat was so clogged I couldn't say a thing, so all I did was nod. And honestly, I'd probably bolt right out of this rickety tub if his hands rubbing my bare torso didn't feel like fucking Shangri-la.

"That's a long time. A lot of betrayal."

Guilt stole over me, and I swallowed again, the sound actually audible over the shower. "I told you I'll go."

"Oh no, Red. You aren't going anywhere."

"They call me that."

He stiffened, hands freezing at my waist. "Who?"

"The, uh..." I couldn't bring myself to say the words. "The team."

He jolted back, leaving me reeling at the loss of his touch. "They call you Red."

The fury vibrating off him made me turn.

"Little Red," I mocked, making a face. "Like I'm some kind of stupid kid. Like I'm not the one doing all the goddamn work."

His silence interrupted my outburst, making my lips press together. His arms were folded over his bare torso, biceps on display. I thought back to the way the veins in his arms had been bulging earlier in his tirade, how fucking hot it had been.

"Don't look at me like that. I'm pissed off!"

Startled, I looked up. The way he was looking at me... it reminded me of something.

Of soap.

"Are you jealous?" I said, mostly in disbelief (and yeah, maybe a little hope).

"No!" he barked.

My teeth flashed in a quick self-satisfied smile. He was totally jealous.

"The first time you called me that, I thought it was because you found me out."

Annoyance pinched his features. "You were scared to tell me."

"Wouldn't you be?"

"No," he deadpanned.

Embarrassment coiled around my ankles like a menacing snake. How much mortification would I have to endure because of him? It was like he fucking lived to make sure I knew he was strong where I was weak.

*But that's what you like.*

I told myself to shut the hell up.

"Whatever. That's great, Shim. You're invincible, better than me." I bitched, grabbing the edge of the curtain to shove it back so I could leave.

His hand enclosed mine, gently tugging it from the curtain. "The only thing I'm scared of is someone taking you away from me."

The underlying fear that came with those words made me shudder. Almost like he'd already experienced heavy loss and he knew the kind of hell that awaited if he had to live it again.

I turned abruptly, wrapping my arms around his waist

and pushing in. He made a crooning sound in his throat—a sound I rather liked—and folded me in, shoving one leg between my thighs.

"I'm not going anywhere, Red. It doesn't matter what you say or what you do. I know you think I'm the one with all the power, but the truth is you own me. I'm not scared of anything you could say because I'll stay. I'll fight your battles. I'll kill to keep you. The only thing that scares me in this world is if for one brief moment I'm not there or I'm not enough and it somehow takes you away."

"Shim." The blunt edges of my nails dug into his back muscles, clinging to him as I'd never let myself before.

And then I was climbing up his body, whimpering until my legs wound tight around his waist and his body pinned my back against the wall. The hard head of his dick nudged my puffy entrance, and I bit down on my lip to keep from begging.

The tension in his body made him vibrate, but surprisingly, he started to pull away. Panicked, I sank, his fat head catching on my rim. Both of us groaned, and I slid farther.

"No lube," he said, voice biting like it took everything he had not to move.

"I don't care," I said, using his shoulders to lever myself up and hold him tighter.

"I do."

"I thought you weren't a gentle man," I said, mouthing at his neck.

"Well, I guess with you, I want to at least try."

I was still stretched from earlier, already sore too. I wanted him so bad I didn't care about the consequences. I only cared about having his body inside mine.

"Please," I whispered.

He groaned and knocked a few things over when his hand fished around. Finding the body wash, he pulled me back slightly, laughing when I refused to pull off all the way.

He drizzled some of the liquid between us. "At least it's organic," he muttered, and I laughed.

I would have taken him bare with nothing but water, but this would work too.

The bottle thumped onto the shower floor when I slid down over him, my ass swallowing his cock like it was hungrier for affection than me.

"It's not," I said, sucking at the side of his neck as he thrust up.

"What?"

"Nothing."

He stopped moving, stopped giving me that delicious friction stretching my walls. I whimpered impatiently, and he made a sound.

Clinging a little tighter, I whispered into his ear, "My dick acts like it likes you more than me, but it's not true, Shim. No one likes you more than me."

His growl reverberated off the tiles, and he pumped into me with enthusiasm. It didn't take long for my body to go boneless, and I was unable to help him hold us up.

With a low curse, he pulled out, pushing me onto my back in the tub. It really wasn't big enough for this, but I really didn't care. I threw my legs up on either side, and he slid back where he belonged.

"Touch yourself, baby," he said, snapping his hips.

Wrapping my fist around my throbbing cock, I pumped in tune with his thrusts. All at once, the orgasm ripped through me, my back arching off the bottom of the tub. Water splattered and splashed around us as I spurted out across my belly. Before I was finished, he was coming as well, filling me just like he promised.

He collapsed on top of me, all his weight pressing me into

the old white porcelain. I had a moment of gratefulness that Ivory insisted on sending a cleaning lady because otherwise I'd probably get an infection.

"This water is ice cold," Daeshim bitched, his body still boneless over mine.

I laughed. "I can't feel it, Shim. You're blocking it all."

He shifted, and a blast of the icy water hit me. I yelled, and he laughed.

"Asshole," I muttered, shivering.

His body fit over mine again, blocking the spray. A pair of pillow-soft, warm lips brushed over mine, and our tongues tangled languidly, making me forget the cold.

When his head finally lifted, water dripped off the long ends of hair at his neck and onto me. "I meant what I said."

I nodded.

"No more secrets from me, Red."

"Okay."

When we were finally out of the shower and towel-dried, I ran a comb through my hair, goose bumps pebbling my skin. "I'm getting clothes," I said, pulling open the door.

He wrenched me back, pushing me up against the closed door. His hand slapped beside my head when he leaned in. "What do you think you're doing?"

I made a face like it was obvious. "Getting clothes before I freeze to death."

"Why were you heading toward the living room?"

First of all, how did he know that? Second of all... "That's where my boxers are."

"You think you can just waltz out there with it all on display?" Punctuating his words, he gazed down between our bodies.

I rolled my eyes. "You were literally just scooping your cum out of my ass with your finger. I think it's a little late for modesty."

"Not the second time," he intoned, leaning in to nibble my lip.

I arched into him. "Huh?"

His amused sound made the base of my spine tingle. "I left it in there the second time. Didn't want you to complain."

I flushed and pushed him back.

He wouldn't let me go. "Earth is out there."

My mouth opened. Closed. Opened again. "He is?"

"Do you really think I'd hustle you into the shower if I thought the front door of our apartment was still wide open and no one was out there to watch our back?"

"Well, considering what we just did in the bedroom…"

He made a rude noise. "No one would dare come in that room."

I didn't argue with him because, really, he was right.

"How do you know he's there?" I asked, blushing profusely. Was this going to be a permanent condition? Fucking red hair.

"Brother sense."

"More like wolf sense," I murmured.

He kissed me quickly. "Point is Earth is out there. And you are *not* walking around naked in front of my brother."

"He's my brother too."

"Wear a pair of mine."

I sniffed. "Maybe I just won't wear any."

His hand came up around my throat, squeezing just enough to get my attention. "You wanna freeball it, Red? Fine, but only when we're home. Alone. I don't share. With anyone. Under any circumstance. You will have two layers covering that sinful stick of yours at all times. You got it?"

How could I be turned on and amused at the same fucking time? I totally was. Was this asshole so possessive I had to wear two layers over my dick? It was borderline ridiculous.

*I love his ridiculousness.*

"And I thought being jealous of soap was stupid."

His hand left my throat, but the heat from his hold still lingered on my skin.

His brow arched. "Jealous of soap?"

"Never mind."

His grin was so big it split his angular face. "Were you jealous of the soap touching my body?" he asked, thumbing over his shoulder toward the shower.

"No!"

He laughed.

*Fuck.*

"Maybe I should let you put some marks on me," he mused, dragging a finger over the massive hickey he'd left on the side of my neck. People were going to think I was attacked.

*I was. And it was so good.*

"You wanna see marks on me too, baby? Hm? Leave something soap can't wash away."

My lips curled in on themselves.

He smiled. "Later." He reached around to open the door.

On my way out, he captured me again, holding me in the doorframe. "Don't you worry, Red. Hickey or no, I've already got your fingerprints all over my heart."

I ran into his bedroom, slamming drawers while pulling out a pair of boxers and some socks. I didn't bother looking for clothes, choosing instead to pull on the ones I'd been wearing before.

When I was done dressing, I looked down at myself. *His.* Everything on my body was his.

And everything *in* it was his as well.

# 25

*DAESHIM*

HE WAS WALKING GINGERLY.

I was the reason, and I liked it. It made me want to bend him over and take him again. It didn't matter I'd gone at him like an animal in bed and then again in the shower. He'd let me. Hell, he wanted me just as bad as I did him.

His neediness was something I did not anticipate. Beau was so calm and collected on the outside, the easy-going brother and friend. Underneath, he was pure chaos, a ticking time bomb of anxiety and panic and a deep-seated, clawing need to be perfect. To be wanted. He practically vibrated when I touched him, even in the smallest of ways. I could literally sense the way he held back from climbing on me, from pushing further into any affection.

He wanted it so desperately but was conditioned to keep it contained. Conditioned to ignore the gnawing need to have someone realize the reason he was so agreeable to everything was that he literally had no room left inside him for any kind of fight.

How exhausted he must have been. Keeping his lies straight was a full-time job, a job he worked overtime at. He expected me to kill him.

Not really a stretch, especially considering my track record and the body literally lying in the living room.

What he did not expect was my acceptance. No. What he didn't expect was for me to protect him even when he didn't deserve it.

It seemed Beau was also conditioned to be pushed away, tossed aside... left alone when he required work.

*Exactly why he tried not to require anything at all.*

How did he get here? Who made him this way?

"Hey." I caught him around the middle, towing him back into the bedroom. He was dressed in my sweats again, and I felt like I would likely have to peel them off his body just to get them into the wash.

*Fucking adorable.*

"What now?" He complained, but his body molded against my front instantly.

"You sleep in this room from now on. Beside me and nowhere else."

He made a rude noise. "Just because I let you stick it in doesn't mean I'll let you boss me."

"Oh, baby," I crooned, licking over the shell of his ear. "I don't have to boss you. You're already primed to obey." Reaching around, I cupped his package through his clothes.

A garbled sound escaped his lips. His narrow hips and ass pushed farther into me.

"You probably won't ever walk straight again," I whispered.

His hand reached around behind us, fingers delving into

my hair to grip my scalp and pull me in, panting as I rubbed against his ass, sucking on the skin just behind his ear.

He had another mark when I lifted my head. Giving his semihard dick a gentle squeeze, I released him, nudging him to go.

The front door of the apartment was closed, only held in place by the secured locks, which was further proven by the chair wedged beneath the door handle as if it were needed to prop it up.

"You're still here," Beau said, stopping several feet from the couch where Earth was sitting like he expected to be there a while.

Despite his lazy appearance, his eyes were sharp when they slid over Beau. "You okay?"

Beau flushed immediately, shifting from one foot to the other. "Why wouldn't I be?"

Earth raised an eyebrow. "You two weren't quiet."

A choked sound filled the room. Every visible centimeter of skin on Beau matched the shade of his hair.

"Where's the dead guy?" I asked, drawing the attention to give Beau a reprieve.

"I got rid of him."

I grunted. "Good looking out, bro."

I held my fist over the back of the couch.

Earth looked at it and then up at me. "Fuck off."

"Pissy."

"Yeah, well, I was scrubbing up blood while you were nailing my best friend in the bedroom."

Beau made another of those choked sounds.

I smacked Earth in the back of the head. "Don't make me kick your ass, little brother."

"So that's how it is, huh?" Earth asked, turning his full stare back onto Beau.

"Yeah," I said, watching Beau work to remain calm under

the scrutiny. Actually, he didn't appear to have to try, but I knew. I would never not know again. "That's the way it is."

Earth stood soundlessly, leaving his leather jacket and blade on the sofa to close the space between him and Beau.

Beau remained rooted in place, his eyes never once wavering from my brother's. In fact, his stare never wavered... unless it was me he was looking at.

Earth's boots bumped against Beau's sock-covered toes. "Since when did you switch teams?"

"Who said I did?" Beau countered, his even voice matching Earth's.

"He force you?"

I cursed, and Beau jolted.

"What?" he asked, shocked.

My hand slammed down on Earth's shoulder, and I pulled him back. Earth grabbed my wrist and twisted it behind my back, free hand grabbing the back of my neck and forcing my head toward the floor. His grip was not gentle, and the coldness wafting from him was so icy it almost felt hot.

"What the hell is wrong with you, Earth? Jesus! Not even I'm that much of an animal."

Earth jerked his head toward Beau. "His neck looks like a crime scene. I bet the rest of him does too."

"He didn't force me," Beau said.

Earth's fingers stiffened. "What?"

"I, ah... liked it."

Earth let me go, and I was up, shouldering in front of Beau to shield him a little. "If anyone else had even dared ask that..." I threatened.

"What?" Earth tossed out, clearly unbothered. "I'd end up like that guy I just dumped?" His eyes rolled.

"I know I missed most of your growing up, but didn't anybody teach you to respect your elders?"

"If you want respect, act like you deserve it!" he spat.

"Where's the body?" Beau interrupted.

"I told you I got rid of it," Earth replied.

"Where?"

Earth seemed irritated that Beau would question him, but he answered, "I put him in the dumpster behind the bar. The truck already came. He's part of the landfill now."

Beau nodded. "That should be good."

"Tired of explaining the bodies?" I teased before thinking better of it.

"Yes," Beau snapped. His own outburst surprised him, and his shoulders sagged. "Sorry."

Pulling his side into my body, I kissed the top of his ear and whispered, "Don't be sorry, baby. I won't tease you anymore."

He started to sink into me but instantly caught himself, staring at Earth who was looking at us like we'd grown tails.

"I called a family meeting." He informed us, still slightly shell-shocked.

"It's the middle of the night," I complained.

"There's a bullet hole in my couch, you just used my blade to butcher someone, and the only reason you even calmed down was because"—he cleared his throat and gestured between Beau and me—"this." Then without even taking a breath, he burst out, "What the fuck even is *this*?"

"He's mine."

Beau made a rude sound.

"You gonna tell me you aren't?" I challenged him.

Beau's eyes slid away, and he said nothing.

Earth looked at me. "You told me you weren't gay."

"I lied."

Earth transferred all his attention to Beau, who straightened. "You want to be with Daeshim?"

"*Earth.*" His voice was plaintive.

Earth's hand shot out to grab Beau, but I stopped him. "Do. Not. Touch," I said, squeezing his wrist.

"Answer me, Beau," Earth intoned, ignoring my crushing grip.

He nodded once. "Yeah."

Earth looked at me. "You serious about this? About him?"

I recoiled. "What are you, his mom?"

"I'm his family, something you've been adamant you aren't."

I released his wrist. "He *is* my family. Just not the same kind he is to you."

"Don't hurt him."

"You're worried about him getting hurt now?" I fumed. "Where've you been the last five years?" I shouted.

Earth's eyes flared.

"Shim." Beau's quiet word and light touch on my chest were all it took to bring me down.

Earth gazed at Beau with questions in his eyes, but there was also a glint of something else. Resolve. "Family meeting. My house. Right now. I want to know what the fuck has been going on. Every last bit of it."

Beau started to shake. I could literally feel the energy around him tremble. "We're coming," he answered.

Earth grabbed up his jacket and weapon and went across the room, wrenching back all the locks and then kicking the chair out of the way. Just as I knew it would, the door sagged out of the frame, the corner of it digging into the floor.

Earth fumed and turned on me. "You do this?"

"Yep." I wasn't even sorry.

"Assholes," he muttered and left.

When he was gone, Beau practically deflated. Catching him around the waist, I let him lean into my body, supporting all his weight.

"That's probably the last time he will ever call me family."

"You should know not to underestimate my brother."

Beau tilted his head back to look up. His green eyes swelled with so much emotion that I found it hard to breathe. His lips parted then pressed together with a small shake of his head.

"What?" I cajoled.

His voice was so small when he worried. "What if he asks you to choose?"

A singsongy croon slipped between us as I reached up to cup his face. "Oh, baby. I'd choose you. Every time."

"I can't let you," he whispered.

"That's why I'm in charge and you aren't."

The fire inside him sparked, and it made me smile. "Don't argue with me," I told him. "We're on the same team."

"Earth doesn't seem to think so," he muttered, blushing furiously all over again.

I laughed.

"He heard us." Beau groaned, trying to duck his face into my neck. I let him because it was too endearing.

Wrapping both my arms around him, I rubbed up and down his back. He stiffened at first but then relaxed into the hold.

Grinning over his head, I told him, "Next time, tell him you're team Daeshim."

Beau snorted. After a few moments of him just soaking up attention, he pulled back, blinking at me with vulnerability shining in his eyes. "You just told him we're together. Just like that."

*Does he really not know?*

"I'll tell the rest of the family in about five minutes."

He bit into his bottom lip. "But are we?"

"Yes. Might seem fast to everyone else, but this has been a long time coming and we both know it. We wouldn't have fought each other so hard and denied being brothers if we were going to end up as anything but together."

"We should go," he said, pulling away.

"Hey." I tugged him back. "I'm sorry it took so long for me to admit this. I'm sorry it took a gun to make me snap. But I'm here now, okay? All in. You aren't by yourself anymore, Red."

Want swirled in his eyes, which clung to mine almost desperately. Dipping my head, I kissed him deeply, swallowing his small whines of pleasure and battling back the anxiety I could feel haunting him.

When I lifted my head, he clutched onto my shirt, not yet wanting to let go. I nuzzled his still-damp hair, breathing in his scent.

"I have to take my PC with me. At least part of it. I can't leave it here with the door like that," he said after a while.

I smiled into his hair, happy he wasn't even going to try and deny our relationship. He really wasn't one for wasting his energy.

"Go get what you need. Get a hat too. It's colder than a witch's tit outside."

"Shim?" he said as we were on our way out.

"Hmm?"

"I'm nervous."

"It's okay." I reassured him, hoping like hell the family we both had come to love didn't let us down.

# 26

I'D CHOOSE YOU.

It wasn't a love declaration.

It was better. Sometimes love felt like weightless words. Anyone could say them. But being a choice? That took action. It took resolve.

If he ever went against those words, all the pieces of myself I managed to hold together would splinter apart and there would be nothing left of me at all.

Even though I hated feeling that way—knowing he had so much power over me, I couldn't change it. Even if I could, I wouldn't. Messed up? Sure. But who wasn't messed up a little bit? And I liked being his mess.

What I didn't like? The severe panic squeezing my lungs and churning my stomach as we trudged up the stairs toward Earth and V's place.

I never thought it would come to this. To me telling them about all my lies and betrayal. It wasn't that I hadn't imagined it. I had so many times. And those visualizations were enough to keep my lips sealed and my resolve to just let the FBI make me disappear someday.

Hurting because I left and betrayed them was less horrifying than actually having to tell them what I did.

I didn't want their ire, though I definitely deserved it.

The door swung open before we were even in front of it. Earth stood there scowling as though he were dealing with a raging case of constipation.

"Should I run down to the store and get you some Ex-Lax?" Daeshim asked, voicing my thoughts.

Earth's face pinched even more. "I wouldn't look like this if you two assholes weren't causing trouble."

The second I was within reach, he took the main case that contained the CPU and storage drive that held most of the important info. He didn't even ask why I was hauling it around. He just took it and disappeared inside.

I went in ahead of Shim, going straight over to a small station near the kitchen where the home security system I'd installed was located. Hitting a bunch of buttons and keys, I checked the whole thing to make sure no one was messing with it or attempting to. I also maybe procrastinated a bit and checked the cameras around the building and then ran through the footage from the day before. No one was lurking around their place, and it made me feel a little less worried.

When I looked up, shock made me do a double take because Ethan was standing there. How he was so big but soundless, I didn't know.

He smirked. "You were very involved with whatever you were doing," he said, hitching a chin toward the monitor.

I cleared my throat and put the equipment away in the cabinet. "Just making sure the security is running smoothly."

"Or buying yourself some time."

My head whipped up.

He smiled, eyes dropping to my neck. "I see you made that choice we were talking about."

I nodded.

He was wearing some kind of black turtleneck sweater, but not the kind that was so tight it looked like it would strangle you. It was a thick knit material, and the neck was loose. As I stood there awkwardly, he grasped the hem and tugged the entire sweater over his head. I gaped, taking in the black T-shirt he had on beneath it.

"What the hell are you doing?"

"You should put this on," he said, extending it to me.

"What? Why?"

"Because frankly, you look like a domestic abuse victim."

I blanched, thinking of Fletcher, V, Ivory, and Emogen. Hell, even Neo.

*Maybe I should cover it up at least until we have this meeting.*

I started to reach for the sweater, but a hand shot out, pushing my arm back to my side.

"What the hell is going on?" Daeshim demanded. "Put your shirt back on."

"I think Beau needs it more than I," Ethan said, casually proper as always.

"The hell he'll be wearing some other man's clothes!"

"Perhaps you should have offered him something with a little more... discretion."

"What the fuck are you saying?" Daeshim wondered.

I couldn't help it. I smiled. "He thinks I should cover up my neck for our little family meeting."

"The hell he will!" Daeshim roared. "I put that there on purpose."

"I never would have known," Ethan murmured.

Daeshim scoffed. "Please. Like Fletcher doesn't run around with hickeys all over him all the time."

Ethan seemed proud of that. "Yes, well, I understand

your… enthusiasm, but…" His eyes strayed to my neck. "That actually looks painful."

Daeshim turned to push my head aside. "Does it hurt?" he demanded.

"No."

"Don't lie to me."

"It's sore," I told him. Then I met his eyes. *I like it.*

I knew he heard the unspoken words because his gaze softened. "I'll be more gentle next time."

"If I can't lie, then you can't either." I smarted off.

Ethan made an amused sound.

"I said a family meeting, not a meeting for the Three Stooges!" Earth bellowed from over by the couch.

Virginia popped up from the couch cushions. "There's coffee and snacks in the kitchen!"

"Don't give them more reason to waste time," Earth told her.

She stuck out her tongue. "It's a family meeting, Earth, not an appointment at the DMV."

Earth made a sound. "What the hell would you know about the department of motor vehicles? You don't have a license, which you prove every time you run over shit with that chair!" He accused her, pointing at the wheelchair parked by the fireplace.

She gasped. "I'm a good driver!"

"Ooh, donuts," Fletcher exclaimed from the island, already shoving a pastry in his mouth.

Daeshim smirked. "Hey, Fletch, can I have a bite?"

"You have some nerve," Ethan muttered.

Daeshim whipped back around to pin Ethan with a look. "Then stop trying to dress what's mine in your clothes."

"Whatever," I snapped, irritation making my lips curl. I left both of them there and went into the kitchen where Fletch flung his arms around me.

"Hey, Beau."

"Hey," I said, returning the hug.

"Here," he said, pushing a glazed donut at me.

I took it and shoved half of it in my mouth. "Thanks," I said, chewing loudly.

"I'll call Marco and have him send you some concealer. A really big pot of it."

I started choking, eyes watering, and Fletcher started banging on my back. I kept hacking, trying to get the stupid donut down my throat.

Suddenly, Fletcher's hand was no longer beating me, and I was up against something warm and broad with a hand rubbing the center of my chest.

I smacked at him, wanting to be free, but he held me tighter.

"You're cute and all, Fletch, but I'm afraid I'll have to stop flirting with you now," Daeshim said, still rubbing against my shuddering chest.

I sucked in a giant breath, and the donut slid down.

Fletcher smiled and shoved the rest of his donut into his mouth. "Okay," he said, going to the cupboard to get some hot chocolate mix.

Once he was busy, Daeshim kissed my cheek. "Don't be jealous, baby. I only flirted with him to piss Ethan off."

"I don't like it," I said, surprising us both. My voice was still strained from all the hacking I'd been doing.

Hands on my hips, Daeshim pulled me around. I was fully aware of the audience we attracted from the living room. Fully aware of the stunned silence they all sat in while Daeshim held me in the kitchen.

But I couldn't look away. I'd been hungry far too long, and he was like a giant four-course meal served on a platter.

Sincerity and the softness he barely ever showed gleamed in the depths of his eyes. His lax whisper sent tingles shooting down my spine. "I'm sorry. I won't do it ever again."

I looked away. He made a low sound, bringing my eyes back up.

His thumb dragged along the curve of my lower lip. "You're the only one I want to flirt with. Okay?"

I nodded once, secretly thankful I was still wearing my beanie because my ears felt hot.

He let me go, and as soon as I turned toward the fridge, Neo bellowed, "What the fuck is going on between you two?"

Ivory sighed dramatically. "I really hope all of you will clean up your mouths before this baby is born."

"We're together," Daeshim announced.

I bypassed the water and juice in the fridge for a beer. I didn't even have the door shut before he was pulling it out of my hand, popping off the cap, then handing it back.

I stared at him, incredulous. "I can open my own damn beer."

He patted me on the ass.

I felt actual puffs of steam blow out of my ears. Lifting the beer, I drained half.

"What the—" Neo glanced at Ivory and grimaced. "What do you mean you're together?"

She beamed as if he'd won the Nobel prize instead of managing to say one sentence without a bad word in it.

"By the looks of his neck, I think you know what he means," Ander quipped.

"Do you need a doctor, Beau?" Emogen asked.

"Isn't anyone wondering why I called you all here in the middle of the night?" Earth wanted to know.

"V, do you want hot chocolate?" Fletcher called.

"Of course," she replied.

Earth glowered at the room. "I cleaned up a dead body tonight, and you all want hot chocolate."

A spoon clattered on the white countertop, and Fletcher gasped. "A body?"

"Way to ruin the mood," Daeshim observed, heading toward the couch.

I got another beer.

"It was your body!" Earth bellowed.

"Maybe we should all talk calmly," Ivory suggested.

All the girls in the room nodded.

"You know your family got drama when no one bats an eye at the mention of a body," Ander mused.

Virginia looked up at Earth. "I thought you were at the bar. What were you doing cleaning up a body?" Her eyes widened. "You aren't supposed to be killing people!"

Earth pinched the bridge of his nose. "I didn't kill him. Daeshim did."

Virginia looked at Daeshim. "You aren't allowed to kill either."

"I never promised that," he deadpanned, folding his arms over his chest.

Virginia frowned, and I opened the new beer to take a pull.

*Just a regular night with the fam, talking dead bodies and murder while hiding the fact I'm a cop.*

"So you killed someone tonight," Ivory said, pointing at Daeshim, and then turned to Earth. "And you cleaned up the body?"

Earth dropped onto the vacant seat next to Virginia.

Ivory turned to me. "Where were you?"

"I was there."

Daeshim made a sound from his place on the end of the sectional, and everyone turned to him. "Someone has been trying to kill me."

"What?" Fletcher exclaimed, nearly spilling the mug of hot chocolate he was carrying to Virginia.

"The first guy came into the bar after closing the other night. And we found this guy in the apartment."

"What happened to the first guy?" Ander asked.

"I killed him too."

After Virginia had her mug, Fletcher came back to grab his off the island. "Were you there that time too?"

I couldn't help but smile a little at the worry in his eyes. "I heard them fighting and ran downstairs."

Fletcher patted me on the shoulder and then took his mug over to where Ethan was sitting, climbing right into his lap.

*How easy it is for him to give and take affection.*

My eyes strayed to Daeshim and his open lap and thighs slightly spread on the couch. One arm was draped over the arm and the other was at his side. I imagined what it would be like to tuck my long limbs against him and breathe in his scent. How comforting it would be to have his body heat for this cold conversation.

Feeling my stare, he looked at me, but I turned away quickly, drinking more beer.

"Why didn't you say anything the first time?" Neo asked.

"I was busy."

"Too busy to worry about someone trying to kill you?" Emogen seemed disbelieving.

"Yes," Shim said, the single word absolute law.

A spark of awareness jolted my stomach at the steel in his tone.

"He was Korean." Earth spoke up. "Was the first guy Korean too?"

Daeshim nodded. "They're Black Rose."

"Dammit, Earth!" Neo burst up out of his seat. "You said there weren't any loose ends."

"This isn't his fault." Virginia defended him.

"When will it be his fault, V? When they come here for you?"

Earth made a rough sound. "They wouldn't dare."

"How do you know?" Neo fumed.

"They're here for me." Daeshim was calm despite everyone else freaking out.

Neo turned on him. "And you know that how?"

"Because I knew them. Both of them."

I stiffened, glancing at him. "You didn't tell me that," I heard myself say.

"I told you that night at the bar."

I nodded, remembering. He did say it was someone he thought of as a friend.

Daeshim glanced at Earth. "You remember Jae-Hee?"

Earth frowned, contemplating, and then a moment later, he nodded once. "Your best friend? The one you went to school with?"

Daeshim made a sound. "He came to the bar. Pulled a knife on me."

Virginia sat forward, clutching the mug, eyes wide. "You killed your best friend?"

"If he pulled a knife on him, he wasn't his best friend," Fletcher said.

"How do you know he wanted to kill you? Did you ask him?" Ivory asked.

Daeshim made a sour face. "I figured when he stabbed me, I didn't need to."

"Seriously, princess, what kind of question was that?" Earth barked. "Should he have asked him to have tea?"

"Well, I didn't know he was stabbed," she insisted. Then to Daeshim, she said, "Are you okay?"

He seemed mildly surprised she would ask but gave a curt nod. "I'm fine."

"Thank goodness," she said, sitting back and placing a

hand on her belly.

My throat tightened, and I looked away.

"And the guy tonight?" Ethan asked. "You knew him too?"

Daeshim nodded. "Kang-Woo. We trained together. I might not have considered him a friend, but I definitely never thought he was an enemy."

"But they came to kill you."

"Exactly. Someone sent them, someone who wanted to shock me by using men I would never expect."

"It didn't work," Ander said.

"Yeah, well, I don't care who it is. They threaten Beau and they're dead."

My stomach flipped over at his casual proclamation as a pregnant pause filled the room.

"They threatened Beau?" Earth's voice was low and cold.

"If they hadn't, I might have had time for tea," Daeshim quipped, glancing at Ivory.

"For heaven's sake," she muttered.

"So you killed them because of Beau?" Emogen asked.

Daeshim shrugged. "I would have killed them either way, but I just did it faster."

"Did you have to make such a mess?" Earth complained.

"A mess?" Neo echoed.

"The second he pointed that gun, his blood was as good as spilled," Daeshim growled, and with it, a blast of arctic air seemed to swirl around the room, swallowing up all the heat the fireplace put off.

Agitated, Daeshim shoved off the couch and paced toward the mantle. The gun seemed to be some kind of trigger for him because every time it was mentioned or he thought about it, his wildness turned unruly.

In the shower, he told me I could ask him anything. I wondered what he would say if I asked about this.

Just as the bottle was about to meet my lips, it was jerked away. Eyes popping wide, I tried to snatch it back.

Shim made a rude sound, holding it farther out of reach. "Switch to water."

"Fuck off," I snapped, reaching for the beer again. He tossed it in the sink, the bottle making a loud cracking sound.

"You're cleaning that up," Earth announced.

He tugged me in, forcing my shoulder to brush into his chest. Leaning close, he spoke low into my ear, making goose bumps race over my skin. "You need to keep a clear head right now, and you're probably already dehydrated from all the puking you did earlier. Switch to water."

Despite the visceral reaction I had to his voice, I forced myself to stay rigid and annoyed. But then he went and ruined all my efforts. "And yes, baby"—his voice was like a quiet massage directed into my ear—"I will tell you."

I shot up so hard and fast I would have fallen back if he hadn't been holding on to me. He said nothing else as I stood there and wondered how the fuck he knew what I'd been thinking. It completely panicked me that he read me so well. I knew I said I'd keep no more secrets, but damn, couldn't a man have some private thoughts?

He held me until he was sure I was steady, then left me standing there to grab some water. Yeah, he twisted that cap off too. "Here," he said, pushing it into my hand.

I took it numbly, still marveling that he read me so well.

"Come on, into the room where everyone else is." He directed me, putting a palm against my back.

"I'm good here." I tried.

He gave me a look that had my feet moving. It was that or have him pick me up. I knew he'd do it.

*I hope he does when we're alone.*

"Can we move this along?" Emogen asked, yawning wide.

The big diamond on her ring finger caught the light when she covered her mouth. "Y'all are lucky I'm off tomorrow."

"Daeshim?" Fletcher asked. Even though Shim looked over at my brother, he still kept his hand settled on my lower back. "Why is the Black Rose trying to kill you?"

"I'm not sure yet," he answered, sitting down and tugging me to sit alongside him.

*I'd rather be in his lap.*

"Maybe they want revenge for what happened to Dae," Ander said, glancing at Daeshim.

I knew he felt guilty about shoving the old hag out the window, but really, the world was better off.

Daeshim grunted. "There's no one left there to care about her. No one liked her anyway. They were probably glad she died."

"Maybe whoever stepped up to lead wants to make a point on how powerful he is by taking you out." Earth hypothesized.

"But Daeshim isn't a threat," Virginia said.

Earth grimaced.

Daeshim smiled, ruefully. "I know you think Earth is the big bad, but in reality, I'm the baddest of them all."

Everyone turned their eyes on Earth as if wanting his confirmation. I made a rude sound and drank the stupid water because someone took away my beer. Daeshim's hand slid over my thigh and gave it a light squeeze.

He didn't care that everyone thought Earth was more threatening. He probably preferred it. But it made me irritated. *Mine!* Mine was the strongest in this room. *Mine.*

"If Daeshim went back to Korea, he'd run it," Earth said.

The water I was drinking spurted out around the bottle top when I sputtered. Droplets clung to my chin and dripped onto my shirt. Daeshim took the bottle and used the sleeve of his shirt to mop up my face.

"I'm not going back to Korea," he told the room, but really, I knew he was reassuring me.

I hated that I needed reassurance.

"So why poke a sleeping bear?" Emogen wondered.

"They obviously aren't very bright." Ivory concurred.

"It's gang shit," Earth said, tired. "We have more to talk about."

"More?" Neo repeated.

Earth's attention fell on me, and my stomach clenched. Adrenaline spiked in my blood as my body literally told itself to flee.

But I couldn't. My own lies had caught up to me, and I was ensnared.

"Beau?" He phrased my name like a question. As if that was all he needed to ask for me to reveal five years' worth of betrayal.

Five years of walking a tightrope between worlds. Five years of lying, hiding, and hearing a ticking clock counting down to this moment.

The moment when yet another family cast me out.

*I made a mistake this time.* One I'd never made in all my life. I became attached. And now when I showed them who the real me was, everything would be ripped away.

# 27

*DAESHIM*

HE WAS SHAKING. BREATHING SHALLOW. EYES GLASSING OVER at an alarming rate.

About two seconds shy of an epic panic attack.

I gave not one shit that the family was staring, that it was the middle of the night and Earth wanted answers. Fuck all of that. Fuck them.

I was barely on my feet when I slid my arms under him and plucked him right off the couch. He didn't even react, just swallowed thickly and blinked like the battle going on inside him was so epic nothing on the outside even registered.

Over my shoulder, I said, "We need a minute," as I carried him from the room.

The first door off the living room was for the bathroom. I kicked it closed behind us and then climbed into the tub, sitting down with him in my lap. The white shower curtain squeaked when I pulled it closed, blocking everything but us.

His lips were slack when I pressed mine against them, not warm at all as they'd been the last time we kissed. Making a soft sound, I tugged the hat off his head, wiggling my fingers against his scalp.

A jolt of awareness washed over him, and I licked across the seam of his lips. A desperate sound ripped out of him, making my heart squeeze. Lips parting, hands sliding up to hold the sides of my neck, he made another frantic sound.

I kissed him deep and fierce, knowing gentleness would never penetrate such severe panic. Fixing my thumbs into the joint on his jaws, I pressed, making him open wider so I could climb deeper inside him.

He sobbed and then started kissing me back, his hungry tongue stroking over mine with wild abandon. The hair on the back of my neck practically stood on end. In my jeans, my dick turned to stone. Planting my feet so they were flat against the tub, I drew my knees in, forcing him closer, giving him a smaller area to occupy in my lap.

His fingers delved into my hair, tugging at the strands. Our teeth gnashed together with a particularly aggressive yank, but I kept kissing, grunting in satisfaction so he knew he could use me in any way he needed.

Refusing to break away, he dragged in oxygen through his nose even as our tongues twisted and one palm wrapped around the back of his neck, squeezing in a reassuring hold.

He sobbed into my mouth and shuddered, ripping at my shirt, trying to find skin.

It took a minute to drag him back, but once my shirt was gone, he was kissing over my chest, latching on my nipple and sucking hard. I grunted, reclining against the wall to give him more space.

He scrambled up so he was straddling my lap and attacked the other nipple with just as much aggression. Palming his head, I pushed him closer, telling him to suck harder. He did, and I moaned, my dick jolting under the extreme sensation.

When his teeth bit down on the already abused pebble, I flinched. The sudden reaction seemed to shock him, and he shoved back, blinking owlishly at me, his cheekbones hot pink. I saw the worry in the wide, hazy stare.

Cupping the back of his head, I smiled. "It's okay, baby. Come on," I said, pushing him back down.

His palm hit my pec, stopping me from guiding him back. "I don't want to hurt you."

My heart turned over, and my stomach somersaulted. "You're not going to hurt me. Take what you want."

Famine flashed in his eyes, so stark it actually robbed my breath. And then he was on me again, rocking his hips and latching on to my collarbone, sucking his way back down to my nipple.

My palm fit just above his ass, holding him as he rocked into me. I closed my eyes at the sensation of his tongue lapping at my flesh.

I knew I had to pull him back. This was going to go too far.

"Red," I whispered, grasping his shoulders. "Come on, baby."

His lips made a smacking sound when they unlatched from my chest and I peeled him back. His eyes were unfocused, hair wild. The panic wasn't in his eyes anymore. Instead, there was desperation.

Reaching behind me, he pulled something back, holding it between us.

Body wash.

I groaned, staring at that fucking bottle, knowing exactly what he wanted. Wanting it too.

"Baby, the whole family is waiting for us."

"Please, Shim," he whispered. "You said I could have what I want."

I was seriously going to have to tell him body wash was not lube. *Jesus.* But later. I'd tell him later.

My hands slid beneath the waistband of his sweats, shoving them down just enough. He whimpered, already melting into my chest, pushing his ass up in the air.

"You have to be quiet this time," I told him.

Earth hearing was one thing, but the entire family? He'd die of embarrassment.

"Okay," he said, wiggling his ass.

The scent of the body wash was very light, and I warmed it between my fingers before slipping them into his crack.

"I mean it, babe. You have to be quiet."

His lips latched on to my chest, and I grunted with pleasure. I went in with two fingers first, knowing we had to hurry but also knowing we'd just had sex a couple hours ago. I groaned when I felt some of me still inside him.

My fingers went deeper when he sat back, his lips parting on a shaky sigh. Then he was ripping at my jeans, freeing my hard length in record time. He started up my body, but I held him back, scissoring my fingers a few more times.

I didn't even have time to coat my dick because the second my fingers were out of him, he was sinking down onto me, his soft sounds of satisfaction directed against my neck.

The second I was completely inside him, he seemed to turn boneless on top of me. Both his arms wrapped around my shoulders while he lazily licked my neck.

It was like it was all he wanted—to have me in him, to have some kind of connection that was harder to break.

"Red?" I whispered.

"You do it," he said, licking over me again.

I laughed under my breath. "You're on top of me."

"Please, Shim."

Digging my heels into the tub, I thrust up, and he groaned. I set a fast pace, fucking up into his body. My legs quivered from the effort.

He stayed plastered against me the entire time, his soft sounds of satisfaction and the feel of his leaking erection between us telling me everything I needed to know.

My hips stuttered, and he pushed his hand between us. The feel of him jacking his rod between our bodies had me thrusting up into him again, rocking hard against his prostate.

His teeth sank into my shoulder, and his entire body went rigid. We were so closely pressed together that I felt his rod jerking with the release before the warmth of it smeared my stomach.

His pleasure triggered my own, and I held his hips down on me as I painted his insides white.

We collapsed against the tub, the air no longer scented with the body wash but heavy with the musk of sex.

We breathed so heavy the shower curtain ruffled a bit from our breath.

A few seconds later, Red pushed up, eyes lingering on his release smeared all over my chest before looking up. His eyes were clearer than before, and the blurred relaxation satisfied me in ways nothing else could.

"I don't even remember coming in here," he whispered, glancing at the tub as though he were seeing it for the first time.

"I carried you."

Something shifted in his expression. "You carried me?"

*He likes that.*

"Yeah. You were about to have a panic attack."

Realization dawned. Some of the panic crept into the edges of his green irises.

I sat up, grabbing his face. "No you don't. You're fine. I'm here."

His cheek lay on my shoulder, rubbing against it. "I like you."

I laughed under my breath. "You're cum drunk."

He whispered, "I'll like you even when I'm not."

Oh my God, he owned me. He owned every fucking cell in my body.

I rubbed up and down his back, not even giving a shit that we were making everyone wait. He'd done so much for these people, and they had no goddamn clue.

The least they could do was wait while he got what he needed.

*Thank God it's me.*

"Look at me," I said.

He made a sound of protest.

"Red."

Grumbling, he sat up. "What?"

"If you don't want to tell them, we won't, okay? We'll figure it out on our own. No one will force you. I won't let them."

"I want to tell them," he confessed. "It's just hard."

"Well, I'm not anymore," I quipped, lifting his hips so my softening cock could fall out. "And if we're doing this, let's go do it."

After a quick cleanup and putting the shower back the way we found it, I handed him his beanie. "You have sex hair."

Smiling, he tugged it on. "We seem to have a thing for tubs."

I made a rude sound. "No, I have a thing for you, and I'll take you anywhere you offer it."

The air around him shifted, and he hesitated. I stilled,

trying not to spook him. When he reached out, I felt like I'd won a fucking medal.

"Shim?" he asked, slipping his hand under my shirt to touch my skin. "Thank you for giving me what I needed."

He leaned in and kissed me. It was soft and short.

It laid me bare.

It took me a moment to recover, and when I did, I cleared my throat. "You ready?"

He nodded, looking much calmer than before.

And then he walked right out into the living room and professed all.

## 28

*Beau*

Being cum drunk was *way* better than being beer drunk.

I marched right out into the living room, ignoring the worried stares.

"Are you okay?" Ivory's voice was laden with concern.

"I'm a cop," I announced.

Silence. It was so loud. So definite. So... unnerving.

*What the hell did I just do?*

A warm presence pressed up close behind me, and I drew in an unsteady breath.

"What did you just say?" Emogen was the first to speak, her voice absolutely bemused.

The words didn't come as easily this time around, but I still spoke them. "I'm an undercover cop."

Fletcher laughed lightly. No one joined in. "You're joking... right?"

"No, Fletch, I'm not," I heard myself say.

Neo fell back into the cushions, wearing a stunned expression. Ander's face wasn't much different than Neo's.

A hard knot formed in my stomach, but that didn't stop everything around it from churning. It didn't stop the low buzzing sensation in the base of my skull or even cool the heat nearly singeing the tips of my ears.

Everyone was staring, completely flummoxed, for once not talking over each other because no one knew what to say. Every pair of eyes assessed me, wondering if they had ever known me at all. I couldn't look at any of them. I didn't even know how to begin to explain.

Like a magnet attracted to metal, I stared at Earth. He was the only one in the room not looking at me. The one whose stare I wanted the most. He sat so rigidly I wondered if it was painful. Boots planted on the floor, hands resting on his thighs, staring across the room but vacant as if he saw nothing at all.

I couldn't read him. He was motionless, cold... flatlined. Even though I could see him, even though he was present, it seemed like he wasn't here at all.

I swallowed, throat so dry my spit scraped down my esophagus, making my eyes water. I started to say his name, but no sound came out.

Neo burst up off the couch, the sudden flurry of movement catching me off guard. I flinched back, my subconscious obviously bracing for an attack.

With a deep growl, Daeshim darted around, using his body as a shield and planting right in front of me.

"What the fuck, Beau?" Neo roared, still approaching.

Daeshim planted his palms on Neo's chest and shoved. "Stay back."

My brother skidded backward, his dark hair falling away from his face. But then he was charging forward again, eyes drilling over Daeshim's shoulder and into me. "I want an explanation."

*Slam!* Daeshim's right hook sent Neo flying sideways.

Ivory yelled and jumped up from the couch, dropping to Neo's side. "You hit him!" she accused, glaring at Daeshim.

"I warned him first."

Out of the corner of my eye, I saw Fletcher start up, but Ethan pulled him back, anchoring him into his lap.

"Earth?" I finally croaked. He was the one I was worried about most.

He remained stone, eyes not once flickering. My heart thudded so slow and heavy that I found myself working to breathe. But then he moved, the granite edge of his angular jaw flexing then sliding back into place.

His eyes flicked up. Bottomless black pools of darkness that made me feel like I'd been pushed into a place where there was no right side up. As long as he stared, I would be left to spiral in the cold nothingness, awaiting my fate.

His words stopped my spiraling but dropkicked me into a freefall. "I knew it."

"What?"

"I suspected, but I just didn't want to believe." The disappointment in his eyes turned wicked, holding the promise of something much worse. "Guess I have to now."

I tilted forward as if his words had made me top heavy and I would faceplant on the floor. But Shim was there, stepping back so I tumbled into him, his body holding mine up.

My cheek rested against his shoulder as I stared off toward the wall, finally free of Earth's iron gaze.

"You knew!" Daeshim accused with rage, but the hand that reached behind him to anchor me against him was nothing but reassuring.

I blinked slowly, my eyelashes dragging against my cheeks before I forced them back up.

"You've got five minutes to explain before I get my knife."

There was some noise around the room, but it was all just background.

Though Daeshim barely moved, everything about him shifted. "You'll have to get through me first."

"You would fight your own brother?" Virginia asked, clearly upset.

"Maybe you should ask your other half the same question," Daeshim rebuked.

"No," I said, a sudden calm washing over me.

No. Not calm. Numb. I grew numb, and frankly, the feeling was a relief.

"Just let me say this, and I'll go."

Fletcher made a stricken sound, and I turned my face away from it.

"When I was three months old, my parents died in a car accident. I had no family on record, and my parents didn't have any friends willing to take in a kid. I went straight into foster care, and I stayed there until I was fifteen."

"What happened when you were fifteen?" Ander asked, and I shot him a small grateful look because he was listening.

"I ran away," I said, rubbing over my arms, suddenly wondering why it was so cold in here. "It was snowing that day. Some kind of freak blizzard. I remember thinking I'd rather freeze to death than spend another night in that house."

Daeshim reached for me, and I stepped away. "Just let me say this," I begged, taking another small step away. A small step closer to the door. I couldn't take his comfort right now. If he touched me, I'd fall apart.

He dropped his hands, but I felt his eyes. They never once left me.

"I was in foster care for a little over fourteen years. In those fourteen years, I lived in forty different places."

"Forty!" Ivory gasped.

Frowning, I said, "At least, I think. I stopped counting after a while. Could have been more."

"Red." Daeshim's voice was strained and rough. He took a step toward me, and I nearly tripped stepping back.

Holding out my palm, I held him off, straightening to my full height. "I was almost adopted three times. Each time, they brought me back. No one wanted me."

Someone sniffled, but I ignored it. I wasn't saying this for sympathy. I was saying this because I had to.

"Sometimes I only stayed in a place for two weeks. A couple times, one night. I was skinny, nerdy, and quiet. I didn't want to play outside. I didn't want to play cars or watch cartoons. I only ever wanted to read... and then later, I discovered computers.

"No one wanted a gangly redhead who never talked, wouldn't socialize, and could hack into your phone without even needing the password. So I bounced around, and in between foster homes, I stayed at an orphanage." I sucked in a breath, feeling my lungs shudder, and pressed on. "When I was fifteen, I went to a foster home where my foster father expressed an interest in, ah, redheads. I think he thought my quietness would work in his favor."

In a burst of movement, Daeshim swiped a photograph off the mantle. The wooden frame cracked, and shattering glass rained across the floor.

"So I ran away. They never came looking. The state was probably glad they had one less mouth to feed."

"Beau—" Virginia started, sadness in her voice.

"Don't feel bad for me," I told her, surprising vehemence in my tone. "I had it no worse than the rest of you."

There wasn't even one crack about how Ethan never had it bad.

"Anyway, I lived on the streets for a couple years. I spent a lot of time in libraries, internet cafes, anywhere I could be on a computer. I'm not real good with talking or people, but coding is something else." I felt a small smile lift the corner of my lips. Computers always were my happy place.

"I did a lot of hacking, illegal shit. Breaking into systems just to see if I could. I never stole anything except a couple times when I was really hungry."

Ethan made a sound, and I plowed on.

"Anyway, the FBI came looking when I cracked into their database."

"You hacked the FBI?" Ander mused, totally impressed.

I shrugged. "Their security sucked. Anyway, instead of throwing me in jail, they offered me a job."

"The FBI offered a seventeen-year-old kid a job?" Neo scoffed.

"I was better than their IT department, and I was young and homeless. They offered me a place to live, a nice computer setup of my own, and three meals a day. I said yes before they even finished asking. It sure beat sleeping on a park bench."

"You slept on a park bench?" Ivory bemoaned.

"Anyway, I went through their training, and after a couple years, they came to me… asked me to do a job."

"What job?" Fletcher asked.

"They, ah, said I was uniquely qualified because of where I'd come from, how young I was, and…"

"And?" Emogen asked.

"My red hair," I muttered.

"Your hair?" Virginia echoed.

I felt my face screw up. "They thought it made me look innocent."

Neo scoffed. "Real fucking innocent."

When Daeshim said and did nothing, I glanced out of the corner of my eye toward him. He'd been quiet and still since the broken photo. He hadn't tried to approach me at all. Insecurity climbed over me like ants on abandoned food. Sure, I'd told him I was a cop, but now he was hearing everything.

Earth still wouldn't even look at me, and now Daeshim wouldn't either.

"Little Red, they said," I told the room. "We want you to go into the forest and catch the big bad wolf."

"Idiots," Ethan muttered.

"I already told you they were."

"And the wolf?" Virginia questioned.

Rubbing the back of my neck, I stared at my feet. "It was Earth."

Neo rose to his feet, staring me down. "You're saying that you've been living with us for five years. Pretending to be our friend—our *brother*—when what you've really been doing is collecting all the evidence you need to put Earth in jail for life?"

I gave one decisive nod. "Yes."

All hell broke loose.

# 29

---

*DAESHIM*

EARTH BURST OUT OF THE STONE MOLD HE SEEMED TO BE CAST in and dropped low, rushing at Beau like a wild bull.

I leaped forward, but Earth had a head start, catching Beau around the waist and rushing him backward, slamming him into the wall across the room so hard the window rattled.

Beau didn't fight at all. He let himself be pinned and stayed upright on his feet as Earth's fist drew back to deliver a blow.

Over my dead body.

I caught his fist, crushing it in mine, and wrenched his arm behind his back. He gave a shout, shoulder dropping toward the floor, and I squeezed his fist tighter. Twisting my free hand into the black hair on his crown, I yanked, forcing his face up so I could snarl down.

"Don't make me do something I don't want to do."

Earth struggled against my rough hands, and Neo rushed

around the couch like he would help him. Making a rude sound, I shoved Earth back, making him tumble into Neo. I didn't wait to see how they handled their collision, too busy whirling around to face Beau.

Wide, incredulous eyes latched on to mine, and oh, what I saw in their expression… Not fear. Not anger. Not even resolve.

Vulnerability.

His lower lip jutted out. "I thought you changed your mind."

*See what happens?* You see what happens when I try and listen to what he wants? Ten minutes without me touching him, and he decides I'm abandoning him.

With a rough sound, I dragged him forward, pushing his face into my neck and locking my arm around his waist, embracing him as if I could banish any and all space between us. "I told you I'm not going anywhere," I said. "Even when you act like an asshole and refuse to let me touch you."

A broken sob pressed against my throat. I could feel his hands clench and unclench with the desire to wrap around me, but he wouldn't let himself.

"By the way, I'm not listening to you anymore," I said, pulling back enough to kiss the side of his neck.

He shuddered, burrowing closer.

Yeah, we all had messed-up lives. Except Ethan. *Freaking richie.* So it wasn't really a surprise Beau was no different, but *oh,* this hit hard. Worse than even the most heinous of crimes I'd committed or punishments I'd endured. This was somehow so devastating.

I wasn't much for kids, but not even I could stand the thought of a tiny red-haired, freckle-faced boy wanting someone to like him.

No wonder he kept to himself. No wonder he never asked

for anything. No one had ever given him anything, and when they did, they took it all back.

And that foster father? His fate was sealed.

"I want you, and that's not going to change," I vowed, keeping my voice for him and him alone.

One of his hands pushed between us so he could take a fistful of my shirt and twist.

"Move out of the way, Hyung," Earth intoned from behind.

Beau started to pull back, but I held him tighter, lifting my head to glare over my shoulder. "You'll have to kill me."

His eyes flickered. "Think I won't?"

Beau went rigid, pushing out of my hold. "No! Jesus, I'm so sick of cleaning up after you."

A pregnant pause filled the room.

Earth folded his arms over his chest. "Excuse me?"

"You think if I was sitting around behind my computers all day *fucking off*"—he air-quoted that last part, and I had to hide a smile—"you'd still be walking around on the street?" Beau scoffed. "Fuck no. You'd be serving twenty-five to life in the state pen."

"What?" Neo said, his shoulder practically colliding with Earth's.

Beau made a rude sound. "And you." He turned his ire to Neo, jabbing a finger at him to tick off his crimes. "Tax evasion. Theft. Breaking and entering. Public vandalism. ATM looting—"

Neo sucked in a sharp breath. "How do you know about that?"

Beau rolled his eyes. "I know everything. And you'd be in jail too!"

"ATM looting?" Ivory wondered.

Neo groaned and shot a look at Beau. "Why'd you bring that up?"

"What about me?" Fletcher asked as if name-the-crime was some kind of game.

"You don't count," Ethan insisted.

"I've done bad stuff too," Fletcher argued.

"You don't count." Beau confirmed.

"Why not?"

"You're the baby!" all of us yelled.

Fletcher deflated. "You guys are so stupid."

Ander chuckled.

Beau's eyes went to him and narrowed. "Please. Your rap sheet is longer than a CVS receipt. Daddy's money sure cleaned up a lot. But then he went and got all tangled up with a loan shark, and you pushed a woman out a window."

Emogen made a tsking sound, likely about to defend her precious beast. A rude sound from his lips stopped her. "Illegal gambling. Conspiring with a known criminal."

Her mouth dropped open. "My pops—"

"Yeah, I know." He cut her off.

Ander sat up a little straighter on the sofa, eyes narrowing on the man I still shielded with my body. "You saying you're going to put us all away?"

Virginia made a stricken sound, and Earth's eye started twitching.

"For fuck's sake!" I burst out, not even giving anyone a chance to answer. "Use your damn brains. It's been five years. *Five.* Don't you think if Beau wanted to put anyone away"—I flicked a hard look at Earth—"he would have done it already?"

"Exactly," Earth said, drawing me up short.

Behind me, Beau shifted, and automatically, my body rotated to match his.

"What?" Beau's voice was wary.

"That's what never made sense. If you really were here to bring me down, then why didn't you?" Closing the small distance between us, Earth stepped right up to me. "Hyung, move."

I measured him for long, tense moments, using all my instincts to feel him out. He was my brother, and I loved him. I would do anything for him. Anything but go against Red. He let me measure him, calm under the scrutiny but anxious to face Beau.

Even after I decided, I glanced behind me, silently asking. He nodded, and I moved so I was at his side, reaching down to thread our fingers together.

Despite the tense moment and obvious stress Beau was under, he abandoned it all to look down. The high points of his cheekbones turned pink, making his freckles look like he'd spent the day in the sun. Cinnamon-colored eyebrows drew down over his eyes and then arched back up as he processed the fact I was holding his hand.

I couldn't help but look at our clasped hands because the way he stared made me think I was missing something amazing. His skin was so pink and fair against mine, fingers long and slender.

All his digits flexed like he was testing the hold. I kept my hand locked around his even as he wiggled. A couple of his fingernails were jagged from chewing, likely a symptom of the extreme stress he functioned under.

*Flex, flex, flex.* His fingers opened and closed against mine. It didn't take him long to understand I wasn't letting go, and when his tired jade eyes looked up, they were shining with awe.

I smiled. A soft curve of my lip, nothing too extreme. But enough for him. His Adam's apple bobbed at the same time his fingers closed around mine, gripping tight.

"Hasn't anyone held his hand before?" Fletcher whispered to no one in particular.

Even though the exchange between us was brief, clearly everyone noticed.

"No," Beau whispered.

"You've been protecting me," Earth said, his voice lacking the brutal edge it had boasted just moments before. "All of us."

Beau nodded. "Of course I have."

"The reason the police didn't come down on me for everything that happened at the tower. The reason everything was so easily cleaned up, including Riley's murder... That was you?"

"Who's Riley?" Ander whispered.

"Earth's old informant," Fletcher whispered back.

"Yes," Beau told Earth.

"Why?"

I could practically hear Beau's lungs shudder with the force of his exhale. Despite the way he clung to my hand, there was a fine tremor in his limbs.

"Do you remember the night we met?"

Earth made a rude sound. "The night you were getting your ass beat?"

Tension bunched in my neck, but Beau laughed under his breath. "Yeah."

"I didn't plan on helping you, but you were getting blood on my street."

"I'd been staking out your street for months. Always trying to get a glimpse of you and trying to hear anyone whisper your name."

Any kind of weird fond thought Earth had about Beau bleeding on his street was wiped off his face and replaced with that cold, blank aura he used, giving nothing away.

Beau must have recognized the look because the trembling in his fingers increased. Without thinking, I started drawing smooth circles over the back of his hand.

"No one knew anything about you, and they were too scared to gossip. I hadn't actually gone looking for you that night, though. The guy who owned the internet café I always used started getting suspicious of me. Couldn't understand why I was in front of a computer all day, every day. He tried to hustle me out of some money, and I ran off. Didn't realize I was on your street until I looked up."

Beau glanced up, seeing everyone was listening, so he said, "I was pissed off and tired, so I pulled my hat off."

"You make an easy mark."

"Yeah. The FBI knew it too. Probably knew I would spend the first few months getting my ass kicked on the regular."

I cursed under my breath, and Beau actually smiled.

"Anyway, I got jumped."

"You fought back," Earth said, a hint of pride in his voice.

Beau made a sound. "I told you I was pissed off."

"You still would have ended up bleeding out in the alley," Earth deadpanned.

"But you stopped them." Beau glanced at me to say, "He just showed up out of nowhere and kicked all their asses."

In that moment, all the years I'd spent worrying about Earth, about where he'd gone and if he was okay, suddenly seemed like a good tradeoff. If I hadn't shot him, pretended he was dead, and gotten him out of the country, he never would have been here to protect Beau.

"I told those assholes to stay off my turf," Earth intoned.

"He protected you." Thoughts were still churning and spilling out through my mouth.

"Yeah," Beau replied. "And then he gave me a beer. The Rotten Apple was such a shithole then."

"You stayed!" Earth snapped.

"You let me," Beau said, far less indignation in his tone. "You never asked for anything from me. Not once. The Feds?

They sent me into the ghetto, but you? You're the one who taught me how to survive it."

"He became your brother," Ivory said, sounding like some sappy Hallmark commercial.

"The Feds must have been frothing at the mouth that you managed to move in with their mark," Neo observed.

"Don't make me come over there, Neo Florian!" Virginia threatened.

"Florian?" Emogen cracked. "Oh, this is gold."

"Of course they were thrilled," Beau answered, ignoring everyone's bickering.

I knew he was tired. I could feel it in the air around him.

"My boss has some kind of hard-on for you," he told Earth. "Guy is convinced you're a murderer."

"How long did it take you to figure out he was right?" Earth asked.

"A year."

The indifferent mask my brother wore so well slipped. "You've known *that* long?"

"I heard you on the phone a couple times," he admitted, then rubbed the back of his neck. "I have some hidden cameras around the bar."

Earth's mood went dark.

Beau shrugged. "I'm good at what I do."

"What *do* you do?" Ethan asked.

"No one ever thought to ask that before?" I asked the room. "All this time and not one of you has ever asked?"

"He told us he was a hacker," Neo said, voice tight.

"Yeah, he would take hacking jobs and then get a cut," Fletcher said. "Was that a lie too?"

"No," Beau said, eyes downcast as his expression turned sheepish. "I started taking jobs because I told you that's what I did."

Ander made a sound. "A cop taking illegal jobs. Do you get immunity for that?"

"He did it so he didn't have to lie to us more." Fletcher defended Beau.

He was cute. But he wasn't Red.

"I do a lot of cybercrimes work. Because I'm so good with a computer and coding, I can move around pretty much undetected. I've actually solved a lot of cases and brought down some bad people."

"But not me," Earth said.

"No. By the time I figured out you were the Huntsman, Neo was here and…"

"And?" Neo goaded.

My back teeth made an audible snap. I hated the way they were pushing him for answers and growing impatient. Yeah, I was impatient with him a lot, but that was different.

I was about to tell Neo to back off when Beau burst out. "And I was attached, okay? I liked you guys. I liked the Grimms. I finally felt like I had a family." His shoulders slumped. "Then Fletch came, and I knew I'd never be able to turn any of you in."

"So he started protecting you. Covering up your crimes," I said, laying it out plain for Earth.

"That true?" Earth asked.

Beau nodded. "My team started getting impatient. Putting pressure on me. Threatening to pull me off the case if I couldn't get anything on you." His foot started tapping against the floor, a clear sign that his agitation was rising. "So I gave them someone else instead."

"What do you mean?" Neo frowned.

"I mean I framed some other people for some of your kills."

Earth sucked in a breath. "What?"

"It wasn't hard. You can do anything with a computer. I

hacked into databases and deleted a few files. Made it look like they got lost in a glitch. I created a couple ironclad alibis by hacking into cameras and splicing footage to make it look like you were somewhere else on the night of a few, ah, kills. One time, I even managed to hack your GPS and triangulate your phone so it showed you on the other side of town." He paused for a second as a cocky glint came into his eyes. "Woods was fucking livid."

"Who's Woods?" Fletcher asked.

"My boss," Beau told him and then turned back to Earth. "I tampered with evidence so it didn't point to you, and yeah... I even framed and put away a few people so the murders Woods was eyeing you for were solved." Then, as if he hadn't just completely shocked everyone, he shrugged. "They can't blame you for crimes already solved, and it shot holes in his theory you were a hitman."

"You did all of this from that desk in your apartment?" Ethan said, clearly impressed.

"Imagine what he could do with a better setup," Ander remarked, and Ethan made a sound of agreement.

"I did the same thing for you," Beau told Neo. Then, turning to the room, he added, "For almost all of you actually."

Ivory sighed. "Oh, Beau."

"The more cases I solved, the less impatient they got to pull me because I was using my cover to solve other stuff. The bureau looked good because they were closing cases, and I got to stay." Taking a deep breath, he forged on. "I understand that I betrayed you all. I might have lied for you, but it doesn't really make up for the fact that I also lied *to* you. I don't expect you to forgive me, and I'm sure, after tonight, you will never want to see me again."

Earth made a gruff sound, and I wasn't sure if it was agreement or something else. Narrowing my eyes, I gave my brother a stark warning glare. I meant what I told Beau before... I'd choose him. I already had.

"I'll go," Beau said quickly, clearly hurt by Earth's indifference. He tried to pull his hand free of mine, but I wouldn't let go. With a frustrated sound, he said, "You don't have to worry about me selling any of you out. At this point, if any of you goes down, I'll go down with you. Just, ah, when I'm gone, maybe dial back on the criminal activity because I won't be here—*oomph*." His words turned into a rush of breath when Earth plowed into him.

The sudden movement caught even me off guard, and by the time I realized he'd moved, he was already hugging Beau.

My mouth dropped open then snapped shut. Earth never touched anyone unless he was causing some sort of pain (except for Virginia, obvi). He definitely, *definitely* did not hug. Hell, even when Fletch hugged him, he mostly just patted him on the back.

So it took me a few heartbeats to actually process what the hell I was witnessing. Earth was full on embracing Beau with his arms wrapped around his shoulders, squeezing tight enough that the muscles in his arms bulged. Their chests were flush, and he made no move to yank away. He just hugged him tight and stared over his shoulder at the wall.

Shock rendered Beau still. His green eyes were wide, face beet-red, and jaw slack. He didn't even hug Earth back but left his arms at his sides, his hand still clutched in mine.

I wasn't letting go.

My little bro was lucky I was letting him hug Beau so tight, but even my jealousy wouldn't let me pull them apart. Beau needed this. He needed it almost as much as anything I could give him.

Almost.

Beau's eyes shifted to me, silently asking what he should do. I just smiled.

"Earth?" he asked.

"I'm so pissed," he demanded, still hugging Beau tight.

Beau's lashes swept down. "I know."

Wrenching back, Earth grabbed his shoulders, giving him a light shake. "You never should have risked yourself for me."

Beau's face pinched. "But, Earth, you can't kill me." His brow furrowed. "Wait. What?"

"I said I'm pissed off you took so many risks trying to protect me. Any of us. What if you got caught?" He fumed, smacking Beau upside the head.

"Ow!" Beau wailed.

"It stops right now," Earth demanded.

"You could have just said thank you," he muttered, rubbing his head. The movement skewed his hat, and some wild strands of his ginger hair poked out around his ear.

Fletcher rushed across the room, somehow slipping between everyone to throw his arms around Beau. "I always knew you were the smartest one in the family. Please don't leave, Beau. You can't!"

Confusion clouded his face as he glanced down at Fletcher. "Aren't you mad?"

"Why would I be mad?" Fletcher asked, pulling back. "You might have lied, but it was to protect us."

Beau's throat worked, and the fingers clutching mine tightened a bit. Automatically, I shifted just a little closer to him.

"But I didn't protect you, Fletch, and it's one of my biggest regrets." Lowering his voice, he said, "I'm so sorry."

Fletcher's eyes rounded. "What do you mean?"

"All that time you were living with *her*—stolen from your real life and being abused—I should have figured it out. I should have looked into her. I should have—"

Beau's body bumped into mine when Fletcher flung himself into him again.

"Don't say that," Fletcher rushed to say. "You didn't know because I hid how terrible she was. And who could have known I was kidnapped? That's not your fault, and it wasn't even your responsibility."

"How'd you figure it out anyway?" Beau directed the question to Ethan over Fletcher's head.

"My PI ran her photo through recognition software."

Beau nodded. "I should have done that."

Fletcher squeezed him tighter, making Beau grimace. "No way! Ever since I moved in here, you've always watched out for me. You let me wear your shoes, your clothes, even your coat. You put money in my pocket every single time I left the house, and you even got an Xbox so we could play together. You took better care of me than she ever did. I don't blame you, Beau. I love you."

Beau's weight rocked back into me, and I widened my stance so I could support both of them. "Fletch..." His voice was hoarse.

"Please don't leave, Beau. I won't let you. I'll even fight Earth!"

Behind them, Earth rolled his eyes, and Neo snickered.

"And you covered up all my crimes too, didn't you?"

"Pickpocketing isn't really..." Beau started but then noted the hopeful look on his brother's face. "Of course I did." He amended, reaching up to ruffle his hair. "I'd never let the FBI arrest you."

"Yes, well, Fig did enough of that for everyone," Ethan quipped.

Fletcher pulled back with a gasp. "Does Fig know you're really a cop?"

"Please, that man probably has to look hard to find his own reflection in a mirror," Beau said, offended.

"He would likely try and argue the FBI wasn't as impressive as a street cop in the Grimms," Ethan added. "He's an egomaniac."

"You can't tell him." Beau reminded Fletcher. The entire room. "You can't tell anyone who I am. It would put a bigger target on my back and put all of you in danger."

"If anyone comes at you, they're going to have to go through all of us," Neo declared.

Varying sounds of agreement went around the room.

Beau glanced at Neo. "Really?"

Neo made a rude sound and came in to hug him. Fletcher was still half hanging on him, so Neo just hugged them both. "You should have told us sooner, bro. You've been doing too much on your own."

"But—" Beau started but was cut off when Ivory added herself to the hug. And so did Emogen and, surprisingly, Ander.

"Earth," Virginia demanded as Ethan came over to stand just behind the massive group hug.

Beau was clearly overwhelmed, shocked, and apprehensive.

"All right, back off," Earth demanded, coming up behind them.

Everyone shuffled back, and Earth carried Virginia over, holding her out.

Beau hesitated for one second, but when he tugged his hand from mine, I finally relented. Reaching out, he took Virginia, lifting her into a bridal-style hold.

Her arms wound around his neck, and she hugged him tight. "I'd tell you you're my favorite brother," she whispered loudly against his ear, "but then Neo would get mad."

Beau's lips twitched. "Thanks for never committing any bad crimes I had to cover up."

"Oh, Beau," Virginia sobbed. "All this time, you made

yourself stay in the background, but you're the one who held us all together."

She sniffed into his shoulder, hugging tighter.

Emotion filled his face, his eyes turning a bit wet. Clearing his throat, he tugged her back, holding her out to Earth. "I didn't do that much."

"Are you kidding?" Emogen asked. "V is right."

Creases formed between his brows. "You mean... you guys don't hate me?"

"Earth has done way worse than you, and we love him," Ivory declared. Then she glanced at me. "Daeshim too."

I thought about giving her the finger, but you don't give pregnant ladies the finger. Especially your pregnant sisters.

Earth's dark glower told me he was having the same thoughts.

"Earth?" Beau looked toward him.

It was my brother's forgiveness/acceptance he seemed to need most of all. Maybe because the betrayal between them was the worst. A cop sent to take down a criminal, a cop who would have done it if he didn't have a heart.

"I told you I'm pissed," Earth spat, but then his voice softened. "But I could never hate you."

Beau's cheeks turned pink, and hope burst around him. "You believe me, then? That I wouldn't turn you in?"

Still holding Virginia, Earth turned, handing her off to Neo before facing him completely. "Family doesn't turn on family," he replied. "And you're family. You always will be."

Beau swayed on his feet, and it was like watching a battery expire right before my eyes. The second Earth offered up that acceptance, all the fear, pain, and anxiety keeping Beau upright drained away. What was left behind was a man made of pure exhaustion.

Anchoring my arms around his waist, I tugged him back, offering support. He leaned in without hesitation.

"Maybe we could finish this in the morning," I said, glancing at Earth, silently telling him Beau had had enough.

He frowned a moment, concern crossing his features as he looked at the man I was holding. "Yeah. It's late." Gesturing down the hall, he said, "Take one of the bedrooms."

"We can go home," Beau offered.

Earth's face darkened. "The hell you will. The door doesn't even latch right, and people are running around trying to kill my brother."

"Probably me too," Beau muttered.

My body jackknifed so hard it bounced him off, making him stumble. Ethan came forward to catch him, but I grumbled, snatching him back and spinning him to face me. "What the hell do you mean *you too*?"

"I'll tell you later."

"You'll tell us right the hell now," Earth barked.

"Don't talk to him like that," I snapped. Turning my full attention back to Red, I said, "Tell me."

"I pissed some people off."

"That's not an explanation."

Shoulders slumping, he said, "I'm tired, Shim."

I cursed under my breath. He wasn't even trying to stall. I literally felt his exhaustion.

"Why don't we all meet up tomorrow?" Ivory suggested, yawning and holding the small of her back. Her stomach seemed bigger than the last time I'd seen her, the baby obviously growing fast.

"Everyone, just stay here. We'll talk in the morning," Earth declared.

"Oh, yes!" Virginia exclaimed. "Ivory and Neo, you can take the bedroom across from ours. There's plenty of pillows," she told Ivory, glancing at the baby bump.

"There's two bedrooms upstairs that are finished. You

guys take those," Earth said, pointing at Ander and Emogen, Ethan and Fletcher. "You two," he said, pointing at me and Red, "take the other one down here."

"I'm too tired to argue." Ivory agreed, turning toward Neo. "This baby has me asleep on my feet."

Once he had V in her wheelchair, Neo went to Ivory, wrapping his arm around her waist. "See you guys in the morning."

They didn't get very far before Ivory turned to rush back and hug Beau again. After a second, his arms wrapped around her, returning the embrace. "We love you," she said. "And this baby is so lucky to have an uncle like you."

He made a noise in the back of his throat. When Ivory pulled back, her blue eyes were sincere, but Beau likely didn't notice. He was too busy staring down at the belly between them.

His hand came up, hovering above it. Swallowing audibly, he glanced around at Neo. Ivory giggled softly and grabbed his hand, pushing it onto her stomach.

Beau's eyes widened, and he glanced up at her then down again. Lightly, his fingers moved, caressing the spot where she held his hand.

Abruptly, he jolted, body colliding with mine.

Ivory laughed. "Did you feel that?" she asked. "He likes you."

"That was *him?*" Beau gasped.

Her head bobbed.

A bolt of energy puffed out around Beau, surprising in its intensity because of how worn down he was. A fierce glint shone in the deepest part of his emerald eyes, and his hand pushed a little closer against her stomach. "I'm gonna make sure he's safe," he said, almost to himself. Then, directing his words to the baby, he added, "I won't let anyone hurt you."

Ivory's eyes filled with tears, but Beau turned, gaze flying to mine. "We should go home. Us being here just puts all of them in more danger."

I frowned. Maybe he was right, but I was more concerned about his safety than anyone else's. And this place had a solid door and a security system.

As if he could read me as well as I did him, he scoffed. "Please, you'd just wolf out at anyone who came at us."

He was right. I would.

"No one is leaving," Earth declared. "The place is on lockdown."

"C'mon, princess," Neo said, leading her into the bedroom.

Virginia followed behind to make sure they had enough blankets. Fletcher leaped on Ethan's back and told him to carry him up the stairs.

Once everyone was on their way to their bedrooms, I felt a tentative touch against my hand.

My heart skipped as I automatically reached for him.

"Hey."

I turned to see Earth standing near the island, staring at us. "What?" I asked.

*Take care of him,* his eyes said.

*With my life,* I replied.

His voice was gruff when he called out a good night.

Beau started to turn toward him, but I swung him up, carrying him past the bathroom we'd had such a good time in earlier and into a dark bedroom.

"I can walk," he complained.

"Yeah, but you don't want to."

When the bedroom door was shut, I put him on his feet and tossed my shirts onto the floor. He watched me kick off my shoes and pants, his eyes hungry on every inch of my body he could see. A familiar craving built low in my stomach and started tingling my sack. I tried to hold it back because I'd already had him three times and he was exhausted.

He was still just standing there staring when I stepped up in nothing but my boxers. I reached for the hem of his shirt, and he lifted his arms overhead.

"You can undress yourself," I teased.

"Yeah, but I don't want to."

I whispered, "That's okay because I do."

When we were both in nothing but boxers, I enclosed his wrist in my hand, tugging him to the bed and pulling back the covers. I nudged him in, following closely behind. I expected to wrap myself around him, thinking he wouldn't reach out.

I was wrong. He turned toward me before I was even settled, pushing me onto my back and practically climbing on top of me. Our legs tangled. One of his hands tucked between me and the mattress and the other shoved beneath the waistband of my boxers to settle in the V of my hip.

I wondered if he could feel and hear the heavy thudding of my heart and the unevenness of my breathing. But if he did, he seemed to like it because he let out a heartfelt, contented sigh.

"Is this okay?" he asked, voice small.

I was so tangled up in emotion it took a moment to find my voice. "Yeah, baby," I finally rasped. "This is good."

# 30

*Beau*

HIS RESTLESSNESS DISTURBED THE HEAVY SLEEP CLAIMING ME from the moment my cheek rested against his chest.

It took a while to rouse me, but the hoarse shout he let loose made my eyes pop open. He was dreaming again, clearly haunted in his sleep. Last time I tried to wake him, I'd nearly had my throat crushed, but I didn't think of that when I lifted my head and saw the stricken look tightening his features.

"Shim," I whispered, voice heavy with sleep.

He thrashed again, my body jostling with the movement.

"Shim," I crooned, gliding my palm across his jaw, the tips of my fingers nudging against his earlobe.

My heart clenched with the distraught sound he made, and the primal urge to comfort took over. Reaching up, I pressed a kiss underneath his chin, then slid to the side and kissed there too. I continued, body straining upward as I pressed gentle, lingering kisses to every place I could reach.

When the underside of his jaw and neck were covered, I shimmied up to kiss the corner of his mouth, cheek, and brow. My body rode the heavy rise and fall of his deep breathing, and his fluttering lashes felt like butterfly wings against me as I pecked a kiss against his temple.

"Red." His voice was like dark velvet, and I'd never liked the dark more.

"You're having another nightmare," I said, pulling back to look at him.

Awareness flickered in his eyes, bringing with it a flare of absolute panic. He moved fast, grasping my face to stare at it intently. "You're okay."

I wasn't sure if it was a question or him reassuring himself, so I just nodded against his hands. Abruptly, he rolled, pinning me under him with a broken, desperate sound. His eyes were endlessly obscure, deep opaque pools where he usually hid most of his emotions. But right now, I felt like I was staring into a translucent ocean, directly into its depths. Right now, he was letting me see something I would never expect to exist within him.

*Fear.*

Buried underneath his trust, overwhelmed with the depth one man could have, I was once again at a loss for words. I was already bad at talking to begin with, but this—*him?* Words just weren't enough.

I did what my instincts always whispered for me to do. I did the thing he seemed to love the most. Lifting my chin, I bared my throat.

The sound he made caused me to shiver, teeth sinking into my bottom lip when he leaned in, nuzzling my exposed jugular. The thick width of his tongue dragged over the massive bruise he left behind, causing a little spark of sore-ness beneath the desire I burned with.

Grasping my chin, he connected our lips in an all-consuming kiss. Hand slipping into my hair, he pulled my head up off the pillow so it was cradled only by him. Our mouths rubbed hungrily, producing warm friction, which turned my limbs and mind heavy.

I surrendered everything to him as we became all lapping tongues and shared breath, until we weren't really kissing but mating in the most basic way. Soon, the inside of my mouth didn't taste like me or even the cottony flavor of sleep but him and nothing else.

The blanket of his presence was reassuring, allowing me to exist here and nowhere else, all the chaos inside me no match for everything he was. Tugging my lower lip into his mouth, he sucked, and I strained upward, trying to give him more.

Our hips settled into a rhythm, dicks rocking together deliciously. I made a frustrated sound when he released my lip, which felt swollen and well-loved. A sound rumbled from deep in his throat, making my hips buck up against his again.

Clutching his hips, I yanked, hissing when his granite dick stabbed against me. His body slid down, disappearing beneath the covers, lips dragging wet kisses down my torso, leaving a trail of saliva as he went.

He was a messy lover, wanting to mark me in every possible way he could. I never thought being covered in saliva, cum, and blood would ever be a kink, but I wanted literally every piece of him I could get.

No one had ever made me feel like this. Wanted. Protected. Recognized. Vulnerability had always been a weakness… until being vulnerable gave instead of took.

My gasp floated up to the ceiling when his wet mouth latched on to my dick over my boxers. Half out of my mind, I started pushing at them, trying to get rid of the barrier between us, wanting his mouth on my skin.

When the fabric was gone, the warm silk of his mouth slid over me in one swallow. My shoulders lifted off the bed, and a silent satisfied scream ripped from my mouth. The slurping sound he made dragging back up my length made me collapse back into the bed. His full lips stopped around my swollen head, locking tight and then sucking like a vacuum.

I whimpered and thrashed, dropping a few F-bombs I probably wouldn't remember. His deep chuckle only vibrated my already sensitive cock and made me moan into the room.

Pulling off, his hand circled the base, pulling my dick straight up from my body. That wicked tongue of his licked over my slit, and my stomach muscles started to quiver.

With a sound, I pushed my legs wide, and his throaty chuckle filled the room again. Wiggling against the bed, I whined, and he tossed the covers off our bodies.

Still holding my dick, which was flushed and glistening, he quirked a brow. "What do you want, baby?"

"You know," I told him, squirming and pushing my thighs even farther apart.

"You're a greedy thing," he mused, giving me a long stroke with his fingers.

My back arched in pleasure, but it wasn't enough. "Shim, *please.*"

A thick finger dragged over my rim, and I sighed happily, melting against the sheets.

"You're still swollen," he murmured. The longish strands of his hair brushed the inside of my thigh when he leaned in and licked.

Grabbing a pillow, I slapped it over my face so it could muffle my groan.

Settling more firmly between my legs, he dove back in, licking and sucking, making my legs quiver along with my stomach. My hole was wet when his tongue pushed inside, and my hips rose off the bed to meet the thrust.

Enclosing my rod in his fist, he began pumping me as his tongue penetrated. Sensation stole over me, and I basically wept into the pillow. When I started to crest the hill, he was so expertly driving me up, I almost didn't realize what he was doing.

"Hey!" I demanded, ripping the pillow off my head and throwing it at his.

It hit with a soft sound and then fell to the side.

He looked up, bottomless dark eyes filled with laughter and desire, tongue paused midlick. I shuddered at the sinful picture he made. Giving a little slurp against my trembling rim, he lifted his head farther. "Do you have a problem with my performance?"

"Yes!" I burst out, the words instantly followed by a rush of heat over my face.

He smiled like a predator, as if he wasn't bothered at all that I'd just basically insulted him. Sitting back on his heels, he slipped the tip of his finger inside me. My dick jerked upward, a fresh bead of precum leaking from the tip.

"Your body seems happy to me."

His husky voice made me look down between his legs where his hard dick was highlighted by the wet spot on his boxers.

"I want you inside me," I said, still staring.

Delving his hand beneath the waistband, he shoved down the black fabric, allowing his thick, straining rod to spill out. He was so hard a vein stood out, snaking down the length and taunting me with its power.

I swallowed, staring, just thinking about that first push when his engorged head would catch on my rim.

"You want this?" he said, wrapping his fist around it and

giving it a squeeze. A pearly bead appeared on the tip, and my tongue swiped over my lower lip.

I nodded.

"I can't hear you, baby."

My voice was nothing but a throaty whisper. "Yes."

"No," he said, the denial slapping me like a cold bucket of water.

Shocked, I ripped my gaze from his center to stare at his face. "What?"

"I told you. You're still swollen."

Tears welled up behind my eyes, and I found myself blinking furiously, wanting them away. As I fought back that reaction, intense embarrassment washed over me. Shame that I was so damn needy that his denial would make me want to cry.

I rolled over onto my belly, burying my face into a pillow and trying to get some of my intense want under control.

I felt him at my back, his chest brushing against me as he lowered toward my ear. "Are you pouting right now?"

I jerked my shoulder, trying to toss him off.

"Are my fingers and mouth really not enough?" he asked.

Right now? No. No, they weren't enough. Maybe they would never be. Ever since he first pushed inside me, it was as if a piece of me caved in, creating a gaping, hollow hole that only disappeared when he was inside me, filling it up.

After facing the family, telling them things I never planned to say out loud and then succumbing to exhaustion while in his arms, it was even worse.

I didn't say any of that because there was no way I could. I couldn't do anything but be at his mercy... and in that moment, I hated it. Hated it even if the mercy he was showing was out of consideration for my body.

An angry sound ripped from my throat, my hands slapping onto the mattress so I could push up and leave the bed.

A hard slap landed on my ass, the smack reverberating around the room. Flesh stinging, I gasped.

"You don't get out of this bed until I say you can," he intoned.

"Fuck off, Shim." I snarled, moving again.

*Slap!* His palm connected with my ass again, and I had to bite back a groan. His entire body blanketed mine from behind, his weight making my arms shake with effort. Curling around my waist, his hand delved down to wrap around my still raging-hard dick.

Fine. Maybe getting spanked was a kink too.

*I hope there's a handprint on my ass.*

"I didn't say no because I don't want you." His voice was gentle against my ear, making my stomach somersault. "I do."

A sob ripped from my throat, and we both tumbled into the blankets when my arms gave out.

"I'm sorry, baby," he crooned, carding a hand through my hair. "I have what you need."

He must have licked his hand because when it went between my cheeks, it was slippery and wet. A noise caught in my throat as he rubbed the wetness around. Against the pillow, I squeezed my eyes closed as unparalleled need built in the center of my chest.

When his legs shoved mine wide, breath caught in my throat. Grasping my hips, he dragged them up and entered me with one powerful thrust.

I shouted into the pillow, the sound mixing with his groan. His arms quivered on either side of me as he held himself still while my body burned and stretched around his.

There was definitely some pain, but it chased off any frustration and anger I felt, leaving behind a tight, overfull feeling. For someone who was also so filled with chaos but painfully empty, it was nothing short of addictive.

"Oh God, Shim," I whimpered, pushing my ass farther onto him.

"How am I supposed to protect you if you're so desperate for me all the time?" His voice was strained.

Turning out of the pillow, I directed the reply toward him. "Protect me from everything. Everything but you."

He rose behind me like a predator overtaking his prey, and anticipation curled my toes against the sheets. His fingers were like vises on my hips, the hold a direct contrast to the gentle way the pads of his thumbs caressed my ass cheeks. "Just remember," he grumbled, "you asked for it."

And then he was fucking into me, hips slamming against my ass so impatiently the slapping of our skin drowned out everything else.

I clutched the pillow as my mouth fell open on a sound-less yell. There was no room for sound or thought against his relentless pounding. My body burned and stretched around him, the sensation so fucking good I couldn't even breathe. Pressure unlike anything I'd ever known built inside me, and every single thrust sent zings of pleasure firing through my sack and into my dick

All I could do was lie there and take it—no, lie there and fucking die for it. My entire body was boneless. The only reason my ass was still in the air was that he held it up.

After a while, the burning turned into discomfort, and his hips stuttered. There was a spitting sound and then some wetness, and he was pounding in me all over again.

I floated off into a place I'd never been but would gladly stay. A heavy state of euphoria that left me weightless enclosed me, and I let myself fall into a place where the only thing that existed was Shim and the pleasure he gave. His voice. His scent. His body filling mine.

I was so blissed out that the orgasm ripped through me unexpectedly, my body spilling out all over the bed beneath me. Dully, I marveled that I'd come untouched, only his cock inside me, but then that thought drifted off too. I'd never felt so relaxed before. It was almost like an out-of-body experience.

Shim's body bent over mine, his chest meeting my back. Reaching around, he palmed my softening cock, gently massaging and making me croon. He said something, and I just purred, not hearing the words but loving the sound of his voice.

The hand on my cock fell away, and his body stiffened, hips grinding against my ass. His hot release pumped into me, and I bore down to drink in every last drop.

We both collapsed onto the bed, his body pinning me in place. Aftershocks made his hips buck occasionally, and my channel tightened around him every time he moved.

Satisfaction unlike anything I'd ever experienced hummed beneath my skin. He kissed my ear, my hair, the back of my neck, and then he lightly bit into my shoulder before kissing there too.

After a while, he shifted slightly, and panic clutched my chest. Reaching around, I slapped a hand against his ass. "Don't leave."

He thrust, pushing his softening length deeper inside me. "I'm not, baby." The covers rustled as he tugged them up, hiding us both from the rest of the world.

"I love you," I told him, the words slipping right out before I even realized I'd thought them. Eyes springing wide, I stared across the room, seeing nothing at all, completely flabbergasted I'd just blurted out something so... big.

*How could I—*

"*Salanghae*," he answered, pushing his arms between me and the mattress, wrapping me up like I was some kind of burrito.

After a moment, I whispered, "That means I love you, right?"

His laugh vibrated against my back. "Yes, baby. I love you."

"You didn't have to say it," I said, the anxiety that loved to plague me rearing its ugly head.

His arms tightened as he nuzzled the back of my neck. "I've never said those words to anyone. Ever. So trust me when I tell you I wouldn't if I didn't mean it."

I was hella comfortable with him wrapped tightly around me, his dick still in my body keeping his release exactly where I wanted it.

But that was some declaration. I had to move. Lifting my cheek, I craned my head over my shoulder to stare into him with one green eye. "Never?"

"I might have told Earth when he was a baby," he muttered.

I wiggled, wanting to roll over, wanting to look at him completely. Obliging, he slid out and pushed up so I could turn under him.

I loved the way he planted himself over me on his hands and knees, caging me in with his body and the blankets. His face was slightly flushed, his eyes heavy with desire. He was beautiful.

Emotion pummeled me like a sudden tidal wave taking over a beach. My heart skipped and then skipped again, my stomach doing a little flip. My entire body started shaking, and another rush of tears welled behind my eyes.

He grunted, shifting so he could spoon me, wrapping his body around mine as tight as possible. "You're okay, baby," he promised, his voice like a soothing blanket. I clutched his arms, afraid he'd disappear. "It's okay. It's the drop."

"The what?" I asked, voice shaky.

"The drop. You dropped into subspace when we were having sex."

I felt my nose wrinkle. "Isn't that like BDSM shit?"

His warm, rumbly laughter against my ear made me sigh and wiggle closer with a yawn.

"Yeah, usually. You're submissive to me, baby. Whether you like to admit it or not. And sometimes subs drop into subspace. I didn't think it was this easy, but you are wound so tight I guess it's not a surprise."

I couldn't even argue about being wound tight. Saying I wasn't would be a lie, and I was too satiated to even bother.

"Did you know when it happened?" I whispered.

"Yeah, but I wasn't sure until now." I felt his fingers on my face, gently turning it so I would look at him over my shoulder. "When you drop like that, you don't really have the ability to, ah, control anything... or consent. I won't ever hurt you if you drop, okay? I won't take advantage of you. I will always, always protect you."

I nodded, chest tight.

"If it happens again, I'll just stop until you come back."

"No," I said quickly, making him smile. "I trust you... more than anyone."

He practically purred his delight, and I snuggled into him with another yawn.

"The aftereffects shouldn't be too bad. I don't think you were under that long, and I only smacked your ass twice."

I hid my face in the bed, making him laugh.

"But whatever you need, just tell me, okay? I'll do my best to read you and give it without asking, but there will be times you're going to have to use words, baby. Okay?"

I fell quiet.

"Red?"

"Have you done this with lots of people before?"

"Have sex?" He wondered.

"Been so good they drop." Insecurity ate me up inside, spreading like some insidious incurable disease. I started to tremble again, thinking of the people who had seen this side of Daeshim, people who were not me.

He grunted. "Only a couple times before, just enough to know what it looks like. I read about it a little too."

I wanted to pull away, but my body wouldn't let me. Every cell in my body wanted his attention even if I had to lie here forced to think about him with another.

He cleared his throat. "It was at clubs… clubs that specialized in that kind of thing. And it was planned. Like there was actual BDSM involved."

Forgetting I was feeling awkward, I twisted to look at him. "You went to a BDSM club?"

He shrugged. "I was curious."

I nodded, realizing there was so much about him that I had no idea about.

"Does that bother you?"

My eyes whipped up, and my mouth nearly dropped open when I saw the insecurity in the depths of his eyes. With a sound, I rolled the rest of the way around so we were chest to chest and I could look at his face. Thankfully, his leg pushed through mine, and his arms slipped back around my body.

My eyes fluttered for a few moments because, really, his touch was just that good.

"Red," he beckoned.

Forcing my eyes open, I looked right into his. "About the club? No, it doesn't bother me. But I don't like thinking about you with anyone else."

He nodded. "There is no one else. Just you."

I pushed my face into his neck to inhale and stayed there when his fingers began dragging along my spine.

"I'm your first man, aren't I?"

I grimaced against him. "Is it that obvious?"

I felt his silent laughter. "No. But everyone thought you were straight."

I made a noise. "I'm team Daeshim."

That earned me a nice pat on my bare ass. "But there've been women?"

"Of course."

He made a rude noise.

"I've never, ah, dropped before."

"That's because you've never submitted to anyone else before."

He was right. I was usually far too in control for that. He was the only one who'd ever made me feel safe enough to let go.

"If you ever have sex with anyone else, I'll kill them."

"There is no one else. Just you," I whispered, rubbing my hand over his chest. "There could never be anyone but you."

Honestly? I was pretty sure I was addicted to him. *Annnd… there comes the panic.* My stroking hand turned into claws against his chest as I pushed out of his hold. "I'm really needy," I burst out. "What if you get sick of it?"

*Jesus, I practically cried when he tried to tell me I could only have a blowjob and not his dick. And now I'm blubbering about being needy!*

*But what if he leaves?*

The warmth of his laughter somehow banished some of the coldness in my thoughts, making me turn outward to gaze into his face.

Have I ever mentioned how handsome he was? His bone structure was angular, wrapped tightly with smooth skin. His dark brows accentuated almond-shaped eyes framed with short black lashes. His Asian features gave him an almost unreal quality, and his lips were plump. His dark hair was on the long side, flopping over his ears and forehead and curling out against his neck. It was shorter when he first got to town, and sometimes I wondered if he refused to cut it out of some weird sense of rebellion.

Following my own train of thought, I reached up, noting how pale I was compared to him as I pushed some of the strands out of his face. "Did they make you wear your hair short?"

"Yeah. You don't like it long?"

"I like it any way you wear it."

He made a sound, pushing his thick fingers into my red locks. "Your hair is like fire I can touch. Saturated in color when most of my world is black and white. It's soft but attacks my fingers every time I push them into it. Everything about you is a fighter, Red. Even your hair. I like it messy like this. I like it when it sticks out around your ears."

I smiled a little, listening to him talk fondly about the hair I'd mostly hated all my life. It made me stand out, it made me different, and sometimes it made me unliked. "I thought about dying it black for a long time."

The hand in my hair tightened, and I yelped a little when he pulled my head back. "Don't you ever." His eyes glittered. "This red is *mine*. I can barely stand it when you cover it up with that goddamn beanie."

His eyes turned soft again when a blush bloomed over my cheeks. "I like that too. How pink you are. How you're covered in millions of freckles." Leaning in, he whispered, "I even like the red trail leading down between your legs."

I ducked back into his chest, but a rude noise and firm hands stopped me. "Did you think I'd forget?"

*Well, I was hoping.* I shook my head.

"You think I'm going to get sick of you," he deadpanned.

My lips rolled in on themselves.

"Red."

"I practically made you have sex with me!"

He laughed. Like full on threw his head back and laughed. I saw all of his very straight white teeth. His evil mom must have valued dental hygiene.

He laughed harder, and my face pinched.

"We were gangsters, not savages."

*Shit.* I said that out loud.

"Let's get something straight," he said, hooking a hand around my neck. Once again, his unrestricted eyes held me hostage. "No one can make me do anything. You're the submissive here, not me. If I really didn't want to have sex with you, I wouldn't. I want you always. Endlessly. I was trying to protect you." His gaze dropped. "Your body. It's your first time, and I've done nothing but go hard at you."

I averted my gaze. "But I need you."

"Yeah, baby, I know," he murmured, kissing my hairline and making my heart patter. "It surprises me how much sometimes, and I'm still learning too. No one has ever needed me like this before."

"Exactly. You're going to get sick of it. I'll try and rein it in."

"The hell you will!" He fumed, eyes furious. "You've spent your entire life being so self-contained you can barely function outside of the tiny world you created. You're so needy because no one has ever met any of your needs. You will not rein it in. Not with me."

I bit into my lower lip, still feeling how well kissed it was.

"I want all of you. All your needs and insecurities. I'll do my best to chase away the chaos, but you have to let me see it. Sometimes we will probably clash because what I think you need isn't what your body is screaming for. But I would not—*will not*—ever deny you something you truly need just because I can."

"I'm sorry I'm like this," I whispered, moving back into his chest.

"I'm not. This is how you survived. Any result of that survival is fucking beautiful to me. And honestly, you needing something only I can give you is a fucking headrush. It makes me feel powerful. I won't ever get tired of it. Of you."

I wound my arms around his waist and squeezed tight.

He went back to rubbing my back, and I relaxed into him, partially drifting, until my hand rubbed over his chest, meeting something warm and slick.

I gasped, noting the red smear on my fingers. "You're bleeding again," I said, looking at the knife wound in his chest.

"It's fine," he murmured, trying to pull me back.

"No, it's not. I'm going to go see if there's a first aid kit in the bathroom," I said, rolling toward the side of the bed, ignoring the way my legs still trembled.

I hit my back, blinking up at his dark expression that filled my entire line of sight.

"I'll go get it. You stay in bed."

"Hurry," I whispered.

He pecked a soft kiss that lingered on my lips.

"Pants." I reminded him.

His throaty chuckle made me burrow deeper into the center of the bed, my arm reaching out to find the body heat he'd left behind.

Movement at the side of the bed made me look up. His covered knee hit the mattress, and a gentle hand stroked through my hair as his lips brushed over my ear. "I'll be right back, baby, but be sure to miss me."

I smiled.

# 31

*Daeshim*

IF A TREE FALLS IN THE MIDDLE OF A FOREST AND NO ONE IS there to hear, does it still make a sound?

Irrevocably, yes. You just have to be there to listen.

That was my Red. Sent deep into the forest, everyone expecting results but not thinking about what he might endure to get them.

He is the quiet chaos of a tree falling in the forest, and the only one there to listen is the predator he was sent to take down. Except not even my brother was listening, too wrapped up in making sure his own ass was being ignored.

I was here now, and what big ears I had. I would listen. I would love. Apparently, I had a big heart too, and Beau consumed every corner of it. Even the darkest parts.

Caution was not my strong suit, but I would have to be careful with him. I was thankful he was so strong because even if I was soft for him, it would still be hard to love me.

*He said he did.*

I couldn't help but smile as I pushed into the dimly lit bathroom. Who knew the key to getting his most vulnerable thoughts to tumble right out was a good ol' drop? Neither of us meant for it to happen, but I was glad it did. Now I knew he trusted me completely. If there was even just the slightest hint of doubt inside him, he never would have gone offline like that.

There was a first aid kit beneath the bathroom sink, and I grabbed it, hearing some muffled sound out in the kitchen. Tucking the red box beneath my arm, I left the bathroom, bare feet quiet over the cold hardwood floor.

Peeking around the corner, I expected to see Virginia but was surprised to see Earth. His back was turned, making coffee at the counter. He was shirtless like me, a pair of sweats sitting loosely on his hips. His back and shoulder muscles were more defined than when I first got to town because he'd been hitting the gym with me, doing it so he could carry V around.

"You just going to stand there?" he drawled, turning around to look at me. Behind him, the coffee started brewing with a glug and hiss, the scent of it bursting into the space.

"I heard a noise. Was checking it out."

His eyes strayed to the kit under my arm, concern drawing his eyebrows together. "Is he okay?"

I rolled my eyes. "It's for me," I said, pointing to my chest.

Earth rolled his eyes. "It's barely a scratch."

"Yeah, well, the blood upsets him."

His lips pursed. "He's very attached to you."

"And that pisses you off?"

"No. I think it makes me feel relieved. And a little guilty."

*Interesting.* I walked farther into the room, stopping on the opposite side of the island. "Why?"

"He needs someone solid enough to withstand his storm." Turning, he grabbed a mug to fill it with the brewing coffee. "Guilty because I didn't see the storm until now."

"You should have looked harder at him," I said, not sugar-coating the fact I was pissed he didn't.

"Yeah." The word was gruff. He slid the mug across the island to me, the dark liquid nearly sloshing over the rim. Then he went back to pour himself a cup.

"Still, you did protect him. He said it himself. You taught him how to survive on these streets. And you also gave him a home."

"It wasn't enough," he said.

"For a while, it was. But I'm here now, and I'm taking over."

Earth drank from his mug, eyes the same impervious color as the brew he sipped. The scrutiny would unnerve anyone else, but not me. I saw the same expression in the mirror every single day. And as I told the fam, they all thought he was the alpha, but I was the alpha's bigger, older brother.

"How'd you know?" he asked, lips barely moving.

I pondered the question even though I already knew the answer. Picking up the mug, I swallowed down some of the black liquid. The mug was warm against my fingers, and I wondered if Red was warm enough in bed without me beside him.

"He bites his nails, is an insomniac, and when he does finally sleep, it's behind that damn desk because he tries to take up as little space as possible." I started around the island as I continued. "He observes everything, processes at a rate that makes me think he might be borderline genius, and wears those headphones nearly constantly to drown out the noise because it's too much for his head."

Setting the mug on the counter, I pulled open the fridge to reach inside. "He functions under extreme stress and is addled with anxiety but still thinks clearly. He's touch-starved, convinced he will be abandoned so he works over-time trying to hold this family together even though he doesn't even think he's part of it."

Earth's mug made a sharp *thunk* when it hit the counter. This time the liquid did splash over the side. "You got all that from what, six, eight months of living with him and arguing like cats and dogs?"

I set what I held on the counter, turning to face my brother. "He's an instinct for me. Gravity. He took my atten-tion so hard and so fast it scared me and then pissed me off. No one has ever gotten to me like this. Maybe you did once, long ago, but I got you out and sent you away, and then there was nothing…"

"How could I not have noticed?" he said, likely hearing everything I said but still beating himself up for not seeing all the chaos beneath the quiet.

I smirked. "Because all I had to do was flirt with Fletcher and everyone was all up in a tizzy. He has this whole family wrapped."

Earth went rigid, eyes narrowing into slits.

I made a rude sound. "Relax. I would take a bullet for the kid too." I paused. "But I'd murder and die for Beau."

He tilted his head. "Mom didn't approve of you being gay."

"Mom didn't approve of much."

"Did you think I wouldn't approve either?"

I shrugged.

"But Fletcher and Ethan—"

I made a rude sound, cutting him off. "Are not me. They aren't your *Hyung*," I said, using the term he always used, the one exclusively for older brothers.

"I don't care."

"I know."

"But you didn't."

I regarded him levelly, letting him see the same hard glint he showed me. "We might have been close as kids, but we're adults now. And we both learned the hard way that having the same DNA doesn't always equal instant acceptance."

"You stayed anyway."

"You're my brother. There wasn't a day that went by that I didn't wonder if you were okay."

"Hyung."

All his hard edges and ingrained aggression drained out of him for a moment, leaving behind exactly who I remembered him to be all those years ago. There was a slight catch in my throat, and I swallowed aggressively, trying to shove it down.

"I'm proud of you," I said quietly, figuring maybe he needed to hear it. Loving Beau taught me that sometimes words needed to be spoken to be heard. "I'm sorry I shot you like that, and I know you felt betrayed. But having you hate me was better than watching as you were lowered into the ground. You're too good for that life. Too good for the Black Rose. I know it wasn't easy, *Maknae*"—*the youngest of the group*—"but look at you now. Living on your own terms, dragging home misfits like Fletcher drags home cats."

Earth scoffed and rolled his eyes, making me smile.

"It's true. That's why everyone looks at you to lead. You brought everyone together, made a bunch of misfits belong. You built a family made of better things than DNA. I would shoot you all over again if it meant getting you here."

Earth bowed his head, digging his thumb and forefinger into his eyes. "Jesus," he swore, voice murky with emotion.

Pushing aside the first aid kit, I shifted forward, catching him by the shoulder and pulling him in for a hug. I smiled over his head when he ducked it into my shoulder. "You did well, baby brother."

"Hyung?" he asked, voice muffled against my shoulder.

"Hmm?"

"It was harder for you when I was gone. She was mean to you."

My stomach squeezed. "Nothing I couldn't handle."

"What did she do?" he asked, hand going between my shoulder blades and fingers grabbing like they wanted to twist in a shirt I wasn't wearing.

I sucked in a breath, not wanting to answer... not sure what to say.

"What are you doing?" a familiar voice demanded from across the room.

Earth yanked free like he was caught doing something illegal, his entire face going sheepish.

Amused, I rotated toward the voice. "I told you to stay in bed."

He made a face. "You were gone a really long time."

*His pouting will be the death of me.*

"Are you pouting?" Earth demanded. Then, bewildered, he turned to me. "Is he pouting?"

"Isn't it the cutest thing you've ever seen?" I asked.

Beau scowled at Earth. "Me? You're the one out here feeling up what's *mine*."

"I was not feeling up my brother!" he barked.

Beau turned glimmering green eyes on me. "He was touching the wolf."

If this was what his drop hangover consisted of, I was going to have to make sure he dropped a lot. Smugness put a little bounce in my step as I hotfooted it over to where Beau stood in the archway leading to the hall.

"I was just hugging my brother, baby. The wolf doesn't even like him. You know all he sees is you."

Behind us, Earth made a strangled sound, but I ignored him.

The closer I got, the pinker Beau's cheeks became. He was embarrassed, but his neediness outweighed it. "Sorry I took so long. I heard Earth in the kitchen making coffee. I got you some."

His lower lip was so supple, like a ripe berry waiting to be plucked off a vine. I swiped my thumb along it, and the jade of his stare turned hazy.

But then awareness snapped back, and he scowled.

Hiding a smile, I turned, showing him my back. He made a sound so soft I was sure I was the only one who heard. He hesitated even as his eyes ate me up, but then his cool fingers brushed over my back almost as if he were petting the wolf.

My stomach bottomed out, and a rush of tenderness squeezed my chest.

"Mine," he whispered, and then the unmistakable pressure of his lips imprinted against my back.

My eyes blew wide, shock and awe pummeling me into the ground. The only reason I stayed steady on my feet was that if I moved, it would dislodge his lips. The kiss lingered for long moments, suspending me in some kind of awestruck state. When he pulled back, he made a satisfied sound as if he proved the wolf was still his.

I was still trying to compose myself when he leaned around my frame, nailing Earth with his stare. "Don't tell anyone what you just saw. And the next time you want to hug what's mine, make sure he has on a shirt."

Earth rubbed a hand over his jaw, speechless. Finally, his eyes lifted to me. "What the fuck did you do to him?"

I was pretty sure I looked like a big dumb idiot standing there smiling, but damn, this was some good shit.

"Where's my coffee?" Beau grumbled, starting toward the kitchen.

My sweatpants hung so loose I worried they would slip off his hips, and he wasn't wearing a shirt.

"What did I tell you about walking around in front of my brother half naked?" I bellowed, staring at his ass.

Earth coughed into his coffee.

"Says the guy out here without a shirt, letting other people touch him," he deadpanned.

"I'm his brother!" Earth implored.

He was lucky I could see the waistband of his boxer briefs. Otherwise, I'd have to spank his ass. Instead, I went into the bedroom, inhaling the lingering scent of sex while taking in the twisted sheets and rumpled pillows.

His T-shirt and hoodie were lying near the door, so I snatched them up, bringing them into the kitchen. Beau was sitting at the island, looking a little hungover.

Without saying anything, I stuffed the T-shirt down over his head, and he pushed his arms in. Next, I did the same thing with the hoodie, reaching down to make sure the hem covered his back.

"Here," Earth said, handing him the coffee he'd originally poured for me.

Beau wrapped his hands around the mug and pulled it in. Grabbing the creamer I'd pulled from the fridge, I popped open the top. "He likes extra creamer in his coffee but refuses to use it," I told my brother while adding a generous amount to Beau's mug.

Without a word, Beau lifted it to his lips and drank with a sigh.

While he drank that, I grabbed a bottle of water, setting it in front of him uncapped. "Drink that. You probably need it after everything."

His ears turned pink.

"I'm making breakfast," Earth announced, banging around in a bunch of cabinets.

"You're still bleeding," Beau said after about half his coffee was gone.

"We're using the shower," I told Earth.

He grunted. "Don't be loud. I'm still traumatized from the last time."

"Fuck you," I told him, bustling Beau, his coffee, and the first aid kit into the bathroom.

The second the door latched behind us, he said, "Don't let people touch you, Shim."

Placing everything on the counter, I pulled him into my arms, reaching behind him to turn on the shower. "Are you jealous?"

"No. But I don't like it."

Chuckling, I stripped his clothes and mine too. "C'mon, this time we're gonna use the body wash to actually get clean."

He groaned when the warm spray hit his back, and goose bumps lifted over his skin. "This shower is way better than ours."

"You feeling okay?" I asked, soaping up his body and admiring all the marks I'd left on his skin.

"I'm sore," he admitted, letting the water saturate his hair.

I hummed in reply, pouring some shampoo onto his hair. "We can't have sex again until you aren't as swollen and there's lube."

His eyes popped wide, flaring with anxiety.

Grabbing him by the back of the neck, I brought my mouth in, crashing over his as the water rained over us both. The kiss was sloppy and deep, tasting of the shampoo sliding over his face and accentuated by the coffee lingering on his tongue.

Pulling back, we both gasped for breath as I pushed the saturated strands off his forehead. "Don't look at me like that. I'll still touch you." Leaning in, I put my lips against his ear. "I'll still love you." I couldn't help it. I sucked some of the water off the shell of his ear, making him moan.

"Turn around," I instructed. He was thin, probably too thin for his height, and his hips were narrow, but he still had enough of an ass I could palm. "Do you want to do it, or should I?"

He didn't even hesitate, just pushed those pale globes farther into my hand. Satisfaction filled me as I slipped into his crack, fingers finding his hole.

His body jolted a little, and I knew it was because he was so sore. He was definitely swollen, but I couldn't bring myself to regret a single moment I'd spent inside him. Hell, I regretted telling him no before and making him so upset. That's why this time I told him when we weren't in the heat of the moment, hoping he would be thinking rationally.

I was careful but thorough as I cleaned him, making sure there weren't any tears. "Okay?" I asked, checking in.

He nodded. "Okay."

When I was done, he sank into my chest, and I held him as warm water wrapped around us both. With a thick sigh, he finally pulled back, grabbing up the body wash to lather me.

"Turn around," he instructed, wanting my back. "I'm washing the wolf first."

I made a rude sound but smiled wide at the shower wall. "Gotta make sure Earth is washed away?"

"Yes," he intoned, the word filled with annoyance.

I snickered until the hands massaging over my back had my chin dipping toward my chest and a low moan of appreciation bouncing around the steamy air.

"Shim?"

"Hm?"

His finger traced down a long scar. I squeezed my eyes shut, knowing what was coming.

"Where did you get these?"

I knew he was curious. He'd fingered them before. I

wondered if he was finally asking because seeing me like that with Earth had somehow made him insecure and this was his way of taking back our intimacy. I didn't ask him, though, because the reason didn't matter. He asked, and I would answer.

"They're lash marks."

His finger stilled. "Like from a whip?"

"Mm." I agreed.

His finger fell away. "Someone whipped you?"

"Not someone. My mother."

The bottle of soap clattered against the side of the tub and slid away. Beau's arms wound around me from behind, his body pressing against mine.

"She… ah," I told him, wondering what to say. "She found out a betrayal I'd committed against the family, and she couldn't kill me, her only heir. So she had me chained up and beaten. She left me there for three days."

*Sometimes my shoulder still aches from nearly being ripped out of its socket for that long by those thick metal chains.*

His arms squeezed so hard my ribs ached, but I liked it. That little bit of pain kept me from tumbling completely into the past.

"It was summer. We were in the middle of a heatwave. There was so much sweat, and it slid into all the open wounds and stung like a bitch." I heard myself recalling how bright the sun was during those three days and how black the nights were. "I bled a lot. Spent probably at least half the time unconscious. And then when my punishment was up, she had her men collect me and drive me to a hospital where I was admitted as a VIP. She came and crooned over her poor injured son as though it wasn't her who did it."

"Shim…"

Reaching up, I patted his hands. "It was a long time ago, baby."

"The betrayal…" He hesitated, and I mentally sent him the strength to ask. "Was it what you did for Earth?"

For a moment, the pride I felt for him eclipsed even that heinous memory of the way the scent of my own blood turned my stomach and I wondered at times how I was still sweating because I was so dehydrated.

I never thought I'd be the type to care about communication. Hell, most times I hated talking to anyone. But Beau being unafraid to ask me anything was something I intensely wanted.

"Yeah. A few years after I got Earth out of the country, the man who helped me was captured and tortured for something unrelated. He gave me up trying to save himself."

"Did it work?"

I barked a laugh. "He ratted out the heir of the Black Rose. Fuck no, it didn't work. He died more painfully than he would have if he'd kept his mouth shut." I grunted. "Asshole."

An inkling of doubt crept in, wondering faintly if Beau could handle my past. Yes, he was real good with wolves and criminals and even killers, but this was a different kind of level. My own mother had me chained up and beaten.

*But they didn't touch my face. Heaven forbid her son appear anything but handsome.*

Sometimes I'd thought bitterly of slicing myself up, of making myself so unsightly she would disown me. Somehow she knew what I was thinking because she told me if I ever did it, she'd be forced to hunt down Earth; she'd be forced to make him replace me as the heir.

Beau slipped around my body, squeezing between me and the shower wall. Wide emerald eyes shone with sincerity along with a hint of sadness. Hand curling around my waist, he said, "I can handle it, Shim. I can handle anything with you."

My eyes snapped up.

He smiled. "You said all that out loud. You stayed to keep them away from Earth."

"She killed my lover," I rasped, the words ripping out of me unplanned.

Beau went still, his fingers slack against my side. "What?"

I nodded once, the steady sound of the shower nearly drowning out my quiet confession. "She was not happy when she found out I'm gay. It's considered an abomination, a weakness..." I shook my head. "She went on a tangent and demanded I stop being that way. The heir of the Black Rose couldn't be gay." Lifting my eyes, I continued. "I was young and cocky. I didn't listen. I got involved with Hoon to prove I could, and she killed him. Had him shot in our apartment. He bled out in my arms."

Beau leaped, and I caught him. He clung, arms and legs wrapped tightly around my body. His skin felt cold, so I backed us beneath the spray, and he stroked my wet hair as he hugged me.

"The nightmares. The reason you hate guns," he murmured. "The reason you went wild when someone shot at me."

Abruptly, I yanked him back, thumbs digging into his ribs where I held. I spoke fiercely, knowing my eyes flashed. "I couldn't protect him. But you? *I will.* I will rip apart anyone who even looks at you sideways."

"You loved him," Beau said, eyes dimming just a bit, touching my face. His lower lip wobbled as he said, "I'm not him, Shim. I'm not Hoon."

His body hit the shower wall, my chest and shoulders pinning him in place. I was rough, taking his face in my hands, squeezing to keep his attention. I let my stare—*my truth*—bore right into him.

"I never loved him. He wanted me to. Sometimes we fought about it. I could never give him what he wanted. I told him I never would. But he stayed anyway, and I let him because it pissed off Dae. And he died for it. For my stubbornness, for his stupidity. Even as he was lying there bleeding out, I couldn't find the love he wanted so badly, and so he died without it. I know you aren't him, and I'm glad. I never loved him because it was *always* you. I'm the type of animal that can only mate once, and it's you, Red... the only one I *can* love. The only one I *will* love. Only you."

The sheen in his eyes could light up the darkest of nights. "You say this after you tell me I can't have you until I'm healed?"

Pulling back, I let his body slide down at the same time I thrust up. His yell bounced around the bathroom, and I didn't bother shushing him. The sound turned into a little whimper as he wiggled down over my fully erect dick and his chin hit my shoulder.

"Don't ever compare yourself to him," I whispered in his ear, thrusting up. "There is no competition... And even if there was, he loses. You win. But even still, I didn't want him to die."

"Shh." He soothed, holding my face to kiss me deep.

I sucked his tongue, small mewling sounds releasing from me for him to swallow down. He began rocking on my dick, thrusting himself on me as I tried to swallow his tongue.

I ripped back, making him blink, and grabbed the body wash, pouring it between us.

Look. Body wash is not lube, okay? Don't try this at home. But it was better than taking him raw, and I had to be inside him.

"I dreamed about it again last night," I said, breathless as I pushed deep. "But it was you in the dream and not him... and you died in my arms, Beau. You fucking died." A broken sob echoed around us, and my hips stuttered.

"I'm here," he promised, threading his fingers through my hair and latching on my neck.

I tilted my head, telling him to suck harder. When he did, I rose on tiptoes, straining into his body.

He panted, a slight sound of discomfort echoing in his throat.

I started to pull back, but he bore down and bit my neck again. "Mark me," he said, releasing my neck. "Fill me up, Shim, and let everyone know I'm yours."

"Bite me again," I demanded.

This time his teeth sank into my shoulder. Pain stung through me, and I grunted in satisfaction and thrust up. The orgasm ripped through my stomach, making my muscles quiver and my knees turn weak. Afraid I'd drop him, I pinned him against the shower wall, emptying into his body as he licked over the damage he inflicted on my shoulder.

When I could think, I pulled back, realization crashing over me. He smiled, a drunken, happy smile that kept a large portion of my guilt at bay. Legs sliding onto the floor, I pulled out gently, anchoring my arms around him for support.

"That was fucking hot," he declared.

"I shouldn't have—"

His hand slapped over my mouth. "Don't ever say that." He was fierce. "This is who we are. This is how we communicate. I like knowing you need me the way I need you."

He was needier than me, but I didn't think it was a good time to point it out.

"There was no way you could tell me about someone else in your past and then not get inside me. You were hurting. I'm too insecure."

"You didn't even cum," I pointed out.

He folded his arms over his chest. "So? I don't want you in me for that anyway."

I crooked a brow, and he made a face. "Well, this time. The tank is empty."

I smiled. "'Cause I milked you dry already."

*Ah, he was blushing.*

"You needed me, and I wanted to be there," he whispered.

Pulling him in, I pressed a kiss to the top of his wet hair. "I mean it, baby. You're the only one I've ever loved."

"I know."

"How do you know?" I demanded.

What? I wanted to know.

"Instinct," he stated, the answer only a mate could give.

We were washing—yet again—when his voice rose over the steam. "I'm sorry. Heinous, violating acts were committed against you and by the person who should have loved you the most. You might not have loved Hoon, but you cared about him, and she murdered him. That had to have killed something inside you. You deserve better."

I swallowed, digesting his words, finding they soothed some of my deepest scars.

He whispered, "I'm going to make sure you have better."

I didn't say anything—I couldn't—just kissed his temple and continued rinsing us off.

"I'm glad she's dead. If she wasn't, I'd kill her myself," he muttered as if he were having some kind of internal tirade.

Knowing him? He totally was.

"A cop committing murder?!" I mock gasped.

"I'm yours first, and I'll do anything for you," he said fiercely.

No one had ever said that to me. Not ever. Even as the powerful heir of the Black Rose—especially as that—people would throw me under a bus if it got them even an inch ahead.

Nuzzling behind his ear, I wrapped around him, smiling. "I don't want anything but you. Let me keep you."

"Always."

After we were both washed and dried off with some towels stocked on a shelf, Beau dabbed some shit on the knife wound on my chest and applied a fresh bandage.

He moved to gather up our clothes, but I wrapped a hand around his arm, pulling him back. "Your turn."

He frowned as I reached into the first aid kit, rifling through to find the packet I saw earlier. The second I did, I held it between my teeth and sank to my knees in front of him.

"What are you doing?" His voice was dubious.

"Turn around."

He hesitated.

I swatted his hip. "Turn around."

With a huff, he did. Using my teeth, I tore open the small packet and squeezed the soothing liquid onto my fingers.

"Shim?"

"It's aloe, babe. It's safe, and it will help with the soreness."

His feet spread, and my heart tumbled. *So fucking trusting.*

"Feels kinda nice," he murmured as I massaged it around. I kissed his cheek before pulling back to wash my hands. Then I handed him a packet of anti-inflammatories. He took it dutifully, ripping it open the same way I had the aloe.

I filled my hands with water from the tap, holding them up. Eyes glittering, he came forward, cupping his hands around mine to drink from my makeshift cup. When he was done, we did it again, and then I used the towel to dry off his chin.

"We need to go home and get clean clothes," I mused, watching him dress in the same thing he'd been wearing for days.

"I like these." He defended himself.

"They need washed." *I'm gonna have to pry them off his crusty body.*

*Bang! Bang! Bang!* The bathroom door shuddered under the intense knocking. "Your breakfast is ice cold, and Virginia fed Snort all the bacon!" Earth bellowed.

"Yeah, yeah!" I bellowed back.

"Is everything okay between you two?" Beau asked.

I thought about the moment we had in the kitchen, how I finally told him the things I really wanted him to know. "Yeah. Everything is good. But hey…" I beckoned, making him turn those killer green eyes on me. "Don't tell Earth what I told you, okay? I don't want him to know." The things I did to protect him were not his responsibility but mine.

Beau nodded, understanding in his expression. "I won't tell anyone."

I kissed him.

He pushed me toward the bedroom when we stepped into the hall. "Put on a shirt before you go out to the kitchen."

Snatching his hand, I entwined our fingers. "Come with me."

His gaze averted, and a small smile turned up the corners of his lips.

"Unless you want to get out there before breakfast gets any colder." I teased.

He didn't look up, but his fingers tightened around mine. "I'll stay with you."

Oh, I was never going to let him go.

# 32

*BEAU*

A PLATE PILED WITH SCRAMBLED EGGS, BUTTERED TOAST, AND bacon slid in front of me. My stomach rumbled in appreciation. The ramen I'd eaten with Shim seemed so long ago.

"Eat." Daeshim's voice was gruff as he dropped a fork beside the plate and then went back into the kitchen to presumably get a plate for himself.

*Thanks* lingered on my tongue, but I couldn't bring myself to let it out. So instead, I sat there clutching the fresh mug of coffee in one hand while staring at the food.

Almost as if he knew I wanted to speak but couldn't, he glanced over his shoulder, catching my eye to wink.

My stomach fluttered wildly, and I lifted the mug to cover up the smile I couldn't stop. The coffee was creamy and sweet, exactly the way I liked it. I didn't know how Shim made my coffee the way I liked it best because not even I could make it that way.

Almost as quickly as that thought appeared, another one came hot on its heels. *Any way he made it would be your favorite.*

I was turning emo. *Is it the dick? Is this why girls always seemed so emotional and dramatic?* God knew I was better at maintaining some sort of composure before I started having sex with Daeshim.

*It's not the dick, dumbass,* I told myself.

*Could be,* I argued.

*He told you he loves you. Even after you told him everything, he still stayed... and he told you about his past. He trusted you enough to confide things he wouldn't even tell Earth.*

"Why aren't you eating?" Daeshim interrupted my internal dialogue, putting down a plate that looked a lot like mine. The legs of his barstool made a shrill sound over the floor as he dragged it nearly on top of mine. "What's the matter, Red?" he asked softly, his shoulder brushing close as he sat down.

"Nothing," I answered, lifting the mug to my lips again.

With a rude sound, he took it away, and I glared. Unimpressed with my annoyance, he plucked a piece of bacon off his plate and smacked me in the mouth with it.

Grease smeared my lips as they parted, and he shoved the entire strip inside.

"I thought Snort ate all the bacon," I said, chomping around the crispy edges.

"I made more," Earth said, drawing my eyes. He'd put on a shirt with his sweats and was leaning against the counter with a mug in his hand.

I wondered if maybe I would feel awkward this morning, if I would wonder what everyone was thinking when they looked at me. But honestly, everything felt like it always did —normal.

"I would never feed Snort all the bacon and leave none for you, Beau," Virginia said. "Earth is dramatic."

"Good morning," Ivory said, entering the kitchen, looking more awake than anyone else and somehow less rumpled even though she was wearing yesterday's clothes like the rest of us. My eyes instantly strayed to the bump in her middle, recalling how it felt when he kicked.

That sweet feeling twisted, making me think of the images on my computer of the sick things people were somehow capable of.

As depravity swirled in my mind, threatening to overtake the few bites of food I'd managed, everyone else in the room carried on as if they had no idea the gruesome shit happening right under our noses.

"I made breakfast," Earth announced.

Ivory glanced into the pan on the stove, wrinkling her nose. "I don't like eggs."

"That's why I made them."

"Earth!" Virginia gasped. "She's our guest."

"She ain't a guest. She's family," Earth countered. "And this ain't some fancy hotel."

Neo swept in, wrapping his arms around Ivory and his baby, kissing her cheek. "I'll make you something else."

"There's pancakes too," Fletcher said from where he sat next to Ethan, shoveling in carbs saturated in sugar.

A reassuring warm pressure enclosed the back of my neck, bringing me out of the half-in-half-out state of mind I was caught in. The hand that was not wrapped around the back of my neck tapped at my temple. "It's a busy place in there, huh?"

I tried to smile, but it probably looked more like a grimace.

His hands disappeared, leaving me feeling irrationally

bereft, but it lasted only a minute because then he was tugging me off my stool and into his lap.

I have no idea how he managed to fit us both onto his seat, but he did, his entire front encompassing my back. For long seconds, relief made me forget everything else, and my head craned back to rest on his shoulder.

Before my eyes slid shut, I realized we were at breakfast and our entire family was staring. Clearing my throat, I straightened a bit but didn't argue when his body followed so it was still plastered against my back.

He really was good at chasing away the chaos.

His lips caressed the back of my ear, causing a tingling sensation to tighten my scalp. So caught up in his warmth, I didn't even see him trying to feed me until a fork filled with eggs pushed against my lips.

My first reaction was to recoil, but his palm slipped around my middle to rub slow circles over my waist. Lips parting, he slid the food in.

"Chew," he instructed.

Everyone did their best to act like they weren't completely captivated by our behavior, but they failed miserably.

"What?" I finally grumbled around my fourth bite of food.

Virginia was the first to speak. "We're sorry for staring," she said. "It's just we've never seen you like this before."

"Like what?" I asked, and Daeshim used the opportunity to shove more food into my mouth. Ripping my attention from the others, I turned to glare at him.

His eyes were filled with merriment, and then his stupid palm rubbed over my stupid stomach again.

*Oh, it is nice.*

"In love!" Fletcher announced.

I sputtered.

"You are usually more, ah, self-contained." Ethan followed Fletcher's declaration.

"And none of you thought to wonder why?" Even though I was sitting with my back to him, I could feel the way Daeshim glowered at the room.

"I feel just awful," Ivory said, dabbing at her eyes. "I could barely sleep thinking about it all."

"I heard you snoring from all the way across the hall," Earth accused.

She gasped. "That was Neo."

My lips twitched because this family was ridiculous.

Ander stood from his place at the island, grabbing up his empty plate to carry to the sink. When he turned, the only side visible was the scarred part of his face, and I couldn't help but look at it, thinking about everything Ferrari put him through.

He'd stopped hiding it around us months ago, finally realizing none of us gave a damn if his previous elite good looks were now marred with scars. Usually, I looked right past them, but for some reason this morning, my eyes couldn't seem to focus elsewhere. When he dumped the plate into the sink, my eyes went to the scars disfiguring his hand.

Guilt crashed over me when I felt his stare, so I forced mine up as he turned, folding his arms over his chest. "It must have been a mindfuck to have to hide the fact you're a cop and not a criminal."

*Only in the forest does being a good guy actually make you bad.* I shrugged. "Betrayal is betrayal I guess, from any angle."

"You didn't betray us, though," Fletcher said.

"I could have."

"You didn't." Neo tacked on.

"Do you all really still trust me?" I wondered. "Like really? I could be lying right now."

"Are you?" Emogen asked.

I sank back into Daeshim, and his other arm wrapped around me so I was folded into a giant bear hug from behind.

"No," I whispered.

"If we can look past the things Earth has done, then why can't we for you?" Ivory's voice was gentle.

Earth grimaced. "She has a point."

"Are you agreeing with me right now?" she exclaimed. Reaching out, she caught Neo's arm. "Neo, write this down!"

He laughed.

"You didn't even do anything, not really," Virginia put in. "Everything you did was to keep everyone together."

I nodded. I guess I just hadn't expected them to think of it that way. I hadn't expected them to understand.

The thought spiked self-doubt and an almost stubborn urge inside me. Before I realized, I was blurting, "I pissed some people off."

*Let's see if they forgive this. You put everyone in danger, Beau.*

I nearly flinched from the ugliness of my own thoughts, feeling browbeaten and downtrodden.

Tension coiled in Daeshim. I felt his muscles ripple with it, but his hands stayed gentle on my middle. Rotating, I bounced my eyes between his. "You're gonna be mad," I whispered, nervous jitters attacking the food he'd fed me, and I grimaced. "I shouldn't have eaten, Shim."

I don't know how he did it, but one of his legs came up to wrap around my lap, anchoring me fully in his. Surprised, I gazed down at how he pretzeled himself around me—on top of a barstool, no less!

"Do you do yoga?" I asked.

His lips twitched, the dark chocolate of his eyes lightening a little. "No."

"Is it because you're Korean?"

He laughed.

"Look at me," he said, his voice probably audible to the rest of the room but making me feel like it was just for me.

The second my weighted stare settled on his, he said, "You're fine, and I'm here. Even if I get mad, it won't be at you, just the situation. I don't care what you do, okay?"

"It's true. He just killed two people," Fletcher told the room.

The reminder of that made me frown. "I don't want you to get involved."

I wanted to protect him. All of them. It was practically my default setting. I was so used to handling everything quietly and alone. But now the truth was out, and in my quest to stay here with them, I'd stumbled into a big case and put a target on my back, which inadvertently put one on all of them. I couldn't be quiet about this. I had to at least warn them to watch their backs.

And Ivory... I turned to her. "Maybe you should leave town for a while."

Neo jolted up, tipping over the chair he'd been in. His aura turned dark and stormy, aggression curling his hands into his palms. "Why? What the hell is going on?"

I glanced at Earth. "Maybe V too."

His jaw turned to granite, eyes glittering like black diamonds.

"Emogen." I'd barely said her name when Ander went rigid, the scars pulling tight across his face.

When I glanced at Fletcher, he shook his head, chin jutting out. "I am *not* a baby."

"Red," Shim summoned against my ear.

My lips curled in on themselves as tightness squeezed my chest. I wanted to tell Shim to get the hell out of here too. If something happened to him because of me, I'd never survive it. But being without him would almost be like trying to breathe without air.

*I never expected to be this attached to you.*

"I'm really glad you're good at killing people," I told him.

His eyes turned into half-moon shapes, and a deadly, flat presence blossomed out around us. It didn't scare me, not at all. I was grateful for it, so fucking grateful he had the ability to protect himself.

"I am, and I will kill anyone who comes close to you." He spoke quietly with no arrogance. It was just a cold, hard fact.

His violence made me calm, and so I held on to that. On to him. "I think I finally hacked someone I shouldn't."

"Get to the point, Beau!" Neo roared.

I nodded, understanding his impatience, especially since he was worried about Ivory.

Daeshim flicked a frigid stare over my shoulder. "Shut up, or I'll shut you up."

My hand pressed against his shoulder. "Shim."

I could feel the pounding of his heart, knew he was also wanting more. He denied those urges to instead say, "Take your time. Tell me."

"I was working on this case for the bureau. I'm actually a federal agent... not just a cop." I don't know why I felt the need to point that out, but everyone kept calling me a cop and I was more.

Neo made a sound of impatience, and I started to turn toward it. Daeshim's hand caught my jaw, pulling me back around. "Eyes on me."

Nodding, I went on. "It was a pretty sensitive case. We knew it would be bad, but no one realized how bad."

Daeshim nodded encouragingly, and suddenly, I really wanted to kiss him. I didn't know how that personal desire somehow showed on my face, but he leaned in, pressing his lips to mine.

"Keep going," he said as he pulled back.

"The more I tried to get into their systems, the harder

they pushed back. I tried stuff that always worked, only to get denied. I knew then that it was going to be big. I mean, you just don't hire top-tier security to bury your files if you aren't hiding something that would basically ruin a shit ton of people."

"You got in," Daeshim said. "That day I found you on the floor—"

"What?" Earth butted in.

His voice was startling. I'd almost forgotten other people were in the room. I blinked. Blinked again.

"What did you see on the computer, Red?" Daeshim asked.

"I used my most aggressive hack and tricks, and it took all night to break in. That morning… I went to my monitor, and it was all there, flooding the screens. Pictures. Videos." My voice went hoarse as I recalled the shit I saw. *The fucking pictures.*"

"What kind of sensitive material are we talking about here?" Ethan asked.

I swallowed, fingers curling into Daeshim's shirt. "Kids," I whispered. "It was a child trafficking ring… but it's way, way more than that."

All the women gasped. A few others dropped some F-bombs. But it was all mild background noise to the things I'd discovered.

"I've never seen such sick shit in my life. I hadn't expected it, and it was all just… there." My chin bowed, but Shim brought my face back up. "Who even thinks of shit like that?" I asked.

"I don't know," he murmured, pulling me in. I shifted, straddling his lap, feet hanging toward the floor behind him with my face buried into the side of his neck.

"I haven't even gone through it all yet. Just seeing what I did…"

"I found him next to a puke bucket," I heard Shim telling the room. "He was damn near catatonic. He wouldn't let me look at the screens." With a noise, he peeled me back, dipping low so he could look at me. "You didn't want me to see that?"

I shook my head. "Protect you."

He groaned, clutching me back into his chest. "You don't have to protect me, baby. Jesus. That's not your job."

"Yes, it is," I whispered.

There were a few blissfully quiet moments, and then Earth spoke. "So you're telling us this scum knows it was you who hacked them? They're coming for you?"

Daeshim went rigid, arms turning to steel around me.

Because I could, I turned my face just a little, pressing a kiss against his neck. A wide hand settled between my shoulder blades and rubbed.

"Beau," Earth reprimanded.

A growl rumbled in Shim's throat, so I kissed his neck again and sat up.

"I don't know if they've found me yet. But if someone hacked your system and found out that kind of crap, wouldn't you be hunting them down?"

"And you think they'll be able to find you?" Ander asked.

I shrugged. "It's not impossible. I'm good at what I do, and I tried to cover my tracks. But they probably have access to tech I don't, and I can't guarantee there wasn't some kind of trail that will eventually lead to me."

"This why the Feds wanted to pull you out?" Shim asked.

"What?" Earth bellowed.

I nodded. "They wanted to pull me out of the Grimms. I'd done too good of a job throwing them off your tail, Earth. They wanted me to finish delving through all the files I hacked in a safe house no one knows about."

"You don't think that would be the best option?" Emogen asked.

Daeshim burst up, bringing me with him. "He's not leaving!"

"I'm not saying I want him to," Emogen sassed back. "But we have to think of *his* safety!"

Unwinding my legs from around him, I took my own weight back, peeling myself off him like a reluctant octopus so I could turn and face the family. "I was selfish."

"You are not selfish!" Daeshim burst out.

"I wasn't ready to leave yet. I didn't want to. So I used the fact someone was trying to kill Daeshim to stay a little longer and investigate."

"Well, if they agreed, there must be a reason," Ethan stated, ever the rational one.

"If I left so abruptly, it would look strange. I haven't deep-dived into everything, and we aren't even sure who the main players are. We just know they are sick fucks," I said, finally finding a little bit of ground beneath my feet. "Just disappearing might tip off anyone and cause more danger. It's risky, but sometimes making no moves is better than doing something too rash. So I asked to stay and write up my report. We aren't sure if anyone has found me yet... but it's not out of the realm of possibilities."

"You thought that guy last night was in the apartment for you?" Shim asked.

I nodded without turning around. If I looked at him again, I'd want to climb back in his lap. "Yeah. He was over near my desk when I went inside. But when I heard him speaking Korean, I knew he was after you."

Neo laughed humorlessly. "You two make a fine fucking pair."

"It's not their fault people are after them," Ivory scolded him.

"He just broke into a child pornography ring, and now

those people are looking at him, which means they're looking at all of us." Neo swung on Ivory. "At *you*!"

Her hand went to her belly, and my stomach soured. The breakfast I'd choked down threatened to reappear.

"He's right," I said, making everyone turn to me.

Daeshim's chest hit my back. "You're blaming him for taking down a bunch of sick fucks?" he said, shouldering past me to Neo.

I grabbed his arm. "Shim. He's just worried about Ivory. So am I." I glanced at the room. "I'm worried about all of you."

There were a few beats of awkward silence. "I think it's best if I go." I came out with.

"If you go, I'm going," Shim said, and I couldn't stop the relief crashing through me. He was willing to just walk away from everything, everything but me.

Tentatively, I reached out, hooking my pinky finger around his. He shifted back so we were side by side, and most of my hand fit into his palm as I clung.

"You think some secret location the Feds come up with is better than family?" Earth scrutinized.

"The Feds aren't completely lacking." I defended them, but even I had to admit, "But they don't exactly understand what it is to survive on the streets, to run with wolves."

"You can't understand unless you live it." Ander's voice was quiet.

"But at least this way I'd be away from you all. If I'm not here, they can't use any of you to get to me."

"But then you'll be alone." Virginia worried.

"I'm used to it," I replied.

"He won't be alone." Daeshim's words overlapped mine.

"No," Fletcher said, his voice strong and earning the eyes of everyone in the room. "You aren't leaving. You stayed with us. You protected us even when we didn't know it. We aren't going to just let you leave because you're the one that needs protecting now."

My chest tightened a bit, and Daeshim grunted in approval. It meant a lot to me that Fletch was willing to stick by my side, but how could I ask them to do that?

I glanced at Ethan, hoping for some help, but all he did was shrug. "He's right."

I gaped at him. "What?"

"You don't turn your back on family," Neo said. "Even when it's hard."

From the corner of my eye, I saw Earth nod.

"But what about Ivory?" I burst out. "The baby?"

"Ivory, V, and Emogen will leave town."

All the girls gasped.

"That is the most sexist thing I've ever heard," Emogen declared. "You can't tell me what to do."

"This isn't something you can just swing a bat at, Em," Ander said quietly. The rumbly tone in his voice brought her up short. "If this scum is willing to hurt kids, imagine what they'd do to women."

"Y'all act like you're invincible because you're men," she muttered but with far less sass than normal.

"Why don't we all just leave?" Virginia suggested, eyes rounding with hope. "We can make it into some vacation somewhere. Let the Feds arrest everyone, and we can come back when it's safe."

"The Feds can't arrest everyone until I give them a list," I said.

*I really should have been working last night. I should spend every second available compiling that list instead of dragging it out.*

*You're slacking, Beau.*

*You're wasting time.*

*More people are going to get hurt because of you.*

My inner dialogue was constant, reminding me of everything I was doing wrong. Letting me know I wasn't performing the way I should.

*And now look. Now everyone is trying to come up with a way to make up for the fact you didn't do your job.*

"Stop." The command cut through the anxiety, and I found myself staring into steady dark eyes. Shim had moved so he was planted right in front of me, my face firmly between his hands. I couldn't see the rest of the family behind him, too ensnared by his attention. "This is not your fault, and you needed some damn sleep. You aren't a robot, even if you sure as hell act like one sometimes. If people are after you, it's because they're shitbags and you called them out. We're all adults here, and if anyone in this room doesn't want to be involved, they can get the hell out." He threw the last words over his shoulder almost like a challenge.

No one moved.

Everyone stayed.

"I'm really worried about the baby," I confessed. My niece or nephew was a serious source of freak-out for me. If those people got ahold of Ivory and her baby, the guilt would kill me... I would kill me.

And yes, I realize suicide is not a joke. I'm not joking. I couldn't live with myself if something—

"Ivory, you have to go," Daeshim said, releasing me to turn and face our sister.

"But Beau—" She began.

Shim made a rough sound, cutting her off. "Beau can't function knowing something could happen to you and that kid."

"That kid is my son or daughter," Neo injected.

"Then you must know how Beau feels," Daeshim countered.

"Please, Ivory," I said, stepping from behind Shim to look

at her. "No one protected me when I was a kid. Please let us protect you and the baby."

Her throat worked, tears welling in her blue eyes. "As long as you know that I'm not leaving you, Beau. I'm just going away to protect the baby."

I nodded, relief making it slightly easier to breathe. "I know." I turned to Virginia and Emogen who stood beside her.

Virginia looked at Earth, who dropped a dirty curse into the room. She nodded. "We can make it a girls' trip."

Emogen nodded.

"I'll hire a team of bodyguards to escort them. They can stay on location with you." Ethan decided.

"And we all can't just go?" Virginia asked again.

I shook my head. "I have to stay and do my job, make sure it's safe for you to come back."

"And we aren't leaving him here alone," Fletcher put in.

"It would be better if you did," I said.

Earth made a rude sound. "No. You said it yourself. The Feds can't handle this. They have no clue."

I looked at Neo.

"I'm staying."

Fletcher and Ethan nodded. My eyes moved to Ander.

"You had my back when Ferrari was threatening me and Em. We barely even knew each other then, but you came. I'm staying."

Emotion lodged in my throat, making it really hard to swallow. "I, ah…" My words faltered. I didn't know what to say. They weren't sending me away or turning their backs. I just… never knew I was worth it to them.

"Thank you," was all I managed, the words gravelly and awkward.

"Don't thank us for doing what family is supposed to do," Earth said, gruff.

I glanced at him, and for a moment, I thought he might try and hug me again. But the thought was gone almost as soon as it appeared as Shim wrapped his arm around my waist, pulling me possessively into his body.

Earth rolled his eyes. "You three," he barked to the girls. "Start packing. And don't be dragging twenty pounds worth of shit. We don't have time for that. You need to be out of here by tonight."

He glanced at Virginia, eyes softening. "Except you, sweetheart. You can pack as much shit as you want."

"I'll call my travel agent," Ivory started, and half the room yelled, "No!"

"That just makes it easier for people to find you," Neo explained gently.

"Oh," Ivory said, crestfallen. He pulled her in, wrapping his arms around her. I could see the worry in his face and how torn he was at letting her go without him.

"You should go with her," I told him.

His eyes flashed to mine, and slowly he shook his head. "I'll stay. The faster we wrap this up, the better."

"I'll call and have my jet readied. We are required to file a flight plan, so I'll say that it's going to Martha's Vineyard. I own property there," Ethan said. "But once you get on the plane, you can tell the pilot a different location, and he will fly you there instead."

"Where should we go?" Emogen asked.

"I have an idea about that too. I know a lot of people, many of whom offer me the use of their exclusive properties. I'll make some calls, secure one of those. It will be ideal because it won't be in any of our names, and it won't need to be booked through an agency."

"Do it," Neo said.

"I'll tell you the location once you arrive at the airstrip."

Ethan agreed. "C'mon, puppy. We have things to do," he said, already moving toward the door.

Fletcher nodded but ran at me, hugging against my side that wasn't pressed against Shim. "See you later."

"Be careful, okay?" I told him, once again unable to swallow the emotion lodged in my throat. As I spoke, I looked at Ethan, knowing he would watch out for Fletch.

Our eyes met and held, and he nodded.

"Guess it's not so bad having a well-connected *richie* in the family." Ethan smirked, glancing at Earth and Neo.

Neo surprised everyone by stalking toward Ethan and holding out his hand. "Thank you for what you're doing for Ivory. For my kid."

Surprise flickered over Ethan's face, but then he smoothed his expression and shook Neo's hand. "Of course. She's my family too." He motioned for Fletch. "I'll have the plane ready by early evening. I'll be in touch."

"Ethan!" Ivory called as they were on their way out.

"Yes?"

"But what should I pack?"

Earth groaned. "You're worried about your wardrobe?"

I couldn't help it. I smiled. Daeshim glanced at me and winked, making my stomach tumble.

"Well, how am I supposed to pack light if I don't even know if it will be cold?"

"It's winter," Earth bellowed.

Ivory sniffed. "Ethan?"

"A valid question of course," he allowed, smiling faintly. "I'll work on a warm location. Might as well get some sun if you have to be in hiding."

Virginia clapped.

"Don't even think about packing a bathing suit," Earth told her.

She rolled her eyes, and Emogen laughed gleefully.

Ethan smiled. "I'll be sure to make sure the place is wheelchair accessible as well."

When they were gone, Earth grumbled, "He makes it hard to hate him."

"C'mon, princess, you need to pack and call that moron of a doctor to make sure you can travel."

I sucked in a breath. I hadn't even thought of that. Daeshim's arm tightened around my waist. "You let Neo worry about her. She's fine."

"It's perfectly fine for me to travel right now, Neo. Why on earth would I need to call the doctor?"

"You will," he insisted.

"You aren't the boss of me."

"I damn well am when my kid is in you!"

"Fine!" she insisted. "I'll call him and let him tell you how dumb you are!"

"If you think me worrying about my baby and his mother is dumb, then I guess I'm as stupid as they come."

"Oh, Neo." Ivory gave in. "You aren't stupid. We love you."

He grunted. "I know. Now come on. We have to pack all your vitamins."

As he was towing her toward the door, her eyes came to me. "Don't worry, Beau. I'll be fine and so will your niece or nephew."

I worried even though she told me not to.

After Neo and Ivory left, Ander and Emogen left moments later, and Virginia went to pack.

"I'll be right there, sweetheart," Earth called as her chair disappeared down the hallway with Snort trailing behind her.

The calico cat, Moxie, who had pretty much been hiding since we got there, suddenly appeared and trailed after her and the dog.

"You guys can stay here," Earth said.

"My workstation is at home," I argued.

Earth glanced across the room where the tower to my PC was sitting.

"I need the other parts to make the whole thing work," I explained. "That just has all the info in it." *And it would be a disaster if someone stole it.*

"Stop at the scrapyard a few blocks down and get a new door. I'll be over after I take care of V."

Daeshim leveled a hard look at his brother. "I can take care of the apartment and Beau."

"I can take care of myself," I argued.

It was true. I might be a mess inside, but I'd basically relied on myself my entire life. I could do it again.

*Can you? Can you really without Shim?*

I shied away from that thought because it scared me.

"I'll still be over."

I nodded. "I'll get to work on the files."

"How long will it take to figure out the main players?" Earth asked.

Daeshim stiffened. "Don't rush him."

"The longer it takes, the more time people have to hunt him down," Earth snapped.

I laid a hand on Shim's chest, trying to soothe his agitation. "I'm not sure. Probably at least a day. Maybe longer. I'll try and go as fast as I can."

Snort barked, and Virginia's laughter floated down the hall. Earth's attention went toward it.

"We'll talk to you later," I said, nudging Daeshim toward the door. "I need my tower."

Without a word, Shim went and picked it up, meeting me at the door.

"Hey, Earth?" I called, bringing his head around.

"Yeah?"

I exhaled. "Thank you for everything. For, ah... forgiving me."

"There's nothing to forgive."

I wasn't so sure of that, but really, I guess it didn't matter. All that really mattered was making sure the family who accepted me didn't regret it later.

# 33

---

*Daeshim*

HE STILL WOULDN'T LET ME LOOK AT THE SCREENS, AND IT WAS driving me batshit crazy. Frankly, it made me want to kill someone.

Instead, I tempered the primal urge to spill blood and fixed the door. The entire time I worked, he did too. I'd seen him behind those monitors thousands of times. Hell, he spent more time behind that desk than anywhere else. His seat had a permanent indentation from his ass.

But seeing him work today hit differently. Seeing that damn beanie pulled low over his brow and the chunky headphones perched overtop didn't represent Beau to me anymore.

No. It represented everything he hid behind. Everything he endured. How much he actually sacrificed keeping everyone together while feeling so apart.

I didn't much care about anyone. We all had our issues, and in my world, it was every man for himself.

But I cared about Beau. The thought of him being alone made me sick inside.

And so did his colorless cheeks.

He was over there right now, pouring through grisly photos and information, surfing the darkest parts of the dark web for the bottom feeders of this planet. And yeah, maybe an inkling of guilt whispered that I wasn't much better than the people he devoted so many years to taking off the streets. I wasn't worthy of him.

I didn't care.

I wanted him. He needed me. I wasn't a good enough man to deny either of us.

And so yeah, it pissed me the hell off he somehow thought he was protecting me by refusing to let me see the shit he was forced to look at. Like he somehow thought I was above it all. I wasn't.

I worked at hanging the door with my shirt off. As much as he used to claim to dislike the wolf on my back, he was doubly attached to it now. He liked when it watched him. He liked feeling its eyes. It seemed the very least I could do was keep it visible so as he sifted through everything he had to, he could look up and see I was here.

Part of me wished the scum he hacked would trace him. I hoped they'd show up to exact revenge. I would end it. I would exact revenge for every kid they hurt and the house of horrors they'd unlocked inside Beau's head.

Hours passed. He remained hunched over, cast in the blue glow of the screens surrounding him. A choked sound brought my head up, and I'd had enough.

A little satisfaction singed my chest when he looked up the second I pushed up off the couch. Even fully involved in what he was doing, he was still very aware of me.

He must have seen the look in my eyes because he shoved one side of the headphones, uncovering his ear. "Shim?"

"I'm coming over there," I announced, not slowing my steps.

Clearly seeing that a denial would be a waste of breath, he turned back to the screens, his fingers flying over the keyboard, probably minimizing some of the shit.

My hand dropped onto the top of his chair and yanked, the wheels sliding back to give me some room. Without hesitation, I lifted him, sitting down where he'd been, dropping him in my lap.

"What are you doing?" he asked, voice a little breathless.

"I'm bored."

"No, you aren't."

"I want to touch you."

He seemed to like that answer and curled into my chest, legs falling over the armrest, cheek meeting my shoulder.

I glanced at the screens, but there were no images pulled up. Just rows and rows of moving code, a bar that looked like it was scanning something, and a bunch of documents filling the screen of another.

"How's it going?"

He didn't answer, and I looked down, noting his downswept lashes. I smiled, taking in the freckles across his cheek, then reached up to pull the headphones and beanie off in one movement.

"You didn't drink any of the water I brought you. Or eat your sandwich," I said, staring at the untouched food.

"I was busy."

My fingers delved into his fiery hair, and he hummed in appreciation.

"How's it going?"

He was silent a moment, then said, "There are some powerful people behind this."

"Anyone we know?"

"The whole country would know some of these names."

"I'm not above it, you know." I kept my tone low, conversational.

He stiffened, arm sliding around my waist. "Hurting kids?"

"No. Seeing the photos. The video. You should let me help you go through it."

"I don't want you to see."

"I've seen worse."

His silence was heavy. I knew he was thinking about the things I told him in the shower. About the things I probably did as a member of the Black Rose.

"Did you... did you ever hurt kids?"

It was the first time I ever felt anything close to shame. The first time I felt a certain remorse for the way I was raised, for the life I'd been taught to live.

And really, the only reason I felt it was because now the man curled in my lap had to ask me... because we both knew I probably wasn't above it.

And because I was the dark soul I would always be, I said, "If I said yes, would you leave me?"

I felt his swallow. It was almost as though his entire chest had to work to get it down. In direct contrast to that action, his cheek rubbed against my shoulder as if I'd upset him but I was also the one he wanted comfort from.

"I don't think I could ever leave you," he whispered.

"No. You'd just live with the guilt of loving such a bad man."

He sucked in a breath, jolting up from my chest. His eyes were wide green pools that seemed a little sunken in his pale cheeks. He was so tired, yet he just ignored it and kept going. "I don't think you're bad. You're the first person to ever really look at me. To see all the stuff I kept private and accept it without even blinking. Maybe you wouldn't have been able to do that if not for everything you lived through. I won't ever feel guilty for loving you because you've given me more than anyone ever has."

My arms wrapped around him, enclosing him tightly. I wished I could tuck him under my skin, use even my own bones to protect him. I wanted so much to be worthy of him, but I wasn't. The least I could do was tell him the truth.

"The Black Rose was involved in sex trafficking. That's what set Earth off and made him shoot Dae."

Beau nodded, likely remembering when Earth told everyone about finding a folder of potential, ah, sales.

He was fifteen at the time.

"I was younger then too. I knew we were involved in all kinds of stuff. Drugs, smuggling, weapons. Sex trafficking. Prostitution. But I hadn't realized some of the victims were teenagers, not until Earth found that folder and recognized some of his classmates.

"He'd, ah, stumbled on some of the women before that were to be sold." I continued. "Our mother was in a coma for a while after he shot her. So once I'd gotten him out of the country, I filled her shoes while she was out."

"Then what?" Beau asked, snuggling into my chest, voice sleepy.

It wasn't lost on me that he was basically cuddling up to me while I told him about my family's crimes. It made me tumble deeper in love with him. It made me want to tell him every dark detail and let him love me in spite of it.

That kind of love was unbreakable. There wasn't much in this world that could live up to that strength.

"I couldn't just let the women we already had go. It just doesn't work like that. It would have gotten me killed and discredited my mother. So I sold them. But then I disbanded the trafficking organization. It caused a lot of discord. People questioned me. My leadership. Someone put a hit out on me."

Beau gasped, dislodging my arms when he sat up.

The outrage on his freckled face was so fucking cute I couldn't help but pat his carroty head. "Don't worry, baby. I killed them first." I smirked, remembering. "That calmed everyone right the fuck down."

Because he was still staring at me intently, glimmering eyes searching behind the cockiness I was showing, I let it drop.

"Sex trafficking is a multimillion-dollar business. But I couldn't do it. They weren't kids... but teenagers might as well be."

"What happened when Dae woke up?" Beau asked.

"I got beat for that too," I mused. "I took the beating and then went into my mother's office all bloody and told her if she started the trafficking back up again, I'd take down all of Black Rose."

"I really hate her," Beau whispered fiercely.

I meant to kiss him quickly, but the second our lips matched up, they fused and refused to let go. I kissed him slowly, delving my tongue deep into his warm mouth, stroking over the roof, twining around his textured tongue, and gliding over his teeth.

*He tastes like a second chance, but he isn't. I don't need a second chance with Beau because I don't have to be anything other than exactly what I am.*

The weight of that was so heavy the chair tilted a bit when I rocked back. Beau followed, hands clasping my shoulders as he hummed into my mouth.

No one ever loved me without condition. Everyone expected something from me. I had to be an heir, a ruthless killer. I couldn't be weak or love who I wanted. I was an older brother, a leader... a criminal.

Everyone wanted something from me. No one ever asked for love.

But Beau? That's all he wanted. In whatever form I could give it.

I ripped my mouth away, eliciting a low whine from him. "I love you," I vowed. "I swear to God, I love you with every single inch of my soul."

"I love you too, Shim."

"I'm not good," I told him even though I knew he didn't care. I had to say it. I had to have the words out there. Not necessarily between us because they didn't have that much power, but it seemed not saying them somehow gave them strength, and I wanted them to be weak. "I've done things I should rot in jail for. I was raised to have as little conscience as possible. I never hurt kids. I wouldn't. But I can't guarantee the drugs we sold didn't get into their hands. I can't guarantee that families weren't ripped apart from some of the shit I participated in. My mother was ruthless, cutthroat, and a total she-devil, but she never started up the trafficking stuff again or anything involving kids. That I knew about at least. I like to think she knew I'd make good on the threat."

"I love you," he repeated.

I didn't miss that life. I didn't miss all the shit I felt I had to live up to. I was a good criminal, but I didn't want to be one. Since coming here, I'd left all of that behind, only tapping into my willingness to kill when people threatened me and mine.

I didn't really know who I was without the Black Rose, but in the last half year, I realized I'd rather not know than be someone I was told to be.

"Aren't you going to ask me to behave? Tell me since I'm dating an agent, I can't commit crimes."

"No."

I tilted my chin down toward him. "No?"

He leaned up to kiss my chin. "No."

"Isn't this better than making me sit over there while you work?" I asked.

Silent laughter moved through him.

I glanced at the monitors again, staring at the code and endless numbers and letters. "You really understand all that?"

"Better than I understand most people."

We fell into comfortable silence for a short while before I patted his hip. "Show me."

I felt his hesitation, but I waited it out. Finally, he leaned forward, hitting a key without having to even look.

Photos flooded the screen, and I let out some dark curses. Fuck, it was just as bad as he said. It actually made my stomach knot, and I was used to violence.

"These people deserve a special place in hell," I said, voice dark.

"Hell is too good for these people," he whispered.

He was right.

"I'm sorry you have to see this, baby," I murmured, kissing the top of his head.

"I should get back to it," he announced, swinging his legs toward the floor.

When I made no move to get up, he looked over his shoulder at me.

"What?" I asked, innocent.

"I have to work."

"I'm not stopping you."

"You're in my chair."

"So are you."

Twin red spots bloomed on his cheeks. His voice rose a little with shyness. "I can't sit in your lap while I'm working."

"Guess you'll have to get another chair, then, 'cause I'm not moving."

His eyes narrowed, and I reached up to tug gently on his

earlobe. I would never, not ever, get enough of his pink and red coloring.

"At least scoot closer," he muttered as if he were annoyed.

Spoiler alert: He was not annoyed.

Chuckling, I scooted the chair closer to the desk, and he wiggled around, making himself comfortable.

"You better watch that." I warned. "You're gonna wake up the wolf."

His hips paused midwiggle, and he glanced over his shoulder. *"Shim."*

My shoulders left the back of the seat when I leaned forward, sinking my teeth into the back of his neck. He let out a moan, body melting.

Reaching around him, I grabbed the water and released his neck. "Drink this."

After a sip, he set it on the desk and reached for his headphones.

"I'm gonna order some pizza later," I said before he covered his ears.

He grimaced. "I can't eat."

I flicked a glance at the images on screen, jaw ticking. "You're too skinny, and I won't have it," I declared.

He jolted, twisting at the waist. "You think I'm too skinny?"

*Well, shit.* I thought he'd get pissy and argue. I didn't think he would worry I didn't like the way he looked.

I released a soft sound and leaned forward to nuzzle my nose against his cheek. "I think I don't like knowing you aren't eating. I worry about you."

His chest rose and fell with his breath.

"What kind of pizza do you want?"

He turned back to the monitors, his reply offhand. "Sausage."

I wrinkled my nose, and almost at the same time, he stilled but didn't turn around.

"I mean, it doesn't matter. Just get whatever you like."

Irritation slammed into me, making my jaw slide forward before I snapped it back. "You like sausage on your pizza?"

He shrugged.

"Beau."

His shoulders slackened a bit, but he still wouldn't turn around.

"We never order sausage on pizza. Not one time has anyone in this family ever ordered it like that."

He said nothing, and my tongue slid over my teeth. "You mean to tell me you won't even ask for the kind of pizza you like when we're ordering it. You just go with whatever everyone else likes?"

"Fletch doesn't like sausage."

"I don't give a damn what Fletcher likes!" I roared.

He winced, starting to climb off my lap.

"Don't even think about it," I ground out, grasping his hips and pulling them into me. "Sit here and work."

After a second, he moved to put the headphones on again. Before he did, he glanced over his shoulder, one green eye seeking me out.

I sighed. Leaning in, I kissed his temple, his cheek, and then his ear. "I'm not mad. I'm glad you're comfortable enough with me to tell me what you actually like."

He pulled the headphones on, and his fingers started flying over the keyboard once more.

I sat back, blowing out a breath. After a little while of watching him, I pulled my cell out of my pocket to order up the pizza, making sure to get extra sausage.

---

## 34

*BEAU*

MY EYELIDS FELT LIKE SANDPAPER, THE SENSATION SO FAMILIAR I almost didn't notice anymore. I'd been sitting at this desk for so long I wasn't even sure what time it was, except to know it was late.

My neck had a kink in it, and my stomach growled. The pizza we'd had hours ago was long since gone.

Shim was down at the bar with Earth, a place I had to practically force him to go. I was a federal agent, for fuck's sake. I could sit in my own apartment alone.

No one seemed to realize exactly what being an FBI agent entailed or that it meant I'd actually been taught how to take care of myself. Okay, fine, I wasn't *that* trained. It seemed the young, nerdy hacker wasn't top priority for field training because they never thought I'd be in the field. They expected me to be nothing but a brain behind a machine all day.

Color them all surprised when they needed me in the field.

My lack of training didn't stop them, though. They sent me anyway.

I didn't realize until years later how fucked up that was. I didn't realize a lot of things until I was in too deep. Were the "good" guys any better than the "bad" if they used me as a pawn too? Sure, they'd taught me how to shoot and a few basic self-defense moves, most of it to probably cover their own asses so if I died, they didn't have to take the blame. They also taught me some profiling, but I didn't have near the training most agents got.

Probably why Earth never thought of it. Why no one around here did. I hadn't been lying when I said Earth was the one who taught me survival. Most of the training I had was literally from being in the field. It was do or die. Eat or be eaten.

*I like when Shim eats me.*

The stray thought made me blush wildly even though I was alone. My God, I embarrassed even myself with how needy I was for him. It was borderline obsession.

I was saved from traveling down that rabbit hole of endless pondering when the monitor to my left blinked and new images opened one after the other, hiding everything else on the screen.

Shifting away from what I was doing, I glanced over, suddenly glad my stomach was empty. It seemed no matter how deep I dug, there was always more to find. I'd managed to sift through a lot, coming up with a sizable list of people I thought were the main players. But I was still missing one— the most important one. There were transactions, astonishing amounts of payments, vague messages… an overall tone to everything that someone was in charge and that someone was purposefully being kept off page.

I could turn in the list I'd curated along with all the files and evidence. The FBI would haul in everyone. Someone would probably roll over. They *might* be able to get a name that way.

I couldn't accept might. I was nearly compelled to keep digging. To keep unearthing hideous details until I found it all. I wanted this guy's identity. I wanted him to know he wasn't powerful enough to be above punishment. I wanted the satisfaction of bringing him down.

*I am just missing something.* The thought was like a worm burrowing through every segment of my brain. It tried to distract me but only served to drive me harder.

A foul taste coated my tastebuds and tickled my gag reflex as I sifted through the newly unlocked images and documents.

*Click. Click. Click. Click.*

Stop.

I clicked back to the previous picture, one I'd deliberately moved by quickly because of its unsettling nature. In my haste, I almost missed it.

The chair creaked as I leaned forward, teetering on the edge as I peered into the background of the image. Heartbeat accelerating, my fingers flew over the keyboard as I sent the photo to the monitor perched in front of me so I could crop it, zoom in, and enhance.

I waited a few breathless seconds, still leaning in as if my eyesight were bad, chest rising and falling with the heaviness of my breath.

*It can't be.*

The pixels on the blown-up image rearranged and cleared almost like I was watching a puzzle come together right in front of me.

And then it was there.

A symbol.

A symbol I knew.

Blowing out a heavy breath, I fell back into the chair, its

wheels sliding away from the desk. Dropping my chin into my palm, I stared at that symbol, partially in shock and totally sickened.

There it was. The missing piece. The missing person.

The one who managed to keep himself off page... until now. And sure, if any other agent had been sifting through these photos, they wouldn't have known. They could have seen the symbol and then maybe gone searching but maybe not. Hell, even I had first gone past, only to stop when my brain told me it recognized something.

The symbol I'd seen inside Blacklight.

I'd only once been to the exclusive club for the city's most notorious criminals. Ander's scars were courtesy of the club owner and biggest crime boss in the city, Ferrari. The only reason we got inside was because Earth came and went there as he pleased.

He and Ferrari had a bit of an understanding. They didn't mess with each other. So when Ferrari messed with Ander, we paid the man a visit. I saw the symbol that night, my mind filing it away without even realizing I would need the information later.

Ferrari had his hands in a lot of illegal dealings, and he was *very* good at keeping them clean. Meaning the cops could never find enough to haul in his dirty ass. I could have taken him down when everything with Ander happened, but the casualties would have been hard to swallow.

Ander's father, Emogen's father, maybe even Em herself. Not to mention the deal Earth had with him. It seemed like a tenuous time to rock the boat. Not only that, but it would have blown my cover sky high and painted a giant target on Earth's back.

But this?

I couldn't turn a blind eye to this.

I stared at the symbol so long my vision began to blur.

*You have to take him down.*

*What about your family? They're already in danger. This will make it worse.*

*They're kids, Beau. Helpless kids. This guy has to be put down. This is your job.*

*You've been protecting your family for years. Just do it again.*

*Figure it out, Beau. Don't fuck this up.*

# 35

---

*Daeshim*

"Why don't you just go back upstairs?" Earth grumped, reaching past me into the cooler to snatch a few bottles.

I glowered at the bottle in my hand.

"I'm gonna be sober by the time you get me another," some drunk asshole on the other side of the bar complained.

I straightened, bringing the bottle with me. The drunk's eyes went wide when I settled the weight of my stare on him, his lips curling in. "T-take your time."

"You got a problem with the service at my bar?" Earth intoned.

"O-of course not."

Instead of popping off the bottle cap, I slammed the neck of the bottle against the corner of the counter. The cracking glass drew some eyes but didn't hold any attention. The top of the bottle, including the lip still sealed with the cap, snapped off, rolling across the counter toward the asshole.

I slammed the bottle down in front of him. "Apologies for making you wait," I deadpanned.

The man looked down at the jagged neck of the beer he'd been waiting on. "How'm I 'posed to drink that?"

I shrugged.

Earth's shoulder brushed mine when he stepped closer. "I'd suggest carefully."

"I paid for that!" the man whined. "What kind of service is this?"

"The kind you get at my bar," Earth stated. "Don't like it? Get the hell out."

The man started to open his trap to no doubt whine some more but thought better of it when he saw us both standing there staring him down.

His Adam's apple bobbed as he reached out to take the hacked-off longneck. "I'll, ah… be careful."

Earth grunted.

When he'd shuffled back to his table, I turned away.

Earth's hand closed around my forearm. "Just go home."

I pulled my arm free. "And do what? Sit there and watch him torture himself with a bunch of pictures?"

Earth stepped away from the counter, and I followed. "You know he has to finish this."

"He does too much for everyone else," I grumped.

Earth's voice was low when he asked, "He, ah, find anything yet?"

"He has a list, but he won't stop digging. I think he wants the guy in charge."

"I thought about putting some feelers out, seeing if there are any whispers on the street."

"No." I cut him off. "It might tip them off." It would bring attention to this family—to Beau, and that's exactly what he didn't need right now.

Earth nodded, grim. "That's why I didn't."

"Just keep your eyes and ears open," I told him as the bell on the door jingled across the room.

"I'm going to get another case," I said, heading to the back. My eyes lingered on the stairs leading up to the apartment as I went.

*I should just go home. Put him back in my lap where he belongs.*

I didn't want to distract him, though. The faster he got this shit done, the less stressed he would be.

The bottles clanked together as I carried the case out behind the bar and started unloading the longnecks into the coolers. A few minutes later, Earth materialized beside me, his foot reaching out to tap mine.

My eyes flicked sideways where Earth settled his hand on the edge of the cooler. One finger gestured toward the right.

I kept my posture casual, pulse hammering as I unloaded the rest of the beer. When I was done, I straightened, bringing the empty box with me to unceremoniously break it down while I stood there.

As I worked, my eyes lingered around the bar as if I were looking to see if anyone needed anything. Finally, my eyes made it to the back right corner of the bar where two men were sitting at a table.

They weren't familiar faces, so that meant they didn't come here often. I might not have thought much of it. I didn't know everyone around here yet, but Earth did. And Earth seemed bothered by their presence.

The men saw me looking, so I hitched my chin at them. "I ain't a waiter. If you're drinking, you're coming to the bar to get it," I called, then dismissed them to turn away from the counter to dump the box near the register.

A few moments later, the two men approached the bar, and my hackles rose.

"What are you drinking?" Earth asked.

"Beer."

Earth set their drinks on the bar top and told them what they owed. The one who ordered pulled some cash out of his pocket while his friend glanced around like he was casing the place.

"You looking for something?" I asked.

The quiet one's eyes snapped to mine, and the urge to leap over the bar and attack filled me.

"Where's your brother, Earth?" the man paying asked.

"Which one?" Earth countered.

"The ginger."

I took a threatening step forward, a growl building in my throat.

Earth shifted closer to me but kept his attention trained on the men. "Why would you be asking about him?"

"Just haven't seen him in a while. Thought it was strange. Doesn't he usually hang here?"

My brother crossed his arms over his chest. "Considering you don't, how would you know if he does?"

"Thanks for the beer," the man said, and they both reached out for the bottles.

We watched them head back to their table.

While their backs were still turned, Earth leaned close to speak out of the side of his mouth. "Those are Ferrari's guys."

My eyes narrowed.

"Ferrari's people don't come here," he added.

But here they were… suddenly asking about Red.

"Fuck," I spat and rushed for the stairs.

# 36

---

WORKING UNDER PRESSURE WAS NOT SOMETHING NEW. I practically thrived under pressure. My body almost thought anxiety was its relaxed state.

*I want Daeshim. I want to feel the heavy eyes of his wolf.* If my thoughts were pure chaos, then those were the beat of my heart.

I knew I could go to him. Hell, I'd probably only make it to the top of the stairs and he'd come running, somehow sensing my need.

But I wouldn't. Putting him in the middle was unfair and cowardly. I might be a needy bastard, but I was no coward.

This was *my* case. This was *my* family. I had one shot to fix it all. And if I failed, then I would go down—alone.

I sent the message, letting them know I needed a meeting, and then paced the narrow space behind my desk, so anxious I could practically feel the blood rushing through my veins. The second the basket came onto the screen, I stopped pacing to stare. In the center, coordinates for the new meeting location flashed, and I barely had enough time to repeat them before everything disappeared.

Grabbing a pen, I scrawled the numbers on a napkin with pizza grease on the corner and then pulled up a map.

After a few minutes, I committed the location to memory and blew out a breath. My legs were stiff from sitting for so long as I moved around the room, changing out of Daeshim's sweats.

After peeling off the hoodie, I laid it gently across the top of my dresser, fighting the urge to pull it back on. It pissed me off that I had to change, but I just used that anger to strengthen my resolve. Once the sweats were traded for a pair of black jeans and a long-sleeved T-shirt, I pulled on my coat and beanie. Instead of sneakers, I put on a pair of boots and laced them up.

When I was finished, I glanced nervously at the door, chewing on my lip. *He is going to be so mad.* I thought about leaving a note but decided against it. He'd just follow me, and I wanted to keep him away from the Feds as much as possible.

Especially if I wanted my plan to work.

I loved Shim, but he had a tendency to piss people off. Pissing off my boss was not good for any of us.

The thought made me stop in front of the door—the door he'd just installed. My chest was so tight it constricted my throat and made it harder to breathe. On impulse, I stalked back to my desk, bumping my chair out of the way with the force of my movements, and snatched up a sticky note. Once I scrawled across it, I stuck it to a monitor and walked away without a backward glance.

My hands shook in the hallway and made me work harder to shut the door quietly. The bar downstairs was noisy and would cover the sound, but Shim seemed above that, and I worried he'd sense me leaving.

*I hope he doesn't think I'm abandoning him.* The thought caused actual pain, and I bent at the waist, squeezing my eyes shut.

I knew what it was like to be abandoned. To be returned. I would never want to cause even a fraction of that for him. Yes, my wolf was very tough... but I sensed I had the power to break him.

*Just go. Get it over with. You'll be back soon, and then you can explain. You can spend the rest of your life making it up to him.*

I crept down the steps, extra light on my feet, pausing only at the archway that led into the bar. My ears strained to hear his voice. My nose inhaled deeply to catch even a hint of his scent. I caught neither while denying the urge to sneak a peek of his face.

Heart thudding, I practically expected to hear him roar my name and come slamming out onto the street after me. The anticipation of it was so great I stopped a few feet up from the bar to lean against a brick building and suck in much-needed lungfuls of air.

It was cold out tonight. So cold every breath I took created white clouds around my head. The air was scented heavily with snow, and the few streetlights that still worked seemed to make everything look grittier than usual.

Once I was sure my heart wouldn't pound right out of my chest, I gave one last lingering look toward the bar and then spun on my heel and fled into the forest.

## 37

*Daeshim*

"RED!" I BELLOWED AS I BURST INTO THE APARTMENT, EYES wild and heart erratic.

My feet skittered to a halt behind the couch the second I did not see his head bowed behind the monitors or hear his fingers flying over the keyboard.

Panic threatened to overtake me, but I beat it back, sucking in a deep breath and rushing into the bathroom.

He wasn't there either.

Or in our bed.

The stillness of the apartment nearly shouted that he was not here.

"Fuck!" I roared, boots pounding over the floor on my way toward his desk, but I only made it as far as his dresser.

Pivoting, my gaze landed on the hoodie. My hoodie. The one he claimed and was loath to take off.

But he did—draping it over the top of the dresser with care.

I stared for long moments, chest clutching so violently I might have thought I was having a heart attack in any other circumstance.

Leaving a sob in my wake, I rushed over to his desk, partly hoping I'd find him slumped on the floor but knowing I wouldn't.

The sticky note stuck in the center of the dark monitor looked like a full moon in a midnight sky. The desk and everything on it rattled when I dropped to my knees, staring at it.

*Love you - Red*

Another sob, more broken than the last, ripped out of me, and I banged the side of my fist on the desk. *What the fuck is he doing?*

*If he took the time to write this down... he was worried he wouldn't come back.*

The roar I let loose propelled me to my feet as Earth burst into the apartment, swinging toward the sound.

"Beau?" he asked.

Ripping the note from the screen, I held it up. "He left."

"Where?" Earth demanded, coming over to where I was. The second he reached for the note, I smacked his hand away, pulling the paper into my chest.

"It doesn't say."

Earth turned toward the desk. "Maybe there's a clue." He glanced at the computers. "How do you turn this shit on?"

Recalling what he did earlier to show me the photos, I hit the same button, hoping maybe everything wasn't shut down, just asleep.

The tower under his desk hummed to life, and then the screens blinked on. The monitor on the left was filled with useless code, and the one in front of me had some kind of picture that showed not much of anything.

"Fuck!" I spat and started rifling through all the shit on his desk.

My eyes strayed to the trashcan nearby and a crumpled napkin lying on top. Plucking it up, I smoothed it out, staring down at the numbers.

"Earth," I beckoned.

"It's coordinates," he said, and I nodded. "What the fuck would he be going out there for?" he muttered almost to himself.

"You know where this is?" I jabbed a finger at the greasy napkin.

*He really liked the pizza. First time anyone had bought him his favorite.*

"It's near where I brew the beer."

"Could be a meeting with the Feds," I said, mind reeling with possibilities. "Maybe he figured it out and went to tell them."

"Without telling us?"

"He never tells anyone anything!" I bellowed, shoving the napkin into my jeans pocket and heading across the room toward my leather jacket and weapons.

"He tells you," Earth deadpanned.

"I never should have left him up here alone." I swore, shrugging into the coat and pulling a black baseball hat over my eyes. "Let's go."

When he didn't immediately fall into step behind me, I swung around, ready to unleash some of the anger burning a hole through my esophagus.

But Earth wasn't even looking at me. He was bent, staring at the computer screen.

"What is it?"

Earth straightened, jabbing a finger at the photo. "That's Ferrari's symbol."

I went back, recalling something else I'd watched Beau do, and hit something to make the photo zoom out.

We both recoiled from the disgusting image that should have never, ever included a child. But yeah, right there in the background of the depravity was the symbol.

"You're sure that's Ferrari?"

"Oh yeah," Earth replied, voice filling with fury. "That sick son of a bitch."

"You think Beau recognized this symbol?"

Earth thought for a moment, then nodded slowly. "He was in Ferrari's office that night with Ander. I'm sure he saw it. Hell, the photo was zoomed in on it."

If Ferrari sent people here to keep an eye on Beau, then they were already suspicious. Hell, they might even know he was the one who hacked them.

"Let's go. We have to get to him before they do," I demanded, this time not stopping to be sure Earth followed.

# 38

*BEAU*

THE MEETING PLACE WAS NOT IN BROOKLYN THIS TIME BUT ON the outskirts of the Grimms, not too far from the rundown place where Earth brewed his beer for the Rotten Apple. I knew as soon as I sent the request that the location would change. We never met in the same place three times, most times not even that often.

I'd taken two cabs to various places, gotten out, and switched to another. Then I spent some time on foot to finally arrive here in the Grimms, though not quite.

It was a pretty rundown section of town but wouldn't stay that way much longer. The efforts that Earth and Neo were putting in to fix up some of the spaces around the Grimms were attracting others to do the same, and it wouldn't be long before this district was bought up.

For now, though, it remained old rundown buildings with one being used as an auto repair shop, which was probably actually a chop shop for stolen cars. I walked right past it, head down, hair disguised beneath the dark beanie.

Earth's building was about a mile down the road and looked abandoned like everything else. Only the inside was fixed up so he could brew his house beer.

I was glad I didn't have to go that far down. I didn't want to look at a place my brother owned because being here made me feel like I was stabbing him in the back.

*But you aren't. You're here for him. For all of them.*

Have you ever noticed rational thoughts have nothing on feelings? I could tell myself everything I knew to the fiber of my being to be true, but if my feelings didn't care, then the truth didn't matter.

I pushed on anyway, tucking my cold fingers into the pockets of my jacket and feeling the familiar weight of the gun tucked into the waistband of my jeans.

Yeah, a gun.

FBI agent, remember?

And yeah, I was going to meet my team, but after this, I was going somewhere else.

*If Woods goes for it.*

*What if he doesn't?*

*He will!*

*But what if he doesn't?*

The constant war within my head made me so weary. And that was why I trudged on, approaching the building sitting nearly on top of the coordinates I'd been given.

I was tired. Done. I wanted out.

The building looked just like every other around here. Like a dark shithole with crumbling brick and broken windows.

Dead weeds waved around the foundation, tangling together in the wintry wind. Flurries of snow had started falling a while back, but I ignored them.

My steps grew slower as I approached, listening for anything that might seem out of the ordinary. There was nothing, though, and I chose a side door to the left of the building instead of walking right up the slanted front steps.

The handle turned instantly, the rusty hinges making me wince when I pulled it back. Dim light shone from deeper inside, so I headed toward it, not even flinching at the heavy slam of the door behind me.

It was just as cold in here as out, so I hunched into my coat a little more as I walked.

The scuffle of feet made me pause.

The light ahead dimmed, then came back as someone moved in front of it. I squinted at the form, unable to make out their features because of how they stood right against the light.

An unscrupulous sensation reached out its boney fingers, tapping against the back of my neck. *Tap. Tap.*

Shivering against the creepy consciousness, my chaotic mind whispered, *It's a trap. Run.*

I went for the gun tucked against my back, but I never made it that far.

*Slam!*

Something unforgiving crashed down on my head, and my legs folded beneath me.

# 39

*DAESHIM*

THE SIDE DOOR TO THE DILAPIDATED BUILDING WAS OPEN. Maybe not something out of the ordinary given the rundown location, but seeing it shudder against the howling wind and falling snow made me cold in a way winter weather never would.

"Beau!" I roared, ripping it back and barreling inside.

"So much for the element of surprise," Earth muttered.

I swung around, grabbing Earth by the collar of his leather, and yanked. "Let them hear. I will kill anyone in this place, so do *not* get in my way."

Earth held up his hands in surrender, and I shoved him away.

"Red!" I spun toward the spotlight shining in the back of the room. It was lying on the floor, maybe fallen over or maybe just because someone laid it there.

I moved in, scanning the darkness beyond the light, trying to sense the perimeters swallowed in shadows. The beam of light was yellow but seemed rather harsh against its inky backdrop. So busy peering beyond it, I barely noticed I'd moved right on top of it until my boot connected with its edge.

Cursing, I righted myself, glaring down at the light and the beam stretching out like a triangle on the dirty floor. A dark spot caught my attention, immediately making my stomach drop and my fingers tremble.

"Earth." My voice was rough as I stalked toward the very familiar spot.

"Is that blood?" my brother asked from a few feet away.

Squatting, I positioned myself so the puddle was blocked by my frame, tucked between my spread feet. *I will protect even your spilled blood.* Heart thudding at an unnatural rate, I felt as if time slowed to a crawl as I watched with an outsider's perspective, reaching out a finger toward the puddle that appeared black but I knew to be crimson. Around it was a smattering of lighter dots, making the concrete look like it had a rash.

*Someone was struck, hence the splatter.*

*Someone fell, hence the puddle.*

My eyes fell onto the smears not much farther away, and I adjusted my body so those were in its protection as well.

*Someone was dragged up off the floor.*

Earth hovered just above my shoulder, staring down at the mess. "It might not be his."

I laughed, but it came out choked and more like a sob. Hunching forward, my palm hit the floor, and my fingers spider-crawled over the dirty cement toward the puddle.

The blood gobbled up the tip of my finger the second I pushed it in almost like it was alive and ready to attack.

*His hair attacks my fingers this same way.*

The thick, sticky substance was still warm, a shocking

discovery against the frosty temperature of every other part of me.

Staring blankly, I swirled my finger in the puddle, pulling back to stare down at the stain. "It's his," I rasped. I just knew. I recognized him even like this. Curling my fingers in, I felt the blood smear against my palm. "He was here."

"I'm gonna see if he still is," Earth said with no inflection, his voice devoid of literally everything.

My heart stuttered and shrank, causing me to clutch at my chest as I pushed to my feet. Part of me wanted him to still be here, and the other part knew if he was but wasn't calling out...

*He's not dead!*

I wouldn't go there. I couldn't.

*If he's dead, I will set this city on fire and then throw myself in the flames. We will all burn together.*

"Daeshim!" Earth called, and I ran toward his voice.

In the back of the building, I found my brother squatting in front of someone, the light on his phone shining up at the ceiling because of the way he'd just laid it on the floor.

The bottom of a shoe was all I saw, and I went near feral. An inhuman sound ripped out of me, and I grabbed Earth, tossing him back so I could take his place in front of the body.

"Red!" I worried. "Red!"

There was a groan, and I practically threw myself at the body, enclosing his shoulders in my palms to pull him up. "Jesus, baby," I nearly groaned.

Realization dawned. The pads of my fingers dug in tighter.

*Not Red. Not yours.*

The instinct slapped me in the face like the buckets of ice water they'd tossed on me after being left in chains for three days.

Horrified, I let go of the man, and he slumped back against the wall. "Who the fuck are you?" I yelled. Then immediately, I pulled him back up. "Where is Beau?"

The man panted, his dazed, blackened eyes opening wide when I yelled. He cowered back, trying to climb into the corner.

"Where is Beau?" I demanded again.

"Hyung," Earth said, dropping down beside me. "He's beat up pretty bad."

I gave the man a shake. "Tell me where he is!"

Earth's hand slapped on my arm and pulled me off the man. The second I let go, he slumped backward once more.

"Daeshim. He won't be able to tell us anything if you knock him out again."

Frustrated, I leaped to my feet, grabbing the bill of my hat and tugging.

"We aren't going to hurt you," Earth said to the man, helping him sit up. "I'm going to call an ambulance."

I made a rude sound.

"Th-they f-f-found him," the man slurred.

"Found who?" Earth pressed.

"Beau?" I said, dropping in front of him again. "Are you talking about Beau?"

The man coughed, blood drizzling out of his mouth, and I had to bite my tongue to keep from yelling. "Yeah. Beau," he finally answered.

How Earth kept any patience, I would never understand. "He's my brother. What happened to him?"

"Don't know. They... j-jumped me. T-took him."

"Who took him?" Earth repeated.

"Don't know."

The yell I unleashed echoed through the entire lower floor of the building, and I began to pace. The ringing of my phone silenced everything, and I damn near ripped my jeans pulling out the device.

*Unknown* flashed on the screen.

"Hello?" I said, picking up before the first ring even finished.

"I know where he is." A low voice filled my ear.

Gut tightening, I hit the speakerphone button, holding out the phone so Earth could hear. "Where?" I demanded.

"Blacklight."

"Fucking Ferrari," Earth swore.

"You better hurry. Not sure how long they'll keep him alive."

My fingers tightened around the phone so hard I was surprised the glass didn't crack. Despite it being on speaker, I jammed the phone against my ear to yell, "Who is this?"

"Someone who thinks that pet of yours is worth more alive than dead."

An inkling of something—*dislike? familiarity?*—rippled over my frayed nerves, but I didn't have time for it. I didn't have time for anything that didn't involve finding Beau. I disconnected the call, still clutching the phone. "Let's go!" I roared, already heading for the door.

"I'm calling an ambulance. They'll be here soon," I heard Earth tell the man on the floor. "What's your name?"

"Rogers," he said, sounding slightly more coherent than before.

"I'm Earth."

The man coughed. "I-I know. He always said you weren't as bad as they thought." *Wheeze. Wheeze.* "Guess he was right."

Earth didn't answer, too busy speaking with the emergency responders he'd dialed. As he did, he went over and angled the light so it was shining at the man.

Despite the near skin-crawling urge I had to rush out of there, I went back to where the man lay. "You know Beau?"

Rogers nodded. "Go. Find him."

"I will," I vowed even as a ticking clock inside my head warned me time was running out. Not waiting another second, I rushed to Earth's vintage black Dodge Charger, slamming behind the wheel. He said nothing when he slid into the passenger seat, just gave me a look. No one ever drove this beast but him.

Not tonight.

"I'm calling for backup," Earth said as I burned rubber out of the lot. Seconds later, he called Neo and had everyone on their way.

When he was done, he dropped the phone in his lap, knee bouncing.

I pressed the gas harder, the car shooting forward. "You just helped an FBI agent back there," I said. "One that has been trying to take you down."

"Beau would have wanted me to."

He was right. Beau would want that.

*Please don't let me be too late to help him.*

# 40

*BEAU*

THAT SYMBOL I WAS TALKING ABOUT BEFORE?

When I finally blinked open my eyes, it was that exact symbol I saw first.

Except this time it was bloody.

No. Wait. That was me. I was bloody. It was dripping over my face, blurring my eyesight.

Love that for me. I also really loved the splitting headache nearly ripping my skull in two. Super good times.

*Daeshim is going to be livid.*

*If he was here, he'd wipe this blood out of my eyes.*

*If Daeshim was here, whoever tied you to this chair would be dead.*

*I want Shim.*

Blinking against the pain, trying to clear some of the blood from my eyelashes, I stared at the symbol proudly adorning the wall. Though my eyes tried to take in every-

329

thing, I remained slack in the chair, relying on the ropes to keep me upright.

I was in Ferrari's office at Blacklight.

*They found me. Probably followed me to the meeting place.*

*No, I was so careful. They couldn't have.*

*Well, the chair you're tied to says different. And that headache? It's laughing in your stupid face.*

Seriously, my brain was not a place I'd wish on anyone. Except maybe fucking Ferrari.

Some of the metallic-tasting blood trailed down my nose and dripped off the tip, splashing against my lips. I didn't react, instead letting the coppery tang force its way into my mouth.

They traced me, followed me, and took me hostage. The thought of my team back at the location made my entire body go rigid.

Had they been there? Did Ferrari kill them?

*Oh my God, did I get my teammates killed?*

*I told you not to fuck this up, Beau!*

"Ah. You're awake."

His voice was like having a thousand black widows unleashed over my bare skin. My lip curled against the sensation, and I lifted my pounding head to meet his stare.

Ferrari sat behind his desk as though we were at some kind of corporate meeting and I didn't have a head injury and wasn't tied to the chair across from him.

"You could have just called," I deadpanned.

"And miss the sight of the scarlet oozing from your head? Never."

"I don't think Earth is going to take too kindly to this," I said, not wanting to mention my brother but having to because the Beau who wasn't a cop would be confused as hell about being here, and he would also use the threat of his brother to try and intimidate Ferrari.

"I think Earth will thank me for getting rid of the cop living in his house."

I scoffed, which sent small splatters of blood out into the air. "Cop? You think I'm a cop? I thought you were smart."

He picked up a crystal tumbler, regarding me over the rim before tossing back all of the dark liquid in the bottom.

Sweat trickled between my shoulder blades, and my stomach roiled with nausea. I was definitely operating with a concussion.

*Focus, Rogen!*

"I'm insulted this is the route you want to go," he said as if his disappointment in me would somehow matter.

"I'm insulted you hit me over the head."

He sighed like he was tired, and I wanted to laugh. *Asshole.*

Ferrari's eyes snapped to something behind me, lifting his chin for a barely-there signal.

That creepy-crawly sensation clamored over every inch of me as the sound of quiet feet made their way across the office, drawing closer to me with every step.

The fact I hadn't known someone else was in here rattled me. I was better than that. I could easily read a room... but not today. *Probably the head wound.*

Muscles tensing, I strained against the rope holding my wrists together against the back of the chair. Not caring if they could see, I twisted and fought against them, hoping to find a weakness in the knot.

Black dress shoes appeared first, walking past me to halt beside Ferrari's desk.

I forgot about struggling with the rope.

For a moment, I was struck speechless, doing nothing but staring.

"McClaren?" I said his name on a whisper as if I couldn't even bring myself to say it out loud.

I might have been thinking a little sluggishly, bleeding

from a gaping wound in my head, but I knew exactly what I was looking at.

"You're dirty?" I asked as if I needed the answer.

"Little Red thinks he's the only one that can go into the forest," McClaren mused.

I licked at my lips, ignoring the sticky substance coating them. "You've been working with Ferrari?"

"How naïve of you to think I wouldn't have eyes and ears on the inside," Ferrari crooned.

"He's a fucking child abuser!" I roared, trying to leap out of my seat. "You help him, you sick fuck!" I lunged again, my feet tangling in the folding chair and toppling over. I landed with a grunt on the concrete floor, my wrists burning from the rope and black spots swimming before my eyes.

*God, my fucking head hurts.*

McClaren squatted beside me, looking very smug despite the yellowing bruise in the center of his face.

I snarled. "If I wasn't tied to this fucking chair, I'd break your nose again."

"That was him?" Ferrari mused from somewhere above me. "I guess it's true what they say about redheads."

McClaren's face twisted in anger, and with a shout, he brought his fist down into my cheek. My face bounced off the concrete floor as more pain exploded in my head.

His fist drew back again, and I got ready to roll, but the punch never connected because Ferrari said, "We need him conscious."

McClaren stood, spinning away from me, and I pressed my cheek against the cold floor, mind reeling.

"How long have you been working for him?" I asked.

*How did I not know?*

*Another fuck-up, Beau.*

"Not going to play stupid anymore?" Ferrari asked.

"Untie me."

Ferrari was quiet a moment. "And why should I?"

"Because I'm not telling you shit down here on the floor."

He must have given some signal because another man—presumably one of his bodyguards near the door—came forward and sawed through the ropes with a knife Earth would have laughed at.

I wasn't laughing, though, because the fucker nicked the pad of my hand and fresh blood welled.

The second my arms fell apart, it felt like a million needles were being jabbed into me as feeling rushed back.

Rolling a little, I kicked the chair, sending it flying toward where the guard was. He let out a low grunt but otherwise said nothing.

I sat up, head swimming, but refused to show just how woozy I was. Pushing to my feet, I straightened, grabbing the hem of my shirt and pressing it against my bleeding palm.

"I always knew you were an asshole," I told McClaren. "But this? Not even I thought you were this bad."

His eyes flickered, and then rage stole over his face, scrunching it like an enraged bull's. "Whatever. You think you're the fucking golden child, solving cases and making us all look good? Fuck you, Rogen! I got sick of you acting like you run the show."

I quirked an eyebrow, ignoring the searing pain the action caused. "That's your excuse? The reason you're helping out a fucking pedophile is that you're *jealous*?" I laughed, humorless. "You won't even make it a week in jail. A dirty cop *and* a pedophile? There won't be anything left of your body."

McClaren lunged, but Ferrari slapped a hand on his shoulder and pulled him back. I kept at him, though. McClaren was a weak link, and I would use it.

"You think he's gonna protect you? Is that what he told

you? You know better!" I roared. "You're just his fall guy, his way to get to me."

Suddenly remembering the gun I had tucked in my jeans, I reached for it.

Ferrari laughed. "You've been relieved of your weapon."

"How'd you even know I figured it out?" I turned to Ferrari. "Figured *you* out?"

McClaren scoffed. "You came a crowing that you finally cracked their system." He held up his hands like I thought I was a big deal. "Hacker king. You should have left it alone, Rogen."

I stared between McClaren and Ferrari for a while. "So you knew even before I did? You knew what kind of business he was running, and you kept your mouth shut?"

"What can I say? He pays better than the FBI."

Puke tossed itself up the back of my throat, and I swallowed it down. It burned so much my eyes watered. "You sick son of a bitch."

Ferrari made an impatient sound. "Yes. Yes, we're all heinous. So you've said. That's not important. What is important is who you've sent the information to."

*Like I'd tell him.* "Everyone," I replied. "Every-fucking-one."

"He's lying," McClaren rebuffed. "That's why he called the meeting. He wanted to tell everyone. Brag some more. He hasn't said shit. He hasn't even sent the info to the FBI yet. He has it stashed in a secure location until he can hand all of it in with his report." McClaren finished, smug, smiling as if he'd just tried sliced bread for the first time.

"Should have surrendered it all when you found it. Now it will get buried just like you," Ferrari intoned.

Death was never really something I worried about. I mean, why bother being scared of it? Sometimes it seemed kinda peaceful. It wouldn't matter if I was alone. All my thoughts couldn't touch me there. Hell, if death wanted me… at least something did.

But being threatened with death right now? It left a chill deep in my bones because now I had something to lose.

*Please let me keep you.* Daeshim's words wrapped around my heart, squeezing, begging it to keep beating, to never leave him alone.

I knew I was needy as fuck, but so was he, and my death would kill him. I would never do that to him. *Never.*

The ear-splitting pounding in my head dulled a little as new resolve took over. Calm washed over me in a weird deadening way. The chaos in my mind quieted to a whisper, bowing down to a wolf who wasn't even here but a wolf who owned me regardless of distance.

"You want to kill me?" I spoke quietly and even, almost as though I were engaged in a boring party conversation. Instead of shifting away from McClaren and Ferrari, I stepped closer. "Go ahead. Try. You might even manage. But that info is as good as released. You think I wouldn't put some kind of safeguard on it? You think I don't have it set up for everything to be emailed directly to several massive news agencies and the FBI if I don't check into my own system every few hours?"

Ferrari's eyes glittered with anger. McClaren's face paled.

"And you," I said, turning to face Ferrari. "You might somehow evade the cops with all your money and power, but you won't ever be free of my brother." I laughed, and I swear the little dark hairs on the back of Ferrari's neck lifted. "You think he doesn't know his own brother is a cop? You think you're the only one with a man on the inside? I thought you were smarter."

Ferrari shoved McClaren, and he smacked into the nearby wall. "You didn't tell me that!" he roared.

"Because he didn't know. I'm a much better cop than he is."

"No fucking way!" McClaren bellowed, lunging at me.

I swung, connecting with his jaw. The hit was solid, and it sent me sagging back onto one knee.

McClaren recovered faster and charged, but I stayed down, dropping onto both knees to catch him around the middle, lifting him and driving him over my head into the floor.

"There's no way Mr. Goody-Two-Shoes Hacker is dirty! No fucking way!" McClaren yelled from the ground.

I turned to Ferrari. "I think you know my brother better than that."

The dark-headed man seemed to mull over everything. "I've always respected the Huntsman, and we've been content to stay out of each other's way. But our agreement was not founded on fear, and if I have to, I will take him out."

Panic seized my lungs, making them shrivel.

"You know too much. I'll take my chances with the info getting out after you're dead. Besides, if I let you get away with this deep of a betrayal, others will think they can as well. I don't have time for that." He smiled. "I have a business to run."

I sprang at him, throwing my fist into his shocked face with a running leap. Blood spurted from his lip as we both fell onto the ground. Grunting, he rolled, pinning me with his weight and slamming his fist into my face. More blood pooled in my mouth, and I spit it at him. I rolled us again, drawing back a fist, but I never got to swing because the bodyguard hauled me off, making my feet swing over the ground like a toddler having a tantrum.

Pissed off, I bent at the waist, reaching into my boot for the knife I had hidden there. I mean, I lived with Earth. Did you expect less?

Tugging it out, I hammered it down into the man's arm, making him howl. I fell out of his grasp and spun, kicking the bleeding guard in the stomach and sending him onto his ass. The other guard was already coming at me, and I braced myself, brandishing the bloody knife.

The office door burst in, and more of Ferrari's lackeys filed in. The knife was kicked from my hand, and I was grabbed from all sides. Fresh blood rushed over the side of my face and drooled from inside my mouth. My cheekbone throbbed from McClaren's hit, and my shoulders screamed under the pressure from the way my arms were being yanked behind me.

Ferrari stalked across the room, the men surrounding me parting to make way for their king to approach. I lifted my chin, glaring at him with a level stare, refusing to show any fear.

"Shame I didn't find you before the Huntsman," he mused.

I spit blood in his face.

The muscles in his jaws nearly protruded from the sides of his face as he worked to keep control of his temper. Slowly, he withdrew a crisp white cloth and wiped some of the blood from his cheek.

"Kill him," he ordered before turning and walking away.

## 41

*Daeshim*

THE BLACK CHARGER DRIFTED AROUND THE BUILDING INTO the slim alley, narrowly avoiding a brick wall.

"Watch it!" Earth shouted, glaring at me from shotgun.

I ignored him and muscled the car down the center of the alley and slammed on the brakes near the entrance to the most exclusive club for criminals in this city. We left the car where it was, Earth reaching across the dash and yanking the keys out of the ignition to pocket them.

I was headed right to the entrance, where I was fully prepared to knock heads to get in the door, when Earth called out.

I turned to see Neo, Ander, Fletcher, and Ethan making their way down the alley toward us. I didn't ask where they'd come from, where they parked, or anything. It didn't matter.

"Is Beau inside?" Fletcher asked, keeping his voice low.

"We think so," Earth said.

"Let's go," Ethan said, dressed more like a misfit than I'd

ever seen before. Gone were his tailored designer suits and fancy loafers. In their place, he wore black jeans, a black T-shirt, and a black flannel over it. He was even wearing a black baseball hat over his blond hair.

"We're pretty sure Ferrari is the one behind the case Beau's been working." Earth warned them.

"I should have just killed him months ago," Ander spat.

"He's as good as dead now," I vowed as Earth beat on the black door.

A small window opened, and Earth gave it the finger. The trap slammed shut, and the door opened soundlessly. The bouncer balked when he saw the group standing there with Earth and started to shake his head.

Whatever little showdown was about to occur—aka me breaking this guy's neck to get inside—was interrupted by the abrupt, deafening sound I hated and feared the most.

A gunshot.

# 42

*BEAU*

"Wait," I said, the single word making Ferrari stop and glance over his shoulder.

He was calm for a guy who'd just ordered my murder.

I was calm for a guy who was just sentenced to death.

*At least I'm trying to appear that way.*

"I'll delete the files."

Ferrari cocked his head, tucked his hands into his trousers, and rotated to face me. "You think I would trust you to do that?"

I glanced across the room at his desk and toward his computer. "You don't need to trust me. I'll do it in front of you. Right now."

"How will I know that you will delete all of them?"

"I don't want to die."

It was all I had, and it was the truth, so I knew when he studied me, he'd see that.

"Do it," he finally said, hitching a chin at his desk.

The man restraining me let go, shoving me so hard I stumbled. The room practically spun as I wobbled over to the desk, blood still sliding over my face, but it seemed to have slowed. I dropped into his desk chair, my weak knees fucking screaming in relief.

Within seconds, the chair was yanked out from under me, and I was on my ass practically under the desk.

"No one sits in my chair but me," Ferrari intoned, standing over me.

I thought about nut punching him right there. I mean, I was at the right level. And any man who was involved with what he was didn't deserve his nuts and berries anyway.

However, I refrained. It was a waste of energy, and besides, I had work to do.

"Whatever," I muttered, rising onto my knees and tugging the keyboard close. When the screen lit up, it asked for his password, and I glanced over my shoulder, quirking a brow.

Ferrari made a sour face but reached around me to type in the code, glaring at me to look away as he did.

I shut my eyes dutifully, trying not to smirk. Once I was in, I wouldn't need that code ever again. It just proved how fucking narcissistic he was, thinking he was better and somehow smarter. Thinking he was getting exactly what he wanted.

Thinking I was stupid.

Deleting these files wouldn't save my life. He planned to kill me no matter what. All I was doing was buying time and doing what I did best.

Once the code was in, he moved back, and my fingers flew over the keyboard. I was so at home with technology it didn't even matter that my thoughts were slower than usual and I was seeing double. I could do this with my eyes closed if I had to.

"What are you doing?" he asked, paranoia high in his tone

as he watched the screen go dark and then a bunch of neon code fill it up.

"Accessing my system where I hid the files," I told him easily.

"That true?" he demanded from McClaren.

I suppressed an eye roll. "He wouldn't know." More code filled the screen, and I did a few more neat little tricks.

"Hey, fuck you, Rogen!" McClaren fumed, his feet scuffling closer.

Ferrari turned away to deal with his idiot on payroll, and I took the chance to send out a message for backup with the location. Then I stripped his pathetic firewall and sent myself access to Ferrari's entire hard drive. That would come in handy later.

"What's taking so long?" Ferrari barked.

The sudden sound of a gunshot echoed through the club, silencing the thumping music. People out in the club screamed.

"Go find out what's going on!" he barked to his men.

"Maybe I should come back later," I said, standing up to leave and, as I did, slyly hitting a few more keys.

His hand slapped onto the back of my neck, fingers squeezing. A panicked sick feeling assaulted me.

*Wrong. Wrong. Wrong.*

As I fought the uncomfortable urge, he squeezed harder, finger digging into the giant bruise Shim left on my neck. I yelped a little in pain but then went rigid because this asshole dared touch what was not his.

In a burst of energy, I spun, dislodging the hand from my neck while plowing his middle with a roundhouse kick. He stumbled back into McClaren, and they both went down in a heap.

"I changed my mind. I'm not deleting shit, you pervert scum," I snarled and leaped over the desk.

Okay, fine. I didn't so much leap as fall over it clumsily, but the result was still the same. Look, this headache was wicked.

The office door was wide open from when the men had left, so I raced toward it but was plowed into from behind. We both fell into a heap with me on the bottom. My chin bounced off the floor, and the cut inside my mouth gushed more blood.

A hard punch slammed into my kidneys, and I grunted as I was yanked to my feet. The cold nozzle of a gun jammed against my temple, stopping any more fight I had left in me.

I was familiar with guns. Not afraid of them.

But the second I felt that metal practically against my brain, all I could think about was Shim. About what he told me in the shower, how he'd lost someone once to a gun. The rawness in his voice when he swore he loved me and only me and how he wanted to keep me.

"You get your ass over there and delete those files, or if you don't, you'll taste the lead of this bullet even after you're cold and dead," Ferrari hissed.

I held up my hands and turned to the computer.

McClaren stood against the wall, his gun also trained on me.

"You ought to be ashamed of yourself," I told him.

"Yeah? Well, at least I'm not the one dying today."

I laughed. "Who do you think he's gonna shoot after me?"

"Delete them," Ferrari insisted, shoving me the rest of the way behind the desk.

"Delete the files that prove you are the headliner of a giant, sick child pornography and trafficking ring? Sure, I can do that."

"It's business," Ferrari ground out.

"No. It's kids."

"Well, they make me more money than anything else."

More commotion from out in the club made me look up.

"Ignore it," Ferrari growled, jamming the gun into my temple even harder.

But I couldn't. I couldn't *not* focus on whatever was going on out there. The loud, wild roar that cut through all the chaos told me exactly why.

My heart rate jackknifed, hammering so hard the blood that had slowed to a leak suddenly started flowing more heavily, the warm substance saturating my hair and slipping down my forehead anew.

One of Ferrari's men fell face-first near the door, but I barely looked at him because every cell in my body focused on the whirl of movement that came right after.

"Red!" Daeshim burst into the office as though he had to plow through a wall to get there. The dark hat pulled low on his head didn't stop him from locking those wild black eyes on me, turning impossibly wilder.

His presence made me scared, but the fear was overruled by sheer relief and the desperation I always knew when he was near.

Despite being the kickass, independent FBI agent I was, I could not halt the small stricken noise that ripped out of me on sight.

He growled, eyes immediately snapping to the gun threatening my temple. I felt rather than saw his panic, but it didn't hinder his determination. If anything, it enhanced it. Lunging forward, he ran at us, readying his body to leap over the desk.

The gun left my head to swing wide, aiming at him.

"No!" I yelled, throwing my body at Ferrari as the gun went off.

We both went down in a tangle of limbs, the world tilting on its axis when I hit. Panicked, I scrambled up, ears still ringing from the close-range shot.

"Shim!" I panicked. "Shim!"

And then he was there, arms recognizable even if I was out of my mind with panic, fear, and pain.

"I got you." His voice was like a blanket, his arms wrapping around me from behind. As much as I wanted to collapse into him, as much as my body practically begged to let him take over, I denied the urge.

It physically hurt to rip myself away, turning in the circle of his hold, frantically patting him down. "Are you hit?" I worried. "Where are you hit?"

His hands caught my wrists, restraining me with no effort at all. "Look at me."

I looked.

"I'm not shot."

I slumped, relief making my legs want to fold.

He caught me, a low sound in his throat.

More movement and chaos filled the opposite side of the room, but it was like I just didn't care. Daeshim was here. My wolf was here, and everything was fine.

Those wonderful thoughts lasted, oh, maybe two-point-three seconds because then Ferrari burst up off the ground, still brandishing that fucking gun.

Daeshim shoved me behind him and kicked out, sending the gun flying. He dove forward, knocking Ferrari to the floor, raining down hits on him right and left.

When he reached behind him and withdrew a rather wicked-looking knife, I snapped out of it. Rushing forward, I grabbed his wrist, not afraid of the blade he held at all.

He glanced at me, his eyes flickering with humanity.

"You can't," I told him.

His upper lip curled. Without turning toward it, I slid my eyes in the direction of the computer, hoping he would understand.

He grunted and shoved up off Ferrari, who was positively unconscious. Dude looked just as bloody as me.

The blade disappeared, and then my face was swallowed up by two large, epically warm palms. "Ah, baby, what the hell happened to you?" He agonized, swiping blood away from my eyes and cheeks.

*I knew he'd do that.*

"I think I might need stitches."

A light croon vibrated his throat, and my lashes swept down for long seconds. When he pulled me in, I forgot we were in the middle of a hostage situation. I melted into his body, inwardly so intensely happy that he was wider than me and could swallow me whole. I looped my arms around him, squeezing his waist with as much strength as I had left, pushing my bloodied head into his shoulder.

I shuddered, and he held me tighter. I made a sound of despair, and he made one of comfort.

"Unhand me!" McClaren's voice boomed through the room. "I'm a federal agent. You are accosting an officer of the law!"

Dude made Fig sound smart.

I pulled back from Shim, looking to where Neo and Earth had ahold of McClaren, preventing him from leaving the room.

Ander had the body of one of Ferrari's men at his feet, and Ethan was standing guard at the office door, looking more like a freaking WWE star than the rich elitist he was.

Fletcher was standing over another body not far from Ethan.

"You know this douche?" Earth asked me.

"He was on my team. He's been working with Ferrari."

"Lies!" McClaren spat.

Neo decked him.

I wobbled a bit, stepping over Ferrari, but Shim was

there, grabbing me by the hips and practically lifting me over his prone form. When I was on the other side, I looked back at him, holding out my hand.

His entire face softened, and he came forward, wrapping his hand around mine. "You look bad, Red."

"I'm okay now that you're here."

His eyes were still hella soft, but he tried to scowl. "We're going to have a long talk about you disappearing like that."

"I left a note."

He pulled the sticky out of his back pocket and held it up. "I know."

McClaren struggled against my brothers, and I stepped up to him. Since there were two of him, I just focused on the center. "You're the one that answered my meeting request. You responded with the location. You told Ferrari I would be there. Hell, you probably told Ferrari I was the one who hacked his shit."

"How dare you act like you're better?" McClaren snarled. "You're dirty too!"

Daeshim bristled, but I laid a hand against his chest.

"You're bleeding here too," he roared, holding up my palm to study the gash.

"Shh." I hushed him, turning back to my old partner.

"The only dirty cop in this room is you. And I'm going to make sure you go down for this."

There was a scuffle at the door, but Ethan handled it quickly.

"We should go," Neo said.

I shook my head. I couldn't go yet. "Backup is on the way."

"What?" For the first time, McClaren looked scared.

To Ethan, I said, "I have some friends coming."

"You're lying!" McClaren yelled.

"He gave me access to his computer. Did you really think I wouldn't send out an SOS?"

"This is all just a big misunderstanding, Little Red," McClaren whined. Daeshim growled at the use of the nickname. "I was just working undercover like you. I wasn't actually going to let him kill you."

"Really? This concussion, rope burns on my wrists, and the gun to my head a few minutes ago really say something different."

Daeshim burst past me, plowing his fist into McClaren's face. The man would have fallen if Neo and Earth hadn't supported his weight.

"I was talking to him," I scolded Shim.

He grunted. "You're done," he declared. "C'mon, you can talk to your friends at the hospital. If you lose any more blood, I might kill someone."

The sound of a gun cocking and Fletcher yelling, made us all swing to the door.

"Ethan!" Fletcher yelled again, rushing forward.

Earth cursed, dropping McClaren and running to catch Fletch by the waist and hold him back.

"Let go!" Fletcher demanded, fighting against Earth.

Slowly, Ethan backed into the room, two guns trained on him and the men attached following.

The second the door was clear, someone new stepped through.

# 43

*Daeshim*

"We meet again."

Shock rendered me momentarily speechless as I stared at the man who had so casually strolled into this crime scene.

*I'm seeing a ghost.*

My mind automatically rewound to the day months ago in the Tower. To the time I'd been sent here to take care of my brother even after I'd gone to such lengths to save him.

*He died that day. He's supposed to be dead.*

"Kwan?" I asked, though it was clear who this was. "I thought you were dead."

He smiled, the action not at all reaching his eyes. "I guess it will take more to kill me than your brother's blade." Smug, he looked at Earth who was just as shocked as me.

He pushed Fletcher in Ander's direction and came to stand at my side. We made a formidable team against the man who had been our father's best friend until our father was brutally murdered and he took up with our mother.

"You thought I was dead because that's what I wanted you to believe," he said, practically crowing his genius. "But it seems the only way to get something done is to do it myself."

"You're trying to kill me," I stated. Not shocked. Not enraged. Not anything.

He made a tsking sound. "You always go right to the bad. What about the good I've done?"

There was not one good thing in this man's body. I crossed my arms over my chest, angling in front of Beau, very conscious that he needed a hospital. "You called to tell me where he was."

"I have to admit I was put off that you didn't know my voice."

"You were watching Beau," I stated, flat.

"Something you should be thankful for. I even distracted these goons to buy you some time to get here."

"That gunfire earlier was you?" Beau asked.

Kwan's attention went past my shoulder to him. "You're welcome."

"Why have you been watching him and not me?" I shifted even closer to Beau. When his cold fingers delved into the hem of my shirt, tangling in the fabric just above the waistband of my jeans, my heart turned over. The need to get him the hell out of here and cover his body with mine was so palpable it was almost distracting.

"We've been watching him for a while now. When you killed your dear best friend for punching him, I figured he might be of use to me."

"You sent my *dear best friend* here to kill me." Something about my own statement hit hard, and the edges of my vision dimmed. "Guess that seemed natural to you considering you're the one who killed *your* dear best friend."

A look of surprise flickered over Kwan's face, and I felt

Earth tense. "You killed our father?" he croaked, likely reliving those gruesome memories.

Kwan divided his stare between us, then settled it back on me. "I didn't realize you knew."

"I know everything," I professed. He didn't need to know I'd just realized. "You had our father brutally murdered and then moved in on his wife."

"He took what was *mine!*" he burst out, shrill and frankly unstable.

It was a new look on Kwan. I didn't much care for it.

"The Black Rose should have been mine to lead! But he got it by default."

I had no idea if that was true, and frankly, I didn't give a rat's ass. "But it didn't work out the way you hoped, huh? He died, and Dae took over. She was far more ruthless than he ever was."

"That woman was a bitch even in death," he spat. "Even though you were such a disappointment to her, even after all your betrayals and how devoted to her I forced myself to be —" He stopped, sucking in a breath so deep his nostrils flared. "She still left everything to you!"

I laughed. It tasted bitter and maybe just a little vindictive.

Red's hand twisted a little tighter in my shirt, and I interrupted this little faceoff to glance behind me. "It's okay, baby." I spoke so low only he could hear.

His eyes were slightly unfocused. There was so much blood on his face I could barely see any of his features. I had no idea what kind of injuries all that blood hid, but it was also trickling out of his mouth.

*I never should have left him alone.*

"So you tried to take over the Black Rose, and you can't because you're broke and all the funds are in my name," I surmised, trying to hurry this along.

"So smug," he muttered, an ugly grimace twisting his face. "I even told them all how you both left me to die. How you stood by and watched your own mother be murdered!"

"My pleasure, by the way," Ander quipped.

"I told them you abandoned this entire organization and weren't coming back." Kwan's chest heaved. "And they still wouldn't follow me!" he roared.

I shrugged, and he sputtered.

*What can I say? Just the threat of me alive and able to show up at any moment is enough to scare the shit out of all of them.*

"I figured once you were dead, they'd have no choice. They can't be loyal or afraid of a corpse. But when I got here and saw your attachment to the hacker…"

I stiffened, backing into Beau a little more.

"I realized I could use him to take everything I'm owed."

"He's not a chess piece," I growled.

"He's the key to unlocking every account Dae left in your name. Millions of dollars. Contacts. Names. Once I have control of all that and you're dead, no one will dare defy me."

*Someone who thinks that pet of yours is worth more alive than dead.*

I recalled what the voice on the phone said. He wanted to keep Red alive long enough so he could use my impending doom as a bargaining chip to get what he wanted from him.

I let out a strangled yell, beyond livid this man would put Beau in the middle of our turf war. He was better than that. So much better.

As I lunged forward, Kwan pulled out a gun, leveling it at me. I was too incensed to care and already barreling forward with unstoppable momentum.

And then everything happened so fast the series of events overlapped:

The gun discharged. Shouts drowned out the deafening

sound. I saw the bullet cutting through the air at me, but I was so enraged I didn't slow.

A body leaped in front of me, jerking when the bullet meant for me plowed into them. The force of his jerk flipped something dark off his head, filling my line of sight with a shock of cinnamon hair. The green eyes I loved so much glazed over with pain, and his body dropped out of the air like a dead weight.

The smacking sound he made seemed to blow apart the jumble of events, and I no longer saw anything but the body lying pliant on the floor.

"Noo!" I yelled. "No!" I dropped to my knees, leaning over his body, leaving just enough space to pull him around. "Red! Ohmigod, Red, answer me!"

I had no idea what went on around us. All I saw was him. All I knew was that if his life was over, then so was mine.

"Red," I sobbed, voice breaking, guilt and despair crashing over me. Gone was the temper; gone was the need for blood and revenge. I sat there hunching over his body, no longer giving one goddamn about anything but him. I pulled his upper body into my lap. "Why?" I begged. "Why would you do that?"

He grunted.

I lifted my head, not even noticing the wetness dripping off my cheeks to mix with the copious amounts of blood smearing his cheeks.

"I'm fine," he wheezed. "I can take a bullet better than you."

"Are you out of your mind? No! You can't!" I demanded. I began patting down his body, fingers shaking as I braced myself to see blood spilling out around his body.

*He's already lost so much. He can't lose more.*

"Where?" I demanded, automatically going to the place Hoon had been shot.

Jesus, not again. Not fucking again.

"I love you," I whispered hoarsely. "I love you so much."

His hand reached for mine where I was patting him down. "Shim."

I stilled as his hand guided mine to the hem of his shirt, the shirt that was saturated in blood. A new sob ripped from my throat.

"It's from my hand," he said, tugging his shirt up. "Look."

Realizing he wanted to show me his wound, I quickly ripped at his shirt to get to skin... Only, there was no skin. Instead, there was a tight black... tank top? I wrinkled my brow, trying to wade through trauma to understand.

"Bulletproof," he said, breathing rough. "It's bulletproof."

"He's okay," Ethan announced somewhere nearby. "He's got a bulletproof vest on."

"You aren't shot?" I said, pulling his body around so I could check his side and back. He grunted in pain, and I pulled him back into my lap.

"I'd never die on you," he whispered, making my heart cave in.

"This is the FBI!" someone announced as an entire team dressed in head-to-toe gear rushed the room. Their guns were pretty impressive. "Everyone against the wall! Hands up!"

"Took you long enough," Beau rasped.

"Rogen! What the hell kind of mess have you made?" some older man bellowed, sweeping into the room.

I felt Beau stiffen, and I automatically curled around him.

"Rogen!" the man roared again, stopping over us.

I started to grumble, hackles rising instantly.

Red reached for my hand, threading our fingers. "Calm down," he told me before ducking out from beneath me to look up at the foul man.

"Maybe we could talk after I've had some stitches."

The man muttered a string of expletives and started ordering everyone around. "You!" he demanded, pointing at me. "Back away from the federal officer."

I didn't move.

The asshole reached for me.

I grabbed his wrist, the snapping sound audible. "Back off."

The man howled in pain, and frankly, it satisfied me.

"Shim!" Beau wailed, then started to wheeze. "That's my boss."

I shoved the man away, letting my eyes burn into Beau's. "The only alpha you have is me."

He nodded once, then lifted his chin, showing me his throat. Leaning in, I nuzzled at the exposed skin, not caring his blood was smearing all over my face.

In my ear, he whispered, "Please be nice to the FBI."

I made a rude sound.

"Shim?"

"What baby?"

"I think I might pass out now."

I made a strangled noise, pulling back to cup his face. "Stay with me, Red."

He tried to smile but didn't quite make it. "I'll be okay because you're here now."

And then he went limp in my arms.

## 44

*B*EAU

S*ILENCE WAS WEIRD.*

Maybe not weird... just not what I was used to. So much so that when my eyelashes first began to flutter, it was the very first thing that came to mind.

I was so used to chaos, thoughts trampling any kind of peace or order inside my head so when everything was bliss-fully quiet, it made me suspicious.

*Am I dead?*

That thought, more unnerving than the last, restarted the noise I was so accustomed to living with. My eyes popped open so quick they didn't see at first, only registering the dim lighting of the room.

*Daeshim.*

I tried to call out to him, the effort only resulting in a pathetic grunt. Turns out it was all I needed because he filled my line of sight instantly. Everything cleared and aligned, all his features crystal clear, a feast for my hungry eyes.

The butterflies in my stomach lifted off, rising into a storm of flight, bounding around everywhere and making my breath shudder.

"There he is," he whispered, eyes shining like he was so proud, and all I did was open my eyes.

*No one was ever proud of me for that before.*

"How you doing, Red?" His voice was soft, as were the fingers that lightly caressed my hair.

Instantly, my gaze fell to his lips, neediness rising inside me like a tidal wave. He chuckled softly, and I dragged my eyes to his, silently begging.

His lips settled on mine with a deep sigh. I felt his breath push into me, and I gulped it down greedily as his tongue swept into my parched mouth. The kiss was tinged with the bitter taste of copper, and memories of everything that happened attacked behind my lids.

Eyes flying open, I felt my nostrils flare. He didn't pull back. His movements were not startled by mine. Instead, his lashes lifted, lips gentled, and I found myself falling into his enigmatic gaze while being soothed from the inside out.

My mouth moved again, rubbing against his for more reassurance, and he gave it before pulling back to lick over the seam of my dry lips.

His thumb came up to swipe the bottom, and a bit of worry filled his gaze. "Are you hurting?"

"I don't know," I whispered, surprised at how raspy my voice was.

"He needs water," Fletcher announced, and when I lifted my head to look for him, I winced.

"Easy," Shim cautioned, slipping an arm under my body to tuck me into his side.

We were in bed together. A hospital bed...

"What—?" I started, wincing again when my head tugged.

Fletcher appeared beside the bed, wide eyes staring at me.

"You're in the hospital. You have a concussion and stitches in your head. Do you want me to get you some water?"

I nodded.

He went off, and I turned my face toward Shim who was still right there. "How long?" I asked.

"Most of the night."

"I'm getting sick of sleeping in these hospital chairs," Neo grumped.

I started to sit up, but Daeshim tugged me back down. Seconds later, the bed started to shift, the top part of the mattress rising so I could look at Neo, Earth, Ander, and Ethan all sitting across the room.

"Oh, how kind of you to let us look at him," Earth pronounced.

"Are you guys okay?" I asked, riding the warm flush through my limbs upon hearing how Daeshim kept everyone back.

"You're the one in the hospital bed." Shim reminded me.

*Well, technically, you are too.* I glanced at him. "Are you okay?"

"As long as you are."

Beneath the blankets, pleasure curled my toes.

"What happened?" I asked, trying to sit up a little more, but Daeshim prevented it.

The door opened, and Fletcher came in carrying a pitcher of water and a cup with a straw. He set it all on the bedside table and then poured a glass.

"Here," he said, holding it out, angling the straw toward my lips.

I glanced at Shim, and he took the cup, holding it for me. The water was cool and tickled going down my dry throat. I coughed a little, and Shim pulled the cup back, thrusting it at Fletch. The warmth of his palm settled over the front of my throat, rubbing just lightly, making my muscles relax.

"You dudes are weird," Ander muttered.

Daeshim flipped him the bird, but I didn't care. I couldn't. Having his hands on me was so good. It felt like an eternity since he'd touched me, and I was back to being starved.

His fingertips brushed over the bruise on the side of my neck, and I was thrown back into the moment when Ferrari grabbed me, and the panic I experienced came rushing back.

Seeing the flip switch in me, Daeshim did the opposite of what you might think he should. Instead of pulling back, his grip tightened, almost like he was anchoring me into the touch.

My stare whipped to his, clinging as his remained calm and cool.

"You're okay," he murmured, thumb brushing along my Adam's apple. The memory of Ferrari faded, and my eyelids drooped. Only then did Daeshim pull away, but I followed, shoving my face into his neck to inhale.

"Maybe you should give us a while," Shim told the room, and guilt assailed me.

*I should be stronger than this.*

I started to pull back, but he gently pushed me back down. "Go grab some breakfast for everyone."

"I gotta call V anyway," Earth said.

"I'll get you guys some clean clothes," Ander offered.

The door latched loudly behind them. As soon as they were gone, I was moving, climbing on top of Shim to straddle his lap. He slid into the center of the bed and adjusted the IV line sticking out of the back of my hand before pulling the blankets up around us.

Tucking my arms between us, I shoved my face back into his neck, feeling the stitches in my head tug but refusing to move. My side hurt like hell, my face was sore, and there was a big cut on the inside of my lip.

None of that mattered, though. I just wanted him.

Out of nowhere, I started to tremble, my entire body vibrating like an exposed wire. I breathed in deeper, and when it wasn't enough, I licked over the side of his neck.

"I'm here," he whispered, delving under the stupid hospital gown to rub over my back.

Reaching up, I yanked at the string holding it around me, letting the fabric fall between us. I shoved it away and pushed Daeshim's shirt until it was practically bunched beneath his armpits. When my skin met his, I sighed in relief and licked at his neck again.

"He touched it," I blurted out, clearly not as relieved as I thought.

Shim went stiff as a board under me, his fingers curling around my upper arms. I felt the way he tried to restrain himself, and in a way, it pissed me off. I wanted the wolf. The one who was rough and demanding.

"What?" His voice was deliciously dark and ominous, making me burrow deeper into him. When his fingertips bit into my upper arms, I smiled into his neck.

He yanked me back, eyes glittering. "Who touched what?"

"Ferrari. He grabbed my neck. It made me panic." Sheepish, I said, "I think that upset me more than getting clobbered over the head."

His eyes turned into half-moon shapes, and his snarl showed the white of his teeth. But the violence of his reaction was short-lived, and his hand was curling around the base of my neck with firm but gentle fingers. "Show me."

I showed him eagerly, and he grunted in approval. He intently studied every inch as if he were making sure no one else left any marks. It made me feel cherished somehow. Wanted to the point that if there was a mark from anyone else, he would eradicate it.

"I think we are weird," I whispered.

He drew me in, nuzzling into my neck and making me

feel like being weird was especially my favorite. His nose nudged under my ear and against the lymph nodes in the side of my neck, dragging down to kiss over the hickey he'd already left, making me wiggle in his lap.

The thick width of his tongue dragged along the column of my throat, and he sucked my Adam's apple between his lips.

"More." I panted, thrusting against his stomach.

With a grunt, he latched on to the spot just below the hickey already there, sucking to the point I knew there'd be another mark. I keened quietly, arching into him, satisfaction zinging down to my balls.

He released me, the air brushing over the wet patch against my skin. "Better?" he asked, trailing kisses over my collarbone.

"Mmm," I hummed, reaching between us to wrap my hand around the erection straining against his jeans.

The muscles in his stomach tightened, and he groaned a warning. "Baby…"

"I need you," I whispered, already undoing the buttons and struggling to pull the zipper over his hard-on.

My body was back to quivering, the need for him so great I shook with it. Pushing my hand away, he opened his jeans, and I lifted so he could push them down his hips. The second they were out of the way, I settled against him again, reaching into the waistband of my boxers to pull out my already throbbing dick.

Squeezing myself, I leaned down to suck his nipple into my mouth. I moaned against his flesh, stroking my cock as I sucked.

His fingertips danced down my sides, flirting over my bare skin and leaving chills in their wake. There was no lock on the door. No curtain over the small window. Anyone could walk in and see us. I didn't care. In that moment, all that existed was my need to have him inside me, to be connected to him in a basic way.

He'd come for me when I needed him. He came faster and without being asked like the FBI. He tracked me down in a way only he could, and then he literally fought his way into the office and charged a man with a gun to get to my side. When I finally passed out, I did so knowing he would stand over me like a shield.

There was literally nothing in this world that was bigger than that. Nothing at all that could compare.

His finger slid into my crack, and I nearly sobbed into his chest. Releasing his nipple with a small smack, I laid my cheek on his chest as I widened my knees around his hips so he had more room to touch.

"Did you miss me?" he whispered.

"So much," I whispered back.

His finger circled around the tight ring of muscle, making it spasm with every pass. When he pulled away, I jerked back, staring with wide, flustered eyes.

Quietly chuckling, he leaned down to fish around in the jeans around his thighs. Seconds later, he held up a packet of lube and smiled. "I'm learning."

My heart tumbled seeing his smile and how he seemed proud to have thought to carry what had almost become a basic need for us.

I leaned in, pushing my tongue inside his ear to swirl it around. He grunted in satisfaction, and then his slippery fingers pressed against my hole. Panting, my forehead dropped to his shoulder, and I waited for that first blissful breech.

He gave it instantly, spearing me with two fingers, the burn and stretch making me cry out.

"Shh," he shushed against my ear, nipping at it before moving away.

Teeth sinking into my lower lip, I pushed back onto those fingers, relishing the way he scissored them inside me, opening me up to take his cock.

A little dazed and with warm cheeks, I sat back, holding out my hand between us. He squirted some of the lube on my hand, and I slathered it all over his dick. He hissed as I pumped, and the two fingers inside me started thrusting.

I started to melt into his chest, but he caught my shoulder, pulling me back. With a rough sound, he tugged my lower lip from beneath my teeth and then leaned forward to lap against it. My tongue went for his automatically, and when he finally gave it, the tang of blood coated his tongue.

"You opened that cut in your mouth. Don't do it again." He warned me, and I shivered with the authority. His fingers pulled free, hands going to my hips. "Come on, then. Come here."

My stomach dipped as I scrambled up, lifting my ass as he pushed his dick up off his body so I could slide down over it.

"Go easy," he murmured, but I didn't listen. I sank down on him in one long motion, nearly coming right then and there from just his intrusion.

My eyes watered from the stretch, marveling at how my body just molded around his, accommodating him as though it were meant to be. All the panic I'd felt before, the exhaustion, and the physical pain from my injuries ceased to exist.

"Jesus, Red." His voice was strained, and his eyes were heavy-lidded.

Bracing my palms on his stomach, I tried to push deeper, but pain in my hand made me grimace. Pulling it back, I stared dumbly at the large bandage wrapped around my hand.

Shim grabbed it, pulling my palm in so he could kiss the injury. "You have stitches there too, baby."

His hips thrust up, giving me the depth I'd been craving

and making me forget all about my hand. As much as I wanted to sit atop him proudly, I melted mercilessly over his chest.

Snuggling in, I kissed right over his heart. "You came for me," I whispered, the words just tumbling right out.

*People always left. They never followed.*

*But he did. He followed me right into a fight.*

"Always," he whispered back, digging his heels into the mattress and thrusting up.

My breath caught, and I bore down, looking at him through hazy eyes. I started to bounce up and down, up and down, short, quick movements that made the base of my spine tingle.

His hands slapped onto my hips and gripped. "That's it. Ride me, baby."

Emboldened, I lifted and then sank back down, my mouth opening but no sound coming out. I did it again and again, reveling in the feeling of being split open every single time. Soon, my dick was weeping against his stomach, the flushed, swollen tip glistening with pre-release.

"Touch me." I panted, grinding down on his stick and nearly wailing when it hit my swollen gland.

He wrapped his hand around my cock, hand hitting the exact spots that were most sensitive. Settling all my weight, I rocked against him, eyes rolling back in my head as his dick assaulted my prostate and his skilled hand milked my erection.

"Shim," I whined, so close but just not quite.

His shoulders left the mattress, our chests colliding. One of his arms wrapped around me, and the other delved into the hair at the base of my skull. I shifted, hooking my legs around his waist and changing the angle of penetration.

"Yes," I moaned, teeth sinking into his shoulder.

"Bite me harder," he commanded, circling his thumb and index finger around my sensitive head and twisting.

I came apart right there in his lap. Shuddering, weeping, and biting while red-tinged saliva literally pooled around my tongue, leaking against the raw bite marks I left in his flesh.

Every single jerk of my dick was magnified. Every single spurt of release felt like fucking ecstasy. My mind turned fuzzy, mouth going slack against his shoulder, and I started to slip away.

"Red," Shim called, and I refocused. "You can't drop right now, baby. Stay with me."

I stuck out my lower lip, and he chuckled, stroking my softening cock one last time before pulling off.

I snuggled into him, and he made a sound. "Not yet you don't," he said, flipping our positions.

I barely had time to untangle the IV line from around his back before he was plunging into me with a single, hard thrust. I cried out, shoving my legs so wide my feet fell off the sides of the mattress.

"That's right," he grunted, pounding into me all over again. "You're mine."

My body bounced against the mattress as he hammered into me, a vein standing out in his temple. When I saw the orgasm crest in his eyes, I reached down and pinched his nipple, and his yell turned into a garbled moan of bliss.

The heat of his release seeped into my channel, giving me the kind of peace I'd only ever known with him. I was obsessed. Addicted. Madly in love.

Heart thundering, cheeks flushed, I dropped against the mattress, totally boneless and satiated. Leaning in, he kissed me again, slipping his tongue to the underside of my lip to lick over the cut once more. He never shied away from any part of me. Blood, cum, severe anxiety, the secrets, the lies... hell, not even the truth.

He accepted me wholeheartedly, and there was no way I would never worship him for that.

"I want to suck your dick," I slurred, still cum drunk from sex.

He paused and glanced down. "What?"

"I want to suck you."

"Baby, my dick is busy inside your ass right now."

"Shim," I said, shy. I don't know why I even got shy still. I mean, geez, my thoughts seemed dirty as fuck.

He laughed, the muscles of his stomach rippling against mine. He was so strong, and I had no idea I'd needed such strength.

"Wait till we get home, okay?"

I made a face.

"They're going to be back soon." He reasoned, pecking a kiss to my temple. "You can sleep with it in your mouth for all I care."

My interest was piqued. I'd never thought of that.

Almost as though he could read my thoughts, he laughed under his breath. "I think you're obsessed with my dick."

I caught his hip, ignoring the sting of pain in my hand as he started to pull out. I pulled him back in. "I'm obsessed with your dick because it's attached to you, Shim."

He lowered onto his elbows, caging me in. "Why, Red, what a big heart you have."

"All the better to love you with."

We were kissing when he slipped out, making my nose scrunch up. Almost immediately, he reached between us and pushed two fingers in me, making sure his seed stayed deep.

I sighed in satisfaction.

"Come on. I'll help you clean up before the room is crowded with everyone again."

"Can I wear your shirt?" I asked.

"It has your blood all over it."

"But it's yours."

"Fine, but that means I'm walking around without one."

"Let me see my wolf."

He quirked a brow. "Demanding today."

I quirked my brow back.

Lips twitching, he turned around, stepping up to the bed so I could see the wolf on his back. Leaning up on my knees, I pressed a kiss against it.

"You've gotta stop doing that, Red." His voice was hoarse.

"Why?"

He turned, picking me up off the bed as if I wasn't almost as tall as he was. Instantly, my arms looped around his neck, my cheek meeting his shoulder.

The aches and pains in my body were loudly making themselves known, but they were easy to ignore like this.

"Because I like it far too much."

I made a mental to do it more.

# 45

---

I KNEW THAT LUBE WOULD COME IN HANDY.

I mean, I'd call myself a hero, but since Red literally took a bullet for me, that would make me pretty lame.

Actually, I was pretty positive Red thought I came to the rescue when, really, he rescued himself. And everyone else in the family... more than once.

Red didn't need anyone to rescue him. He needed someone to want him. To love him. And to have lube around 'cause boy was thirsty.

But only for me, so don't be getting any ideas.

And yeah, maybe he needed someone to charge into dangerous places, willing to break necks to make sure he walked out. I could do that. I would do it.

He was mine.

But seriously, he better never get in between me and a bullet ever again.

Fuck, when I thought he'd been shot, my entire world

crumbled right there. But no, of course not. Mr. FBI Genius himself had on a discreet bulletproof vest. Know why? Because *I'd never die on you.*

I didn't even know they made that shit. They do. I googled it when he was passed out and drooling on me in the hospital.

He was sporting a nasty bruise, though. He was lucky his ribs weren't broken.

Fuck, I was lucky to have him.

His legs were unsteady, his body weak, so I washed away what was left of the dried blood, which was more than I liked, as he sat on the small bench in the bathroom shower.

"Head wounds bleed a lot," he said, likely noting the way I scowled at the blood, which was fucking everywhere.

"Who the fuck hit you?"

"I'm not sure. I didn't see it coming."

"I am so pissed you left without a word."

He opened his mouth, but I made a rude sound. "A note doesn't count," I insisted.

"But it said I love you."

Goddammit. How the fuck was I supposed to be mad? Lowering the handheld showerhead, I lowered to my knees between his spread legs. "I know, baby, but you almost got killed."

His brows knit together. "I didn't know McClaren was dirty."

I finished washing him, even washing all the blood out of his hair while taking care to avoid the stitches. There were twelve of them. Fucking twelve. And five in his hand.

"Shim?"

"Hmm?"

"Are you still really mad?" he asked.

"Yes."

"Will you still have sex with me?"

I laughed. How the fuck could I not? "You know I won't deny you."

His hand settled against my hip, and the energy in the small shower shifted. "You know I wasn't abandoning you, right? I was always coming back."

It took one second to place the showerhead on its hook and one more to squat in front of him. "I always knew that."

He nodded, emotion seeming to bubble up inside him so much he seemed overfull. I realized then what leaving must have done to him. Why instead of telling me where he went, he told me he loved me instead.

To Beau, having me know he loved me was more important than anything else because no one ever loved him.

"Hey," I rasped, lifting him off the seat to sit with him in my lap. His long legs straddled my hips, and his chest was close to mine. "I love you... even when I'm pissed off that you almost got killed. Even when you do shit I don't like. I love you no matter what, Red. I never, not once, thought you weren't coming back, okay? I know you won't leave me. I need you to know I won't leave you."

"I know it. I do."

"Knowing and believing are two different things." I cautioned him.

"It might take me some time," he confessed, lowering his eyes.

Gently, I pushed his chin up. "It's okay. I'm here for that too."

His eyes glinted like sunlight on a rare gem, and the awe I saw in their depths made my heart clench. "I'm probably going to be riddled with anxiety my whole life."

"I'll make sure I stock up on lube."

He smiled.

"I love you just as you are, including your anxiety. Okay?"

He nodded, lips curling in. "Could you maybe be done with being mad at me?"

I made a face. "Not even going let me be mad until the stitches come out?"

He pleaded with tired jade eyes, the bruising across his cheek and the freckles on the other fighting a battle he didn't even have to try and wage.

Giving in, I pulled him down for a slow, deep kiss that required exhaustive use of my very skilled tongue. When at last I drew back, he sighed, a signal that I'd manage to give him some peace. I held him a while, stretching out my legs, letting the spray rain down on my ankles and feet while he languished against my chest.

I wasn't sure if he was aware, but every few minutes, he'd kiss the side of my neck.

A knock on the bathroom door didn't even rouse him, and I called out from inside the shower.

"I have your clothes!" Ander announced. Then the bathroom door opened, and I heard a thump before the door shut again.

Then the door flung open again. "Food's here!" Fletcher announced. "I got you a muffin, Beau!"

"Shut the damn door," I hollered.

"I can't believe they forgave me," Beau said, voice lazy.

"They love you. But not as much as me."

He snorted.

After peeling him off me, I quickly washed—I had his blood all over me too—and then shut off the water. Once we were dry, I rummaged through the bag of clothes Ander had tossed inside, surprised to see he'd gone all the way to our apartment to get our stuff.

Beau's face brightened when he saw the hoodie he'd left draped over his dresser, and he reached for it as though he'd won the damn lottery.

It was hella fucking cute.

"That's dirty," I grumped.

"I'm wearing it."

"Put this on too," I said, thrusting a T-shirt at him. He balked, and I gave him a questioning stare.

His eyes strayed to the other shirt in my hand, the one that was mine. Tenderness oozing from my heart, I tossed his shirt down and pulled mine over his head. Then I helped guide the hoodie he loved so dearly over his stitches and chest.

When that was done, he sagged into the counter, out of breath.

"You need some pain pills."

"Didn't they give me some?"

"Last night. You probably need more." Squatting, I helped him step into some sweats and then dressed myself under his watchful gaze.

"Come on. The doc needs to look at you now that you're awake. Probably needs to change the cover on those stitches. I got it wet."

"I want this out," he complained, flicking at the IV line and glaring coldly at the pole parked nearby.

I swept him up into my arms and grabbed the pole he despised. Everyone was in the room, and all of them stared when I carried him to the bed to put him down.

Instead of going to find the doctor, I hit the call button for the nurse and then snagged a coffee off the table. Fletcher carried a paper bag and paper cup over to Beau, holding the drink out. When he took it, Fletch opened up the top of the bag and set it in his lap.

"Are you doing okay?" He worried.

"I'll live," Beau told him, taking a tentative sip of the coffee.

I watched him closely, waiting to see if his stomach would rebel. Dude seemed to have a sensitive stomach lately.

"Is it okay?" Fletcher asked.

"It's good."

Fletch took that as a sign he could launch himself at Beau, throwing his arms around his shoulders. "We've been so worried!"

The nurse came into the room, glancing at the bed. "Oh, you're awake!"

"Yes," Beau said as Fletcher pulled back.

She bustled around, asking some questions, checking some monitors. Then she declared she'd have the doctor come check in.

When she was gone, Beau glanced at the room. "What happened after I passed out?"

"I was about to gut Kwan like a fish, but the FBI showed up and ruined it," Earth complained.

"Yes, such a shame you weren't able to add another body to your already impressive count," Ethan countered.

Earth grunted. "He was already on there, but since the bastard is alive, I have to scratch him off."

Fucking Kwan. I should have killed him myself, FBI be damned, but the second that bullet slammed into Red, I thought of nothing else.

"The FBI arrested him?" Beau asked, looking at me.

Anxiety tightened the corners of his lips, so I went across the room and sat on the side of his bed. The paper sack fell off his lap when he scooched over to me, plastering himself against my side. "Yes, they did. Ferrari too and most of his guys."

"What about McClaren?" Beau asked.

"Him too."

Ethan made a rude sound. "That man was already trying spin some tale about how he was working the case."

I stiffened, thinking of the way he'd betrayed Beau.

Beau's hand slid across my lap, patting my midsection. "It won't matter. He can't get out of what he did."

"Throwing his own team under the bus," Neo bickered.

Beau shot up, wincing against all his aches and pains. I made a sound, sliding an arm around him, offering to support his weight.

"What about Rogers?" Beau fretted. "Did he get jumped at the meeting place too?"

Earth nodded. "Yeah, we found him, called an ambulance."

Beau jolted, then reached up toward his head.

"Be careful," I warned, taking the cup from his hand and forcing him to lean into my chest.

"But is he okay?"

"He was conscious when we left him waiting for the ambulance. He's fine." I assured him.

Earth slid me a glance, and I practically dared him to tell Beau how beat up the man was.

"How did you know where he was?"

"I found your coordinates in the trash. We followed them."

"And we saw Ferrari's symbol on your computer," Earth added.

"Earth called Neo and Neo called all of us and we met them at Blacklight." Fletcher supplied the rest.

"So you went to the meeting and found Rogers. Did he tell you I was at Blacklight?" Beau questioned, trying to piece it all together.

I almost told him not to think so hard, but really, this was probably nothing compared to the inside of his head. Besides, he'd just be anxious until he had all the answers he needed.

"He didn't know. Just that you'd been taken. Since we saw

the symbol, we figured that's where you would be," Earth said.

Ethan leaned forward in his chair, coffee clutched in his hands.

"You look like one of us," Beau mused, taking in his black street clothes.

"He is one of us," Fletcher said, offended.

"Well, usually he dresses like a richie," Neo quipped.

Ethan rolled his eyes, and Ander laughed.

"Thank you for coming," Beau said, drawing Ethan's eyes. "Seriously. You didn't have to, but you did."

Ethan's eyes softened, and my upper lip curled. "I told you we will always be here for you, no matter what."

"When did he tell you that?" I demanded.

"When Beau asked him for sex advice," Fletcher stated as he plowed through a blueberry muffin.

"What the fuck?" I roared, shooting up off the bed and stalking toward Ethan who leaned back in his seat, watching me with a smug look on his face.

"You talking to Beau about sex?" I glowered.

Ethan grimaced. "It was me or Google."

Earth, Ander, and Neo howled with laughter, and behind me, I was pretty sure Beau groaned. "I told you to never speak of this again!"

"He had it coming," Fletcher said, still smacking his lips. "He flirted with me so much."

Beau gasped, but it turned into a wheeze, and everyone stopped heckling to look toward the bed.

Dropping a curse, I spun away from everyone to go to Beau. He was hunched over, one hand on the place the bullet had smacked him and the other near the stitches in his head.

Sighing, I sat down, pulling him into my lap. Pinning Fletcher with a hard stare, I said, "Go get some ice for his head."

Fletcher was out the door in a flash, and Beau collapsed into my chest. As I gently rubbed up and down his arm, I shot Ethan a harsh look. "I'll deal with you later."

Ethan merely smiled.

He wouldn't be smiling if he knew about the murderous thoughts I was having.

Asshole smiled wider.

Fletcher came back with the ice, rushing over to hand it to me. I gave him a sour look, and he turned sheepish. "Sorry, Beau."

"It's okay, Fletch," Beau said, voice hoarse.

The door opened, and a man in a white lab coat strolled in, carrying a tablet that he used as a chart. "Ah, you're awake," he announced, his eyes sweeping around the room. "And you have a full house."

"You can just examine me," Beau said. "No point in telling them to leave."

It took him about ten minutes of poking, prodding, and ignoring my watchful gaze to announce Beau would be fine. Then he said he would send someone in to remove the IV soon and administer more pain meds. The best news was, barring no more complications, he could go home later this afternoon.

As soon as the doctor left, Beau wilted into me, turning to inhale at my neck.

"So," Earth said after a few quiet moments. "I'm assuming this means the case is wrapped up?"

Everything beneath Red's skin went taut. He vibrated like a live wire. "Uh, yeah. Almost."

"You said when the case was over, you had to leave." Earth continued.

"You can't!" Fletcher burst out.

"He's an FBI agent." Neo reminded the room. "If he stays,

he's going to eventually have to give up some dirt on one of us."

Beau's hand slid up over my chest, hooking around my neck. I tried to ignore the way his trembling fingers grappled against my skin, but it was damn hard.

"Beau?" Ander prompted, all of them clearly wanting some kind of answer.

Exhaling roughly against me, he forced himself out of the circle of my arms. "Well, I—"

"Everyone, out!" a loud mouth commanded, his words booming into the room the second he yanked open the door.

We all turned to see the man Beau called his boss striding into the room. Everyone but Beau.

Beau started shaking again.

# 46

*Beau*

No rest for the wicked. Not for anyone.

Woods strolled into the room as if he owned it, sweeping everyone with a self-important, dismissive stare and casually ordering away everyone I loved.

It wasn't because he wanted me. He didn't. He only wanted to use me. He'd chase off any kind of life I'd managed to scrape together, and then when he got everything he wanted, he'd toss me away like he was trying to toss them.

I was exhausted. Weary. Torn in two but wholly wanted to be just one. I was at the point now that I had to choose. No. The choice had been made, but no one knew it yet.

As determined as I was, there was still fear. I'd been afraid my entire life in one way or another. I'd grown used to it, sometimes relied on it. I didn't want to do that anymore.

I didn't have to.

I had Shim now. The very wolves I'd been thrown to had made me one of their own.

So no. No, *Little Red* wouldn't leave the woods. Red would stay where he was fated to be. And I would use everything I ever learned even if it scared me.

"Who the hell are you?" Earth deadpanned.

"Octavius Woods," my boss answered, puffing out his chest. "Director of the Federal Bureau of Investigation and Rogen's direct superior."

Fletcher's nose wrinkled. "Why do you keep calling him Rogen?"

"That's my last name," I explained. "My real last name."

"O'Brien isn't your last name?" Fletcher seemed surprised.

"No," I replied. *I've lied about so many things.*

"Is Beau your first name?" he asked.

"Yeah, I kept it. We just changed my last name."

"I would advise against divulging any pertinent information about your cover or this case, Rogen," Woods instructed, turning hard eyes on me.

Over my shoulder, Shim made an aggressive sound, drawing Woods's eyes, making them widen.

"How's the wrist?" he inquired, clearly proud of himself.

*I'm kinda proud of him too.*

Woods's face darkened. "Broken."

"Shame."

I guess it was too much to hope he'd be nice to the FBI. It really would make things much easier.

"Get out!" Woods roared, waving around his newly cast wrist.

"We aren't going anywhere," Ander announced.

I watched in surprise as all of them punctuated the declaration by settling deeper into their chairs.

Woods's bloodshot eyes nearly bulged out of his ruddy cheeks. "That's a direct order! I'll haul you all in on obstruction of justice."

"This is my hospital room. Not the station," I said, not an ounce of give in my words. "They're here because they're family."

Woods looked at me as if I'd grown another head instead of having this one stitched back together. "Family?" He scoffed. "The FBI is your family."

"No," I declared. "My family is the people who taught me how to survive when you tossed me to the wolves."

I could practically feel Daeshim's pride. I definitely heard a small purr deep in his throat at my words. It made me feel stronger.

Woods blanched. "Rogen. I understand you've been through a lot, five years—"

"I wouldn't even finish talking." Shim cut him off, speaking very quietly.

I sighed, then looked around the room. "Can you give us a few? I do need to talk to him."

"It can wait," Shim said.

"No," I argued. "It can't."

Woods preened like a stuffed Thanksgiving turkey. It was like he didn't realize everyone was about to eat him.

I really didn't like him much. I tried. I really did. But he made it hard, and I was just so tired.

Everyone filed out of the room, Earth pausing beside the bed to look at me. "I'll be right outside. If you need anything, yell."

Gratefulness swelled in my chest, reinforcing that I was doing what was right.

Woods made a rude sound. "The person he needs protection from is you."

I stiffened as Earth stepped up in front of the agent who had long since gone gray at his temples. "I hear you've been wanting to meet me," he said, mild.

I reached for Shim's hand, clutching his fingers, hoping

he knew he might have to pull Earth out of the room. Leaning close, he brushed his lips against the shell of my ear, humming softly. It was all it took for me to relax.

"Name's Earth. I own the Rotten Apple in the Grimms. Stop by sometime. I don't usually let law enforcement drink free, but for you, I'll make an exception."

Woods's face flushed nearly purple, the shade so dark I worried the man might asphyxiate on his own shock.

Earth smiled peacefully, then left the room without a backward glance.

When we were alone, Woods turned his purple-hued face to Daeshim. "Get out."

"No." He refused almost like he was bored.

"You two a thing, Rogen? Is that what this is?" Woods wagged his finger between us. "This is a conflict of interest."

"Yes. We're involved. And he already knows I'm an FBI agent," I said simply.

"You told him classified information?" Woods accused.

"No. *You* told the entire room back at Blacklight." I reminded him. He didn't need to know I'd shared with the fam before he did.

Woods blanched, clearly remembering his little slip. "This is still confidential business."

It was, and I knew the law. I also knew that I had to lose some battles to win the war.

Turning slightly, I faced Shim, his eyes suddenly guarded. "Just give us a couple minutes, okay?"

"You want me to leave you alone with him?" He was incredulous.

"No. But I want this to be over," I said, hoping he would understand.

He frowned.

"Trust me," I implored softly.

"I do."

*Love you,* I mouthed.

Shim sighed, pecked a kiss to my nose, and then untangled himself from the bed. "I'm waiting right outside the door."

"Okay," I told him.

Woods made a rude sound, which thankfully Shim ignored.

When he slipped out, I turned my eyes to my boss. "What's the status?"

"Ferrari is in custody. He's going away for life. DA might even go for the death penalty."

"It's warranted," I said, hoping they threw the book at him.

"I got the files you sent. The lists too."

"You gonna be able to arrest them all?"

Woods made a sound, scrubbing a palm over his face. "You saw those names, Rogen. What a fucking shitshow. One's a senator, for Christ's sake."

"One's a judge," I added.

"Fucking scum."

I made a noise, agreeing with him.

"I've handed over all the files. Warrants are being issued. The bureau is trying to keep it all quiet until it's all in stone so no one flees," he told me.

I nodded. "You got the cam footage from Blacklight?"

One of my neat tricks while in Ferrari's office was to turn on the desktop microphone and camera. The man was so arrogant he didn't even notice.

Woods nodded. "That was good work, Rogen. We got a little on the camera. A lot of it was out of frame, but the audio was clear and is all we need. They won't get away for what they did to you and Rogers."

"How is he?" I asked, my stomach knotting.

"He'll be okay. A head wound, some broken ribs, and a

broken leg. The rest is superficial." Woods made a face that had my pulse thumping.

"What? What is it?" I demanded, thinking there was something else about Rogers no one had told me.

You'd think the man had a raging case of rancid gas when he said, "He helped him."

Confusion made me blink. "What?"

A strangled noise ripped out of him. "That no-good killer helped him! His brother too. They found Rogers and called an ambulance, got him help. Might have bled out if he lay there undiscovered any longer."

I couldn't help it. I smiled. "Earth and Daeshim helped one of us, and you can't stand it."

"It's the first thing Rogers said when he came out of surgery," Woods reluctantly admitted. "Rogen was right."

I pressed my lips together.

Earth helping out the FBI. Now there's something I never saw coming, but damn if it didn't back up everything I'd been saying.

"I'm right, you know. I told you. Earth is no killer." I'd said it so many times I didn't even feel bad for lying anymore.

"He isn't innocent."

"No. No one in the Grimms is."

"That boyfriend of yours is worse." Woods fumed, holding up his wrist. "I ought to have him arrested for assault."

My lips drew into a hard line. "He was protecting me, and you know it. It was a high-octane situation, and I'd just been shot."

"How much do they know?" Woods asked, the question hanging heavy in the room.

I weighed my answer, then settled on, "Some. Not everything."

Clearly unhappy, he said, "They should know nothing."

"Well, when you burst into the room yelling FBI, you had to know there would be questions."

"You told them more than you should have."

I shrugged. "They're my family."

"You'd really choose them over us?"

I looked him dead in the eye when I answered. "Yes. Consider this my notice. I want out."

He turned purple again. He started pacing and then bumped into a rolling cart and shoved it so hard it crashed into the wall.

The door to the room opened, and Daeshim appeared, eyes going right to the bed.

"I'm fine." I assured him.

"Out!" Woods roared.

Daeshim came the rest of the way inside, shut the door, and leaned against it, crossing his arms over his chest. "I'll stay."

I didn't bother arguing.

Woods looked murderous, but Shim didn't understand that was his usual expression.

Woods swung to me. "You can't quit!"

"I just did."

I felt Daeshim's shock from the door, but I couldn't look at him yet.

"Have you been covering for them? For those... misfits?" Woods demanded. "Is that what this is? You think you can clear your friends of all crimes and walk away, leaving the FBI high and dry?"

"No—"

"Because I'll take you down too!" Woods cut me off to rant. "I'll dig until every one of you is behind bars, and you'll never see any of them again!"

His words hit their mark. My heart. The soul no one realized was so fragile. My biggest fear was not being wanted, being abandoned. Now that I felt like I finally had a family that wouldn't leave, someone was threatening to take them away.

A cold draft whipped through my suddenly hollow middle, and that small place behind my heart began to shrivel. Fingers curled into my palms, and not even the sting of the stitches in the meat of my hand was enough to keep me from spiraling inward, to keep me from internally freaking out.

A familiar scent filled my nostrils as the strong wall of a body I'd come to rely on filled my sight. Bending at the waist, his palms flattened on the mattress as he pushed into my personal space. Desperately, I sought the strength in his eyes, and when I found it, my lungs expanded because not only did I find strength but also love.

"Don't you let him push you around, Red. Remember who you are," he said, one finger hooking around mine.

Determination suffused me, and the chaos withered. I met Shim's eyes, letting him see that I was good, and nodded once.

Pride lit his face, and he moved across the room toward the window. In one last show of solidarity, he tugged the shirt over his head to stare out the glass with his back to the room.

Woods was staring at me like he was expecting me to crumble.

Instead, I pushed out of the bed, forcing my unsteady legs to remain stable as I moved around the side under the watchful eyes of my wolf.

*Remember who you are.*

*I'm Red, and I run with the wolves.*

I smiled, and whatever it was that showed in that expression made Woods blanch.

Tearing my eyes from the wolf so proudly watching from across the room, I straightened and faced my former boss but *never* my alpha.

"Here's how it's going to go," I said quietly. Confidently. "You're going to acknowledge the fact that you threw a barely legal, undertrained kid on the streets of the roughest ghetto in the country to catch a killer you only thought existed. You're also going to acknowledge that even though you pressured and browbeat me into turning in a man I'd told you was innocent time and again, I still managed to solve cases, more than you have solved in your, what, thirty years with the bureau?"

"Why you little—"

"I'm not finished, Octavius."

He shut up.

"I closed cases you didn't even know existed, and I found the actual perps of cases you tried to pin on a man that has a solid alibi for half of what you think he did. Is he an innocent lamb? No. No one in the Grimms is, and you damn well know it. But they are not killers, and your hard-on for my brother wilts right now."

"You think I can't bury you?" Woods intoned.

"No. I know you can't. I have more computer skills in my little finger than you do in your entire brain. Every case I've worked, all the proof I have, is backed up with solid documentation and a trail of proof no judge would ever overrule. Not to mention I literally just handed you the biggest crime boss in this country and a list of his known associates so you can shut down a major child abuse ring. Take the info. Take all the credit. I'll even testify in court it was you who figured it out."

Woods was intrigued… but also suspicious. "What do you want?"

"I want out of the FBI. I want you off my ass. I want you

off the ass of my entire family. No more witch hunts for Earth, and don't even think about looking at Daeshim. I want immunity for every little discretion you think they've ever committed. Forget you know us. Focus on actual criminals that are committing actual crimes."

"You think I can give you that?"

"I know you can."

"And if I don't agree?" he asked.

Out of the corner of my eye, I saw Shim stiffen, but I had this. I had him.

"I'll make sure the FBI knows their director isn't as squeaky clean as they think."

He scoffed.

"You think I don't know you've been skimming ten percent off literally every single paycheck I've ever gotten from the bureau?"

He sucked in a breath.

Across the room, Daeshim growled.

"That's ten thousand dollars a year, Woods. I've been working for you, what… six years? That's sixty grand. And let's not forget about that bonus I was apparently awarded for outstanding fieldwork that you never told me about, pocketing the entire check."

All the purple he'd been suffused with suddenly drained away, leaving him ghostly pale. "H-how'd you know?"

"You underestimated me, Woods. I'm not just some dumb kid," I deadpanned. "So unless you want me to file a suit with the FBI that you owe me roughly ninety thousand dollars and show them every receipt and every bank statement I have, even the ones of your secret account in the Maldives, well, you might want to take the deal."

He rushed me.

Daeshim slid between us, shoving him back. "I will break the rest of the bones in your body," he threatened.

Woods turned slitted, angry eyes on him, so I spoke, taking back his attention. "Your freedom for mine seems like a fair exchange," I told him. "Especially since I haven't done anything I really need freedom from."

"You son of a bitch."

"That account has a pretty big balance," I said, overlooking his anger. "Who else have you been skimming from? I don't think the FBI would like to hear about how you're taking advantage of agents who are literally in the field risking their lives and trusting you with depositing their hard-earned pay. They probably won't be as accommodating as me either, letting you keep the money."

"Fine. You have a deal," Woods declared.

"I expect to see a severance package on my desk in two days."

"Severance?" He nearly choked.

"Consider it a finder's fee for the gangster I'm letting you take down."

"You think you're so smart," he bickered.

"No. I think I'm taking what I deserve."

"When they subpoena you to testify, you better be there."

"I won't go back on my word," I promised. "Make sure you don't either."

"Good riddance," Woods said, stalking toward the door.

"Octavius?"

His whole body tightened, and he turned. "What?"

"What's the status on Kwan?"

He pursed his lips, sliding a glance at Daeshim and then back to me. "You tangled up with the Black Rose?"

"Pretty sure we've already been over that," I deadpanned.

His face soured. "Yeah, yeah. You're all innocent. Even this one with the black rose tatted on his chest."

"Coincidence," Daeshim quipped.

Woods snorted. "Kwan is in custody. We're shipping him back to Korea."

"I want him barred from re-entry to this country."

"Whatever. They were doing it anyway."

"I guess I'll see you in court, then," I said, my battery draining fast.

He turned to leave but turned back, hand on the doorknob. Noting his attention, I straightened, strengthening my walls.

"You really surprised me, Little Red."

"Guess I'm not as little as you thought."

He made a rude noise and left.

The second I was sure he was really gone, I sagged. "Shim."

Daeshim was there, wrapping me against his chest and kissing my forehead. "Damn, baby. You fucking beat him down and didn't even have to lift a finger."

I laughed under my breath. "I just did what I had to do."

"You protected everyone again."

"I protected myself by protecting all of you."

Shim pulled back, staring down into my face. "He really steal that much money from you?"

I nodded. "Oh yeah. He thought I wouldn't notice. I wasn't lying either. I have all the transactions and info to prove it."

"Why didn't you just steal it back?"

"'Cause the info was worth more than the cash he stole." *Freedom isn't free, but in my case, it doesn't have a numerical value either.*

"Devious." Shim grinned. "I like it."

"Shim?" My voice was small and hesitant.

"Just ask, baby."

"Hold me."

A gruff sound filled the room, and he pulled me to the

bed where he climbed in first and spread his legs. I crawled between them, grimacing at the stupid IV before pushing as much of myself onto him as I could.

His arms wound around me, and his chin rested on the top of my head.

"How's the head?" he asked.

"Hurts."

"How's the heart?" he asked.

I smiled. "Never been better."

# EPILOGUE

*Daeshim*

WHAT DO RED AND HIS WOLF DO WHEN THEY WANT TO START their happily ever after?

Escape to a private island.

Okay, well, they go there to fetch their sisters. Some of the men in the family thought the girls were necessary for the aforementioned happily ever after. Me? I didn't care. I had Red.

But my Red had never seen the beach before, so instead of going home from the hospital, we got on Ethan's private jet.

Don't worry. Beau's doc said it was okay.

We could all use a vacation after this shit anyway. Well, again, I didn't care, but having sex on the beach seemed pretty good.

I packed lube. Lots of it.

Ethan had stashed the girls on some swanky private island in the Caribbean that was likely owned by some snobby, rich do-gooder who would have a stroke if he found out the heir of a notorious Korean mafia was running around with some of his less notorious but still notable criminal friends.

But what the guy didn't know wouldn't hurt him.

Besides, I was free of the Black Rose now. The minute Kwan was sent back to Korea, he was as good as dead, even if he went to jail. There would be no safe place for him to hide. He was sent to challenge the alpha and didn't come home with his head. That meant he lost.

Frankly, he was lucky I didn't kill him. I would have if the FBI hadn't been in residence and Beau hadn't asked me so cutely to be nice.

I was really gonna have to start curbing the urge to kill first and ask questions later. It caused anxiety for Beau and made him think he had to be the one to clean up the messes bodies left behind.

In fact, this whole family was going to start shaping up. I was putting my foot down. And if they didn't listen, that foot was going up their asses. Except the baby. And no, I didn't mean Fletch. I meant the actual baby that was coming soon.

Beau was done running around behind everyone with a damn mop and broom. He deserved better, and I would make damn sure he got it.

I was gonna have to get a real job. Nothing too crazy, though. I didn't need the money, and I couldn't be away from Red longer than roughly ten minutes at a time. You saw what happened when I was. Maybe I'd brew some beer, my own label like Earth. We could serve it at the bar too. *Red Wolf Ale* had a nice ring to it, right?

It was dark when we flew in, so we couldn't see the ocean from the plane. The island had its own private airstrip and some golf carts to drive up to the massive house perched in the center.

"You want me to drive it down to the beach?" I asked Red

who was plastered against my side under my arm with his head lolling on my shoulder.

"No. Just go to the room," he said, looping an arm over my waist like a little seatbelt. He was way cuter than Fletcher.

It was too dark to really see anything anyway, so I followed the others up to the house where the three girls waited on a white stone parking pad, jumping around as though they hadn't seen us in a month instead of just two days.

Women were a bunch of drama. I was thankful to be gay.

We were surrounded the second I stopped, all of them rushing to Beau's side to coo and worry over him. He blushed furiously under the attention, hugs, and exclamations about all his stitches and battered appearance.

"I'll explain everything in the morning," he promised, glancing around to me for help.

"We'll tell them everything tonight," Earth said. "You've done enough for us."

The girls backed off to fawn over the men who were not mine, and I bent low in front of the cart, offering him my back. "Come on, Red. We're going to bed."

He slid across the short bench seat, grabbing the hem of my shirt.

"What the f—" I started but then realized what he was doing. Chuckling, I tugged the shirt off, and then he climbed onto my back, wrapping around the wolf.

I mean, I always liked this tattoo, but I sure had a new appreciation for it now.

"Oh, Daeshim!" Ivory called, making me turn back. "Your room is in the left wing. Just take any of them. They're all empty."

"Sounds good," I called and climbed about a thousand stone steps to the mansion.

"You aren't as skinny as you look," I muttered.

Red reached down to take the single bag we'd brought with us. I tsked and slapped his hand away.

"Did you tell everyone on the plane what happened with Woods?" he asked as I wandered through the fancy left wing. I wanted the room at the end of the hall. It probably had the best views.

"Yeah," I answered. He was sleeping, and there was no reason for him to have to go through it all again.

"Thank you."

"Anything for you, baby."

Finally, I came to the last room and pushed through the double doors. There was a light switch nearby on the wall, so I clicked it on, lighting up the massive room.

"Who the hell is Ethan friends with?" Beau wondered.

"Probably some president." I chortled as I set him down and then tossed the bag toward what had to be a custom-made gigantic bed. It had four posts and white sheers draping the entire thing.

There were some elaborate-looking sconces on each side of the bed, so I switched on one of those and killed the overhead. The room dropped into a softly lit space, the entire wall across from the bed made entirely of sliding glass.

I went to it, sliding open one of the doors, and the scent of salty sea air immediately swirled in. The roar of the ocean came in with the air, making the curtains around the bed flutter.

Noticing Red was basically still standing where I left him, I went back, reaching for his hand. "You want a shower or bed?"

Clutching my hand, he pulled me around and then swiftly shoved me against the closed double doors. Surprise rendered me momentarily speechless, and I only snapped out of it when he dropped to his knees in front of me.

I gasped as his hands caught in the waistband of my sweats, tugging them down in one swift movement. My heart thundered, and I let out a groan when he leaned in to nuzzle my rapidly hardening dick over my boxers.

"What are you doing?" I asked even though he was making it hella obvious.

Wide green eyes looked up from beside my cock, and all the breath in my lungs evaporated. "You said I could suck you."

"You just got out of the hospital, babe. You have a cut in your mouth."

"You never minded my blood before."

Oh, I was weak for him, and I'd been imaging his mouth on my dick, the feel of his tight throat squeezing my girth, for so damn long.

I nodded, and his eyes went hazy, and any blood left in my head rushed south.

His breath was hot when he latched on to my dick. The cotton dampening to stick to my skin was foreplay I never knew before. My fingers threaded in his hair, and he moaned like a freaking slut, and my hips pushed off the door toward his lips.

Impatient, he yanked the boxers down, going as far as making me step out of them so there was not a scrap of fabric between us. When he yanked my socks off, my feet hit the cold stone floor, and I frowned, looking down at his knees.

"I like it," he said, fingers caressing my sack. "I like being on my knees in front of you."

"Shit."

He smiled, those pink lips stretching as the tip of his tongue coated them with shine.

"Get busy," I growled, grabbing my rod and yanking it down so it was pointing right at him.

Staring up my naked torso, he leaned in and licked over my head.

I was still shuddering when he reached out and wrapped his long fingers around the base to pull it back. *Liiick.* Another long swipe of his tongue over my fucking slit and I groaned.

"I love you," he said almost like he was praying and my dick was his altar.

And then he fucking attacked.

For all his shyness, this man knew how to fucking suck a dick. Jesus Christ, if the door wasn't at my back, I would have been on the floor.

Two licks was all it took for him to decide this was his new obsession, and he swallowed me down like he was famished. Lips locked tight, his head bobbed relentlessly. The sucking sensation he somehow created made me feel like I had a vacuum attached to my rod. His mouth was so wet. The taste was so good he was dripping with it, and when he pulled off, it trickled down my length, pooling around the base.

"Am I doing okay?" he asked, a hint of that shy man I knew gazing up for approval.

I grabbed his face, squeezing his chin. "Who taught you how to suck a dick like that?" I demanded.

A little insecurity shone in his eyes, but he blinked it away. "No one. I just wanted to be good for you."

"Oh fuck, baby. You're perfect. The best I've ever had."

He smiled, eyes lighting in a way I'd never seen, and then swallowed me down again, shoving so his nose was buried in my pelvic bone and I felt his throat spasm around my head.

I muttered a few more curses, burying both hands in his hair (keeping enough mind to avoid his stitches), and anchored him to my crotch. When I felt him gag a little, I pulled back, but he made a sound and pushed himself onto me again.

I wasn't sure what kind of sounds I made, but *oh*, I made them as I rocked my hips slowly, his throat cradling my head like the tightest of cages.

He pulled back, sucked in air, and then did it again. Over and over until tears spilled down his cheeks and saliva coated his chin.

I was sliding down the door when he pulled off, licking me like I was a melting ice cream cone. I was two seconds away from blowing, and I wasn't sure I'd be able to hold off if he wrapped those sinful lips around me one more time.

"Shim…"

God, his voice was wrecked like I'd fucked even his vocal cords into submission. His pupils were blown wide, lips swollen, and an out-of-focus look filled his expression.

"Let's go to bed," I said, dick pulsing.

"Fuck my mouth. I want to taste you."

"You can't say shit like that to me."

He opened his mouth, sticking out his tongue.

I grabbed his head and shoved. Both of us groaned as my hips started thrusting. I was sloppy and rough, and he kept his jaw relaxed and throat open.

"I'm gonna come," I warned, and his palms slapped against my ass, pulling me even deeper into his throat.

I erupted with a yell, body rigid as I poured down the back of his throat. I was so deep in him I heard him choke, but then his throat was working, swallowing me down like he refused to waste even a drop.

My eyes were watering, and I slid down the door onto my ass, not even registering the cold floor. Red moved with me, moving between my legs, gently sucking my softening cock, lapping at the tip until there was nothing left.

He curled up between my legs, cheek on my thigh, cock

still in his fist. Breathing still erratic, I glanced down, noticing the wet spot in the front of his pants.

"Eyes on me," I said, still breathless.

His face turned up, and he was just as wrecked as me. Hazy, satisfied, and looking like I'd just fucked him silly. But I hadn't even touched him.

"Up," I said, standing and dragging him along with me. "Strip. On the bed."

He pulled at his clothes, leaving a trail on his way to the bed. Then he climbed on the bed on all fours, presenting his ass like a trophy.

I smacked it, and he moaned. So I smacked it twice more.

Then I grabbed his thigh and flipped him onto his back. Looming over him, I gazed down. "Your head okay? Want to stop?"

"If you stop, I'll cry," he admitted, tears already shimmering in his blown-out gaze.

"Shh." I soothed him, leaning in to kiss him softly. "I won't stop. I just want to make sure you're okay."

He nodded eagerly.

Slipping down his body, I sucked a hickey on the inside of this thigh and trailed my tongue into his crack. He cried out and spread his legs, and I settled between them and started to feast.

His hole was drenched and soft by the time I pulled my tongue back, his legs quivering around my head. I slid down over his throbbing rod at the same time I slipped two fingers inside him.

He bucked up off the bed, and I pushed him back down, sucking hard, curling my fingers against his prostate.

He came fast and hard, shooting across my tongue as he groaned my name. When his body went boneless against the mattress, I nudged his gland again, and more salty release dripped over my tongue. I swallowed him down, carefully pulling my fingers out but sucking him just a little bit longer.

The second I moved up beside him, he curled into my side, tangling our limbs and sighing deep.

"I love you, my Red," I whispered, the words blending with the sounds of the ocean waves, which seemed kinda perfect because my love for him was as vast as the sea and as unending as the current.

---

*BEAU*

STRONG ARMS LIFTED ME OFF THE CLOUDLIKE MATTRESS, MY sleep-addled mind barely registering the faint whispering of the white cotton sheers draped around our bed. The sound of ocean waves was distinct even though it was an unfamiliar sound.

The balmy breeze brushed over all my bare skin, prickling it with goose bumps, and I curled a little tighter into my safety net.

I was aware of being carried, the motion just as lulling as the steady sea. His footsteps changed a little partway down, but it didn't alarm me because, with him, I knew I was safe.

The scent of saltwater and the rush of wind grew stronger. I lifted my head out of the crook of his neck. "What's going on?"

He lowered us to the ground, pulling his legs in and sitting me in their center. A soft blanket draped over my bare chest, and his husky morning breath brushed over my ear.

"Wake up, Red. Wake up and see."

I blinked, the first hint of peach piquing my interest. Opening my eyes wasn't harsh or intrusive because the light was low, the sky just now waking and bringing with it the soft pastels of day.

My breath caught, sleep instantly slipping away as I studied the peachy pink and yellowish tones blending up into a dark sky. The beautiful colors met the horizon, which bobbed and never stilled. The ocean stretched out so wide in front of us it seemed to swallow me whole.

"Holy shit," I whispered, taking in the white-capped waves cresting and crashing on a smooth, sand-filled beach, rushing up toward us but not quite in reach.

"The sun is about to come up right out there," he whispered, pointing back at where the colors all met. "Your first time seeing the ocean, and it should be like this."

Eyes still stuck on the horizon, I breathed in salt as I unfolded my legs to hang them out of his lap, jolting a little when the millions of textured grains rushed between my toes. "It's cold!" I exclaimed, leaving my toes buried anyway but pushing my back farther into his chest.

"It won't be when the sun comes up."

Beneath the blanket, his arms wrapped around me, making him better than any blanket would ever be. We sat there kissed by the breeze off the ocean, toes buried in sand as the sun introduced me to the sea for the very first time.

The higher the sun rose, the more the water sparkled like gems. Birds soared just over the waterline, and a dolphin jumped a few waves. We sat there long enough that the orange and pink sky gave way to a lilac hue and then faded into a blue so clear I wouldn't have believed it without seeing it.

"I had no idea the sky could look like this," I said, completely amazed.

When he didn't say anything, I sat up to look over my shoulder.

My mouth fell into a little O. "Shim?" I asked, scrambling

around because of the tears shimmering in his eyes.

"You're missing the view, baby," he said, emotion clogging his throat, and gestured for me to turn back around.

"Your eyes are more beautiful than any ocean I could ever see."

He tackled me into the sand, taking care to shove the blanket under my head to protect my wound. We kissed until my lungs were about to burst, and then he rolled off me so we were both on our backs and staring up at the sky. His hand curled around mine, and we lay side by side.

"You know we would have worked it out if you wanted to stay with the FBI," he told me.

I knew. I knew he'd stay no matter what I did. They all would. But the job wasn't worth it to me. There would always be more danger.

"I don't want the FBI. I just want you."

He sat up and tugged me between his legs. "What do you think of the ocean?"

"It's better than what Google said."

His laugh was a rumble against my ear.

"What's this about you asking Ethan for sex advice?"

I groaned. "Oh my God. I didn't! I mean, I guess I did." I sputtered. "I was nervous!"

"Nervous because of me?"

"Of course," I exclaimed. Who else would it be?

"Are you still nervous?"

Tingles raced over my scalp, his voice like a massage for my ear. "I thought you wouldn't like me because I don't have experience."

"I prefer it."

I turned, eyes wide. "Ethan said that."

He made a face. "Don't talk to Ethan about sex."

"I didn't really believe him anyway," I admitted.

Shim laughed as though this news made him unbearably

happy.

I started to turn back to the view, but he pulled me back around. "He was right. I like knowing no one else has touched you like me, that no one ever will."

*Well, I guess when he puts it that way...*

"Do you think the Black Rose will be a problem?" I asked, turning back to the amazing view.

"No. But I'm going to send a clear message. I was hoping a certain hacker might help me."

I gazed at him out of the corner of my eye. "How?"

"Shut down all the stuff Kwan was going on about. Delete it all. There won't be anything left. If they want to start another organization, they will have to do it from scratch."

"And all the money?" I asked.

"Technically, it's mine. Dae left it to me."

"How much are we talking?" I wondered.

"Probably around eighty million."

I gasped, sand kicking up when I sat forward. "Are you shitting me?"

"Think that makes me richer than Ethan?" he asked, grinning.

"Not if you combine all his assets, like all the hotels they own. And not Ivory."

He raised an eyebrow. "You know how much they're worth?"

I shrugged. "I like to know things."

"I was thinking maybe I'd donate some of it. A lot of it. It won't make up for the shit I've done, but it's something."

"I love you."

"Even if I use some of it to buy us a nicer place with a bigger shower and bed?"

I nodded. "I have about half a mil saved up." Then I almost spilled out some other thoughts but decided against it and pressed my lips together.

"Tell me," he said, tugging on my ear.

"It's stupid."

"I like stupid."

I stared out over the ocean. It was this incredible shade of teal. "I was thinking about maybe trying to create a video game."

"That's not stupid, baby."

Wide-eyed, I turned to him. "You think I could do it?"

"You're a fucking genius. Of course you can. But no pressure, okay? Just do what you want. Do it for fun."

I launched into a long explanation of my ideas and the certain code I already memorized and wanted to use and how I was going to ask Fletch to help come up with some of the specs because playing games was what we did together... And then I realized I'd totally geeked out and talked probably more in the last half hour than I had our entire relationship.

*Relationship.*

"Are we in a relationship?" I burst out.

He scowled. "Now see here. Your nerd talk is cute as hell, and I want to hear it always, but that question? I don't want to hear it again."

"I just wanted to be sure," I muttered, turning away.

Arms wound around me from behind, pulling me into his body.

"Marry me."

I sucked in a breath, so shocked I couldn't even turn around to face him. "W-what?"

"Marry me, Red. I'll put a ring on it, and you can look at it every minute of the day so you know I won't ever leave. So you will know how much I want you. You're mine, and that will never change."

Finally, I turned, knees folded into my chest so I could be closer to his. "You really wanna get married?"

He smiled. "Let's get married before anyone else and piss

them all off."

I laughed. "That's not a reason to get married."

Warmth lit up his expression, making the darkness of his eyes seem warmer than the sun. "Then marry me because I love you."

My heart trembled like there was a little earthquake in my chest. "Okay," I said, my voice shaking just like my heart.

"Really?"

I nodded, glancing at his hand. "Will you wear a ring too?"

"Do you want me to wear a ring?"

"Yes. A red one."

"Consider it done."

Happiness suffused my chest, and I felt near to bursting. Never in a million years did that little freckle-faced, skinny, red-haired orphan think anyone would ever choose him as their own. Choose him *and* keep him.

And really, not just anyone did.

I was meant for the big bad wolf, and all the walking alone in the dark forest was worth it in the end.

"Take me back to our room. I want you," I whispered against his lips.

He lifted me. My legs locked around his waist as he kicked up sand running back to our room.

I couldn't help but smile.

I didn't just run with the wolves anymore... I was part of them.

And we lived...

*Happily ever after*

# BONUS EPILOGUE

## THE LITTLEST MISFIT

*The Littlest Misfit*

*Beau*

The muffled yet strong sound of cries reached into the hall. My stomach knotted instantly. Sensing it, Shim pushed off the wall we leaned against to turn toward me. His fingers tangled with mine, and his chest brushed my shoulder. The smooth skin of his nose bumped my cheekbone when he leaned close.

"She's fine, and clearly so is the kid. Listen to those lungs." He spoke reassuringly and soft.

Leaning farther into him, I let his lips brush my cheek as I absentmindedly twirled the red wedding band on his finger. It had become something of a habit.

Okay, I was obsessed with it just as much as I was the rest of him. And really, twirling that ring was probably the least embarrassing way I could assuage my anxiety with him in public.

"There's a supply closet at the end of the hall," he whispered, tugging my earlobe between his teeth.

The ring stopped twirling, and I glanced at him out of the corner of my eye.

"I know what you need," he murmured.

The door to Ivory's hospital room opened, and all of us collectively pushed off the wall, but Shim's hand stayed wrapped around mine.

"It's a boy," Neo announced, eyes bright but face pale. Just as soon as he told us, he disappeared again into the room.

"I knew it!" Virginia exclaimed, smiling wide. Reaching for Earth's hand, she gave it a tug. "We have a nephew."

Earth seemed equally as pale as Neo. I would have laughed, but as I said, my stomach was in knots. "Thank God it's not a girl," was all he said.

Virginia rolled her eyes and wheeled her chair right into the room without hesitation.

I gaped after her. "Can we just go in there?" I asked.

"No one is gonna tell her no," Earth said.

"Well, after nine months of waiting and guessing if it would be a niece or nephew, I'd also like to get a look at him," Ethan mused. "I hope he looks like his mother."

"I heard that!" Neo barked.

The baby let out a wail, and Neo started apologizing profusely. Ivory's light laughter followed.

"Can we go in now?" Fletcher asked, bouncing foot to foot.

A nurse dressed in scrubs with bears on them popped her head out into the hall. "Come on in. But only for a few minutes."

Ethan and Fletcher went first, Emogen and Ander following just behind them. Earth looked like he'd rather swallow antifreeze, but Virginia whisper-yelled his name.

"If I have to go, then so do you," he muttered as he passed.

Shim made no move to hustle me in the room, just waiting… knowing. I turned unsure eyes to him.

"Maybe once you see the kid, you won't be so anxious about him."

"You think?" I asked, hopeful, not even sure why I was so stressed about Ivory having a baby. I mean, I took down Ferrari. He was currently awaiting the death penalty in a maximum-security prison. McClaren was also in jail and not faring well the last I'd heard.

I'd cut off the danger closest to her.

*But babies are so fragile. Small. Helpless.*

A lot like I'd been when my parents died and left me an orphan.

"Baby, tell me what you need," Shim cajoled.

"Can I see it?" I whispered, completely embarrassed and vulnerable.

He didn't say anything or even act like it was a strange request. It really wasn't except for the fact we were in the middle of a hospital hallway. Shim merely untangled our fingers and stepped gracefully in front of me, showing me his back. I lifted my hand, but that was as far as I got.

*This is ridiculous, Beau. It's just a baby.*

Sensing my inability to reach out, Shim grabbed the shirt at the back of his neck and tugged. The fabric pulled up, revealing the watchful eyes of my wolf.

I sighed a little at the snarling tattoo, finding comfort in its perpetual aggression.

Almost as soon as we got home from the little island vacation, Shim went out for a while and came back with it altered.

My wolf had red eyes now.

*Why?* I asked him.

*Because all he sees is Red.*

If people were frightened by the ferocious wolf before, his demonic red eyes made it worse.

To me, though, it made my wolf look in love.

We got married two days later. Daeshim was thrilled because everyone was pissed we got together last but somehow got married first.

I dragged my fingers down the center of his back and then tugged his shirt back into place. "I'm good now."

His arm settled around my waist, and we went into the room where everyone was crowded around the bed.

"He is the most beautiful baby I have ever seen!" Virginia cooed, practically half on the bed as Earth held on to her.

"He's okay," Earth grumped.

"That's your Uncle Earth. He's mean to everyone, but he loves you." Ivory's voice was soft and sweet.

I couldn't even see her because everyone was crowded around, but Neo stood near her head, arm draped over the top of the bed, which was tilted up so she was sitting. His body was angled down, hunching close to his wife and son.

Yeah, they got married not long after we did. Thankfully, it was a small ceremony for just family, but the big society wedding was coming. *Joy.* Apparently in the Upper East Side, the only thing worse than not having a huge society wedding was having a baby out of wedlock. So marriage, baby, and then a big uppity wedding. All I knew was I was going to have to wear a tie.

Neo seemed to not even see anyone but the two people caught in his gaze, looking absolutely besotted and a little worn around the edges. Poor guy. It wasn't even my baby, and I was stressed.

"Beau, come on. Come see," Emogen said, glancing around at where Shim and I hovered. She tugged on Ander's arm, and they backed up. Earth pulled V back, and then suddenly I had a full view of Ivory and the littlest misfit.

He was wrapped up in a blue blanket, and all I could see was a hint of his pink cheek. I expected Ivory to look like...

well, like the first time I'd met her. A mess. But she was practically glowing. Her snow-white cheeks were flushed, blue eyes bright, and bow-shaped lips curled up into a loving smile. Her black-as-midnight hair was long and fell around her shoulders.

"Beau," she said softly, not looking up from the bundle. "Come meet your nephew."

I hesitated but then moved to the side of the bed and leaned in.

"Oh. He is cute," I said, taking in his perfectly round head with a dusting of dark downy hair. His cheeks were pink and so were his lips. The second I spoke, deep-blue eyes fastened on me.

I froze as though I'd been spotted by an alien race.

"That's your Uncle Beau. He's very brave," Ivory told him.

He was still staring, and I didn't know what to do.

"He likes you," Ivory said. "Here. Hold him."

"I can't!" I exclaimed, shifting back into Shim who had somehow formed a wall at my back.

The baby fussed.

"You offended my son." Neo glared. "Now he thinks you don't want to hold him."

My heart pinched. I didn't want him to think that.

"I'm sorry," I told him, leaning back in, feeling a heavy weight when he looked at me again. "I like you a lot," I whispered.

He made a small sound, and I glanced at Neo. He nodded approvingly. "Watch his head."

And then Ivory was passing him into my arms, and I was freaking out. "Pull him into your chest," she said, calm as though she had every confidence I wouldn't drop him.

"I've never held a baby before," I admitted.

Daeshim's arms came around me from behind, and he gently helped pull the baby into my chest.

He was staring again.

"Why does he keep staring at me?"

"Maybe he likes gingers," Shim quipped.

*Oh. Maybe he does like me.* I tucked him a little closer and smiled down. "I guess I'm your uncle." He wiggled a bit in my arms, and I sucked in a breath.

Daeshim tucked the blanket closer around him.

*He totally likes him too.*

"I'll always keep you safe," I whispered to the baby.

"*We* will," Shim said over my shoulder.

The ball of stress in my belly relaxed, and I smiled.

Ivory started sniffling, and I glanced up, alarmed. Neo sat on the bed, pulling her into his side. "I'm just so happy he has all of you."

"I've never held a baby either," Fletcher said, coming to my side to stare at the baby. "Let's name him Spider-Man!"

"No," everyone said at once.

"Can I at least hold him?" Fletcher lamented.

I glanced at Ivory and Neo, and they nodded. Gently, I passed the baby to Fletcher, who pulled the bundle right in and started rocking him like a natural.

"Hi! I'm really glad you're here. You can be the baby now, and I'll be your fun uncle. We can watch Spider-Man since they won't let me name you after him."

Behind us, Ethan made a small sound, and Fletcher turned, still rocking him. "This is your other uncle, Ethan. He will buy you whatever you want—" Fletcher stopped talking. "E? What's wrong?"

Ethan looked the way Neo had just moments ago, completely besotted. His blue eyes actually seemed a little glassy, and his face was all gooey-looking.

Concerned with his silence and trying-not-to-cry face, Fletch stepped closer. "Ethan?"

A small sound made it past his lips as he took in Fletcher

standing there with a baby in his arms. "I, ah…" he stuttered. "You just look…"

"Dang. I thought we'd be next, but it looks like it's gonna be them," Emogen quipped.

"Everybody beating us to the altar and now to the nursery," Ander mused.

"What?" Fletcher wondered, and the baby made a little sound. "He likes me!"

"How could he not?" Ethan whispered.

"I hope you want kids," I told Fletch.

"Me?" he echoed. "How would I have kids?"

"A surrogate, of course," Ethan said easily, totally giving away he was already thinking about it.

"A surrogate," Fletcher echoed.

"It's my turn!" Virginia interrupted, making grabby hands at the baby.

"I'll play with you later," Fletcher promised.

Ethan's eyes literally tracked Fletcher's every move as he handed the baby over to Virginia who was beside the bed in her wheelchair.

"Oh, Neo. He looks like you," V crooned, leaning down to kiss the baby on the forehead. "Oh, you are just so perfect," she whispered, gently touching the baby's cheek.

Earth cleared his throat.

"Do you want to hold him?" Virginia asked.

"No," Earth deadpanned.

"Ethan, you want to have a baby with a surrogate?" Fletcher said, clearly still over there pondering what he'd said.

"Well, how else would he pass on his elite breeding?" Shim cracked.

Ethan made a face. "Why on earth would I want a copy of me when I could have one of Fletcher?"

"You want my baby?" Fletcher seemed shocked.

"Well, who else's?" Ethan wondered.

"I'd rather have yours," Fletcher told him.

Ethan went back to looking dopey and smiled softly. "One of each, then," he decided.

I gazed at Fletcher, waiting for him to freak. But he didn't. He looked back at the baby and smiled.

*Maybe they will be next after all.*

"You aren't gonna ask me for one of them, are you?" Shim whispered in my ear, sending chills racing across the back of my neck.

Panic slapped me, leaving me slightly breathless. Okay, *a lot* breathless. Before I knew it, I was back in the hallway, back pressed into the wall with Shim's hands caging in my body.

"Eyes on me," he commanded.

My stare crashed into his. "You want kids?"

He tilted his head to the side, studying me like he was trying to read me but couldn't because the chaos was just too stirred up.

*Good.* "Tell me what you feel, not what you think I do," I said.

"Honestly? No. I don't want kids. But if you do, I'll come around. But it would have to be your kid. Hopefully, he'd have red hair." He grimaced, a low swear echoing beneath his breath.

"Shim?"

"Look, I can't promise I would take it too well, seeing some woman knocked up with your kid. Even knowing it was—"

I shoved off the wall so hard our teeth clashed when I pushed my lips onto his. We kissed hungrily, forcefully, as I tried to fill my bottomless need for him.

Spoiler alert: I would never be full.

When I pulled back, his eyes were slightly unfocused, and

his tongue came out to lick what was left of me off his lips. "I don't want kids either," I confessed, slightly relieved. "I don't want to share you. And I don't want any part of me inside anyone else but you."

He arched a brow, and I felt my skin catch fire.

"Shim," I admonished.

"Baby, we both know what you really want is me inside you," he purred.

"But no one else." The fact was he offered many times to let me top... but he was right. I wanted him in me.

He smiled. "Never."

"Just me and you, okay?"

He kissed me softly, and my heart turned gooey like Ethan's face. "Always."

In the room, the baby started crying.

"You're holding him wrong," Earth announced.

Shim and I looked at each other and rushed into the room just in time to see Earth reaching into Emogen's arms to take the baby.

"I'm a nurse. I know how to hold a baby," Emogen told him, glaring.

"Well, then he just doesn't like you," Earth grumped, but it was much softer than usual.

When he straightened, the room kinda went quiet, baby included. Earth, seemingly realizing he'd just picked up the baby, stood frozen, staring down at him.

He looked funny in his leather jacket and jeans with his honed features and rough exterior. The blue bundle in his arms was everything he wasn't... yet he held him with care and a little bit of awe.

I tore my eyes away to glance at V, and she was wiping her eyes and smiling as though she'd never seen anything better.

"What are you looking at?" Earth asked the baby.

The baby gave a yell.

Earth grunted. "Just like your father."

Neo came around the bed. "Quit hogging my son." His arms were gentle when he pulled the baby against him.

When the infant was settled against Neo, his palm cradled around his head, he glanced at Earth. "I'm glad you like him."

"I'm not changing his diapers."

Neo chuckled and carried the baby back to the bed, sitting down with him in his arms beside Ivory. Ivory sighed, laying her cheek on his arm and putting one hand on her son.

"What are you going to name him?" Ander asked.

"Finley Thomas Arthur Adair," Ivory told the room. "He has his own name and the names of his grandfathers."

"And my last name of course," Neo added on like we all thought it would be White and not his.

"A very strong name," Ethan said.

Virginia sniffled. "Mom and Dad would love him."

Emotion passed behind Neo's eyes, and he pulled the baby a little closer against him.

The nurse from earlier came into the room. "Okay, everyone out. Baby needs to come with me, and then mom has to feed him."

"We'll come back in the morning. If you would like us to bring anything, just call," Ethan told Ivory, leaning in to kiss her head. "Congratulations. He's just beautiful. I'm very proud of you, and I know Arthur would be too." He pulled back and reached for Fletcher.

We all said our goodbyes, leaving Neo with his wife and son.

From here, our family would probably continue to grow. How big, I wasn't sure. But it didn't matter because our house of misfits would always have room, and we would always belong together.

# AUTHOR'S NOTE

*Once upon a time...*

A redhead left fingerprints on Daeshim's heart. And mine too.

It's always the quiet ones. Am I right? Man, did Beau sneak up on me. I was watching him, and I still didn't see it coming. In a lot of ways, Beau got to me like Trent (from the *Hashtag* and *Gearshark* series) who many of you know is the most favorite character of mine.

Trent was very quiet too, staying in the background of the family, always there, but never saying much. Beau was like this too. He was on my radar since book one in this series (*Ivory White*). Something about him made me curious. I thought about him often, asking what his story was, trying to pin him down. He stayed so quiet and never answered. I actually got really worried he would never show up or let me write his book. I worried I would eventually write everyone else, and he would remain unwritten. I never planned to write Beau last, but the quieter he became, the more accepting of if I was, thinking maybe he just wasn't ready to tell me.

But I did kinda pick at him. I threw Bre into his arms in *Prince*, wondering if perhaps she was the one for him—going as far as coming up with a title for their book—but Beau never quite fit into the story I was trying to create. I asked him if he was gay, and he told me no.

Toward the end of *Huntsman*, I started to wonder if perhaps Beau had a hidden identity, if perhaps he was an undercover cop. I played with the idea, mulled it over again and again. He was always there when things went down. He always seemed to smooth everything over. Maybe he wasn't just agreeable and easygoing. Maybe he had a purpose. Then I tested him out with Winnie in *Beast*, and that only made him uncomfortable.

By that time, Daeshim had come ripping into the series— a bad guy but a reluctant one. A guy raised and trained to be ruthless and uncaring, but like Earth, he was never quite able to turn off all his emotions.

Despite his flirtatious ways with Fletcher, Daeshim was VERY clear in my head. He was also VERY loud. Beau was his and only his. He would accept nothing less. I was a little concerned because Beau didn't really seem too interested in anyone... but Daeshim was persistent.

I began to think maybe the only one that could really see Beau was the man who had just arrived, the man with instincts that had been honed through his years in the mafia. He pushed all of Beau's buttons. They bickered and fought, argued and annoyed each other. Daeshim wore him down, silently watching him and seeing things no one else ever had.

I genuinely think if not for Daeshim and his pushing and prodding, Beau might never have told me anything. Because really? Beau didn't tell me his story—he told Daeshim. He trusted Shim with his deepest secrets and fears. I still recall early in the book (truly, I was sitting in front of my treadmill, tying my running shoes) when Beau started whispering. His tender feelings and vulnerable voice literally made me clutch my chest. In that moment, I asked him to trust me enough to write his book, and I asked him if it was okay that I listened to everything he told Daeshim. He let me in. Maybe because he knew Daeshim would protect him. I hope maybe because he knew I would too.

So yeah, born was a small, freckled orphan with no one to love him but with a heart desperate for love. How could he not slide right in there behind Trent? And despite all his insecurities, anxieties, and chaos, he was strong. A freaking FBI agent living a double life.

Thrown to the wolves, maybe to be eaten, maybe to fight back... No one thought he might become one. But he did.

In a sense, I relate to Beau in a personal way, which sounds odd because I am not a gay man, not a cop, technology hates me (seriously, I can't even format my own Word document), and I don't have red hair (a shame really). But I think this just goes to show that it doesn't matter *what* you are but *who* you are. I really identify with his quietness, the way he likes to just observe. He internalizes literally everything, and people don't realize how that is actually very painful. I mean, the guy has a perpetual stomachache... Me too, Beau. Me too. He'd rather be the stressed-out one instead of causing someone else stress, and he would rather suffer in silence than try and put to words the chaos inside him.

And oh, the chaos. His outward appearance may be calm and quiet, but inside is a completely different story. I identify well with that too. So maybe this is also why I felt a particular... protectiveness over his story and the things he finally shared. Because to him, even his most random thoughts are so private that letting anyone see them can hurt. I can completely see how Daeshim's ruthless and decisive personality was such a strength for him. *wipes eyes*

Beau and Daeshim have fated mate vibes for me even though this is a contemporary story. They are each other's instinct. I love their possessive/obsessive type of relationship. I love how Beau melts when Shim touches him. I love how he learns to depend on him and lets himself need him.

I think Daeshim loves his vulnerability and knowing he can protect him. Daeshim was never allowed to be vulnerable, having it (literally) beaten out of him. I think he sees Beau's vulnerability as beautiful and wants to protect it because no one ever protected his.

He has so much fierceness in him, so much alpha. It's exactly what Beau needs. Daeshim has no boundaries, which is kinda perfect for someone who has so many because he will plow right through them without even thinking twice.

I love these two together, more than I realized I would. I also realize now Beau's book could never be anything but the end of this series because he literally tied up every loose end and also told us how the hell they all managed to stay together through everything.

I hope I was able to convey all the emotion these two made me feel. I spent 80% of this book having to pee and starving because I absolutely could not get away from the laptop. They gave me butterflies, made me laugh, and made my heart hurt. Not to mention the freaking sparks. Good lordy, they got some chemistry. Amen.

I did my best with the plot as well, hopefully wrapping it up in a way that didn't feel dragged out but still answered all the questions and put away the bad guys. In truth, Daeshim wanted to kill most of them. The time I didn't spend having to pee and wanting to eat I spent trying to control Daeshim's urge to slaughter everyone who looked at Beau.

Even now he is grumbling that he didn't kill Kwan or

Ferrari, but really, the FBI was involved, and Beau didn't need to be cleaning up any more murders. Lol. Besides, as much as Shim is willing to break necks—he loves Beau more.

How surprising—but not. A man that feels such rage and violence can surely feel that depth of love.

So sadly, *Red* is the end of House of Misfits—a series that has come to mean so much to me personally. It started as a beauty and a group of savages and morphed into a family filled with unlikely characters and memorable stories. I doubted I would be able to finish this series. It was tough and at times discouraging. I will confess I wish it got more love. I feel it deserves it (yes, I'm biased). But this was also the series I sort of "came back" with. I had a lot of health issues, suffered some writer burnout, and, in 2019, only managed to release *Ivory White.* But I kept going, one foot in front of the other, one word after another. I slowly started to bounce back and feel more like myself again, and this series was with me every single step of the way. In a way, we did it together.

It's bittersweet to step away now, which is ironic because I'd thought many times of putting the series down. But family doesn't quit family, and this series—these characters—are my family.

All of them left some sort of imprint on my heart—most of all Beau. And come on, that's BIG because this series also has Fletcher. I really love him too.

If you're here and you read this series, thank you. Sincerely. You were part of my journey. Part of this family. Your support and love for this series are something special for me. I hope you enjoyed *Red.* And I hope that even after you close this series, you will carry with you the underlying theme of all these books: Go on strongly despite the fear.

And remember, you can always come home again because you will always belong with the misfits.

Thank you for reading. For supporting.

Until my next book,
*Cambria*

Oh, PS: my daughter insists I tell everyone Beau and Daeshim (aka #beaushim) are her most favorite characters of mine she's read (she's read them all). They beat out Arrow and Hopper and Nate and Aerie for her.

# ABOUT CAMBRIA HEBERT

Cambria Hebert is a bestselling novelist of more than fifty titles. She went to college for a bachelor's degree, couldn't pick a major, and ended up with a degree in cosmetology. So rest assured her characters will always have good hair.

Besides writing, Cambria loves a pumpkin spice latte, staying up late, sleeping in, and watching K drama until her eyes won't stay open. She considers math human torture and has an irrational fear of chickens (yes, chickens). You can often find her running on the treadmill (she'd rather be eating a donut), painting her toenails (because she bites her fingernails), or walking her chihuahuas (the real bosses of the house).

Cambria has written in many genres, including new adult, sports romance, male/male romance, sci-fi, thriller, suspense, contemporary romance, and young adult. Many of her titles have been translated into foreign languages and have been the recipients of multiple awards.

Awards Cambria has received include:

Author of the Year 2016 (UtopiaCon2016)
The Hashtag Series: Best Contemporary Series of 2015
(UtopiaCon 2015)
#Nerd: Best Contemporary Book Cover of 2015 (UtopiaCon
2015)
Romeo from the Hashtag Series: Best Contemporary Lead
(UtopiaCon 2015)
#Nerd: Top 50 Summer Reads (Buzzfeed.com 2015)
The Hashtag Series: Best Contemporary Series of 2016
(UtopiaCon 2016)
#Nerd Book Trailer: Best Book Trailer of 2016 (UtopiaCon
2016)
#Nerd Book Trailer: Top 50 Most Cinematic Book Trailers
of All Time (film-14.com)
#Nerd: Book Most Wanted to be Adapted to Screen: (2018)
Amnesia: Mystery Book of the Year (2018)

Cambria Hebert owns and operates Cambria Hebert
Books, LLC.
You can find out more about Cambria and her titles by
visiting her website:
http://www.cambriahebert.com

## ALSO BY CAMBRIA HEBERT

The Heven & Hell series

The Death Escorts series

The Take It Off Series

The Hashtag Series

The GearShark Series

The Amnesia Duet

The Public Enemy Series

The BearPaw Resort Series

The House of Misfits Series

Westbrook Elite Series

Standalone Titles:

*Moth To A Flame*

*Mr. Fantasy*

*Distant Desires*

*Maneater*

*Blank*

*Whiteout*

Check out all these and more here:

https://books2read.com/ap/RQDG6x/Cambria-Hebert